THE
BEAUTIFUL
AND THE
CURSED

PAGE
MORGAN

Doubleday
Canada

Doubleday Canada and colophon are registered trademarks of Random House of Canada Limited

Library and Archives Canada Cataloguing in Publication

Morgan, Page
    Beautiful and cursed / Page Morgan.

Issued also in electronic format.
ISBN 978-0-385-67908-4

    1. Paris (France)—History—1870-1940—Juvenile fiction.
I. Title.

PZ7.M7542Gr 2013   j813'.6   C2012-906560-9

This book is a work of fiction. Names, characters, places and incidents are products of the author's imagination or are used fictitiously. Any resemblance to actual events or locales or persons, living or dead, is entirely coincidental.

Front jacket art copyright © 2013 by Marilen Androver, City Images/ Shutterstock; back jacket photograph © 2013 by Getty Images, manipulation by Michael Wagner; front flap photographs © 2013 Shutterstock, manipulation by Michael Wagner

The text of this book is set in 11-point Hoefler Text.
Book design by Melissa Greenberg

Printed and bound in the USA

Published in Canada by Doubleday Canada,
a division of Random House of Canada Limited

www.randomhouse.ca

10 9 8 7 6 5 4 3 2 1

For Willa Belle

I WEPT NOT, SO TO STONE WITHIN I GREW.

—DANTE

The boy was late.

Brigitte crossed the folds of her sable cape to shut out the creeping frost. It was still and quiet within the walled garden, the hollow sort of quiet that arrives just past midnight. Swaths of snowy burlap covered the rose shrubs, making them look ghostly under the bright moon, and wisps of clouds scudded through the sky.

She felt like a fool. She'd actually believed he would come.

He had to have been trifling with her in the markets the day before, when they'd met. Brigitte usually sent servants there, but she was bored with the shopping arcades, and her friend Jacqueline had suggested they go. When Jacqui had wandered off to look at some inexpensive paste rings, Brigitte had noticed the boy standing behind his barrow of parsnips and potatoes.

She had willfully overlooked his work-roughened hands, his threadbare tweed coat and trousers. Instead, she focused on everything north of his shoulders. He was glorious, his eyes and hair a golden shade of brown that put the finest tiger oak to shame. She knew the boy was unsuitable—he hawked vegetables!—and unworthy of her attention. Perhaps that was exactly why she so eagerly wished to bestow it. Before she knew it, she'd given him her address and a time to meet.

And here she was.

But where was he?

Brigitte stared at the garden gate, the arched planks overrun by withered grapevines. She suddenly wanted nothing more than to be indoors, out of the cold, and safe. She started a slow retreat toward the house. If only the barrow boy had been of her class, they could have met during daylight. Even the garden of Brigitte's family estate wasn't completely safe, not now.

The girls who had gone missing over the last two weeks had all disappeared from their own homes. The Blanche girl was the latest to have vanished. Brigitte had known of her, had seen her at parties once or twice. No one knew where the girls had gone, but the police were starting to suspect foul play. Perhaps it was better that the barrow boy had not come to take her from the walled garden.

That was when she heard it: the sorrowful call of an owl. She stopped, her heart along with her feet, it seemed. The barrow boy had said he'd give an owl's hoot three times. After the third cry rang out, the owl fell silent. Uncertain but hopeful, Brigitte went back to the gate. She lifted the hinge, the iron latch cold through her soft kid gloves.

"I'm sorry." His voice came from the left. "I hope you haven't been waiting long." He emerged from the shadows and once again Brigitte was struck mute. He was magnificent. She wanted to twist his hair around her fingers. Feel the silk of it.

"I haven't," she managed to say. "Will you tell me your name now?"

He hadn't at the markets. *A mystery to keep you tempted,* he'd said. He looked like a Jean or a Hugo or an Amato. Whoever he was, he pulled her away from the gate and shut it with care. Brigitte felt a moment of hesitation as the latch fell into place. But the girls who had been taken had all been alone, with no one to protect them. She would not be alone.

"You must guess my name," he said, leading her down the short slope of lawn toward the orchard lane. His hand was a pocket of warmth, his touch heating her to her core. His long hair shimmered in the moonlight, as if each lock had been glossed with fairy dust.

"Amato?" Brigitte instantly knew that it wasn't right. He let go of her hand as if to punish her.

"Try again," he said, before slipping behind the craggy trunk of an apple tree. Its leafless limbs were black and bent. Brigitte's heel crushed a frost-withered apple in the overgrown grass and slipped in the pulp.

"Jean?"

His silence lingered. No. Not Jean, then. The moon fell behind a knot of clouds and the orchard lane became an inky blot.

"I am finished guessing," she said, tired of the silly game.

The lane stayed dark. The barrow boy made no noise at all. Where had he gone? "Tell me or . . . or I'll go back."

The frost bit at the tip of her nose. Brigitte winced. Coming out here had been pure folly. This boy could be anyone, anyone at all, and his coyness was quickly curdling the thrill Brigitte had first felt.

She took a step backward. The clouds parted and the orchard lit just enough for her to see movement behind a tree to her right.

"I'm leaving," she announced.

The bare limbs creaked. Still the barrow boy didn't respond. The clouds raced back over the moon. Awkwardly, Brigitte kept backing away, a cold sweat dampening her chest. Something felt wrong.

She hadn't gone back three more paces when she slammed into something solid—and a cold, sharp pain burst through her abdomen. Brigitte opened her mouth to scream, but a hiss of air was all that escaped. Her shaking fingers slipped over a pair of smooth rods, one embedded below her navel, the other where her rib cage split. In the moonlight, the rods gleamed bright as elephant tusks. A thick black swell flowed down each tusk. Blood. *Her* blood.

She heard a low growl and gagged at the hot gust of rancid breath. Just as Brigitte realized that she would never make it back to the walled garden, the thing with tusks jerked her off her feet. *Such folly,* she thought as the world spun away from her. She *was* alone.

Just as all the other girls had been.

CHAPTER ONE

So this was what a nightmare looked like by the light of day.

Ingrid stared through the window as the coach drew to a halt along rue Dante's snowy curb, a single block from the ice-crusted Seine. Mother could not be serious. This place, this *ruin*, was to be their new home? Ingrid rubbed the fogged glass and saw the ancient and desolate abbey clearly.

"You've completely lost your mind," Ingrid whispered. Her mother ignored her and continued to gaze out the coach window.

Pockmarks riddled the blocks of dirty gray limestone, leaving the abbey looking like a ravaged victim of the pox. The four front-facing arched windows held dull and warped stained glass that had more cracks and gaps than lead and glass. The two planks of desiccated wood acting as doors had been left slightly ajar, as if beckoning someone, anyone, to enter. Ingrid didn't think she'd ever seen a lonelier place.

Her mother's eyes began to mist over. "Isn't it marvelous, girls?"

"Mama, please don't start crying again. You've gone through all your hankies." Ingrid's younger sister, Gabriella, opened her beaded reticule for one of her own.

Their mother, Lady Charlotte Brickton, had been sniffling ever since their steamer had reached Calais and her feet had met solid French soil for the first time in over sixteen years. She was overjoyed to be home. Ingrid was just relieved to be gone from London. She never wanted to go back there. Not now, not after what had happened and what she'd done. But this abbey . . . it only added insult to injury.

"Marvelous? It looks condemned," Ingrid said.

The place was a hulking wreck. Even the new layer of powdery snow couldn't soften the blow. It coated the spikes of a tall wrought-iron fence like icing. Thick twists formed the gate, which was draped with ivy, roses, and thorny vines forged from the same metal. It was all as cold and uninviting as the white-capped waters of the English Channel had been.

"It's absolutely horrifying," Gabby whispered. An awestruck grin bowed her lips. Ingrid's sister pressed the tip of her nose against the cold pane of glass to get a better look.

"Gabby, among the sane, horrific things don't generally bring about smiles." Ingrid flipped up the black mink hood of her cloak.

Gabby pushed out her full lower lip. "It has charm."

"If you find abandoned and haunted churches charming," Ingrid shot back.

Their mother spared them an irritated glance as the footman opened the coach door. "Don't be so dramatic, girls. The abbey is a masterpiece, and entirely fitting for my gallery."

The footman kicked down the short flight of steps and helped their mother to the curb. Behind them, a second carriage carrying their lady's maids and luggage rolled to a stop.

"Do you really think it's haunted?" Gabby asked. "We'll have to ask Grayson if he's sensed anything. Oh! I know—we'll host a séance!"

Ingrid sighed and held her tongue. Her twin brother, Grayson, would have better luck talking Gabby down from her idea of a resident ghost. Not even eighteen and without so much as one personal servant, Grayson had been sent ahead of them to Paris two months before to scout out a location for their mother's art gallery. Both the trip *and* the art gallery had been planned in a snap. Ingrid hadn't been able to believe that her father, Lord Philip Northcross Waverly III, Earl of Brickton, had finally decided to fund her mother's lifelong dream of opening a gallery of her own. He'd turned the idea down year after year—patronage of the arts was his wife's torch, not his, and he wasn't certain he wanted the Brickton name associated with such a bohemian endeavor.

So when Grayson had rushed off less than two days after their father abruptly announced his support, Ingrid had started to wonder if the art gallery was being launched more because of the growing rift between Papa and Grayson than because of Mama's dream.

Things had never been easy between her father and brother, but within the last year or so their quarreling had escalated. And taking to life as a wild, pleasure-seeking rake had only worsened Grayson's standing with their father. Ingrid hoped it was just a rebellious phase, but Papa had no tolerance for it. He might have sent Grayson to Paris with this task to occupy him, or maybe just to get him out of his hair. What Ingrid couldn't stop wondering was why everything had happened so quickly. Grayson hadn't confided in her before he left, and for the last two months she hadn't been able to shake the feeling that something secret and serious had happened to spur everything on.

The footman helped Ingrid navigate the steps to the curb. The December cold ate through her burgundy velvet dress as if it were a sheer slip of silk. She stared at the abbey, at the frescoes that had crumbled into unrecognizable scenes, and at the dozens of slates missing from the ramshackle roof. What had her brother been thinking when he'd chosen to invest in this heap? Ingrid was only thankful Papa couldn't see it. Some business with his seat at the House of Lords had kept him from escorting them to Paris as he'd intended. He'd come later, he'd assured them. Definitely for the gallery opening.

"Where is Grayson? I thought he was to meet us here," Gabby said as she lighted on the curb. Her ruffled pink parasol was already open against snowflakes drifting from the platinum clouds.

With her smoky eyes, short, slightly upturned nose, rosebud lips, and hair the color of golden rum, Gabby was a fifteen-year-old replica of their mother. Ingrid stood out in sharp contrast to them. Her hair, flaxen like Grayson's and Papa's, was only a shade lighter than her fair complexion. She'd been told more times than she cared for in her seventeen years that she was the epitome of English beauty: all cream and roses and soft petal-pink lips. With it came the expectation of a sweet disposition—an expectation those who met Ingrid dismissed immediately.

"It's too cold for Grayson to stand out here all day waiting for us," Ingrid answered.

She clenched her fingers into fists, hating the buzz of anxiety she hadn't been able to cast off for months. It always flared at the mention of Grayson, turning her blood into a glass of frothing champagne. The jittery feeling didn't worry her. She'd had this sixth sense for as long as she could remember. She and Grayson shared it, the same way they'd shared a womb, a nursery, and, before his recent rebellion, a personality. No, what worried her was what it always meant: that something was wrong with her twin.

The sooner she saw Grayson, the better. And then maybe she could finally get answers about what had happened with Papa.

Mother spoke in her native tongue to the footman, gesturing toward their bags, boxes, and trunks strapped to the top and rear of the servants' coach. Ingrid couldn't understand the fast flow of French. She'd never quite grasped her lessons the way Gabby and Grayson had. She could only guess that her mother was instructing the footman to have their drivers go around to the abbey's rectory. Grayson had written in his letter, that it sat kitty-corner to the abbey on the property. They would all live there while Mama managed the abbey's renovations, which would definitely be more extensive than Ingrid had imagined.

Her mother pushed the great iron gates ajar. The hinges squealed, disturbing a flock of blackbirds on the copper gutters, oxidized to a sickly green, that ran along the abbey roof. The sudden movement led Ingrid's eyes upward. The cloud of fluttering black wings cleared, revealing massive statues crowning each of the abbey's twin bell towers.

Most of the statues—angels, most likely, as Ingrid could make out the shape of wings—were covered in white powder, but a few smaller ones sat on the jutting ledges at the bases of the rectangular towers. The snow had blown free of these and Ingrid saw them clearly: not angels. Gargoyles.

Their mouths had been carved into wide, silent screams, tongues rolling from between daggerlike teeth. They had bulging eyes, clipped, doglike ears, and talons curling straight into the roofline's stonework. The wings were spread open on some, while on others they'd been sculpted into folds behind their hunched backs.

Ingrid stood outside the gate, her stomach in a knot. Why would anyone put gargoyles on a church? The stone creatures were hideous enough to cause the small hairs on her arms to prickle. She turned her eyes away. The abbey sat at the head of an intersecting street lined with grand pale stone buildings. Apartments, Ingrid supposed, terraced here and there, with ground-floor shops and colorful awnings. There were a few people out, but the wide avenue looked mostly stark. Much like the abbey that crowned it.

Gabby and their mother had already reached the abbey's vaulted double doors. They disappeared inside. Ingrid slowly followed their tracks in the dusting of snow. She wanted to get to Grayson. She wanted to keep moving. Every step took her farther from London, their home on Grosvenor Square, Papa, even her dearest friend, Anna Bettinger. She'd miss her friend, but honestly, the trip to Paris couldn't have come at a better time. She could never face Anna again.

Not after what Ingrid had done.

She took a deep breath, pushed back her shoulders, and stepped over the threshold and into the vestibule. Her gloved fingers were numb, and the air in the vestibule was just as cold as it had been outdoors. On top of that, it was dark and damp. Ingrid could barely see a thing inside the nave. Little light fell through the grimy, cracked stained-glass windows running up and down each side of the abbey. Behind the pulpit, a large rose window of pale-yellow glass bloomed at the center of the apse. Ingrid wrinkled her nose against a damp, musty odor.

Gabby's voice echoed off the vaulted ceilings. "It's even more terrible on the inside. Don't you think, Griddy?"

Ingrid's shin struck an overturned pew draped in shadow. She hissed an unladylike word. "Please don't call me that. It's bad enough the horrid nickname caught on in London."

Lady Griddy—rather than Lady Ingrid Waverly, the title due to her as the daughter of an earl—sounded like the name of a wizened old dowager.

Their mother appeared from behind a column, running her hand along the creamy swirls of marble.

"This will be the main gallery. Oh, I do think Grayson chose well, didn't he, girls? It simply aches with character. And we have quite a while before your father arrives for the opening, plenty of time to make all the repairs it requires."

Ingrid stared at her mother, doubt plain on her face. Her mother waved it away. "Honestly, Ingrid, must you be so contrary? Think of Paris as a fresh start." She turned away before continuing. "Leaving London for the winter was in your best interests, dear, especially given what happened with Mr. Walker."

Heat flooded Ingrid's cheeks. Her fingers clutched the curved arm of a pew. *Mr. Walker.* Jonathan Walker.

"Mother," Gabby said.

No one had spoken Jonathan's name since the disastrous gala and the event that had marked the death of Ingrid's spotless reputation in London.

Ingrid fought her rising blush. "It's true. Leaving London was the best thing for me."

With her eyes cast down, she continued toward the pulpit but veered to the right, into the transept, before reaching it. Beyond, there was a wooden door. From the heavy silence behind her she knew her mother and sister were exchanging wide-eyed glares and emphatic arm gestures. Gabby wanted to tiptoe around the subject; her mother wished to chastise Ingrid for being too bold and public about her feelings for Jonathan. Neither approach would change a thing. Ingrid had wanted to marry Jonathan, and Jonathan had proposed—to Ingrid's closest friend, Anna Bettinger.

And then Ingrid had set fire to Anna's house.

It had been an accident. A horrific accident that Ingrid would never forgive herself for. But it didn't matter. She was finished in London.

Ingrid shoved open the transept door and the sudden brightness of the snow-dusted churchyard nearly blinded her. When her eyes adjusted, she saw a two-story Gothic-style stone rectory just behind the abbey's glass-and-iron rotunda. Their coach footman stood in the rectory's open doorway with a tall, muttonchopped man. The man blended into the bleak surroundings in his gray broadcloth suit and gloves and gray domed hat.

"Who is that?" her mother asked as she came into the churchyard behind Ingrid. She hurried forward as fast as her stout hour-glass figure could go in her restrictive trumpet-shaped skirt and fitted S-bend corset.

"Mama shouldn't have said anything," Gabby said quietly as she and Ingrid trailed her at a distance.

Ingrid tightened her cloak's collar around her neck, avoiding her sister's frank gaze. "She can say whatever she pleases. I'm past it."

She was an awful liar. Gabby knew it, too, but was gracious enough to let the matter drop.

When they reached the doorway to the rectory, their mother and the stranger were finishing introducing themselves.

"Girls, this is Monsieur Constantine," their mother said with a wide smile. "Your brother's estate agent."

Monsieur Constantine took Ingrid's hand and bowed over it. "*Enchanté,* my lady."

She muttered a distracted bonjour and slid behind her mother to enter the rectory. Meanwhile, Gabby captured his attention with her natural charm, wide smile, and perfect French.

Ingrid drifted deeper into the large foyer. A young woman in a plain gray dress and black pinafore curtsied and then wordlessly went to work stripping Ingrid of her cloak and gloves. It was only slightly warmer in the rectory than in the abbey. A Persian rug covered the stone floor, and thick, peacock-blue drapes cordoned off two rooms extending from the foyer.

"Your other portmanteaus arrived two days ago and have been brought to your rooms," Monsieur Constantine said, this time in English. "Your lady's maids are being shown about the premises."

Ingrid peered up the flight of stairs, which were covered in lush, cardinal-red carpet. "And where is our brother?"

Her nerves jumped and itched. The hollow sensation she'd learned to live with the last two months yawned wide within her. She was more than ready for it to be filled, and the only person who could do that was her twin.

Monsieur Constantine took a deep breath and held it. That was the moment Ingrid began to suspect something was wrong.

"I am afraid Lord Fairfax is not here," he answered, referring to Grayson by the courtesy title every heir apparent to the Brickton earldom had used for generations. Her twin preferred the less imposing "Grayson" but had long given up lobbying for people to use it.

"Not here?" their mother echoed. "My son knew we were to arrive this afternoon. What was so important that it has drawn him away?"

Constantine smoothed his silver, dart-shaped beard and rocked back on his heels. "My lady, I do not wish to upset you; however, it seems your son has not been at the rectory for nearly four days."

The brewing storm Ingrid had been feeling, the one whispering Grayson's name, suddenly made sense. Startled, she looked to her mother. The Countess of Brickton rarely allowed emotion to color her expression, but at that moment anxiety fired her eyes.

"If he hasn't been here, then where exactly *has* he been?" she asked.

"I know only what the staff tell me," Constantine answered. "From what they say, it seems that your son attended a dinner last Thursday evening. The driver said that after the dinner concluded, there were no signs of his lordship. When he inquired, the driver was told he had disappeared before the first course was served. Everyone in attendance assumed he'd left."

Ingrid frowned. "Monsieur Constantine, where was this dinner? Were the hosts friends of my brother's?"

She didn't like the blank look that fell over the man's face. "All I know, my lady, is that it was within the Fourth Arrondissement. Not very far from here. And the driver tells me the hosts were people his lordship was acquainted with."

"Where is this driver?" Ingrid's mother asked. *"Je veux lui parler immédiatement."*

Monsieur Constantine parted one set of blue drapes and called out. In less than a minute, a small group of men and women flowed into the foyer. The men removed their patched tweed caps and the ladies clasped their chapped hands in front of their starched pinafores.

"I've hired your staff, Lady Brickton, and as requested, they all speak English very well. Bertrand drove Lord Fairfax to the Fourth last Thursday." He snapped his fingers at an older gentleman. The man had a horseshoe ring of thinning black hair running back from his temples. He kept a stranglehold on his cap.

"My lady," Bertrand said with a low bow.

"Has my son sent any word at all?" Ingrid's mother asked, her voice shaking.

Ingrid's stomach tightened. She'd hoped something minor would be the cause of her intuitive jitters. Nothing more than a broken heart or, at the very most, a broken bone. Grayson was supposed to be here, sweeping her into one of his dizzying hugs. But Bertrand voiced exactly what Ingrid feared.

"*Je suis désolé, mais non,*" he answered, shaking his head as an afterthought in translation of his words.

"We will resolve this, Lady Brickton," Constantine said quickly and earnestly. "There must be an explanation for his absence. If you wish it so, we can ask the police for their assistance."

"Why haven't they already been alerted?" Gabby asked, a fervent shine in her eyes.

Constantine fumbled with a few words in his own language before switching to English. "I have been told," he said, "that an absence like this is not unheard of with Lord Fairfax. He is rather . . . *tempestuous,* the servants say. Here one moment, gone the next. Sometimes for a day or more."

Ingrid let out a disappointed sigh. She'd hoped her brother had learned to tame his appetite for parties, clubs, and gambling halls. That hope crumbled at Constantine's explanation.

An awkward silence fell as their mother tried to weather this statement of her son's reputation with grace. After a moment, Constantine helped her by leaping in with lengthy introductions to the staff he'd worked with Grayson to prepare: the housekeeper and the butler, the cook, a kitchen maid, two housemaids, two footmen, a livery boy, and a driver—Bertrand. Their names were a flurry of accents and sounds to Ingrid as she looked from face to face, trying to follow who was who. Constantine's rambling seemed to hush as her gaze tripped over, and then locked with, another.

Instantly, everything stilled—her mind, the room, her breathing. The eyes transfixing hers belonged to a young man. The irises, luminous green and gold flecked, were earthy and vibrant, like a patch of pale forest moss long forgotten by the sun. Thick charcoal lashes shaded them.

He didn't look more than a year or two older than Ingrid, and he watched her with unsettling inquisitiveness. She stared back, sensing hostility in the way he looked at her. His lips weren't set in a grimace, but the flare of his nostrils expressed clear contempt. As if Ingrid had somehow wronged him. Which was absurd. She had never met this boy before.

Ingrid finally forced her eyes to detach from his, only to find herself looking into the foyer's rococo mirror. She saw the high color over her cheekbones. Blasted skin. She couldn't be angry or embarrassed without showcasing it before everyone in the room.

"Ingrid, you look flushed," her mother said once Constantine had finished his introductions. It only made her cheeks burn hotter. "You're upset about your brother. You need to rest. Madam Bertot, could you see to it that Lady Ingrid receives tea?" She then turned to Ingrid's lady's maid from home. "Cherie, do draw a hot bath for her."

For some reason, Ingrid's complexion and slim physique caused people to believe she was frail and more likely to fall ill than her curvaceous sister. The assumption was wholly unwarranted, too, considering that Ingrid hadn't been sick a day in her life. Nor had Grayson, in fact. Their physician had often marveled at the twins' perpetual good health, but it never stopped their mother from fretting.

"Mother, I'm fine." But Madam Bertot, who must have been the cook, and Cherie had already disappeared. The others, including the young man with the lime-gold eyes, remained.

"You mustn't neglect your health, darling," her mother said.

"My health is *fine*," Ingrid ground out. "I think I would like to go for a walk, actually." She needed air. Lots of it. Ingrid turned to Constantine. "Is there a bookshop close by, monsieur?"

Her brother liked books almost as much as he liked to breathe. If there was a bookshop nearby, Grayson would definitely frequent it. Anything she could do to track him down would be worthwhile.

Constantine glanced at the servants and cleared his throat. They took it as an order and filed back through the drapes. Except for the young man. He stood rigid, those curious eyes of his rooted on Ingrid.

Constantine followed the path of the young man's stare before clearing his throat a second time. "Luc? Is there something you wish to say?"

Luc lowered his eyes in answer, to which Constantine replied impatiently, "Then you may leave."

Luc disappeared through the drapes, leaving behind an uneasy silence. Constantine filled it by dismissing Ingrid's question.

"It is nearly nightfall, and the Préfecture de Police has been circulating a notice for people to stay indoors after dark."

Gabby and Ingrid met each other's gazes with raised eyebrows.

"A few incidents have made night travel unsound," he said in response to their confused expressions.

"Do these incidents have anything to do with my son's disappearance?" their mother asked.

Constantine ushered them from the foyer into the sitting

room. The place looked straight out of a castle, utterly medieval, with its tapestries, mullioned windows, and walls of roughly cut stone blocks. They soaked up the warmth of the fire, a natural barricade against the raw winter twilight.

"Certainly not. I am afraid, Lady Brickton, that your son leads a rather colorful lifestyle here." He guided her to the sofa nearest the hearth.

"He's young," their mother said with practiced defense as she sat. It was the same excuse she often tried using on Papa. It worked better on Constantine.

"That he is," he replied. "Lord Fairfax is a fine young man, and certainly not involved in these recent incidents."

"What has been happening?" Gabby asked. She perched on the arm of the sofa at their mother's side.

Constantine shuffled in place a moment, reluctance twitching at the corners of his mouth.

"A few young ladies have been reported missing. The papers print nothing but rumors, of course, and I do not like to speculate, but there are whisperings of violence having been involved."

Their mother drew herself up with a shudder. "I do not wish my daughters to hear any more on the matter. They will stay indoors for the time being. Thank you, Monsieur Constantine."

He made a deep bow. "Please, do not concern yourselves. You have had a long journey and, just as her ladyship has said, are in need of rest."

Their mother rose to see him to the door, leaving Gabby and Ingrid alone in the sitting room.

"Did you hear him?" Gabby shot off the arm of the sofa. "'*Do not concern yourselves.*' He tells us our brother is missing, and that we should avoid the darkened streets of Paris for fear of losing our lives, and then tells us to never mind!"

Ingrid didn't respond. Sometimes it was best to let Gabby's outbursts just fizzle. Instead, she went to the window. The bottom sash had been rigged with wooden shutters painted the same peacock-blue as the drapes. Ingrid ran her fingers over the flaking paint in thought. That was what Ingrid did—she contemplated while Gabby took action.

Behind her, Gabby paced the room. "And I don't care what Grayson's reputation is. Four days gone without a word? It's too long. The police should have been called by now."

Through the top panes of the mullioned glass, the snow covering the churchyard looked pale violet. A stone fountain had been turned off, and snow-crusted apple trees and boxwood shrubs lined the yard. Four days. The effects of any wild soirée Grayson might have attended would have worn off long ago, and besides, Ingrid's sixth sense was positively humming.

"We should find out more about these *'incidents,'*" Gabby said, nervously patting the sides of her skirts. "I hardly know what to think."

Ingrid did, however. Something bad had happened to her brother. It wasn't a knowledge she could put into words. It was only something she could feel, just as when, after they'd left the nursery for their own bedrooms, Grayson would wake from a nightmare and Ingrid would instinctively wake as well. Even if her dream had been a happy one, she'd know somehow to leave it so that she might tiptoe into Grayson's room and climb into bed beside him, assure him it had only been a dream.

Ingrid stared up at the ruined abbey, at the series of stone gargoyles stamped darkly against the twilight. The sight of them made her shiver, and she started to look away.

From the corner of her eye she saw the wings of one hunched black statue flutter up.

With a gasp, Ingrid turned back. She pressed closer to the glass, straining to see through the failing light. The gargoyle's wings were no longer up but were hanging like curtains. What had she just seen?

Ingrid closed her eyes and leaned her forehead against the

cold glass. *Nothing*. She'd seen nothing. She was just overwhelmed and the poor light had been playing tricks on her.

Her brother was missing. There might be a kidnapper—or a murderer—stalking the girls of Paris. And Ingrid was confined to the rectory for the night. Come morning, first thing, she'd set out to find Grayson.

CHAPTER TWO

This was hell.

It had to be.

Grayson turned his face into the hard-packed dirt beneath him and moaned. God, it hurt. His whole body throbbed like one giant, pulsing open wound. He couldn't remember how it had happened, but he knew that he was dead.

Grayson tested his limbs, curling in on himself. He moved easily enough, though it left a dull ache deep in his bones.

"You are strong."

He opened his eyes. A voice. A woman's voice.

"You have lost much blood, yet you do not expire. You merely sleep. Are you awake now?"

His cheek, pressed against the ground, was hot and dry. The only light was an incessant, flickering blue glow. It reminded him of heat lightning during a summer storm.

"I—I'm not dead?" Dirt coated his lips. He felt a twinge of

relief, quickly followed by fear. If he wasn't dead, then where was he? What had happened to him?

Grayson's foggy vision cleared and he saw the silhouette of a cloaked and hooded figure crouching beside him. He couldn't see her face; it was set too deeply within the hood for the rippling blue light to touch it.

"I would be very disappointed if you were dead, Grayson Waverly," the woman replied. Her voice had an echo, he realized, as if it were carrying across some deep valley instead of bouncing off the low dirt ceilings of the cave they were in. Her voice reverberated in Grayson's head and strummed his eardrums.

"Where am I?" He attempted to push himself from the floor. The ache seared him inside. He felt exhausted and empty. Even stranger, he felt hungry.

A dinner. He'd been at a dinner.

The memory eddied away as someone strong seized him by the shoulders and jerked him to a sitting position. Not the hooded woman—another person. A man. His fierce grip slid down to Grayson's forearms. The pulsating light threw blue and black shadows over the man's face.

Grayson squinted. There was something wrong with the man's mouth. His lips were stretched too wide over his teeth, almost as if he had a wedge of orange rind hidden there and was waiting to flash an orange smile to win a laugh. But the stench of him—Grayson had never smelled anything so putrid.

"Unhand me and move aside," Grayson ordered, putting on his father's imperious tone. He jerked his arms back but winced as the man's fingers became as unyielding as an iron manacle.

"You will be allowed to leave in time," the hooded woman said, her words rolling and silky. "All in time, Grayson Waverly. Now hold still. We must begin."

The man let out a low, lasting moan. To Grayson, it sounded like pleasure. It was the same sound he and his sister had made when their governess wasn't looking and they could sneak treacle toffees. As the man's lips drew apart, the idea of the absurd orange-rind smile crashed.

A pair of pearlescent-blue canines curved over the corners of the man's lower lip. Grayson wrenched backward as a second pair of fangs erupted from the man's lower jaw, rising past the canines and stopping only when each needlelike tip had crested the man's top lip.

No. It wasn't a man. It was some sort of monster.

Its jaw sprang wide to emit a coarse growl, the sound of stones scraping and digging into a pane of glass.

"No!" Grayson strained to free himself. "Stop!"

The creature tore one of Grayson's sleeves back, ripping it along the seam.

"You will come to understand," the hooded woman said, her voice glassy and calm over Grayson's screams. "This is all for the best."

The creature snapped its head forward and punched its fangs through Grayson's flesh.

Luc rolled aside the doors to the carriage house hayloft and stepped to the precipice. He leaned into the night wind. Usually the air alleviated his bad humors. Not tonight. Stars knifed through the heavens, and a stream of clouds streaked across the sky. Luc breathed in deeply. His nostrils flared at the unpleasant scent carried on the wind.

They were close. Very close. Just beyond the walls of L'Abbaye Saint-Dismas. The hallowed ground was the first line of protection against the creatures that had broken through the barrier between this world and the Underneath.

Luc was the second.

He looked toward the rectory, which sat less than twenty yards away. Most of the first floor was dark, but the second-floor windows, where the bedchambers were located, showed low, guttering lights inside. The Mesdemoiselles Waverly. The dark-eyed one and her pale older sister had arrived, just as Grayson had said they would. Luc had expected them, along with their mother and servants, but he certainly hadn't *wanted* them. As if Luc didn't have enough troubles to plague him already. Humans. That was what they had become, really—a sort of never-ending plague.

Grayson Waverly. Lord Fairfax. Future Earl of Brickton. Whoever he was, Luc had failed to protect him. There had been consequences for it, too. Mistakes happened, of course. Slips. Accidents. There were always punishments to endure for such missteps.

Luc had not been excluded.

The lamps along the second floor snuffed out one by one, except for the chamber set in the far western corner of the rectory. The pale one was in that room. He could feel her. Her restless energy filled him.

The abbey and rectory had lain abandoned for decades, and during that time Luc himself had lain dormant. But a few months ago, when Grayson Waverly had purchased the rectory and spent his first night beneath its roof, Luc had awoken. The familiar sense of *knowing* had returned. He hadn't wanted it back. Luc had grown used to *not* knowing. To not feeling that uncontrollable, undeniable urge to protect.

It made Luc sick with fury at times that someone else—some*thing* else—directed his mind. His actions. Luc hadn't missed being one of the Dispossessed in Paris. He would have much rather spent his eternal punishment high in the rafters of the north bell tower, curled up like one of the hunched granite gargoyles along the roof, wings wound tightly around himself, his scales slowly crusting over to stone.

But now he was awake, and in charge of whoever inhabited the abbey and rectory. Protecting his last humans, a decrepit Sorbonne professor and his nearly blind wife, had been effortless. It would not be that way with Grayson's sisters. The pale one had battled Luc's fierce glare with eyes that held far too much intelligence and curiosity. She'd looked at him as if she already knew his secret.

Luc breathed in the frost. He liked winter best, when there were fewer scents to decipher. He could better smell the dangers lurking outside the abbey's hallowed ground when the air wasn't perfumed by clipped grass or the summer primroses that climbed over the high stone walls enclosing the churchyard. He didn't like how close the Underneath demons were tonight. It was as though they knew the Mesdemoiselles Waverly had arrived. That new, young blood filled the rectory.

"Vultures."

Luc didn't flinch at the gravelly voice. He'd already sensed Marco's arrival, and he wasn't alone. Yann and René were with him, as they usually were. The hot, chiming pulse that registered at the base of Luc's neck whenever another Dispossessed was near had become as wearisome as the humans themselves.

Marco swayed through the loft, Yann and René crossing the wide plank floors behind him.

"I'm surprised you walked," Luc said over his shoulder. "Can't you smell the demon hounds tonight? There must be at least five swarming rue Dante alone."

The three of them could have come in true form. The Dispossessed could shed their human skins whenever they wished, and night was the best time for it. Dark skies and fewer eyes helped hide their existence from the rest of the world—just as the Angelic Order, their masters and commanders, had dictated. Luc preferred true form. The tempered-steel-like scales in place of skin, the muscles cut from stone. The cold feeling of invulnerability.

Marco shrugged and flopped on Luc's worn cotton-stuffed mattress. He hiked a boot on top of the wooden trunk at the foot of the bed. "It seems the beasts are too focused on the comings and goings of the abbey residents to bother with our lot." Marco raised his thick, dark brows. "Are your new humans that tantalizing, brother?"

René stepped up beside Luc. "We already know they have an appetite for British blood."

Luc stared straight ahead. He knew better than to react to one of René's goading remarks. All of the Dispossessed in Paris, including Luc, believed Grayson Waverly had been taken by a hellhound, one of the Underneath demons. Monsieur Constantine and the police could search all they want. They would never find him.

At least Grayson wasn't dead. Irindi, the angel of heavenly rule, had said as much when she'd paid Luc her required visit and scorched him with an angel's burn, the obligatory punishment for failing his human charge. Grayson was alive, a prisoner in the Underneath—a place where no angel or Dispossessed, regardless of rank or power, could trespass. But how a hellhound had eluded Luc's senses, and why it had snatched Grayson in the first place, remained a mystery.

René clapped Luc on the shoulder. "Lighten up. At least you're one human freer."

He was a head taller than Luc, heavy with muscle, and had a coarse, unapproachable manner. He, Yann, and Marco weren't friends. They were allies, and for the Dispossessed, allies were much more useful than friends.

"You have quite a burden to oversee," Marco continued. "One human down, six more added to your flock. Are you certain you're up to it?"

"I'm not an infant," Luc replied, wanting nothing more than for his three uninvited guests to be gone.

"No. But you've woken from a long hibernation to a houseful of charges and an apparent outbreak of hellhounds. And they seem to be concentrating on your abbey," Yann stated. His voice always surprised Luc. His human form was short and slim, yet whenever he spoke, which wasn't as often as his two counter-parts, his voice was deep and echoed like a canyon. It gave weight to whatever he chose to say.

"And you've already failed one," René said with a smug grin. There had been a time when Luc would have been stupid enough to try to punch it off his face.

Luc shoved away from the hayloft door. "I don't need reminding."

No doubt Marco and the others were amused by the news of this failure. Grayson didn't matter to them. He didn't matter all that much to Luc, truth be told. Humans were nuisances. They were an endless obligation, and protecting them was the cross he was forced to bear for what he'd done when he'd been human himself. But he had never lost a charge before. Until Grayson, Luc had never failed.

"All we're trying to say, brother," Marco said, his heel grinding into the trunk's lid as he slowly rotated his ankle, "is that we are in a position to help you. My charges have deserted Hôtel Dugray until spring, Yann's bridge is under reconstruction and closed off to the public, and René's square is nearly deserted during the week. We could lend a hand in watching over your humans."

Luc resisted the urge to swipe Marco's boot off the lid of his trunk. He knew Marco well, and knew that he spoke on behalf of the Wolves, Marco's caste within the Dispossessed in Paris. The Wolves weren't known for their charity. Why would Marco propose to help him?

"They won't be here long," Luc said, dismissing the offer.

Marco snorted. "You don't think the girls will look for their brother?"

Of course they would. They'd have hope. It was such a predictable human downfall. But they wouldn't find him. Their brother wasn't anywhere on the Earth's surface. If he had been, Luc would have been able to feel his presence, his emotions. His exact location. Luc's ties to those who lived within the walls of the abbey and rectory ran that deep. It had been that way for 327 years. Since the very day Luc, just seventeen, had died and been barred from heaven and, consequently, cast into the Dispossessed.

The day Luc had become a gargoyle.

"Leave them to me," Luc said. He planned to show the Waverly women that hope was futile. Once they saw that their brother wasn't coming home, they would leave the abbey. The servants would leave next, and the place would fold back into the neglected, fenced-off property it had been for the last thirty years. Parisians would once again walk past it without seeing its crumbling walls, without noticing that it even existed. And Luc would slip contentedly back into hibernation.

Marco pushed himself up from the mattress. "Do what you want, they're your humans. But remember my offer if they prove stubborn."

Luc nodded, though he had no intention of inviting Marco, Yann, or René to oversee the Waverly women. As inconvenient and unwelcome as they were, these were still Luc's humans. He was compelled to protect them in a way no other gargoyle would have been.

Luc looked back to the flickering light inside the pale sister's room. *Ingrid.* He tested the name out in his mind. His tie to her was already stronger than the one to her sister. He connected to a human through scent, all gargoyles did, and one breath of her had nearly paralyzed him. It had been a long time since he'd smelled anything so light and clean, with the barest trace of dark soil and sweet spring grass. And yet beneath that clean scent there was some unidentifiable tang, something that made the ridges of his spine shudder with the urge to coalesce.

"They are wrong for this place," Marco said, so agile and stealthy that he'd come up behind Luc without him noticing. "I can feel it. Their brother was as well. You're blessed to be through with him so easily. Perhaps you will be blessed a second time?"

The darkness in Marco's suggestion struck Luc as keenly as the winter air. This was why his offer to help made no sense. Luc dipped his chin as a tremor worked its way down the length of his spine. He felt his vertebrae expand, the bones inside his hands begin to shift. The skin over his cheeks tightened.

Marco visibly tamped down a grin. "I meant no harm. Keep your bones in *humana forma*. You know how ugly you Dogs are when you shift."

René snorted at the insult to Luc's caste, but Luc felt no shame. If one looked close enough, they would notice that the grotesques all along the abbey roofline had pointed ears, muzzle-like noses, and sharp canines. Luc had been appointed to the abbey for a reason. A gargoyle's caste spoke volumes about the kind of person he had been in life. Dogs were fiercely loyal and unrelenting in battle. Wolves, like Marco and René, were powerful, persuasive leaders. Chimeras, like Yann, were two complex halves melded together—he was a griffin, with the body of a lion and the head and wings of an eagle. Noble and predatory.

No matter what his caste, every Dispossessed had at least one thing in common. While alive, they'd all committed the same sin: the cold-blooded murder of a man of the cloth.

Luc's urge to coalesce faded. His shifting bones and vertebrae settled back into place. His skin loosened around his cheekbones and chin. Marco backed up toward the ladder. "I didn't mean to overstep. They are your burden, and so I'll leave you to them."

Marco reached the ladder, but a shift in the air alerted Luc. He cocked his head and traced the gray, smoky scent of another one of his human charges. This one slept in a small corner of the carriage house, one used originally as a horse stall.

"Bertrand is awake," Luc said. "You can't leave the way you came."

Marco motioned to Yann and René, and the three of them promptly began stripping off their clothes. Marco was tall and strapping, the muscles in his chest and thighs impressive compared to Luc's more lithe, compact build. Luc waited patiently for them to shed their last articles of clothing. There was no room for embarrassment among the Dispossessed. They were all men who went unclothed far too often for modesty.

"Thank you for your hospitality," Marco quipped as he strode easily toward the open loft door, his clothing and shoes bundled in his hands.

"As always," Luc replied.

The three of them stood at the loft door, their bodies rimmed by the pearly moonlight. The transformation unfolded within a matter of seconds. In simultaneous motion, Marco's spine lengthened and arched; René's arms and legs extended, his face morphing into a wolfish snout; Yann's fingers and toes mutated into deadly claws. After countless shifts over centuries, their bones, joints, and tendons now moved with ease, gliding from one place to another, springing cartilage where their human forms had none.

Marco's skin hardened over with a thick jacket of rusty golden scales the color of a midsummer sunset. The new skin stretched tight around the shifting bones of his face. And then, in the space of a heartbeat, two scale-covered wings unfurled from his back. The same happened with René, only his scales were a shade lighter, shimmering like spun gold. The stone grotesques, all cast in dull gray, would never be able to capture the magnificent colors of a flesh-and-blood gargoyle. Their individual colors, exaggerations of their human coloring, almost made up for just how hideous their gargoyle forms were.

Marco's wings snapped open. The tip of each scaly copper wing brushed the ceiling. Yann's feathered wings, each plume razor edged, were streaked with silver, just as his black human hair was. He took to the air first, followed by René.

Marco dropped into a crouch, his spine a prominent ridge.

He glanced back at Luc, his thin lips parted to expose two rows of needle teeth, and screeched. It would sound to a waking Bertrand like the shriek of a hawk. But Luc understood the language perfectly: *"Drive them out quickly, brother."*

Marco leaped from the edge of the loft and soared into the night sky.

CHAPTER THREE

Morning dawned with fickle sunshine and a whipping wind. The thin panes of glass in Ingrid's bedroom windows had let in both, and she'd woken shivering. Hers was a small room tucked in a corner of the rectory, two doors down from Gabby. Ingrid had tried to arrange her things the night before when she'd been too restless to sleep, but it had been impossible. She suspected the butler's pantry at Waverly House was more spacious than her new bedroom. She'd slept with dresses laid out at the foot of her bed, with books piled into towers on the floor, shoe and hatboxes on the pillows around her, and the silver-framed photograph of Grayson—one he'd given her a few years before—in her hand.

After carefully setting the photograph on her vanity stand and dressing in a heavy Indian silk dress, Ingrid's determination to hunt down a bookshop returned. Grayson had roamed London's bookstores, and she was certain he'd made a habit of that here as well. The chances that he'd become friends with shop owners were better than good—Grayson was the sort of person who made friends at the drop of a hat.

People were drawn to him, to his easy charm and genuine interest. The courtesy title of Lord Fairfax truly didn't suit him. It made him sound pompous, when really he would give discussions of taxes with their family accountant and of boxwood pruning with the family gardener equal attention and curiosity. Ingrid loved that about him. It was one of the things that, to her, made Grayson the better of their two halves.

She would track down his friends and find him.

After an indecent breakfast of hot chocolate, croissants, and jam (sausage and eggs would not be found on any proper Parisian breakfast plate, Madam Bertot had explained indignantly), Ingrid left for the carriage house. Gabby had not been at the breakfast table, and Ingrid decided to let her sleep. She'd likely stay at the rectory anyway, insisting that bookshops were a dreadful bore. She cared to gobble up only the romantic novels Ingrid dutifully brought her.

The air was frigid despite the sun, and the half-inch of snow on the ground had blown into little crests, making the churchyard look like a shore of bleached white sand. Ingrid hurried toward the stone carriage house with the single-minded need for warmth. She barged through the door and slammed it behind her. The servant named Bertrand jumped out from behind a landau carriage, and she realized just how loudly and inappropriately she'd charged inside. She should have sent one of the footmen, whose names she still didn't know, for the carriage. It had been completely improper for her to come fetch it herself. But she'd been too focused on finding Grayson to stop to think.

Bertrand crumpled a cloth in his hands, one he'd probably been using to polish the carriage's deep-green varnish. He was an older man with a red nose and fleshy cheeks. He turned his lips up in a small, hesitant smile.

"Ah . . . bonjour, monsieur," she said, nervous about her French. *"J'aimerais . . . ah . . . manger des livres aujourd'hui."*

Bertrand's smile deepened. He turned his head to the side. Ingrid saw his shoulders shake. He wasn't . . . he couldn't be . . . was he *laughing* at her?

A voice resounded from the loft. "You just said you would like to eat books today."

The handsome boy from the day before, the one with the green eyes, was leaning against the bare, rough beam of the loft railing. His dark curls veiled half of his face. The color of his exposed eye was just as vivid as Ingrid remembered.

"Obviously I didn't mean that," she said.

The boy—Luc—continued to look down his nose at her. As before, his expression was filled with loathing. "Next time, speak English. In case you've forgotten, Constantine made sure that *we* could understand *your* language." He let go of the railing and disappeared from view.

Ingrid bristled, at once humiliated and livid. She wasn't used to being chastised, especially by a servant.

She raised her voice so Luc could hear from wherever he'd gone. "I meant to say that I would like to go to a bookshop today. One my brother is familiar with."

"Bertrand will take you," Luc called, still out of view. His English was impressive, his accent slight. She pushed aside the fleeting notion that it was charming.

Bertrand stepped forward, setting his polishing cloth inside a large box of tools. "Le Livre Rouge is just a few streets away. I can have the landau ready in five minutes."

His voice was kinder and more attentive than Luc's. But it wasn't open or friendly. Ingrid was an outsider. A foreigner. A job to be taken care of.

"And my brother frequents Le Livre Rouge?" Ingrid asked as she followed Bertrand around the rumble at the rear of the carriage.

His eyes skittered away from hers. "Yes, but Lord Fairfax visits a number of bookshops in the city."

Of course he did. Grayson would have scouted them all out for himself and for Ingrid. "We'll try Le Livre Rouge first," she said. Bertrand gave an obedient nod and Ingrid backed away.

Dash propriety—she wasn't about to go outside and wait in the cold for five minutes. She chose a spot near the door where she would be out of the way.

Ingrid had lived with a staff of servants at Waverly House. They'd had three times as many as Monsieur Constantine had hired. But never had she felt like a burden to them. When Ingrid had been a little girl, Edna, the Waverly House cook, had often hidden a sweet for her beneath the napkin on the trays sent up to the nursery; and Robert, their driver, had good-naturedly teased Ingrid and her best friend, Anna, about their addictions to Bond Street whenever he'd driven them to the shops.

The memories had her longing for home, for Anna and her soft smile. While Ingrid was practical, blunt, and reserved, Anna was pleasant, prim, and fawning, just as fine English girls were born and bred to be. Anna had been happy to bend to London's rules for young society ladies instead of fighting them. She had looked forward to the teas, the dress fittings, the dinners—all the things Ingrid had found insufferable. Anna had been so much better at it all, and she'd been rewarded for her efforts.

She'd be marrying Jonathan Walker before the winter was over.

Ingrid didn't understand how she could both love and hate Anna so much at the same time.

Bertrand had left to go to the stables, leaving the carriage house's large double doors wide. Wind nipped Ingrid's cheeks. The loft stairs to her left creaked. She saw Luc from the corner of her eye but didn't acknowledge him. If he was going to be rude, well, then Ingrid could dish it out in equal doses.

He stopped on the second-to-last step and watched her. Ingrid felt his incandescent eyes on her, scrutinizing, but pretended to be looking over at the landau.

"The stove is farther in. You should wait there," he said. Ingrid peeked around the bare wooden structure of the stairwell and saw a blazing stove, a few mismatched chairs, and a patched couch. She was freezing and the stove looked wonderful.

"No thank you," Ingrid said stiffly. "I'm not cold."

Luc came off the steps and advanced toward her. "Yes you are. You're shivering. And besides that, you're in my way."

Ingrid had been shivering but now stopped. "Excuse me?"

He gestured to the wall behind her. "I have work to do. You're in my way."

Ingrid turned and saw a pegged wall holding leather and metal tack and carriage accoutrements and shelves filled with tools. She moved to the side, toward the underbelly of the steps. She grappled for something cutting to say in return but came up empty-handed. And then the moment passed. Luc took down a length of leather, a round tin of polish, and a rag and kicked out a stool stored beneath a shelf. Ingrid stayed under the steps as he set to work.

His green eyes flashed up at her. "Do you really think you're going to find your brother holed up in some bookshop?"

Ingrid set her jaw. She searched the yard beyond the open carriage house doors, impatient for Bertrand to return with the horses. A gentleman Luc was not. He spoke too boldly, too familiarly with her. And yet, Ingrid stayed put.

"You seem to be under the impression that I have nothing but cotton fluff between my ears," she replied.

Luc looked up from the strip of leather he'd coated in beeswax. The air of loathing had burned off. "I am under no such impression. But I do think you're wasting your time."

He went back to rubbing the leather with smooth strokes, working the yellow wax into the grain.

"What would you suggest I do, sit inside and twiddle my

thumbs? Maybe stitch a little needlepoint? Oh, I know—I could have a tea party!"

Luc's hands paused at her outburst. She knew she was over-reacting, but she didn't care.

"He is my brother. My *twin*. I'm going to find him." She swallowed the unexpected knot in her throat. "Besides, it's not as if anyone here has gone out of their way to search for him. The police haven't even been called upon yet."

For a reason, she knew. Constantine had made it clear that Grayson had kept up his roguish ways in Paris. Still, a little concern for Grayson's well-being would have been nice.

Luc didn't defend himself or any other servant at the rectory. Instead, he sat with still hands and a dark, somewhat confounded expression. He studied Ingrid carefully, the way someone might peer at a strange insect.

"The police are busy lately," he finally replied.

"Do you think . . ." She stopped. She was conversing far too much with someone she'd planned to ignore.

Luc chased away an itch on his cheek with the back of his hand and left behind a streak of polish. The urge to rub her thumb over his cheek and wipe it clean filled her. When Luc spoke, Ingrid's attention roved to his lips.

"Do I think what?" he said.

She tore her gaze from his mouth and battled a rising blush. "That my brother's disappearance could have something to do with the other disappearances Monsieur Constantine told us about?"

Luc capped the tin of beeswax. His fingertips pressed hard on the tin cover, denting the metal.

He still hadn't given her an answer when Bertrand led two black mares through the carriage house doors.

Gabby whipped in on his heels, wrapped in ivory mink from head to foot, looking like a snowdrift. "There you are, Ingrid!"

Luc rose from the stool and set the tin of wax on a shelf. Quietly, as if he wished the words to reach only Ingrid's ears, he said, "They don't have anything to do with your brother."

He was gone, already rattling the steps on his way to the loft when Gabby reached her. Gabby looked after Luc, frowning, and then turned to Ingrid.

"Where are you going so early?"

Ingrid missed a beat, distracted by Luc's answer. He'd sounded so confident. And for some inexplicable reason, she believed him.

"A bookshop," she answered.

"To search for Grayson?" Gabby asked, brightening. "Bring me with you! Mother is having Monsieur Constantine call for the police. I can't imagine why he hasn't called for them before now. Oh, and let's find a café somewhere along the way first. I'm starving. Did you see Madam Bertot's breakfast? Where in the queen's name were the eggs?"

Gabby, whose thoughts all too often streamed from her lips without censor, didn't mention Ingrid's flushed cheeks. She must have assumed the brisk air had colored them, not Luc.

Bertrand was ready within a few minutes and was given new instructions to take them to a café. He drove down the short gravel-and-brick drive rimming the abbey's churchyard and through the unkempt break in the hedgerow, then turned right onto rue Dante. Gabby yawned. Sleep fogged her eyes, making her look even more beautiful than usual.

"We're riding alone," Ingrid whispered, feeling a thrill of freedom. "In London we couldn't even sneeze without a chaperone being there to hold out a hankie."

"Which is absurd. Thankfully Paris and Mama are far more forward thinking," Gabby replied.

Ingrid's first instinct was to object. Chaperones were a sensible notion. She was surprised their mother hadn't decided to bring one for Gabby. Ingrid didn't need one, of course. She was only seventeen, but word had spread like the fever about that engagement gala and Jonathan and how Ingrid had . . . reacted.

There hadn't been a newspaper or scandal sheet in town without a story about it. They'd been awful, and the bald rumors that Ingrid had purposely set the fire were damning. Nevertheless, her ruined reputation didn't matter a whit compared to the damage the fire had done.

To the people it had injured.

There would be no prospects for Ingrid anytime soon, even after their planned return in the spring. She was perfectly content with that, too. She deserved much worse.

"That boy back there," Gabby began. Ingrid's chest tightened and she stared out the window, at the sidewalk crammed with foot traffic. She didn't want to talk about Luc or how rude he'd been. "What's wrong with him?"

Ingrid glanced up from where she'd been worrying her thumb along the trim of her white ermine cloak. "Wrong?"

"He looks odd."

The carriage rumbled down the boulevard, past poster-plastered lampposts, a shopkeeper sweeping snow from his salmon-pink window awning, and a cluster of barrows holding hothouse flowers. Nothing familiar. Everything intimidating. Just as Luc had been.

"I suppose his eyes are an odd shade of green," Ingrid allowed.

Gabby sighed. "Yes, that. But his face, too. It just looks . . . sharp. Defined. *Strangely* defined. Does he have an accent? Maybe he's from the Greek islands. That would be rather exotic."

Ingrid hadn't noticed anything but Luc's eyes and his unruly hair, and the way he'd scorned her with a single glance.

Bertrand stopped the horses just outside a bustling café. As soon as they stepped to the curb, an intoxicating scent of bread and coffee wrapped itself around Ingrid and pulled her through a pair of double doors with the name Café Julius etched in red on the glass. They must have appeared decidedly English to the waiter, because he broke from his own language to take their orders.

"And for you, *chérie?*" he said to Gabby once he'd memorized Ingrid's request for tea, brioche, and an egg.

A slow smile worked its way across Gabby's lips. Ingrid had seen that smile before; it was just as flirtatious as the waiter's own cocky grin. He turned his tall, lanky frame toward Gabby, his shaggy blond hair down to his shoulders, his black trousers held up by a red sash tied around his narrow waist.

"I'll have the same as my sister," she answered. She then made a show of being interested in something outside the window. Ingrid rolled her eyes. Gabby had acted this way around the young men in London, too: bored as a Persian cat batting around a ball of yarn.

"Perhaps a chaperone would have been best," Ingrid muttered after the waiter went to place their order.

Gabby huffed. "You *are* my chaperone."

Ingrid sat back in her chair. "I'm nowhere near on the shelf! I'm not even eighteen yet."

She might still make a match. Someday. Perhaps in America—or more realistically, the North Pole.

"I know, Griddy," Gabby said. "But you're an iron shield against flirtation and temptation. We all know it, and so do you, for that matter. You wouldn't let that scoundrel step out of line, now, would you?"

Gabby sat up in her chair and searched for their waiter. Ingrid had to admit that her sister was right. She wouldn't. Still, she didn't enjoy being likened to an *iron shield*. Iron was cold and unfeeling and hard. Was that how people saw her? Was that how *Jonathan* had seen her?

For weeks, Ingrid had forced herself not to think of him. Not to go back in her mind to the time they had spent together: countless summer picnics, invitations from his mother and sister to afternoon teas, Sunday-morning jaunts through Hyde Park, dinners and balls at Waverly House.

There was little in the world Ingrid despised more than

feeling like a fool. She wanted to be angry with Jonathan for tri-fling with her, making her believe he had feelings for her and then carelessly ripping them away. But she couldn't. Ingrid hadn't been trifled with. She'd been blind, and only after her heart had been crushed had she seen what she'd so naïvely overlooked: Anna Bettinger.

Anna had always been with them. For the picnics, the teas, squeezing onto the bench seat of Jonathan's new motorwagen as they'd puttered through Hyde Park. Jonathan had been falling in love right in front of Ingrid's nose, and she'd been certain that *she* was the object of his affection. The whole situation would have been comic if it didn't stir up tears every time she thought of it.

"What is your name, *chérie?*" the waiter asked Gabby as he returned with their food. "You must tell me or I will not be able to think of anything else for the rest of the day." He had his hip against the rim of their round table. The café was abuzz, but he didn't seem to care about rushing off to see to the other patrons.

"My name is Lady Gabriella," her sister said. The waiter lifted Gabby's hand from her lap and put it to his lips.

"Lady Gabriella, I am Henri. It is a pleasure."

Ingrid parted her lips to divert his attention but saw Gabby's eyes flick to hers. Ingrid stopped. An iron shield she was *not*.

"You are new to the Latin Quarter, *oui?*" he continued.

Gabby nodded, her hand still tucked inside his. "Our mother just purchased an old abbey on rue Dante. She plans to open an art museum the same week the Exposition begins."

Henri's shoulders stiffened. He lowered Gabby's hand. "L'Abbaye Saint-Dismas? The one with *les grotesques?* The gargoyles?"

"They are quite noticeable, aren't they?" Gabby answered, wrinkling her nose.

Ingrid remembered the evening before, when she'd imagined that one of the stone creatures had actually moved. *Grotesques.*

The French word for them seemed more appropriate than the English one.

Henri's coy playfulness fled. "I thought a young man had purchased that abbey."

Ingrid lowered her teacup. "Our brother."

"Lord Fairfax," Gabby added with proud flourish. "Do you know him?"

Henri tucked his circular tray beneath his arm. His eyes roamed over both of their faces with new interest. "You are Grayson's sisters?"

Ingrid leaned forward eagerly, pressing her hands against the copper tabletop.

"You know our brother?" Gabby asked. "Have you seen him? He's been missing for days." Her raised voice had caught the attention of the patrons at another table.

Ingrid widened her eyes. "Gabby, you don't need to air our laundry so thoroughly."

"Why not? Someone could have heard or seen something."

Ingrid doubted the people sitting next to them knew anything that could help. And any rumors they started certainly wouldn't do any good, either.

Henri's blond brows pulled together. "I'm sorry, I have not seen him."

Ingrid exchanged a pensive glance with Gabby before dropping her gaze to the warm, buttery bread and hardboiled egg on the plate before her. She didn't think she could eat a bite now. Henri bowed and walked away, quickly threading around the tables, toward a zinc bar set along the back wall.

Gabby ripped off a corner of her brioche. "Did you hear him call Grayson by his given name? The cheek of it."

"You know Grayson," Ingrid said with a shrug, watching Henri join a girl with short, dark hair behind the counter.

Gabby scowled. "What do we do now? Where the devil is he?"

Ingrid cut her eyes away from Henri. *"Gabby,"* she whispered.

"Did you even notice how nervous that waiter acted once he'd stopped flirting with you?"

Ingrid glanced back toward Henri. He was leaning close to the dark-haired girl, whispering in her ear. As his lips moved rapidly, the girl's round brown eyes coasted over the tables and came to rest on Ingrid and Gabby.

"You think he knows something," Gabby said.

Ingrid pushed aside her breakfast. "I do. Something he doesn't want *us* to know."

CHAPTER FOUR

Le Livre Rouge turned out to be a hole-in-the-wall at two intersecting rues, and exactly the sort of shop that would have drawn Grayson like a moth to flame.

It was set in the corner of a building that jutted out in a prominent triangular tip. A small sign, carved in the shape of a book, hung over the door. The devilish red paint was severely chipped. The metal hooks from which the sign hung, looped through the black-painted book spine, looked as if they had rusted multiple seasons ago.

Inside, the shop was hardly bigger than the sitting room at the rectory. The counter was empty, though stacks of books sat at each end. One was open to a center page, as if someone had just been standing there, reading. Ingrid glanced around at the closely set shelves, each one positively stuffed with books. Tall bookcases blocked the windows and the morning sunlight. Gabby wrinkled her nose at the musty scent of old books and leather. Ingrid breathed it in. If knowledge and curiosity had a scent, it was this.

Ingrid dipped into a darkened aisle and crooked her neck to read the spines. The shelves had been categorized by subject and then by title rather than author. Just as Ingrid and Grayson preferred. The shelves in front of her, lined with the faded and frayed cloth covers of brown and green tomes, were dedicated to theology. She had just tipped one out to slide it from the shelf when she heard a man greet Gabby.

"Bonjour, mademoiselle," he said, then continued in a string of French. Gabby stopped him, and after Ingrid heard a few words she knew, like *anglais* and *soeur,* it was clear Gabby was informing him that her sister, hidden within the shelves, required English. The man laughed. Embarrassed, Ingrid carefully tucked the theology book back between its neighbors and walked toward the aisle opening, a forced grin on her lips.

"Forgive me, I should have asked. It's just rare to find a patron here at such an early hour, if at all," the man said to Gabby. His accent wasn't French—it was the swift, hard lilt of an American.

Ingrid exited the aisle and stopped short when she saw him. He wasn't the dusty, middle-aged man she envisioned as a bookshop keeper. He was young, perhaps a few years older than her. He balanced a stack of books in one hand as he spoke to Gabby, pushing his wire-rimmed glasses higher on the bridge of his nose. It was a strong nose, sharply defined, like his cheekbones, and he had a shy smile.

Ingrid was still staring at him when he turned that smile toward her—and almost instantly, it crashed. He stared at her, recognition firing his eyes.

"You're Grayson's sister," he whispered. He turned back to Gabby. "His sisters."

He set the stack of books on the counter in front of him. They slid into a cascade. Ingrid held still as his eyes skipped from the tip of her head to her toes in close inspection. His eyes were the color of hay, a brown so pale they bordered on gold. He frowned at her, making her think that something about the way she looked was terribly wrong. She glanced down at her dress, her cloak, even her gloved hands, but all was spotless and the height of fashion. What was it, then? Henri had looked at her in the same puzzled way.

Ingrid started to speak but found her concentration dashed. "Yes, I am. We are. I'm looking . . . *we,* I mean. We're looking not for a book, but—" She stopped, flustered. "Who are you, the owner?"

Heat crept up her neck. She was being a complete, bumbling *idiot*.

"No, but I run the place." He scratched the side of his head. "I'm Vander. My uncle, the owner, lives near Vichy now." His eyes moved to the side, as though someone had walked up behind her. Ingrid couldn't help but follow his gaze, but the space was empty.

"How did you know we are Lord Fairfax's sisters?" Gabby asked, but Vander's attention was fixed on Ingrid.

"You look just like him, of course. And forgive me, I know titles are important to your lot, but Grayson insisted I use his given name."

There was a beat of uncomfortable silence.

"Have you just arrived in Paris?" he asked, his voice as tense as his expression.

"Yesterday afternoon," Ingrid answered. "But Grayson hasn't been at the rectory. We're told he's missing—"

"Is this your first time leaving the rectory?" Vander cut in, even more sharply. Ingrid looked sideways at him. What sort of question was that?

Gabby, her temper igniting, spoke first. "Our brother is missing. We aren't about to sit inside the rectory and wait for him to turn up."

Ingrid jumped in to soften her sister's attack. "We didn't leave the rectory last night, of course. Our brother's acquaintance, Monsieur Constantine, advised we stay in."

Vander nodded as he eased himself from behind the counter. He was tall, his shoulders broad. He looked like everything she'd imagined a boy from the American West might look. Ingrid could no longer ignore how handsome he was.

"Good. Constantine is right." The strain in Vander's shoulders, and then the firm line of his brow, relaxed. "I'm sorry. I don't mean to be rude, but in the last few weeks a number of young women have gone missing. Grayson was a friend. I wouldn't want either of his sisters to find themselves in any danger."

Ingrid stepped forward. "*Was* a friend?"

A moment ticked by before Vander mumbled, "Constantine is a mutual friend. He told me Grayson is missing."

"And now you speak of him in the past tense?" Ingrid asked.

Vander took off his glasses and rubbed the lenses with the trailing end of a red sash, each side trimmed with gold thread. He had the sash threaded through the loops of his trousers. Henri had been wearing a similar one.

"I certainly didn't mean to," he said.

"Our mother is speaking with the police right now," Gabby cut in. "We only thought to do some searching for ourselves."

Which now seemed thoroughly inadequate and ridiculous. If anything, Ingrid was more baffled than before.

"Did he tell you we were coming?" Ingrid asked.

Vander replaced the glasses on the bridge of his nose. Somehow, the return of those wire frames pulled the features of his face back together, into a whole. His looks struck her again, this time as even more fetching.

"He did. He was looking forward to not living at the abbey all alone," Vander answered.

"Why? Was there something about the abbey Grayson didn't like?"

Ingrid knew she was being too brusque with her questions,

but she didn't care. Vander rubbed the back of his neck. His lips parted as he sought an answer.

Gabby helped him along. "Personally, I can't stand those gargoyles all over the place. Ugly little things. Mama should tear them down before opening the gallery."

Vander speared Gabby with a deadly-serious glare. "She can't do that. Those gargoyles have adorned the abbey for centuries. It's one of the city's oldest, most important pieces of architecture. They belong there. If your mother has an eye toward art, she has to see what masterpieces they are."

"Masterpieces?" Gabby shook her head. "Hardly. They'll scare off the gallery patrons if we leave them up."

The smallest, briefest smile crossed Vander's lips before they sealed again into a taut frown. "They're of historic importance."

"You aren't from Paris, or even France, for that matter," Gabby said. "Why do you care so much?"

Ingrid silenced her sister with a pointed look as Vander disappeared behind the counter. She wanted to pinch Gabby's arm. Her sister had a fire inside her that flared at the worst moments. Vander was no doubt ruing the moment they'd walked into his shop.

"You're right, I'm from Pennsylvania," he answered as he shuffled through a stack of books along a back shelf. "But I've lived in Paris long enough to appreciate the value of buildings like L'Abbaye Saint-Dismas. Do you have any idea how old that structure is? The foundation dates from the early part of the tenth century."

He extracted a book from the bottom of the stack, not bothering to right the ones he upset in the process. He moved briskly from behind the counter. Though Gabby had been the one to disparage the gargoyles, Vander extended the book toward Ingrid.

"If you read through this, you'll understand what I mean," he said.

Ingrid took the large, square book, its leather spine hanging limp from loosely sewn vellum pages. Vander kept hold of one end as Ingrid inspected the faded, ancient black cover. No title had been embossed along the spine or on the rubbed-worn leather cover.

"Oh. Very well, then," she said. "How much do I owe you?"

He smiled. "Not a sou. The book's not mine, it's your brother's."

Ingrid frowned. "I don't understand. Did he lend it to you?"

Grayson wasn't usually one to lend books. He treasured them too much to chance that they wouldn't be returned.

"He purchased it here, brought it home, read it, then gave it back," Vander explained.

Ingrid was even more confused now. He *gave* the book *back*? Unheard of! He'd have held on to even the dullest of books, including Gabby's dramas.

"I don't intend to frighten you," Vander whispered before releasing his grip on the book. Ingrid parted her lips to ask what he meant, but he began speaking again too quickly. "Your brother was fine living alone at the rectory. He was curious about its history, so he came here, searching for literature. He spoke of you often. He missed you." Vander cocked his head to the side, still holding her gaze. "Understandably."

Ingrid widened her eyes, stunned by his boldness. A warm trickle of unexpected pleasure filled her chest. Blasted skin! She'd be the color of beet juice in less than two seconds. She folded the book against her chest and cut her eyes away from Vander's.

"Thank you for your time, Mr. . . . . Vander." The heat rushed to her face even faster.

"Griddy, his name isn't Mr. Vander," Gabby said.

Ingrid glared at her sister. "And mine isn't Griddy." Ingrid forced herself to meet Vander's gaze once more. He was smiling, apparently enjoying her discomfort. "My name is Ingrid," she said quietly, dispensing with the more formal *Lady Ingrid* she was used to.

"I know," he said. "And my last name is Burke. But please, just call me Vander."

Ingrid nodded, watching as his slanted smile straightened out. Once again he seemed to be taking stock of her clothing, her hair. Looking at everything but her face. Did he think her strange for some reason? If Grayson was his friend, had her brother shared anything personal with Vander? Ingrid fidgeted with the heavy book. Had her mother written to Grayson about what had happened with Anna, and had Grayson spoken of it to Vander?

She hadn't intended to ruin Anna's engagement announcement; she had simply been trying to flee the ballroom before anyone could see her dissolve into tears. Ingrid shut her eyes against the wretched memory. The table she'd caught her hip against, so small and unsteady, the candelabra she'd overturned in the process. The curtains of the nearby window wild with fire. Ingrid still didn't understand how the candle flames had reached the lengths of red damask.

"If there's anything I can do to help you find Grayson, just ask." Vander's voice extinguished the memories. Ingrid opened her eyes. "And I'll call on the rectory soon. If that's acceptable?"

Gabby wrapped her hand around Ingrid's elbow and tugged her toward the door. "Of course, Mr. Burke. Thank you."

Gabby hardly gave Ingrid a chance to stammer good-bye before pulling her out of the shop and rushing back to the carriage.

"What a pity," Gabby said, sighing as Bertrand latched the door and climbed up onto the driver's bench.

"What do you mean?" Ingrid pulled the window curtain aside to peer through the mullioned windows of the bookshop.

"It seems a waste. To be so handsome and yet such a dreadful bore."

Ingrid peeled her eyes from the bookshop's windows. "You wouldn't be saying that if he'd been flirting with you instead of arguing."

Gabby snorted. "Did you hear him? *'They're of historic importance.'*"

Ingrid couldn't help but laugh. Her sister did do a fine American accent.

"Well, perhaps they are," Ingrid said, running her ivory glove over the book's cover. She opened to a random page and sat back in the seat at the sight of the illustration that met her eyes: the intricately drawn face of a gargoyle, its blank, globelike eyes bulging, its doggish snout shriveled into a fierce grimace.

Gabby knocked her elbow into Ingrid's, the impact causing the cover to crash down. "And now he has a reason to pay the rectory a visit, doesn't he?"

Ingrid delivered a stronger blow with her own elbow. "The only reason I would hope for a visit from Mr. Burke would be because he has news of Grayson."

She folded her hands over the cover. What did architecture matter? With every passing hour, the fist inside her chest tightened a little more. Her brother was missing. There had to be something she could do, and she was certain the police wouldn't want her involvement. Grayson needed help. *Her* help. With or without the police's consent, she would give it.

The wounds were slow to heal, and the punctures weren't given enough time to stop seeping blood before the monster with fangs returned.

Grayson held out his bare arm and flexed his hand. At least a half-dozen four-pronged bites riddled his skin. The constant blue-black flickering light made each one look cavernous against the pale violet of his skin. The creature was drinking Grayson's blood, but it was like no vampire Goethe, Lord Byron, or even that new fellow, Stoker, had imagined. And instead of making Grayson feel drained and weak, he felt better now than when he'd awakened in this strange place. Stronger, somehow.

Grayson folded his arm against his stomach. Wherever he was, he had to figure a way out. The thing with fangs, the hooded woman . . . they weren't human. None of the creatures Grayson had spied crossing back and forth in front of the entrance to the dark, tunnel-like cave were. Some whose spines were out of joint, some who had no spines at all, some whose bodies were misshapen, others with more appendages than Grayson could count before they disappeared from view.

The ancient book he'd found at Vander's shop had mentioned otherworldly beings, but Grayson hadn't wanted anything more to do with that book after reading about the gargoyles and then seeing the dark wings atop the abbey. After, he'd realized that what the book said—what Vander and his friends had told him—was real. But what exactly had they told him? Why couldn't he remember?

He squeezed his eyes shut. Whole blocks of his memory were missing, especially about the night he'd been brought here. Scattered images came to him, though it was like trying to see through frosted glass: his reflection in the foyer mirror, his black silk top hat that looked like it belonged on his father rather than on him. The starched wings of his collar hadn't been pressed evenly, leaving one triangle larger than the other. He reached up and felt the now soiled and tattered dress shirt, its crisp collar and cuffs lost.

I was too trusting. The thought fell from his clogged memory and landed heavily. He'd trusted someone, and it had been a mistake. He clasped the buttons of his shirtfront. But who? Who shouldn't he have trusted?

A flash of movement at the head of the cave stole his attention. Instinctively, Grayson dropped his hand and wedged himself as far back into the corner as possible. It didn't matter. The fanged creature was back, walking toward him on two legs, standing as erect as any human. And yet its hands were covered in tufts of shiny, greasy fur, nails extended into sharpened claws. And its fangs.

Grayson knew those fangs best of all.

CHAPTER FIVE

Gabby ignored the cold sweat breaking out beneath her camisole and satin coutil corset. Giving in to nerves wasn't going to get her the information she had just risked sneaking out of the rectory for. Still, the spacious carriage closed in on her as Bertrand called the horses to a standstill. The fleeting thought that it might have been better to invite Ingrid was gone before Bertrand had even hopped down from the box.

Her sister's eyebrows would have leaped clear off her forehead had she seen the dress Gabby had changed into: an evening gown of profane red satin with a black lace overlay and a plunging, black lace–trimmed neckline that accentuated her rather voluptuous décolletage. The gown wasn't appropriate for a girl just shy of sixteen to wear in midafternoon.

But then again, a visit to Henri's flat wasn't appropriate, either.

No. It was better that she'd come alone. Ingrid would have accused Gabby of being selfish and brazen. Of only wanting to see the flirtatious waiter again and not caring enough about the welfare of their brother. *Ingrid*. She could be so starchy. So presumptuous.

Grayson was her brother, too, wasn't he? They couldn't finish one another's sentences or gabble on for hours about the history of some insignificant country or person, but she loved Grayson just the same. And whether Ingrid liked it or not, she *did* share something with Grayson. Just like him, Gabby was spirited and mischievous and bold. If gathering information called for a little recklessness, she would gladly oblige.

Gabby slid the small scrap of brown butcher paper from her cloak's pocket. On it, the slanted handwriting read *Hôtel Bastian, 95 rue de Sèvres, apt. 3. 18h00. Soirée.* She ran the note between her thumb and forefinger, remembering how Henri had slipped the missive into her palm that morning when he'd taken her hand and kissed it. Feeling the paper there after had given her an unexplainable thrill. She'd been dying for a moment's privacy away from Ingrid's judgmental eyes to read what the boy had written.

When she was finally able to, Gabby had decided she would go—but only to ask more questions about Grayson. Henri knew him. Perhaps his friends at this soirée would as well. The only problem was the time. It was barely three o'clock now.

Bertrand opened the carriage door. The air had bite. It was so crisp and cold her lungs wanted to reject it. The party would not be under way for many hours, at a time when her mother wouldn't have let her out of the house. So she'd had to come now—but this was just fine with Gabby. She had an address, a suggestive invitation from Henri, and a dress that would get her whatever information she sought.

Hôtel Bastian wasn't a hotel in the English sense but a five-storied town house with a façade of whitewashed brick and iron terraces, topped by a black mansard roof. It was one of many along the rue, some sporting shops with colorful striped awnings on the ground floor, others with gray stone stoops. Stark trees lined the street, their thin trunks and bare branches reaching toward a bank of snow clouds.

Gabby climbed the steep steps to the double front door with windows outlined by intricate lead work. There was no bell button to ring and no knocker, and, after a moment of waiting, it appeared there was no doorman, either. Feeling quite scandalous, she opened the door herself. She resisted looking back toward Bertrand. She would do this. How could she ruin her reputation in Paris when she didn't yet have one?

A black-and-white-tiled floor filled the oblong foyer, a single round red tile at its center. Oddly enough, there were no doors or rooms leading off the foyer. Gabby wondered at that a moment before moving to the twisting staircase that led to the upper floors. Lifting the edge of her gown off the dingy marble steps, she ascended to the second level. Here, doors lined the walls, though, like the front door, none bore numbers, doorbells, or even knockers.

Gabby hesitated. She needed flat number three, according to Henri's slip of paper. Her best guess was the third door on the left. Gabby raised her hand to knock.

"Can I help you?"

Gabby shrieked and spun toward the stairwell and the sound of the deep voice. The only things she could see as her heartbeat slowed to a normal rhythm were piercing blue eyes fringed by long, coal-black lashes. The boy had spoken in English, though with an accent.

"I—" Gabby fumbled for poise. "I'm looking for someone."

The boy, who actually looked to be a young man about her brother's age, nodded to the door behind Gabby. "That flat there belongs to Henri."

He inspected her velvet cloak and the deep-red gown beneath. His thick black brows pressed together in what looked very much like judgment.

Gabby's cheeks burned. "Yes, well, I happen to be looking for Henri, so thank you."

The man kicked up a corner of his mouth but seemed to be fighting the rest of his grin. "He isn't here, lass."

A Scotsman. Gabby drew closer to Henri's door as the Scot took the last step up the stairs and strode past her. He had an easy stride. It positively dripped with arrogance.

"I understand his soirée doesn't begin until six o'clock," she started to say, attempting an excuse for why she was so elegantly dressed. She also needed an excuse for arriving so early, without a chaperone, and knocking on the door of a young man's flat.

The Scot only half glanced back at her as he approached the second flight of twisting stairs. Still, she saw the humor in those morning-glory-blue eyes of his. His smile revealed gleaming white teeth, a dimple pressing into the corner of his ruggedly cut chin.

"Soirée?" he echoed, one of his large hands gripping the stairwell's iron railing. He parted his lips as if to say something, but then sealed them. "Never mind. Come back at six, lass. *If* you can escape your mother's skirts."

He started up the steps, soles scuffing the marble. Gabby rippled at the insult to her age. She colored at the fact that he'd *known* her age. She'd been so certain she'd made herself appear at least a handful of years older.

Gabby did what she usually did when insulted and humiliated. She fought back.

"I am quite old enough to be free of my mother's supervision," she called after him. "And if you knew anything at all, you would know that it wouldn't be my *mother's* watchful eye, but that of my *governess*."

Gabby fluttered her eyes closed. Governess? That was even worse. Why not just say she still had a wet nurse, too? The Scot's feet came to a halt. They held still a moment before they turned and slowly navigated back down the steps. He held his tongue until he came off the last step, but his eyes glittered with mischief. Gabby wished she'd kept her mouth shut.

"I know plenty, lass." He kept advancing toward her with that relaxed, arrogant gait of his. "I know about the note Henri slipped you saying there would be a bash at this address at six o'clock."

Gabby would not let this Scot see her surprise. "Hardly a difficult conclusion to come to. I've practically told you as much."

He clasped his hands behind him and, still all good humor, began to circle her. She shied to the side.

"I know that this *soirée* of Henri's will consist of two people— you and Henri," he said, arching one of his brows. "I know that at first you'll be spitting fire, ready to give him a good slap, just like the other girls he's pulled this sham on. But he'll work his charm like a puppet master, that boy will. You'll get all tangled up in it, and you'll eventually succumb and stay." The Scot stopped and met Gabby's now infuriated stare. "Just like the other girls."

Her blood ran hot, her embarrassment high.

"I am not like other girls," she said through clenched teeth.

His eyes raked the front of her cloak and the glimpses of gown underneath. "I see that."

The cheek! Gabby squared her shoulders. "If you think I came here for a tryst with Henri—"

"Now, what would make me think such a thing?"

"—a boy I hardly *know*," Gabby continued.

"A fine English rose like yourself."

"Stop that!" Gabby stamped her foot and instantly wished she hadn't made such a childish move.

The infuriating Scotsman held up his hands in submission. He bit back a playful smirk, the defined curves of his full lips quite distracting. His nose slanted to the left, as if it had once been broken in a fistfight. The imperfection made him look wicked and much older than his nineteen or twenty years. Gabby raised her chin and tried to regain some semblance of control.

"I only came to learn what Henri might know about my brother."

The Scot crossed his arms. Gabby couldn't stop her eyes from roaming toward the magnificent broadness of his chest and shoulders. He was as handsome as he was maddening.

"Why would you need to ask Henri about your own kin?"

It was the first sincere thing the boy had said since *Can I help you?*

"I don't believe it's any of your business," she said, cutting away from the Scot's imperious gaze.

His eyes were knives and they'd set about peeling away Gabby's ruse: her upswept hair, her too-mature and persuasive gown, the rouge on her cheeks and the stain on her lips. Even her show of bravery. She suddenly felt absurd, far younger than a couple of weeks short of sixteen, and playing at some silly game.

"Tell me your brother's name and I might be able to help—although I'll admit Henri's *party* might be worth waiting for," he replied, with just enough humor to vex her.

"At the moment, I don't see anything worth waiting for. If you'll excuse me." She gathered her skirts and brushed past him.

"You've got a bit of flint in you, haven't you, lass?"

She stopped. He was right. She did have flint in her. But she'd come here to talk to Henri and she hadn't so much as knocked on his door yet.

Pivoting on her heel, her gaze aloft the Scot's bemused eyes, Gabby went right back to where she'd been standing and brought her gloved knuckles down upon the door three times.

The hinges squealed as the door drifted inward. Gabby felt, more than saw, the Scot step up behind her.

"Henri doesn't get back from the café till four, at the earliest," he said.

The first thing that ran through Gabby's mind was that the flat had been burgled, the door left ajar in the thief's hasty retreat. She shrugged off the notion. This wasn't one of the many novels she indulged in. This was reality, and the answer was probably the very boring prospect that Henri had returned home earlier than usual.

Gabby nudged the door open even farther. "Bonjour. Henri?"

"Wait." The Scot bumped into Gabby as he inserted himself between her and the mouth of the darkened flat. "Henri?"

"He invited me, not you." She edged past the Scot's sturdy frame and went fully into the flat.

Frames of weak sunlight bordered the windows, the drapes being drawn. It was a single-room flat, and poorly furnished. There was a settee with ratty winged arms and a table with mismatched chairs. Gabby smelled the noxious odors of turpentine and oil paints before she saw the easel in one corner of the room, glass jars of paints and brushes set up along the floor. Henri was an artist. It didn't surprise her; he had that flair about him. In the opposite corner there was a four-poster bed, the linens mussed and a bulge in the sheets.

"Henri, rise up, lad. You've got yourself company," the Scot said. Gabby bristled at his emphasis on *company*. No doubt he imagined Gabby was the sort of tartlet who would happily flounce her way straight into that four-poster.

"I'm hardly staying more than a few minutes, and I'm not sure I'll be very good company at that," she said, moving purposefully toward the bed. She saw Henri's head of tousled blond curls buried deep in a pillow. "Henri, I apologize for arriving so early, but I need to ask you about my brother—"

Gabby reeled to a stop.

Henri's body was all wrong. He lay flat on the mattress, his chest facing up, arms splayed out to the sides. But his head . . . it was nose down in the feather pillow.

"Oh my—" Bile filled Gabby's throat. She barely felt the Scot jerk her to the side, away from the edge of the bed.

"He's . . ." Gabby shut her eyes. "Is he dead?"

The Scot ignored her. He went to the window and yanked the

drapes aside. Milky light spilled over the bed and Henri's twisted form. Another lurch of sickness rose up in Gabby's throat. She clapped a hand over her mouth but didn't turn away. He was fully dressed in his café uniform, his shoes still on and laced. Six hours before, he'd been flirting with her. Now . . . Gabby couldn't comprehend it.

The Scot crouched next to the bed and stared at Henri's body. At Henri's one, half-lidded eye that looked dully out at the space before him. "What did you do, Henri?" the Scot whispered.

"What did *he* do? He's been killed. We have to call for the police," Gabby said, backing up. "I'll go."

The Scot shot to his feet. "No. No police."

"But they need to know. Someone needs to come see to his"— she lowered her voice—"his body."

"I'll take care of him."

Gabby, despite not wanting to view Henri again, rounded the foot of the bed.

"You? How?"

"Listen to me, Miss . . . ?" He waited for her name.

"Waverly," she whispered.

The Scot's gaze sprang from the bed and speared her. A half beat later, he turned away.

"He can't tell you anything more about your brother now," he murmured. Then, louder: "It's best you leave."

She stared at the rumpled linens surrounding Henri's broken body, her pulse skipping. She *did* want to leave.

"And it's best if you forget the last ten minutes of your life completely," he added. Gabby nodded weakly, though she knew she'd never be able to follow that command.

The Scot raked his fingers through his crop of hair. "Do you have a carriage waiting for you?"

"Yes."

"Then get to it."

"But I—"

He swung his arm out to silence her. "Please. You have to go, lass."

Though his tone had softened, his level glare brooked no argument. Gabby's eyes skated over Henri's body one last time before she gathered her skirts and staggered out of the flat. She made it all the way down the stairs and through the front door, breathless, before she realized she'd never asked the Scot for his name. It didn't matter, she reasoned as Bertrand shut her safely inside the carriage. She didn't plan to return to Hôtel Bastian ever again.

Ingrid twirled the nib of her pen over the linen paper she'd spread out on her brother's desk. She'd written the date (*3 December 1899*) and a salutation (*Dearest Father*) but nothing else. How should she word the news that Grayson was missing? Ingrid let the pen clatter to the desktop. A telegram would be better, with its short, abbreviated sentences. Absent of emotion. Of panic.

Ingrid and Gabby had returned from Le Livre Rouge to find their mother practically tossing two police officers out the front door. Lady Charlotte Brickton was no shrinking violet, and so when she had been told that there was no reason to panic when a nearly eighteen-year-old male who had been living on his own for months did not check in with his mother for a few days, she had all but dragged them from the parlor by their ears.

"Write to your father," she had instructed Ingrid as soon as the two girls had walked into the rectory. "Scotland Yard won't take the disappearance of the Earl of Brickton's only son as lightly as those arrogant, good-for-nothing peacocks!"

Ingrid and Gabby had stared, speechless, as their mother waved her hands to hurry them along and then announced she was going to the abbey. Ingrid highly doubted it was to pray. Rather, she was sure Mama would be flinging around pews and debris in an attempt to exorcise her frustration.

Ingrid picked up her pen and noticed with dismay that a splatter of indigo ink had arced across the desk and landed on the cover of the untitled book Vander Burke had given her. *Returned,* she corrected herself. The black cloth was already ruined—a few more stains wouldn't matter.

The gargoyle etching she'd opened the book up to on the carriage ride home came to mind. Architecture and Parisian history didn't interest her at the moment, what with everything else falling apart. But the unsightly image of the dogheaded gargoyle did. She had to have been seeing things the evening before when she'd thought she'd spied movement along the abbey buttresses. Perhaps the thing with fluttering wings had only been a particularly large raven.

Ingrid carefully flipped through the near-translucent pages, each bordered with what looked like hand-painted gilt. The book had to be hundreds of years old. And yet, her brother had returned it to Vander instead of shelving it as a collector's piece.

She flipped to another section of the book. The pages landed with a *thud.* She'd come to more images of gargoyles perched along a roof and another on a bridge rampart. The rooftop gargoyles had feathered heads and necks and long, sharply pointed beaks. The rampart gargoyle looked much less frightening, with its clownlike monkey head and chubby cheeks.

The text was in French, but there was a handwritten column in English along the inch-thick white border outside the painted frame. The slanted, cramped script brought a smile and the threat of tears. Ingrid knew her brother's handwriting as well as she knew her own.

The first note at the top of the page read *Presence of gargoyle statue marks a protected dwelling*. Below that: *Intentionally monstrous faces scare off evil spirits*. Then: *Heightened senses . . . smell, vision.*

She ran her fingertips over the letters. It had always been Grayson's habit to jot notes and thoughts and questions along the margins of books. It drove Ingrid crazy, especially when he did it in the margins of her treasured books. But what did this mean? That he'd intended to keep this book and changed his mind? It didn't make sense.

Farther down the page's border there was one last question. It stole the breath from Ingrid's lungs: *Transformation from stone form to flesh?*

She read the notes a second time, then a third. Grayson couldn't have been serious when he wrote this. A stone gargoyle transforming into a flesh-and-blood creature?

Ingrid read the notes once more before glancing at the sketches within the gilded frame. The gargoyles had been colored using a pattern of inked dots that made them look cold and solid. Carved from stone.

Perhaps he'd been foxed. Ingrid had seen him stumble into Waverly House reeking of spirits plenty of times. Living here alone, he could have imbibed as much as he liked, whenever he liked. But Ingrid knew she was grasping for an excuse. Grayson wouldn't have been able to maintain his usual neat, perfectly formed letters had he been drunk. What had led him to take this book from Vander's shop and research gargoyles? Ingrid sat straighter in the leather-cased chair.

Unless he'd seen something along the abbey roof as well.

Ingrid went to the window and searched for the corner buttress where she'd seen the fluttering black wings. Of course there was nothing there except for the ancient statues. She pressed her forehead to the glass. He'd have had to be mad to believe the stone gargoyles could spring to life.

The sun had set, and steel-colored skies rolled like a sheet over Paris. Gabby still hadn't returned from wherever she'd sneaked off to. Her sister could be so infuriating. Not even sixteen and driving about Paris all alone. Anything could happen to her. Gabby never stopped to think, so Ingrid always felt the need to do all the thinking for her. All the worrying, too.

Ingrid needed Gabby home. Not just because she felt caged

and restless with worry, but also because she needed Bertrand and the carriage. She'd tried to hunt down the address of Grayson's last dinner party, but Bertrand was the only one who knew it. Ingrid had to get to that address and speak to the hosts.

Ingrid opened her eyes and was rewarded with the sight of Bertrand clearing the hedgerow. Quickly, she closed Grayson's book and raced to the foyer. She barreled through the front door before their butler even appeared, not stopping as she swung her sapphire cloak over her shoulders and pulled on her robin's egg–blue gloves. She was hatless, but she didn't care. Their mother could step out of the abbey at any moment, and if she did she would no doubt forbid Ingrid to leave alone after nightfall.

The carriage came to a halt just in front of the rectory door. Bertrand regarded her with a trained look of compliance as he shoved on the brake lever.

"Do the horses require rest?" Ingrid asked, one eye on the abbey's transept door.

"No, my lady," he replied.

"Excellent," she said, ready to open the carriage door and extract her sister herself if Bertrand didn't move along. "Can you take me to the address of last Thursday's dinner party?"

He froze, a frown sinking the corners of his mouth. "But, my lady, the time—"

Before Bertrand could finish objecting, Gabby pushed open the carriage door. "I'm coming with you."

Ingrid reached for her sister's hand, stopping short of kicking down the steps herself.

"No, you are not. How could you make me worry like that? You're staying here to cover for me should mother ever come out of that dungeon," Ingrid replied with a nod toward the abbey.

Bertrand helped Gabby down and Ingrid noticed that her sister's dark-gray eyes were wide and red rimmed.

"You've no idea what just happened, Ingrid."

"There isn't time. Tell me all the wretched details when I return."

"But, my lady, we will be out past sundown, and the police notices advise against it," Bertrand successfully cut in. Ingrid didn't have the patience for this.

"I realize that, Bertrand, but I still require that we go. Now." She hated the imperiousness of her tone, but it was the only way he'd listen. She couldn't stand the thought of passing another night without being any closer to answers about Grayson.

Bertrand sealed his lips and helped her into the landau. She looked again toward the abbey, but her eyes snagged on the carriage house, where Luc leaned against a doorjamb, watching them. Even with the corner of the churchyard between them, Ingrid felt his sharp stare. His chin was tucked in, his arms were crossed, and he wore an expression that exuded disapproval.

"But, Ingrid, it's going to be dark soon!" Gabby cried.

"I'll be perfectly fine. This is important, Gabby," Ingrid replied, and gave Bertrand a nod. He closed the door.

In another handful of seconds they were coursing down the drive, Gabby frowning in their wake. Luc had disappeared from the carriage house door. The landau turned toward the Seine and left the monstrous gray abbey behind.

Leaving it made the ache in Ingrid's chest loosen, if just a bit. But slowly, as Bertrand steered them toward the island in the river, the Ile de la Cité, the unease dripped back in. The carriage started over the one-arched bridge crossing the languid, ice-crusted Seine, and Ingrid felt even more weighed down with worry than before.

Lord, but was it dark. The sky had gone from steel to smudges of coal, like a funeral cloth wound over Notre Dame's great spire and twin bell towers. Theirs was the only carriage crossing the wide square in front of Notre Dame. There wasn't any foot traffic, either; no tourists or artists folding up their easels now that the light had gone.

As they rolled over the second bridge that connected the island to the city's Right Bank and began trotting through streets, Ingrid noticed with mounting disquiet that nearly all the sidewalks and corners were clear of people and carriages. A few restaurants were nearly vacant; shop windows were dark, with awnings drawn down for the evening, a few baskets of unsold baguettes lolling on their sides.

A small group of people stood bathed in the light of one streetlamp suspended from a large curlicued hook at the top of an iron post. Ingrid's spirits rose but then flagged. It was a group of women, their hair hanging loose over their mushrooming bosoms, all of them cackling obscenely. The sight of these women did nothing to set Ingrid at ease.

The Parisians certainly were taking this rash of disappearances seriously. She'd thought Vander had seemed unreasonably concerned earlier, but perhaps the recent incidents were more serious than Monsieur Constantine had led them to believe. Ingrid grew tense, the lacquered wood walls of the carriage all of a sudden too thin and vulnerable. She'd be relieved to arrive at the address, conduct her interview, and return to the rectory.

The click of hooves over the pavement mixed with the horses' heavy snorts of exertion. A low whistling from the driver's bench cut through the uneasy quiet. Bertrand's tune was unfamiliar, but it made Ingrid feel slightly less alone. The sound gave a bit of substance to the world outside the carriage.

And then it all stopped.

Bertrand's whistling clipped into silence. The horses whinnied and came to a halt. The carriage chassis rocked violently and then sat still. Ingrid straightened, wondering if perhaps they had arrived—but somehow knowing that they had not. That they were sitting in the center of a street. That something was wrong.

"Bertrand?" she called.

No reply.

"Bertrand, what's happening?" Ingrid slid forward. It was as if every inch of her body had decided to pulsate and sweat. She'd felt this panic before. The uncontrollable humming of her veins and the prickles of electricity. The last time, it had been at Jonathan and Anna's engagement party, just before she'd tried to flee the ballroom.

"Get hold of yourself," Ingrid whispered, tugging off her silk gloves as her palms and fingers became too hot and damp for them. Bertrand still hadn't answered. The horses hadn't whinnied or made any shuffling sounds at all.

Swallowing her fear, Ingrid reached for the handle and pushed the door ajar. She peered through the sliver of an opening. The clusters of globe lanterns topping each lamppost along the street brought out a rippled shine along the varnish of the deep-green wood.

"Bertrand?" Her voice was small, her lungs having shriveled to what felt like the size of figs.

Ingrid kicked the door out the rest of the way. The frosty night air crawled inside the warm carriage and pushed her out. With the flight of steps tucked underneath the chassis, she was forced to leap the two feet to the ground. Her high-heeled boots smacked onto the pavement. She wobbled as the heel on one boot cracked and broke off.

"Blast!" she cursed, keeping tight against the giant spoke wheel as she hobbled toward the driver's bench. The carriage lamp burned brightly, showing her driver sitting on the seat at the reins.

"Bertrand, what on earth is happening? Why have we stopped, and why haven't you been—"

Ingrid held her next words. Bertrand hadn't moved at her voice. Now that she'd drawn closer, she saw he wasn't so much sitting as he was slumping. She went forward, toward the brake lever. It hadn't been thrown, and yet the carriage had stopped completely.

That was when Ingrid saw the horses. She let out a short

scream and stumbled back. Both animals lay crumpled on the street before the carriage, their reins and hitching gear still attached. The street lanterns washed a yellow light over the pavement and showed a vast black pool leaking out from under the horse closest to her. *Blood.*

Panic twisted her stomach. Ingrid searched the street in both directions. Not a soul in sight. If what Monsieur Constantine had said was true, shouldn't the police have been out patrolling the streets?

It was cold. Close to freezing. And someone had just killed the horses, maybe even Bertrand. Ingrid had to find out for sure. She climbed onto the runner and up to the bench, her heart thrumming wildly in her chest. Bertrand's shoulders had shrugged forward. His head drooped like a heavy apple on a thin branch.

She poked him in the arm cautiously. "Bertrand?" His face was mostly buried in a threadbare wool scarf, but as Ingrid leaned closer—close enough to smell the stale scent of ale and pipe smoke on his skin—she saw his eyes were open. They were wide, filled with such fear and surprise Ingrid had no doubt that he'd died of it.

My God. Bertrand is dead.

The scrape of something hard against the pavement startled her. Ingrid's sudden movement set the seat creaking on its springs. A gurgling groan and a wet snort followed. The sounds had seemed to come from all around her. Her eyes settled on the splayed-out horses, the black pool of blood. What could possibly have taken such large animals down so quickly and silently?

Ingrid had to find help, had to get home. She had to *move.*

She climbed down, forgetting her broken boot heel and stumbling once again. Ingrid turned her ear toward another gust of heavy breathing. It sounded like air being sucked in and blown out through a wet snout. *A pack of wild dogs,* she thought. But they couldn't have attacked and killed the horses. There would have been more noise, and Bertrand wouldn't have—Ingrid's head swam—he wouldn't have been scared to death of dogs.

She didn't want to consider what *had* scared him.

The street's shop doors and windows were a black blur of nothing as Ingrid ran past them. The low gurgling came again. It drew into a deep and husky growl, but Ingrid couldn't determine where it was coming from. It was behind her, beside her, ahead, past the next dangerously dark alleyway. The soles of her boots slapped against the pavement, joining with the scratch of paws, of long nails steadily clicking.

Behind her.

She pricked her ears and listened closely. Yes, it was definitely behind her. Ingrid glanced over her shoulder, expecting to see a dog—a pack of them, even—all matted fur and scrub-board ribs. Her feet tripped to a halt.

That was *not* what she saw.

CHAPTER SIX

Luc spun the squared-off edges of the note between his thumb and forefinger. A messenger boy had just been at the carriage house, holding out an envelope the shade of fresh blood. Sealed inside, Luc had known, would be a matching blood-red card—the calling card of the Alliance.

They were humans, and meddlesome ones at that, but the Alliance was the closest thing to an ally that the Dispossessed had. There were underground factions of the Alliance all over the world, just as there were Dispossessed all over the world, and they fought the Underneath demons to keep the populace safe. The gargoyles and the Alliance had many things in common, but that didn't necessarily translate into friendship. It was more like an eggshell partnership. Each side knew to tread lightly around the other. Things were always tense, and the fact that one group consisted of humans and the other of monsters was the largest reason why.

Tonight was not a good night for this, Luc thought, again

reading the two-sentence summons: *You are needed at Hôtel Bastian. It involves your humans.* Luc sat heavily on the edge of his mattress. Of course it involved his humans. And he knew precisely which ones.

Grayson's sisters were walking disasters. The younger one had snuck out of the rectory earlier looking like a strumpet. Then the older one had gone and done the same thing. She'd been dressed more suitably, but her risk had been doubled simply due to the time. Sisters. Luc knew how vexing they could be.

Suzette.

Even now, centuries later, she came to him with piercing clarity. Most memories of his human life had faded or gone completely, but not the memories of his sister. Ebony hair. Eyes the color of Connemara marble. That little impetuous grin that made her cheeks look like rounded peaches. She'd been so much like Gabriella. Daring. Mindless of any sort of consequences.

A glance outside the loft door showed him a bruise-purple sky and wine-colored clouds.

Luc should coalesce. He should locate Ingrid and be there, circling in the sky for the moment she needed him, because he had the distinct feeling that she would.

He held the red card to the candle flame and watched the note burn and curl until he finally had to drop it to the floor and grind the cinders out with his boot heel.

Luc didn't understand why his connection to Ingrid outshone those he had with the other humans in the rectory. It wasn't her beauty—though she did have that in spades. Her corn-silk hair, aubergine eyes, and dove-white skin had been imprinted in his memory almost as forcefully as her scent. Luc had lain awake the night before, surfacing her scent time and again, trying to understand what that underlying tang was. Obsessing over it. Overwhelmed by it.

He'd never had so many humans to protect at once, and never anyone like Ingrid. Still, he didn't want Marco's help. Trusting a gargoyle from the wolf caste would be a foolish move. Whatever the reason for Marco's offering his assistance with the Waverlys, Luc suspected it was self-serving. How so, Luc couldn't begin to imagine. He just knew he didn't want Marco anywhere near Ingrid.

Bertrand's scent rose fast. It filled Luc, drowning out the ever-present bite of rust from the loft's ancient pulleys and the smooth scent of seasoned wood. It had shuttled up into his consciousness on its own, followed by a thunderous heartbeat and the sensation of tight, burning lungs—both Bertrand's sensations, inescapably mirrored within Luc. Even if he'd wished to stamp them out, to *not* know what his humans were doing or feeling at any given moment, he could not have. It was a part of him, built in like a sixth sense.

Luc stilled, tried to grasp the old man's scent. But the sweet trails of pipe smoke were gone fast; the rolling fear Bertrand had just been experiencing was replaced by unnerving calm. The echo of his heartbeat suddenly fell quiet. Luc tried to call up Bertrand's scent and failed.

Ingrid's scent surfaced next, followed by the panicked rhythm of her heart. Something had happened to Bertrand, and Ingrid needed Luc. Now. He swore beneath his breath as he felt the order to coalesce trigger deep inside his core. Luc shucked his shirt and trousers and lobbed off his boots within a matter of seconds. It was all the time he had before the shift completely obliterated his human form.

In well-practiced harmony, his pale skin rippled into a sheath of jet scales, his spinal column popped and cracked as it lengthened to support the rocklike muscles reshaping his arms, legs, and chest. The cartilage and folded bones of a pair of featherless obsidian wings split through the plates on his back. They erupted like charred black mountains and unfurled to a wingspan longer than Luc's human height. The bones of his skull and face parted and slipped like fault lines shaken apart by an earthquake into the shape of a dog's head—crumpled snout, pointed ears, and all.

He knew he was hideous to behold, and as he approached the loft door at a run and leaped into the night, he had every intention of using the terror his appearance inspired to battle whoever—or whatever—threatened Ingrid. He hooked his wings to catch an updraft of wind and went soaring above the carriage house weather vane. He knew exactly where she was. His inner homing ability found her as easily as if she were lit like a beacon.

Luc only hoped he wasn't too late.

Ingrid stared in awe. It was a wolf, with long, shaggy black fur, clipped ears, and a snout. It stood on four legs and had paws. But even in her worst nightmare she could never have imagined a wolf this monstrous.

The animal's legs were as long as Ingrid's, its bulbous paws tipped by wicked-looking claws. The ridge of its back stretched long and wide to rounded and well-muscled hind flanks. It bared its teeth and Ingrid gasped. The animal's fangs were long and needle sharp, curving over the bottom row of teeth like the illustrations she'd once seen of prehistoric saber-toothed tigers. Its bottom jaw had two thick fangs, bent so far to the sides that they were nearly horizontal, extended like two swords. As if its fangs alone weren't enough to slow her heart, she then saw its eyes. Dark, blood-red eyes, rimmed with black voids.

This wasn't real. It couldn't be. But then the animal advanced, its thickly muscled shoulders rising and falling with the movement. Its fur glistened under a nearby cluster of globe lanterns. Curling clouds of mist jetted from its flared nostrils. A putrid stench permeated the air.

Ingrid stumbled backward. The enormous hound followed, another drawn-out growl building in the back of its throat. She turned and kept walking, forcing herself not to run. Animals enjoyed the chase, didn't they? If she didn't run, perhaps it would lose interest. She glanced back to see if it had gone.

It hadn't.

The animal followed, slipping through the shadows between lampposts. Its eyes cut the dark as if they'd been cast of red glass and illuminated by a lamp inside its skull. The hound was getting closer.

Ingrid sped up, still having no idea where she was or where she could go for help. Her lungs burned and her eyes began to water from the cold. The animal's massive paws scratched faster along the pavement.

She broke into a run—and immediately regretted it. The creature growled and yipped and took off after her. A rise in the pavement caught her toe and she went sprawling. As her cheek slid across the street, she thought she heard the shrill cry of a hawk from above.

Two seconds. It was all she had until the hound was on top of her.

Ingrid closed her eyes, rolled over, and threw up her hands as a pathetic barrier against the beast. Roaring heat ran over her palms, and she felt as if something had slammed against them. The force of it was strong, and her back slid along the cold pavement. A few untamed heartbeats later, no snapping teeth had come.

She peeked out from behind her arms and saw the animal a few yards away, lowered into a crouch. Patches of its fur sparked and smoked like embers. Ingrid was still trying to understand what had happened when the shrill, hawklike screech grated on her eardrums again. She twisted around, and what she saw drove the breath from her lungs.

Another creature stood within the hazy light of the next lamppost. A creature with wings. Mammoth, outstretched wings.

Its dog-shaped head was bald, with a pair of sharply pointed ears set midskull. It crouched low, its long, muscular legs tight to its chest. Ingrid couldn't breathe. Couldn't move. She recognized this creature. It was one of the abbey's stone statues come to life. It was a gargoyle. Living. Breathing. *Real.*

And then the space above Ingrid turned wild.

The hound leaped over her, colliding with the gargoyle, which had flown forward to meet it. Ingrid saw a flash of the gargoyle's razor talons before she rolled to the side. The two unnatural creatures slashed, growled, and screeched at one another. The hound raked its claws along a featherless wing the color of glimmering jet, slicing open the gargoyle's scaly skin. A screech of pain ripped out of the gargoyle's throat.

Ingrid sprang to her feet and ran. She'd gone fewer than five strides when another gargoyle landed with a *whump* on the street before her. Its scales were a deep cinnamon, its skull a different, more wolfish shape. It spread its batlike wings and the streetlamp beyond glowed through the thin, featherless membranes, silhouetting slender bones running like columns through each wing.

Ingrid pivoted on her broken-heeled boot and disappeared into the gap between two buildings shouldered up next to one another. There were no electric lamps along this route; not even a single sputtering gas jet. Ingrid ran blindly, the smell of trash filling her nostrils, the snarling of the hound tunneling down the alleyway behind her. She didn't have a chance against its speed. The hound's breath gusted low against the backs of her legs, and then pain lanced through her left calf, hot and brilliant. She reeled forward.

Before Ingrid could hit the ground, sharp talons pierced her cloak, stopping her fall. They latched onto her shoulders, jerking her up and into the air.

Immediately, another pair of talons dug through the heavy folds of her silk skirt. They clutched her thighs and lifted her legs away from the hound's leaping swipe. She screamed and thrashed, but the talons only dug in harder. One by one, the talons pinning her shoulders released and two stony arms laced across her front to draw her up, pressing her firmly against its rock-solid body.

The ground swirled away, the rooftops shrinking, the tops of lampposts whipping by as she hurtled over them. Ingrid could barely breathe, let alone scream, as the gargoyle flew higher and faster. It was the first gargoyle, she realized, its onyx wings beating the air on either side of her. What had happened to the other one?

Ingrid thought she saw the bridge over the Seine and the teardrop-shaped Ile de la Cité, but those things were so far down that the lamps on the bridge ramparts looked like little more than pricks of light.

Ingrid squeezed her eyes shut to the jerking rise and fall as they coasted blindly through the clouds, the frigid wind offset by the creature's furnacelike warmth.

A dull ringing in her ears drowned out the flap of wings and violent fluttering of her skirt. She was going to faint. But then the gargoyle descended, slanting downward toward the twin bell towers of a church. *Her abbey.*

The gargoyle had taken her home. But how had it known where to go? They approached the rectory churchyard at an alarming speed. The talons still digging into Ingrid's thighs released. Her legs pitched forward and her skirt and petticoats billowed wide. The remaining heel on Ingrid's kid boots grazed the top of the stone fountain and sent her whipping from side to side. The gargoyle hovered over the walk leading to the front doors of the rectory, descending lower and lower, until her feet scuffed the gravel. The arms clutching her torso released and she crumpled to the ground. Her legs were weak and numb, except for an intense burning in her calf.

The beat of wings churned the air above her, blowing Ingrid's loose hair across her face. She pushed it back and tried to see the gargoyle again. But all she caught was the very tip of its long, thin, dragonlike tail as it streaked away into the night sky.

And then there was silence.

Except for her rampaging heart, her choppy breathing, and her burning calf, the chaos of the last few minutes had ceased. The night was still again.

Ingrid looked out over the churchyard, toward the carriage house. With a pang deep in the pit of her stomach, she remembered Bertrand. It was her fault. She'd made him go out when he'd warned her they shouldn't. He was dead because of *her*.

Ingrid bounded to her feet and rushed into the rectory, wishing she'd listened. Wishing she'd never left in the first place.

CHAPTER SEVEN

Luc rolled the loft door shut with a thrust so powerful he nearly sent the whole thing off its metal track. What the hell had just happened out there?

He snatched his clothes from the floor. His talons snagged and ripped the patched linen of his shirt. His throat ground out a frustrated shriek instead of a growl. Ingrid had done something . . . something with her hands. From where he'd been, spiraling in fast toward the ground, Luc had thought he'd seen *lightning* streak from her palms. The beast had been thrown back, its fur sparking, its body jerking wildly.

Luc stalked the loft, needing to slow his heart and urge on the reverse shift to human form. The movement helped his vertebrae slide into place, his shoulder blades tighten, his muscles reshape. Whatever Luc had seen flow from the centers of her palms, the fact remained: because of the girl's stubborn disregard for her own well-being, Bertrand was dead.

His death wasn't Luc's burden to bear—the Dispossessed

weren't punished if their humans died from heart failure, or if their humans injured themselves. But *her*. She'd made herself such simple prey for the hellhound. Luc had smelled the demon's unmistakable stench from the air. Fur, rot, and blood. He'd almost been too late, just as he'd been too late to protect her brother.

And Marco. What the hell had he been doing there?

Transformation finished, Luc tugged his trousers on. How was he to watch over these new humans when they insisted upon such reckless behavior?

Luc felt a stirring inside him. Unlike Ingrid, he paid attention to his instincts. They were sharp and clear. Irrepressible. Right then, they sensed Ingrid near panic, agitated, and in pain. Her leg. Her calf, he pinpointed, noticing a dull throb in his own left calf muscle. Luc couldn't have hurt her on the flight back. Everything he was forbade him to harm his humans. So why was she hurt?

Luc shook his head and pulled on his shirt. Did it matter? She was alive. He'd seen to his duty. Now he just wished to sleep while he could, before Bertrand's body was discovered. Before Lennier, the elder leader of the Dispossessed, summoned him for questioning. *Your human is dead,* Lennier would say in his raspy tenor. *Two horses mauled by demons in the middle of a street. What can you tell me?*

Luc's mattress caught him as he flopped down. He crossed his arms behind his head. The frantic gallop of Ingrid's heartbeat slowed. The sensation of pain as well. Good. It couldn't have been that bad, then. He took a deep breath and let it out slowly, recalling her scent. Light and sweet. Springtime and verdant earth. It surfaced effortlessly, his trace on her the clearest one he'd ever had with a human.

Luc let go of her scent, knowing it was a mistake to focus so much on one of his humans. Instead, he surfaced her sister's scent. It came through with less definition. Gabriella's was just a shade lighter than Lady Brickton's heady floral perfume of hibiscus and water lily. Complicated. He preferred Ingrid's scent. But then, Gabriella's was still hand-over-fist better than that daft old pastor's from the early twenties. That one had smelled of horse manure. Luc huffed a laugh. How fitting: a man of the cloth with an essence of shit. Why not? He'd shoveled the stuff down his parishioners' throats with all his fanciful theories regarding heaven and hell, good and evil, and the fear of God. As if it were God the humans needed to fear, and not his army of angels.

Luc closed his eyes and concentrated on the bouquet of hibiscus and water lily. But unwanted images of Ingrid interrupted: her running along that dark Marais street; her corn-silk hair slipping from combs and pins, leaving the curls to bob wildly against her shoulders; the demon beast closing in on her. Luc opened his eyes and sat up. He raked a hand through his hair as if he could rake the images away as well. *Hibiscus and water lily,* he reminded himself. And finally, he landed a better trace on Gabriella. She was fine. Concerned about something, but not in any danger— at least, not for the moment.

"Luc Rousseau."

He shot from the mattress and spun toward the loft stairs. A blast of fierce white light hit him square in the face. It was like being licked by a tongue of flame. *And the humans believe* hell *is hot.*

Luc loathed the way angels appeared out of nowhere. He especially loathed being visited by them twice within the same week. Luc cowered against his will as the light burned hotter and brighter. The angels held sway over him and the rest of the Dispossessed, just as gravity held sway over the world.

"Irindi." Luc felt his head pushed low in a reverent bow. Perhaps he'd been wrong. Perhaps the angels *could* punish him for Bertrand's heart failure.

The burn of Irindi's white light faded, but the brilliant shine of her blazing pearl silhouette remained—a tall, lithe figure, outlined by silver contours. It was impossible for Luc to look directly into an angel's luminosity. The Dispossessed were forbidden to, deemed unworthy of it. He could only look at the angel of heavenly rule from the corner of his eye.

The floorboards shuddered beneath Luc's bare feet as Irindi's voice flowed. "You have erred."

Though her voice was powerful enough to shake his eardrums, it still rang hollow, like the echoing chimes of the abbey's long-dormant north tower bell.

Reflexively, Luc tried to face Irindi and the accusation leveled against him. An invisible force slammed into him and drove his head back down. It held firm. Resentment and humiliation festered inside him. Irindi and the other angels treated him like a mangy dog caught pissing down a drinking well. They treated all the Dispossessed this way, especially those who'd failed their humans.

"His heart quit of its own accord," Luc growled. "There was nothing I could do."

There was a half beat of silence; then Irindi's voice boomed through the loft again. "Of which human charge do you speak?"

The people inside the rectory would not be able to hear her mighty monotone voice. To them, it came through as an onslaught of wind, a sudden storm that would spend itself when Irindi went.

"Bertrand, of course," Luc answered.

The invisible pressure on his chin eased. Irindi's white fire guttered but flared again as she replied in her steady, emotionless voice, "I speak of the child christened Ingrid Charlemagne Waverly."

Luc balled his hands into fists. "How then, exactly, have I erred? I saved her from a demon less than an hour ago. She sits inside the rectory right this moment."

Irindi ignored him. "Her wound. It is a mark against you."

"What wound? The insignificant one on her *calf*?"

But Luc knew angels were not in the habit of suffering the objections of the Dispossessed. They simply punished.

Luc seized as a scorching pain seared the full width of his upper back. He fell forward, arms flat against the floor, as the angel's burn tore through his human skin, traveling slowly and purposefully from one shoulder blade to the other. The scar would carry over when he coalesced, appearing as a deformation in his scales. And from the feel of it, this one would be directly below the one Luc had received for failing Grayson. Luc wouldn't be able to hide them from anyone—the brands of failure.

"See to her care," Irindi said. The angel's burn continued to sizzle and throb.

"Wait," Luc gasped, battling stunned tears of pain. He'd already been punished for failing Grayson, but Irindi hadn't said whether the boy had lived or died. "What about . . . What of Grayson Waverly? Is he dead?"

To Luc's surprise, Irindi actually answered. "The child christened Grayson Fairfax Waverly is beyond our reach and is no longer the concern of the Order. Continue."

Irindi vanished just as quickly as she had materialized, and the loft dropped into cold blackness. Released of her hold, Luc pushed himself to his feet. *Beyond our reach.* Grayson was still alive and somewhere in the Underneath. A place no Dispossessed could trace him to. A place where the Angelic Order did not trespass. Luc had called up the imprint of Grayson's scent dozens of times, the crushed tea leaves and bitter green bark of sapling pine, but without a single result. The same thing had happened when he'd tried to call up Bertrand's scent, of course. But Irindi hadn't come about Bertrand.

Luc went to the hayloft door and rolled it open. He eased out of his shirt and let the intense cold act as a salve for the angel's burn. The one he'd received the night Grayson disappeared had almost healed. Two angel's burns in one week. Luc had never failed before, and he had no desire to be a gargoyle whose back was lined with multiple brands. Those gargoyles, shunned by the other Dispossessed, lived as shadows.

Luc stared at the bright windows of Ingrid's room. He'd investigate this wound of hers—and whatever she'd done with her hands—tomorrow. In human form. Or perhaps his true form would be more effective. Only twice had he shown himself to his human charges. Both times the humans had fled the abbey, and the city, within days.

See to her care.

The best thing for Ingrid and her sister would be to leave this place. Paris wasn't safe, not with this odd influx of hellhounds. Apparently, being compelled to protect his humans wasn't enough. Luc's ability was lacking, just as Marco had implied.

Luc surfaced Ingrid's scent once more. Bright-green shoots of spring grass, freshly tilled soil, the barest hint of nectar. And that tang. Luc shoved it all away at the unexpected skip of his pulse and cinch of his stomach. He needed to be relieved of her.

He took a last glance at Ingrid's windows and shut the loft door.

Pain seared through Ingrid's calf. With every passing second it felt as though the wound were growing wider and deeper. As Ingrid came off the stairwell's top step, she collided with her sister's lady's maid.

"Oh! My lady!" Nora cried as her sewing basket toppled onto the carpeted hallway floor.

Ingrid winced and immediately shushed her. At least it was just Nora, Gabby's maid, and not Maureen, her mother's. "Where is her ladyship?"

A harried glance at the foyer's tall case clock had showed her it was just past five. She'd been out for less than one hour.

And in that one hour the whole world had shifted.

"Dressing for dinner, my lady," Nora answered, rushing to pick up her basket and sewing notions. She looked askance at Ingrid's tousled appearance: Her hair, a mess of loose tangles. The front of her blue silk dress wet and dirty from her fall in the street. A sting rose from her cheek like a blush and Ingrid remembered scraping it along the pavement.

She kneeled to help Gabby's maid. "And my sister? Please tell me she didn't go out again."

Ingrid went cold at the idea of her sister accidentally meeting with that monstrous hound.

"Lady Gabriella is in her room. I thought you were abed with a migraine, my lady, but—"

Relieved, Ingrid handed Nora a needle-filled cushion from the floor. "I am. That is exactly where I've been. I still have the migraine, too, so I'll be skipping dinner tonight. Tell Cherie I don't wish to be disturbed."

The maid nodded, and then Ingrid limped quickly down the hall before swinging inside her brother's study. With unexpected focus, she closed and locked the door and went to the desk for one of his monogrammed linen handkerchiefs. Next, she moved to the glassed-in cabinet set between two tiers of bookshelves and grabbed a bottle of Chivas Scotch whiskey. She swooned halfway back to the desk but grasped the chair and hung on until the spell passed.

With shaking hands, she uncapped the whiskey and, without an ounce of decorum, put the rim to her lips and drank. She gagged, her throat now burning as much as her calf. She propped her foot on the leather seat of her brother's chair, lifted her skirt hem, and rolled down her stockings. On her calf was a bite wound coated with dried blood.

She doused the handkerchief with a heavy splash of whiskey. The injury wasn't what had her truly shaking. It was what she'd seen. The rational, logical side of her mind kept insisting that gargoyles didn't exist. That they weren't *real*.

Ingrid eyed the book Vander had given her, lying on the desk where she'd left it. Her brother had made those cryptic notes. *"Transformation from stone form to flesh?"* But the statues that trimmed the abbey and appeared in the sketches in Vander's book were small, spindly creatures with hunched backs. The creatures Ingrid had seen that evening had been tall and muscular and proud. Disturbingly human.

She pressed the handkerchief against her calf and stiffened, expecting pain. But oddly enough, the throbbing began to lessen. Ingrid felt a shiver of nausea as she leaned forward for a better view. Her calf had two deep punctures, set at least a hand's span apart. The animal's fangs should have done more damage than this—it was a nip, at best.

Ingrid frowned, prodding the wound. She didn't exactly want the pain to return, but it would make more sense if it did. As if anything that had unfolded in the last hour had made any sense at all.

Ingrid closed her eyes and leaned her forehead against her bare knee. Bertrand. Oh, poor Bertrand. The image of his terror, of the horses lying in the slick of their own blood, wouldn't go away. She had to tell someone what had happened. Someone had to go fetch Bertrand and the carriage and the horses.

Another wave of queasiness hit and she lost hold of the doused handkerchief. Something wasn't right. Flowers of sweat dampened the underarms of her dress. She felt both hot and cold, wanting to throw off her heavy silk dress one second, her teeth chattering the next.

The urgent need to see to Bertrand, to be responsible, evaporated, and Ingrid left her brother's room. She stumbled along the hallway in a dizzy, shuddering stupor, closing and locking her door behind her.

Her room was dark, and Ingrid's shins upset a few piles of stacked books on her way to her bed. The floor seemed to tilt dramatically, and the last thing Ingrid saw before dropping unconscious was the white eyelet duvet on her bed rushing up at her.

The hooded woman stood in the corner of the cave, her arms folded across her chest. Even her hands were covered by the cloak, Grayson noticed as he leaned his head against the roughly cut dirt wall. His eyes throbbed, the flickering blue light never ending. How long had he been languishing in this cave—days? Weeks? Was he in some cavern deep beneath the city of Paris? He'd heard tell of unorthodox groups living and meeting within the Parisian catacombs. He'd started to think he'd been taken to one, the victim of some vile secret society.

A society of inhuman monsters.

The hooded woman lowered one of her cloaked arms and rubbed the fanged man's head. With a gentle nudge, she urged the creature toward Grayson. He no longer tried to resist.

"Why are you draining me?" he murmured as the creature crawled toward him, on all fours this time, his legs bent like the hind legs of a dog.

To Grayson's surprise, the hooded woman was not the one to answer. A rasping growl from deep within the creature's throat transformed into words Grayson could understand: "I'm not draining your blood."

The creature stopped a mere inch from Grayson's face and bared its teeth. Rivulets of thick black liquid jetted down each long fang.

"I'm improving it," the creature said before throwing back its head and burying its fangs in Grayson's neck.

CHAPTER EIGHT

Ingrid jerked awake at the sound of his scream.

"Grayson?" Her parched throat burned, but the rest of her was cold. So very cold.

She wasn't on her bed. Instead of resting on a pillow, her cheek was pressed against the floor. Her hip bone ached from its awkward angle against the hard surface. She breathed in a dank, musty odor, and grit dug into her palms as she pushed herself up. She wasn't even in the rectory, let alone her room.

Panels of stained-glass windows surrounded her, the leaded scenes glowing dusky blue, silver, and rose in the moonlight. *The abbey*. She was sitting on the marble tiles in the center of the abbey. Other than the stained-glass glow, the church was pitch-black. How had she gotten all the way from her bed to . . . *here*?

A cold sweat had plastered her cotton chemise to her skin, and her feet, covered only by a pair of silk stockings, were painfully cold. Had she walked out of her room? Out of the rectory and across the churchyard? The stiffness in her back and neck hinted that she'd been on the abbey's tiles for quite a while.

Ingrid rubbed her legs and feet to warm them and tried to gain her bearings. She ran her hand over the back of her calf and the tender puncture wounds announced themselves. She remembered the otherworldly hound, its red lantern eyes and rotten stench. The fuzzy, dreamlike feeling she'd woken with hardened over completely.

Ingrid got to her feet. The rustling of her skirts rebounded off the vaulted ceiling, coming back at her like the flap of wings. Another memory spiraled to the surface: jet scales and membranous wings. An impossible flight through the inky sky. Ingrid closed her eyes and held her head steady with her palms. Would this wretched night never end?

She must have sleepwalked. She had never done it before, but then, this had been a night of revelations. She had to get back to the rectory before she caught her death. Ingrid's thigh hit the edge of a pew and she stumbled into a scattering of rubble. Her stocking feet crunched over sharp debris.

"Damn!" Her oath echoed into the great stone void until it finally broke apart. As it did, another sound took its place.

"Ingrid."

She drew in a short breath. That voice. She knew it. "Grayson?"

The scream she'd woken to—she'd been certain it belonged to him.

"Ingrid. Hurry, this way."

Grayson was in the abbey! Ingrid's eyes swam with tears.

"Grayson, where are you? I'm coming!" She surged forward, not feeling the sharp rubble this time. Right then, she would have gladly crossed a field of broken glass to get to her brother. "Which way? I can't see a thing!"

Her voice bounced back at her, vibrating against her ears as she groped her way through the dark.

"Help me, Ingrid." The strain in Grayson's voice pulled her through the black-as-pitch nave at a reckless speed. He sounded like he was in the chancel, near the time-battered choir stalls, perhaps.

"I'm coming!" she called again, but her toe caught on a rise in the floor and she crashed onto a short flight of stone steps leading to the pulpit.

Her shins were throbbing when unfiltered moonlight flooded the abbey. The transept door had flown open and cracked against the freestone wall beside it. A black figure filled the entrance.

Luc.

His long strides ate up the marble tiles between the door and the pulpit steps. He hooked Ingrid's elbow and hauled her to her feet. "You shouldn't be here."

"I heard Grayson's voice." She wrenched her arm free. "He's here in the abbey. Help me find him. Grayson!"

Luc shackled her elbow once again. "The voice doesn't belong to your brother."

"I *know* my brother's voice. Please. He sounds hurt." She twisted her arm, but Luc's grasp was unyielding.

"That's only what it wants you to think," Luc replied with a strange hint of exasperation.

Ingrid fell still. *"It?"*

She looked at him now—*really* looked at him, without trying to break away. Even through the dark, she saw the pale-lime gleam of his eyes. No one's eyes could possibly be that luminescent. A gentle tug was all it took for Luc to coax her off the pulpit steps.

"It's a trick," he said. "There's an entrance to the catacombs beneath the abbey. You don't want to find yourself lured there." Luc dropped her arm. "If you do, a small wound on your leg will be the least of your problems."

She let out the breath she'd been holding. It came out in a short, croaking gust. "I— Why would you say that? How did you—"

Her brother's pained voice came again. *"Ingrid! Please, hurry!"*

Her heart felt as though it were physically stretching toward the sound, reaching out with grasping fingers. But now, with Luc's warning, she noticed the muffled quality of the words, as if they were coming from somewhere much farther away than the chancel. She knew, of course, of the vast network of tunnels and caves beneath the city, where the limestone used to build Paris had been quarried long ago. When the deposits were finally depleted, parts of the honeycomb of tunnels had become a burial ground.

Ingrid held her place at the bottom of the pulpit steps. Her frozen feet were heavy, leaden as her heart.

"How do you know about my wound?" she asked.

Luc backed away, toward the open door. "I don't suppose you would agree to return to the rectory and pretend this night never happened?"

It was a sarcastic question, posed as if he knew she would decline. And of course, she would. How could she forget? This night had changed her world.

Her silence was her answer.

"Very well, then," Luc said. He sounded offended, as if she had just insisted upon taking part in something vulgar. She heard him rummaging around—how could he even see?

Luc struck a match and Ingrid winced at the sudden flare of light. He crouched and ran the flame over the wicks of old prayer candles that had been unceremoniously left on the floor. As Ingrid's eyes adjusted to the low, flickering light, she saw that Luc was dressed little better than she for the cold. He wore no coat; his white shirt had been rolled and cuffed at the elbows, and the top buttons were undone. He looked like he'd raced out of the carriage house to come fetch her. But what had drawn him? Something told her she'd been in the abbey for a length of time already, every last window dark.

The candlelight threw shadows over his face. He was scowling at her, yet again. She didn't understand why. It wasn't as though she'd called on him for help.

"I'll tell you how I know about your leg, but only if you promise me two things," he said, standing up.

"It depends on what the two things are." She was far too prudent to blindly jump into a promise.

Luc stepped toward her. She felt heat radiating from his body. "Don't scream."

Her pulse skipped. Would she have a reason to?

Luc's glare softened. "And don't run away." He licked his lips, and for the first time Ingrid saw a trace of vulnerability. "Don't run away from me."

Ingrid puzzled over his conditions. Not to scream, not to run away from him. These things should have frightened her, and they did. Partly. But Ingrid was too curious to do anything other than nod.

Luc moved backward and left the circle of flickering candlelight.

"Where are you going?" Ingrid asked, panicked as the phantom of her brother's voice once again sounded through the abbey.

"Ignore it. Stay where you are," Luc quickly said.

Ingrid's bare feet throbbed as she stood on a square of tile. The dull ache of the cold seeped up her ankles and through her bones. She had to get warm.

"Would you please just tell me what you're doing? I'm freezing," she said, impatient for the rectory, for her slippers, a fire, and a heavy blanket.

Luc didn't answer. Instead, something crept forward into the ever-changing light of the prayer candles. Ingrid's throat dammed up as the obsidian-winged gargoyle—*her* gargoyle—edged into the space Luc had just abandoned.

Her body drained of all feeling. The painful cold, gone. The shivering, annihilated. The confusion, lost. The creature she'd seen on the Right Bank street, the one that had flown her back to the abbey, took a last, precarious step into the circle of candle-light. Its wings, folded behind its back, showed only as an arched tip rising over each sinewy shoulder. The creature's head dipped into a submissive bow, and ridiculously, Ingrid's first thought was that it was scared. That it was cowering the way a battered dog would before its enraged master. But as she forced herself to take a breath, she realized how inane the notion was.

The gargoyle towered over her. Ingrid had to crane her neck to see that its pointed, doglike ears disappeared into the blackness that filled the rest of the abbey. Jet scales sheathed its body—a body that looked even more human up close than it had earlier. The creature stood erect, on a pair of legs that, though scaled and ending in taloned feet, looked very much like those of *Homo sapiens*.

The creature was built of muscle. Its chest and stomach, each thigh and calf, forearm and bicep sculpted as magnificently as Michelangelo's famed *David*. Except, Ingrid noted with detached wonder, that this creature was completely devoid of reproductive organs. And instead of white Carrara marble, there were over-lapping scales. They made up a tightly knit pattern that reminded her of snakeskin.

The moment Ingrid's widened eyes finished sliding over its features, the gargoyle's wings snapped open. The *crack!* echoed through the abbey, and Ingrid leaped backward. The black can-opy of wings was easily the width of her rectory bedroom.

Ingrid tried to call out for Luc, but the only noise to escape her throat was a thin, reedy hiss. The gargoyle shifted to the side and started to wind its way around her. She remained silent, a scream locked in her throat. She'd promised not to scream. She'd promised not to run. Ingrid's thrashing heart tripped and floun-dered. No. She had promised not to run away *from Luc*.

Ingrid shied to the left as the gargoyle rounded her right side, then to the right as the tip of its wing brushed her left shoulder.

This creature couldn't be Luc. Could it? She forced herself to take a closer look at the gargoyle's face. She tried to meet its eyes, but they were still cast down, as if in deference.

Ingrid pitched her voice just above a whisper. "Luc?"

The gargoyle stopped its rotation and lifted its eyes. Pale-green jewels set under a prominent brow. Ingrid's voice failed her. She mouthed his name.

And then the creature began to melt. Ingrid skittered back on her numb heels as the gargoyle lost its intimidating height, shrinking nearer to her level. The ridges of its shoulders and arms shaved off into lean muscle. The talons along its toes and fingers retracted, and its doggish ears rounded out as the rest of the gargoyle's face finished losing its angular edges. Lastly, the obsidian scales flashed over to pale white skin. Human skin.

Luc stood before her. A sheen of sweat glistened over his bare chest. His eyes were rooted to hers in that intense, demanding way of his.

"You can run now," he said, and then waited, eyebrows vaulted, for her to do just that. But Ingrid could hardly breathe, let alone run. With jagged breaths, she took in the creamy white of his arms and stomach and—

"Oh, good God!" Ingrid pivoted to face the darkness.

He was *naked*.

A short report of harsh laughter filled the abbey. "A monster doesn't frighten you, but an unclothed man does."

Ingrid was too stunned to even blush. "You're the gargoyle. You're the one who . . . You were there. You saw the hound. But how can you—"

She forced her lips shut. She was babbling again, just like she had that morning at the bookshop with Vander Burke. Of course, that time had been different. Vander had at least been clothed—and human.

"If I were to explain what I am and why, we'd be here past dawn. And you'd catch pneumonia by then," Luc replied, nearly growling with frustration. "You can turn around now."

Ingrid took a skeptical glance over her shoulder. Luc had tugged his trousers back on, as well as his shirt, and was finishing with the metal buttons. He left the collar open and slipped his bare feet into a pair of worn, unlaced boots. "That hellhound had time enough to kill you, but it didn't. Why?"

Ingrid shivered. The shock was wearing off, and the cold had started to creep back in. "I have no idea. I don't even know what a hellhound is! It bit me—isn't that bad enough? And you . . . you *changed.* People don't do things like that. It's not possible."

Luc ran a hand through his long dark curls. Each strand was as black as the scales that had just covered him. He looked like he was fighting the urge to argue with her.

"As you just saw, it *is* possible. And hellhounds are demon dogs, sent from the Underneath on tasks from their masters—also demons," he explained with forced restraint.

Demon. Ingrid rolled the word around in her head, again seeing the animal's red lantern eyes and dripping fangs. Of course that was what it had been. If there were gargoyles in the world, why couldn't there be demons? What other mythical creatures were more than just stories on paper, handed down from generation to generation?

"What about Grayson? The voice I just heard?" she asked.

Luc nodded toward the chancel and choir stalls. "Just a delusion demon trying to lure you off hallowed ground with its siren song. Demons can't tread here like they can in parts of the catacombs."

It hadn't been her brother's voice, then. To have heard his voice—a perfect replica of it—and then learn it had just been a trick hurt. It ached worse than the cold gnawing on her bones.

"But this church has been abandoned for decades," she said, switching over to logic as soon as her throat and tongue felt thick with a repressed sob. "It can't still be considered holy ground."

"It fell out of use but was never deconsecrated," Luc explained. "You should be thankful no bishop ever bothered to perform the ritual. It gives whoever lives here added protection. And believe me—you sorely need it."

Ingrid was still contemplating silently when Luc came before her, lowered himself to one knee, and hiked up the hem of her dress. She shrieked as he roughly grabbed her calf.

"Give off! How dare you!" Ingrid kicked out but Luc only tugged her leg back toward his chest and pushed her hem up farther.

"Hold still. I need to look at the bite."

Luc's fingers dug through her silk stocking for purchase as she jerked her leg back again. "You most certainly do not!"

"Stand still or else you'll—"

Ingrid gave another kick and tug before she felt her balance give way. She fell backward, windmilling her arms, squeezing her eyes shut in anticipation of her tailbone smashing against the marble tiles.

It didn't happen.

A muscled arm caught her like a sling around her ribs. When Ingrid opened her eyes she saw she'd stopped just short of the floor. She also saw Luc at her side. He'd let go of her leg and leaped forward to intercept her fall. His saving hold on her was awkward and, to Ingrid's immediate discomfort, extremely intimate.

"Or else you'll fall," he finished his prior warning, his breath husky and sweet.

She parted her lips to thank him—and he withdrew his arm. Ingrid flopped to the floor.

"Your leg, please," he said, the very picture of chivalry now. He was crouched at her side, his hand palm-up and waiting.

Ingrid pursed her lips. This boy rubbed at her like no one else. But he was so insistent about seeing her wound. She wondered if he had an important reason. Her pride already dashed, Ingrid lifted her hem. Her stocking, loosed from its garter, was gathered in a frumpy silken cowl at her ankle. How humiliating.

"You could have asked the first time, instead of acting like a Neanderthal," she said.

He lifted her leg with markedly more respect, sparing her only a brief, maddened glance. His touch scorched her numbed skin.

"You're ice," he muttered. "Why did you come out here without shoes on?"

"It wasn't intentional. I sleepwalked."

Luc's fingers brushed over the punctures, mindful of the pain they could cause. "Demon poison," he said. "The hound injected you."

"Why would it do that?"

"A human has to have demon poison in their veins in order to cross into the Underneath. I'm sure the hellhound was trying to prepare you for the journey."

Luc continued to stroke the punctures, sliding his thumb down the curve of her calf again and again. Ingrid's stomach tightened. His hand was so warm, and she was so cold. And the cinching of her stomach wasn't entirely unpleasant.

"The punctures are practically healed. Odd," he said softly to himself. "Just in case . . ."

Luc brought out a small penny knife and flicked it open. She jumped as he closed his hand around the blade and drew it down sharply, slicing into his palm.

"What are you doing?" she cried. He clamped his bloody hand around her calf.

"Stop!" She tried to jerk free of his steel grip.

"It's the only way to purge the demon poison," he said with what seemed like bored calm.

"With blood?" she gasped as the burning pain began to fade.

"*My* blood."

How disgusting! She didn't want his blood mixing with hers. Ingrid tugged her leg again, and again, but his grip was iron. She gave up, and then dragged in a gulp of air as Luc traced the two strawberry birthmarks on her calf. Other than Grayson, no one had ever paid her marks this kind of attention. As children, they had sometimes sat side by side, inspecting their matching birthmarks, trying to find even the slightest variations. They never could.

"Not very long ago, some people believed a baby born with a permanent mark had been branded by the Devil," Luc said.

She slapped his hand from her calf, this time without contest, and tugged down her hem.

"Those people were superstitious idiots," she whispered.

Luc glanced at her, unable to hide his surprise. He stood out of her way as she stumbled in an effort to stand on her stiff feet. She had to get inside, out of the raw cold, but she also had so many questions for Luc. Foremost, what *was* he?

"You're not human," Ingrid blurted. Heat zinged to her cheeks, but she forced herself to keep her gaze steady with his.

"Not anymore," he replied. Luc didn't look all that upset about it, either.

"Why did you rescue me?"

"I had no choice. The only reason I'm here at all is to protect the humans living within the abbey grounds. I'm bound to it." Luc looked at her pointedly. "I'm bound to *you*, considering you are one of my human charges."

Sparks licked deep in her stomach. *Bound to me,* she thought. So he was a guardian of sorts. Very odd sorts, Ingrid conceded as Luc crossed his arms and threw his attention somewhere off into the dark.

"And what of Grayson? Does he need your protection?" she asked. His arms, crossed as they were over his chest, coiled tighter.

"The only one who needs my protection at the moment is you," he said, his voice flinty. Ingrid blinked and caught herself smiling. Did that mean Grayson wasn't in any danger?

"Do you have any idea where he is?" she asked.

Luc paused, as if the question had taken him by surprise, before answering, his eyes still averted. "We're not all-knowing."

"How many of you are there?" she asked, not sorry in the least that she was barraging him with questions.

"There are hundreds of us in Paris, probably thousands of us the world over. We guard any place that has effigies of gargoyles." He rushed through his answer, treating the revelation with insignificance. "Let me see you back to the rectory. If you develop frostbite—"

He chewed off the rest of his sentence.

"Does it hurt?" Ingrid asked.

Luc frowned. "Frostbite?"

"No." She waved her hand through the air. "Changing. What you just showed me. When you . . . become something else."

Ingrid bit her lip. Maybe she shouldn't have asked. Maybe the question was as inappropriate as a man asking a woman how uncomfortable her monthlies were. The puzzled expression Luc wore, the one that seemed to be cut from stone, made Ingrid itch.

"Never mind," she said quickly. "I—I need to go. I need to tell someone about Bertrand and the horses. My God, it's been all night."

She passed him, head down, and headed toward the transept door. She felt wretched, and not just because every step felt like icy daggers knifing through her legs.

Luc followed her hobbling footsteps. "Don't worry about explaining Bertrand's absence. I have a feeling it's been taken care of." Luc ignored the inquisitive stare she threw back at him and continued. "I hope it goes without saying that existence is better for the Dispossessed when the majority of humans don't know we exist."

The Dispossessed. Was that what the gargoyles were? Outcasts? Exiles?

Outside, the moon was high and clear, the windows of the rectory blacked out. Even without a clock she knew it was the small hours of the morning. Before three, she'd wager.

"If that's the case, then why did you show yourself to me?"

She stepped out onto the snow-covered bricks. Her soles lit with a cold burn, and the rectory's front door suddenly seemed a torturous distance away. She let out an involuntary whimper.

"Because I want you to leave Paris," Luc said. Before Ingrid knew what was happening, her feet had been swept off the wintry ground. She fell awkwardly into the crooks of Luc's arms.

"What— Put me down! What are you doing?"

He carried her swiftly along the brick path, unruffled by all her squirming. "I'm saving you from a case of frostbite. I can't afford another one of your injuries tonight."

Ingrid had no idea what that was supposed to mean, or why he wished for her to leave Paris, but she did know that he had put his hands on her far too much for one evening. He held her firmly around the ribs and under her knees, not allowing her to wriggle free.

As they approached the front door Ingrid noticed it had been left open a few inches. Apparently, closing it hadn't been important while sleepwalking. Luc nudged the door wider and walked straight into the black foyer. The sudden warmth set Ingrid's whole body throbbing, especially her feet. Luc lowered her, and she sprang from his grip.

"Why should I leave Paris?" she asked as soon as she'd landed on the Persian carpet. She kept her voice low, not wanting her mother or sister or any of the servants, housed in the ell, to hear.

Luc's whisper was firm and smooth. "The hellhound that practically snapped your leg off wasn't reason enough?"

Ingrid crossed her arms. "It was a simple nip."

Luc cocked his head. "It would have been much worse if you hadn't done what you did. Which begs me to ask—how, exactly, did you do that?"

Ingrid closed the door and gestured toward the drapes that cordoned off the sitting room. Their voices wouldn't carry so much from in there.

He followed her inside and drew the drapes together. Ingrid's pulse spiked at the sound of the copper rings sliding along the rod.

"What . . . ah, what was your question?" she asked.

Luc arched one of his thick dark brows. He should leave. The swimmy feeling in her stomach confirmed that she'd had a momentary lapse of judgment in letting him stay. He was too handsome. He wasn't *human*.

The moonlight coming through the shuttered windows fell in a slatted pattern along the floor. Luc stepped forward, letting it ripple along one half of his body. "Your hands? The lightning?"

Ingrid stared at him blankly. What was he carrying on about?

He took a step closer. The muscles in his forearms tensed. "I told you my secret. Don't you think it's common courtesy now to tell me yours?"

"What secret? What lightning?" She could barely concentrate. A wall of heat simmered in the spare inches between them. Heat she sorely needed. Ingrid didn't know if she was afraid of or entranced by it.

"The lightning you threw from your hands. The lightning that struck the hellhound," he explained. Ingrid shook her head, unable to comprehend.

"I didn't. I couldn't have." Luc had to be mistaken. People didn't throw lightning. *And gargoyles don't exist. Demons aren't real.* Or so she'd thought. Before tonight. She flexed her hands into fists, remembering the heat that had lapped her palms earlier, the singed fur on the hellhound, the curtains in Anna's ballroom as they went up in flames. And Anna's skin. Her best friend's hands and arms, burned to a raw, painful pink.

"Normal humans can't do what you did," Luc said.

Ingrid turned away from Luc so he wouldn't see her face or the panic transforming it. "You dare call me a freak?"

Luc circled into her line of vision. His bright eyes sparked over to sooty emerald. "Do you think a creature like me has any right to call you that?" He let out a drawn breath. "I just want to know what you are."

His eyes roved over her, as if searching for some telltale sign. They came back to rest on her face, her lips.

"I'm just a girl," she whispered.

Luc's eyes clouded. "I wish you were." He took something out of his trousers pocket and held it up between them. It was a small, corked glass vial. "Take this. Empty it into a perfume bottle or something you can easily spray. Carry it with you."

Ingrid took the vial from his fingers. The teardrop-shaped glass was cold.

"It's blessed water," he answered her unspoken question. "That and blessed silver are the only things the Alliance knows of that can destroy demons."

She looked up at him. "What is the Alliance?"

Luc backed away, toward the drapes. He began to undo the buttons on his shirt. "You'll know soon enough, I'm afraid." He parted the drapes and started to slip into the foyer. He stopped and half turned back to her, his eyes on the floor. "It doesn't hurt."

Ingrid stood still, uncertain what he meant.

"You asked if it hurt. Coalescing. It doesn't, not anymore," Luc said, and then, after a pregnant pause, he let the curtains swing closed behind him.

Ingrid waited, her palm slippery against the vial. Was he changing again? She wanted to race into the foyer to see but held back. He'd be unclothed. And then he'd be different. A monster that wasn't truly a monster. What had made him this way? Ingrid drew back her shoulders and went into the foyer, ready to see the gargoyle again. But the foyer was empty, the front door closed. She opened it a crack, in time to see dark wings soar over the abbey roofline and out of sight.

CHAPTER NINE

To the ignorant humans winding along boulevard Saint-Michel, Hôtel du Maurier was nothing more than a rotten tooth in the mouth of a noble and beautiful queen.

Constructed just inside the verdant hectares of Jardin du Luxembourg, the mansion had once been as lovely as the gardens Marie de Médicis envisioned and nurtured in the early sixteen hundreds—a time, Luc thought ruefully as he coasted through the pink-streaked skies toward the gardens, he had witnessed. His gargoyle existence had gone on for so long, the years outnumbering those of his previous life to such exponential numbers that he could hardly remember what being human had been like. Had *felt* like. He figured most of the Dispossessed suffered from this same loss of memory and feeling, and there were a great number of gargoyles that had been around even centuries longer than Luc.

Lennier was one of them.

Luc had received the elder gargoyle's summons a few hours

before, just after Ingrid's panicked heartbeat had jumped to life inside him. He'd traced her to the darkened abbey as a gargoyle had flown over the carriage house and a screech had rained down. Luc had understood the goyle language with a sinking sense of dread.

The common grounds, the gargoyle had called, and then the chiming at the base of Luc's skull had ebbed as the gargoyle winged away. Lennier had learned of the hellhound attack, and possibly that Ingrid had seen a gargoyle. Marco had been there. He could have told Lennier as much. Most likely, Lennier just wanted to remind Luc that he must use even greater caution now that one of his humans had been awakened. That Luc should not, under any circumstances, reveal his secret to Ingrid.

Luc would just have to lie convincingly. Ingrid had seen more of his world in one night than most humans ever did.

And yet she hadn't run away.

Luc shouldn't have made her promise not to run. Wasn't that what he wanted? For her to run all the way back to England? But she hadn't. She'd kept her promise, even when his beastly shadow had fallen over her. Ingrid had looked at Luc and she'd allowed her eyes to see everything. She'd stared at him as if he was fascinating instead of repulsive.

The marble balustrades atop Hôtel du Maurier came into view. The building was a square mansion with a shaft cut down the center forming an inner courtyard. Luc remembered the way it had been before he'd last entered hibernation: four stories of impeccable limestone, soft light radiating from tall casement windows enclosed by ornate iron balconies, arcades leading into the public gardens.

When Luc had risen from hibernation this time, he'd learned that the place had become the new communal ground for the Dispossessed. It had turned into such an eyesore that no humans, save a few homeless inebriates, trespassed there.

Luc arrived at the site in his scales, his clothing and boots clutched in the crook of his arm. Dawn was restless on the horizon as he dropped into the inner courtyard from the sky.

Brittle vines scaled the neglected limestone now. They knotted around the rusted bars of the iron balconies and crept indoors where the windows were either open or shattered. Luc dropped his legs into a landing position as he cleared the shaft entrance and spread his wings. Pockets of air filled them and slowed his descent so that when he touched down on the white stone gravel, he was able to at least maintain the appearance of calm.

But what was going on? There were at least fifty, if not a hundred, Dispossessed sitting or standing in their human skins around the courtyard centerpiece, a crumbling statue of a nine-headed Hydra monstress. Luc had thought he'd been summoned to explain the hellhound attack, but perhaps the gathering was for something different. As Luc shed his scales, the Dispossessed watched in silence. With uneasy movements, he tugged on his trousers and slid his arms into his rumpled shirt.

Marco stepped out from a pillared doorway. "Lennier summoned you long ago, brother."

"I was detained," Luc said as he slipped into his boots. He scanned the hostile faces closest to him. They had been waiting for him. It wasn't an auspicious start.

"Another attack on one of your humans?"

Those who had been seated quickly jumped to their feet at Lennier's raspy whisper. Luc felt his own shoulders stiffen, his chin rise. It was something Lennier's presence could command, almost the same way Irindi could turn Luc's cheek and force him into a bow.

Luc could not yet see Lennier, but it wasn't wise to let one of his questions go unanswered. "In a way, yes. But she's fine. Restored to her room at the rectory."

"And she knows nothing?" Lennier asked.

"Nothing," Luc answered, then pressed his lips tight together.

The crowd split apart to allow Lennier to pass through. He shuffled past the Hydra statue to another fountain, this one carved in the smooth limestone block of an exterior wall. The fountain's shape wasn't recognizable upon first glance. But if one stared long enough, it became clear that the top was a pair of globelike eyes set under arched brows. Below, chiseled creases and humps had created cheekbones and a nose. The flared nostrils had once dribbled water into the fountain basin, which was the wide-open maw of a gargoyle's mouth. Its lower lip acted as the rim.

It was a perfect throne for Lennier. He lowered himself to sit in the dry basin and crossed his arms. He wore the same black hooded cloak he had worn as long as Luc had been one of the Dispossessed. He had the wrinkles, loose jowls, and long white hair of a man entering his sixth or seventh decade, but Lennier had far surpassed that age now. No one knew for certain, but it was rumored he was nearly a thousand years old.

"Your humans know nothing, and yet they have a connection with the Alliance," Lennier said. Luc kept his jaw locked and Lennier went on. "Yesterday, a member of the Alliance was found murdered. A young woman and another Alliance member discovered the body."

Luc recalled the red note delivered by the messenger boy. The Alliance had summoned Luc to Hôtel Bastian. *It involves your humans.*

"I trust I do not need to tell you which young woman?" Lennier asked.

Luc closed his eyes and rubbed them with the heels of his palms. *Damn. Gabriella.*

"What does this Alliance death have to do with us?" Luc asked. Other than the unlucky fact that his human found the body.

Which Alliance member had been killed didn't matter. There were fewer than a dozen in Paris, their ranks thinned out by intra-Alliance political warfare that Luc couldn't care less about.

Lennier paused. "They suspect one of us was involved."

A tense rumble worked its way through the crowd. With the rising light, Luc could make out movement in the windows and balconies above. Were *all* of the city's Dispossessed present?

Yann stepped forward from beside Lennier's fountain throne. "Our relationship with the Alliance is already fragile. If they believe a gargoyle murdered one of their own, they could retaliate."

"They would be idiots to make a move like that," Marco said with the confidence and passion Yann lacked. "There are hundreds of us. We could destroy them with less effort than we spend on taking a piss."

Appreciative laughter came on the heels of Marco's comment, but it was sliced off by Lennier's response. "We do not act against the Alliance. Ever."

Luc tended to agree. As meddlesome as it often was, the Alliance had its uses. Having a tangible connection with humans never hurt. But over time its members had learned a great deal about the Dispossessed. They knew the gargoyles' strengths. Unfortunately, they also knew their weaknesses.

At Lennier's reprimand, Marco pressed his lips together and gave a lopsided bow of his head. A proper, if not heartfelt, gesture of deference to his elder.

Luc stepped forward. "The Alliance has proof, then?"

Lennier nodded. Of course they did. It would be naïve to approach the Dispossessed elder without it.

"The Alliance Seer has assured me of it," Lennier answered. Luc sighed. The Seer—Vander Burke. Ingrid had already met the bookseller, but she didn't yet know who he was. What he could do. Luc did. And if Burke said a gargoyle killed the Alliance member, then a gargoyle it was.

"Does anyone wish to confess?" Lennier asked.

Heads turned in search of the one gullible enough to do so. The punishment for a rogue action like the murder of a human—

and an Alliance human, at that—would be dire. It would make an angel's burn look like a slap on the wrist.

"Very well," Lennier intoned. He craned his neck to look up the shaft to the open sky. Dawn had fully broken. "The sky would reveal us, so we will part ways as men. Luc, remain a moment."

Luc waited while the Dispossessed drained from the courtyard, some of them leaving through the front door, more exiting through the arcades that ran straight onto the grounds of the Luxembourg Gardens. Though Luc would have preferred that he leave with the others, Marco didn't move from his spot against the columned doorway leading into the vacant mansion.

Once the courtyard was silent again, the way it usually was for Lennier, who guarded this territory, Marco pushed off the column and came forward.

"We want to know about the human girl."

Luc faced him. "Which one?" he asked, though he knew which girl Marco meant. He'd been there. He'd seen the hound attack.

Luc felt something hot and complicated settle in his chest.

"If your humans are friends to the Alliance, they will know about us in time," Lennier said. "That isn't my concern. What does concern me is what Marco has imparted: that she repulsed a hellhound with lightning."

Luc stayed firm. "I don't know what you mean."

The elder gargoyle didn't react. He was too ancient to react, Luc supposed. "The city has eyes, and last night it witnessed your human conjuring lightning in the palms of her hands."

"Humans can't create elements of nature," Marco said. "How did she do it?"

"What were you doing there?" Luc countered.

"Roaming freely," Marco answered, flashing a flippant grin. "My burden is considerably less than yours. *How* did she do it, brother?"

More like roaming with malice and intent, Luc thought.

Marco's territory was near Montparnasse, far from the street on which Bertrand's carriage had been attacked.

"I don't know," he answered. But even if Luc *had* known, his answer would have been the same. He wasn't going to share anything about Ingrid with Marco. Or Lennier, for that matter.

"You must find out." The elder gargoyle rose slowly from the cracked fountain. "Luc, you have a difficult task before you. I've seen this before, when a Dispossessed loses control of his own territory."

"I'm not losing control," Luc said before he could tamp down his fury. He regretted it, too. He'd sounded like a rabid dog.

Lennier only smiled. "Most humans are simple, Luc. There are so many of them, and yet, in all my years and in all the years that came before mine, most of humankind has never learned that we exist. Do you know why?"

Lennier waited for Luc or Marco to answer. He wouldn't continue speaking until one of them did.

Luc tossed out a guess. "Because we hide so well?"

"Of course not. Humans see us all the time, wings and all. They simply choose to look the other way. They choose not to trust what they've seen. They don't trust *themselves*. And so we have power over them." Lennier held up one craggy finger. "But there will always be humans out there who see us and refuse to turn away. We don't have the same power over those humans."

Ingrid was one of them. She'd already proven that she wasn't going to look away and forget.

Lennier, trapped for eternity in a body that had aged, weakened, and finally failed him, let out a great sigh. "Go now. Discover how the girl makes lightning." He started toward a pair of fractured glass doors but stopped and turned. "And do nothing to anger the Alliance."

Lennier disappeared inside the condemned building. Homeless vagrants and drunks came around just often enough to keep the ancient gargoyle from slipping into hibernation. Should that happen, Luc didn't know which elder would take his place. There were a number of gray beards and creased faces among the Dispossessed, proving that not every man who had taken the life of a holy man had died in his prime. Many of them had lived out their lives and expired of old age, maybe even believing their sin had been forgotten or forgiven. If he'd been lucky at all in life, Luc figured it was to have died young.

He started for the arcades and the lawns beyond. His humans would be rising soon, and he still needed to stop in at Hôtel Bastian.

Marco fell into step behind him.

"You had no reason to be there last night," Luc said as he marched forward. "Are you following her?"

They passed between the columns that held each arch aloft.

"My, my, aren't we paranoid." Marco sniffed. "Your human girl is fetching, but I happen to have been tracking the hellhound. The only creature, I might add, that wanted a taste of her last night. Unless . . ." Marco paused. "It *wasn't* the only creature?"

Luc reached the grass, browned by autumn frosts. He wheeled around, taking care not to slip and look like a fool.

"Don't bait me, Marco."

Marco came up close, his chest thrust out, as if goading Luc to shove him. "Then don't be ignorant. She's the first young woman to live in the rectory for as long as you've been a Dispossessed. You can't tell me you haven't noticed how beautiful she is."

"I've noticed how human she is," Luc shot back, but he'd already turned toward the boulevard. Of course Luc had noticed Ingrid's beauty. Her slender neck and delicate skin, the proud lift of her chin, the fullness of her lips. Luc didn't like that Marco had noticed as well.

"I'm wanted at Hôtel Bastian," Luc called back.

He heard Marco snort a laugh. "And now you know what it is the Alliance wants to tell you. Forget them. Are we their dogs to be beckoned?"

Marco's words struck a chord deep inside Luc. He'd heeled and rolled over for the Angelic Order, the Alliance, and even his human charges countless times. It never ceased to gnaw at him.

Luc reached the boulevard and left Lennier's territory behind. Marco was right, at least about this. He wouldn't go to Hôtel Bastian. The Alliance didn't own him. Answering to Irindi and his humans was trial enough.

What might it be like to be free of that? Free without the void of hibernation, still awake to the world? Marco knew, at least during the six months of the year when his humans lived elsewhere. Yann and René, whose territories were public places, never formed the kind of restrictive bonds that Luc or any of the residential Dispossessed did. But the Angelic Order had assigned him to L'Abbaye Saint-Dismas straight out of the gate, for reasons unexplained, and had never seen fit to reassign him elsewhere. Maybe there was a reason Luc was at the abbey. Maybe every Dispossessed was assigned with thought and calculation. Or maybe the Order just tossed them wherever and however. None of the Dispossessed really knew.

The sidewalks were white with frost, bright posters advertising the upcoming show at l'Opéra pasted on every bronze lamppost. The wide boulevard felt abandoned, but Luc knew it would last only another ten minutes at the most. The first rays of sun settled in a mantle of pink and orange on the pale stone apartment buildings thrown up side by side, without so much as a seam between party walls. To the right, the dome of the Sorbonne flashed in the coming light. Luc kept his chin down, his cold hands deep in his pockets, and lamented that he couldn't fly back to the abbey. Walking was tedious. It brought him close to humans who weren't his own, something he didn't enjoy.

The rumpled wool lapels of his coat fluttered up against his cheeks in the freshening breeze. He was coming upon a crowd and decided to cross the boulevard. As he stepped around a steaming pile of manure, he glanced at the commotion he'd avoided. It was a swarm of blue uniforms, along with a growing crowd of men and women, their ruddy faces and red-tipped noses standing out in the clear morning light. Two police officers each held a corner of a threadbare blanket; their intent, Luc assumed, was to block something on the sidewalk from general view.

It wasn't working.

A few maids wrapped in shawls balanced on the balls of their feet to peer over the ratty woolen shield. A man in nothing but shirtsleeves and suspenders, a cold choice for the December dawn, plucked back the edge of the blanket and raised a flat box he held in his hand. There was an open flap in the center, and protruding from it was a strange device. It looked like a miniature version of a daguerreotype camera Luc had seen before his last hibernation, only this one was small enough to fit in the man's hands. Amazing what thirty years could do.

"*Dégage!*" one of the officers snarled, shoving down the man's contraption. The pugnacious man ripped back the blanket with more force. The officer took another swipe at the camera-in-a-box. His hand connected with it, and a bright flash exploded before the camera clattered to the sidewalk. The officer lost his grip on his corner of the blanket and it collapsed.

Luc came to a halt as a chorus of shrieks pierced the air. The maids, all of them in instant hysterics, skittered away, clinging to one another. In the few moments it took for the officers to fumble around and raise their makeshift screen once more, Luc saw what it had hidden: an arm, dismembered at the elbow; a ropy length of bluish intestine strewn across the sidewalk; and a woman's head, its tangle of long blond hair matted with blood.

"*Qui est-ce?* One of the missing girls?" the cameraman badgered the officers. "Have you found the rest of her?"

Luc walked on, though the images of the murdered and discarded girl pressed against him. He knew what sort of creature it would take to tear a human apart like that—a demon. Any number of them had the strength, but only one variety would be so messy as to leave pieces of its meal behind: a hellhound.

The blood-matted blond hair and the ethereal skin of the dismembered arm had made him think of Ingrid. If he hadn't arrived in time the night before, she could have been torn apart just as that unknown girl had been.

Quickly, he surfaced Ingrid's essence. She was barely awake. She was fine. Of course she was fine. He relaxed the muscles in his hands. He hadn't realized he'd been balling them into fists. As a knot in the pit of his stomach unraveled, Luc slowed his pace. He usually kept his emotions turned off. Gargoyles didn't need them and were better off without them. But just then, Luc had been worrying.

The last time he'd felt such a pointless emotion he'd been human, and the object of his worry had been his sister. What was it about Grayson's sisters that kept digging up the memory of his own? Suzette wasn't someone Luc wanted to think about. He had no one but himself to blame for his transformation into a gargoyle, but it had all started with Suzette.

And Ingrid and Gabriella were making him remember everything he wished to forget.

CHAPTER TEN

Gabby waited behind her bedroom door with one ear pressed to the carved wood panel. It was nearly nine o'clock. She could smell breakfast wafting up from the dining room and kitchens through the heating grates, and yet she couldn't think about eating a single bite of the chocolate-filled croissants Madam Bertot had no doubt laid out for them. She couldn't close her eyes without seeing Henri's twisted neck, his face buried in the pillows. It twined her stomach tight with nausea every time.

When Gabby was certain the second-floor hallway was empty, she clicked open her door and scurried toward Ingrid's room. Her sister had avoided her all night. Nora had broken down and admitted to Gabby that she'd run into Ingrid in the upstairs hallway. That her sister had seemed out of sorts. But Ingrid's door had been locked and she hadn't answered Gabby's knocks. Then, just past dawn, she'd tried again, tiptoeing along the cardinal-red carpet and the creaky floorboards beneath. The door had still been locked, and her soft rapping had again gone unanswered.

Keeping the knowledge of Henri's murder bottled up felt like trying to hide the Crown Jewels in her reticule. She wanted to scream through Ingrid's door: *Someone we know has been murdered!*·

Just as she was about to bring her fist down on Ingrid's door, it swung open. Her sister jumped back, a hand fluttering to her chest.

"Gabby," she said, closing her eyes with relief.

"Why did you lock yourself in your room all night? I need to speak to you. *Immediately*," Gabby stressed.

Ingrid stepped into the hallway. "I need to talk to you as well. I needed some time to think about how to tell you what I need to tell you." She walked slowly along the hallway, worrying her bottom lip.

Her hair, usually neatly done up into a chignon or loose bun, was styled a bit oddly this morning. She'd teased down strands of curls so that they framed her face. It wasn't like her sister to be so casual. Ingrid distractedly pushed one of her tresses behind her ear. Gabby gasped.

"Your cheek!" She hauled her sister to a standstill. "What happened to it?"

Instantly, Ingrid shook the tress forward, but Gabby had already seen what it so cleverly hid: an inch-long track of raw pink scrapes.

"I'll explain it when we talk," Ingrid answered, her voice lower now that they stood near the top of the stairwell. "After breakfast?"

Ingrid, usually so cool and unaffected, looked hopelessly frazzled. Gabby nodded, clamping down on her urge to spill the news of Henri's death. Whatever Ingrid had to say, it was just as big.

"After breakfast. Why don't we meet in—" A voice from downstairs hacked into Gabby's reply. She turned her ear toward it. Male. A deep tenor. An accent.

Ingrid listened intently as well. "That doesn't sound like Monsieur Constantine."

It didn't. Not at all. Gabby swept down the steps, her heart hammering in her chest. She came to a reeling stop in the open entrance to the dining room. Conversation crashed to a halt around the table. Monsieur Constantine dabbed at his silver dart of a beard and pushed back his chair to greet her. Two more chairs screeched back, and their occupants rose as well.

It was *him*.

"What are you doing here?" Gabby blurted.

The Scot she'd met at Henri's blinked. Vander Burke, beside him, cleared his throat. And Gabby's mother's jaw practically fell unhinged.

"Gabriella!" she cried. "What has possessed you to speak to our guests in such a manner? Apologize at once."

The reprimand made the Scot's infuriatingly full lips twitch. *Out from underneath my mother's skirts indeed.* Gabby drew herself up and directed her attention toward Vander.

"I apologize," she said. "I'm simply a bear before breakfast."

Vander smiled and took his chair, while the Scot bent forward in an exaggerated bow. What the devil was he doing at their breakfast table?

"Why, good morning, Mr. Burke," Ingrid said brightly as she entered the dining room. Vander shot to his feet once more and nearly knocked his chair backward in the process.

"Lady Ingrid. Good morning." He sent her much more than the polite smile he'd given Gabby. He fairly beamed as a footman pulled out a chair across the table and waited for Ingrid to sit.

"Darling, I'm so very happy you visited Mr. Burke's shop yesterday," their mother said. "He took it upon himself to contact his private investigator friend, and then asked Monsieur Constantine for an introduction at the rectory."

Gabby slid into the chair next to Ingrid and across from the Scot. She smoothed the napkin in her lap and eyed him as she poured a cup of steaming Earl Grey. The bergamot scent perked her up and helped her focus.

"Private investigator?" Gabby echoed.

"Yes. Girls, this is Mr. Nolan Quinn," their mother replied. "Mr. Quinn, these are my daughters, Lady Ingrid Waverly"—she waited for Ingrid to smile and nod—"and Lady Gabriella Waverly."

Nolan Quinn. A private investigator. He picked up his teacup around the middle, ignoring the curved handle altogether.

"You've got a pair of bonnie lasses, Mrs. Waverly." He sipped his tea, his rich blue eyes peering out over the rim and lingering on Gabby.

"Thank you, though only my daughters carry the Waverly name. It's a bit of peerage fuss, but my husband and I carry the title of his earldom—Brickton."

Nolan gave a short nod to show he understood.

"You're a bit young to be a private investigator, Mr. Quinn," Gabby said, jumping the gun with all the patience of a barely broken mare.

"Gracious, Gabriella, hold your tongue!" her mother cried. Ingrid nudged Gabby underneath the table. Of course, how could Ingrid know that she and Nolan had met the day before and that he'd antagonized her to no end?

"We can't all be as seasoned as Sherlock Holmes," Nolan replied. "But I do have a knack for logic and deduction."

Gabby sipped her tea for lack of anything to say in response. He certainly had figured her out the day before. He'd taken one look at her and known everything, straight down to the reason she'd arrived hours early. As he looked at her now over the break-fast table, he seemed to be doing the same thing. Taking her apart, piece by piece, carefully examining her, and then reconstructing her.

"The police are inundated with the recent disappearances. They want to clear everything up before the Exposition begins this spring," Constantine said after an awkward pause around the table. "In fact, Mr. Burke tells me a few cases have been handed to Mr. Quinn."

"Yes, but I still have the time and resources to help you look for your son," Nolan was quick to add.

Their mother, who was seated on Vander's right, brought out one of her lace hankies and flapped it in front of her face to hide her welling tears.

"I'm sorry, Lady Brickton," Vander said. "We should have waited to bring up the topic."

He turned toward her, creating a wall between her and Nolan, and began to ask questions about Grayson.

"Did he write letters home?" he asked, and their mother began to tell him about the numerous letters that had arrived. As she spoke to Vander, Nolan leaned slightly forward in his seat and spoke to Ingrid.

"Lady Ingrid, you're fond of books?" Nolan asked—rather loudly, Gabby thought.

"I am," Ingrid replied with guarded politeness.

From down the table, Vander asked, "And Monsieur Constantine, did anyone Grayson met during his travels come to visit him here in Paris?" Vander leaned so far forward now that his elbow was propped with dreadful rudeness on the table linen. Constantine began to formulate an answer while Nolan sat back in his chair.

"Mmm, good. Listen." Nolan lowered his voice. "I need you both to come to Hôtel Bastian this morning. As soon as possible."

Gabby set her cup down with a clatter. "Are you—"

Nolan silenced her with a pointed look at Vander's back. The bookshop keeper was artfully engaging their mother and Constantine in a conversation at the far end of the table, and Nolan's demand hadn't been overheard.

Gabby lowered her voice as well.

"Are you insane? I'm not going back there, not after what happened yesterday."

"What happened yesterday?" Ingrid asked quietly.

This wasn't how Gabby had wanted to tell her sister, but it seemed she didn't have a choice. "Henri? The waiter? He'd been killed. I found his body."

Ingrid blanched.

"*We* found his body," Nolan clarified. "And the Alliance needs to speak to you. Both of you."

Ingrid sucked in a sharp breath.

"So you've heard of the Alliance, then?" Nolan asked.

Gabby didn't like the intense stare her sister and Nolan had locked themselves into. "Well, *I* haven't. What is it?" she asked.

Just then, Vander worked another burst of sniffles and tears from their mother, covering their fast, hushed conversation.

"It's a small band of resistance fighters that helps keep Paris safe," Nolan answered, his lips hardly moving as the vague answer traveled over the platter of soft cheeses and bread between them. "Pass the milk?" he added loud enough for the others to hear. The footman moved to comply, but Gabby was too quick.

"But of course," she said gaily, and held the silver creamer out to him. Then, softer: "Why should this Alliance concern us?"

"Aren't you kind!" Nolan returned with glossy enthusiasm. Gabby wished for legs long enough to kick him in the shins. His next words were so hushed, Gabby almost had to read them as they came from his lips: "Because we know where your brother is."

She sat up straight. He knew where Grayson was? Why the devil hadn't he said anything before now? Nolan nodded toward Ingrid, also rigid in her chair. "And because last night, we helped save your skin."

Gabby whipped her gaze to her sister, whose cheeks had colored. She could read Ingrid's emotions easily; her snowy skin made her an open book.

Ingrid's secret wasn't just big. It was *huge*.

"We'll come, but we'll have to hire a hackney," Ingrid whispered. Gabby frowned. Why would they need to hire a coach?

"Your landau is in the carriage house," Nolan said swiftly.

"But Bertrand—" Ingrid started.

"Is taken care of."

"The horses?"

"Replaced."

Gabby's eyes darted back and forth from Nolan to her sister; she was completely confounded.

Ingrid suddenly pushed back her chair and stood. Vander and Nolan launched themselves from their seats as well, followed by a slower-to-rise Monsieur Constantine.

"Excuse me," she said. "I—I think my migraine is returning. It was a pleasure meeting you, Mr. Quinn."

Her eyes skipped briefly to Vander, who shifted his footing as if he wanted to go to her. Unless he wished to climb over the table and crush breakfast with his knees, he was trapped. Ingrid left the room. The men were just sitting down when Gabby's mother rose from her chair. They shot back up, napkins in hand.

"All this talk about her brother has upset her," she said, shuffling around the table and toward the foyer. "I'll speak with her, if you'll excuse me."

Before any of them bothered to sit again, the men turned to Gabby with expectant expressions. It was almost comical.

"I'm staying," she assured them. Vander and Nolan took their seats, but Constantine folded his napkin.

"If you will excuse me, mademoiselle. Messieurs," he said, and exited the rapidly emptying room.

Vander relaxed into the cushion of his chair. "Well, that makes things a bit easier."

"You did well," Nolan said with a sly grin. "You should be onstage, Burke. I'm sure you could find work as an ogre or hunchback or some other disfigured beast, what with that ugly mug of yours."

"It would be a shame to go onstage alone," Vander said. "You could take the female role and finally show off those stunning legs of yours."

Gabby couldn't believe their easy banter. "Do you two mind?" She glanced at the footman, standing by the door leading toward the kitchens. "You're dismissed. Thank you."

The footman, though appearing startled by the dismissal, followed orders. Gabby lowered her voice in case he was listening from the other side.

"Mr. Quinn, if you know where Grayson is, why haven't you told my mother?"

His lopsided grin evened out. "*Mr.* Quinn is in Rome with the heads of the Euro-Alliance. I'm his son, Nolan. And I haven't told your mother because she wouldn't believe a damn word of it. She'd likely toss me out on my ear."

Vander propped his forearms on the table's edge. He split a croissant in half with fingers that, Gabby now noticed, were stained at the tips with indigo ink. He took a bite, watching her as if he expected her to lose her temper.

She mustered the last of her patience. "Forget your ear. If you're lying to me, I'll toss you out on some other, more southern part of your body entirely."

Nolan rubbed his chin, covering the amusement Gabby continually seemed to inspire in him. That cocky grin irked her. The black stubble along his cheeks and chin irked her. The careless look of his rumpled clothing, his uncombed hair, his slight Scottish brogue. All of it irked her. But the one thing she disliked the most about Nolan Quinn, private investigator and mysterious Alliance member, was that whenever he looked at Gabby, it was as if he saw straight through her. His eyes rendered her transparent and self-conscious. For some strange reason, he made her feel insignificant. No boy had ever made her feel that way.

Vander stood up while taking a last swig of his tea. He had on the same brown tweed suit from the day before, gone soft and baggy from too much wear. His mustard-colored waistcoat could have done with new buttons and his silk tie with a fine steam pressing. She wondered if this was his only suit.

"I'll call for the phaeton," Vander said, and he dashed through the servant door toward the kitchens. He also required a serious tutoring session in etiquette.

"He can't go through the kitchens like a common servant," Gabby said.

"Of course he can. If you haven't yet noticed, we aren't exactly of your status, Lady Gabriella," Nolan replied.

She floundered for a response that wouldn't also be an insult. "Then tell me who you are."

Nolan pushed his teacup and saucer aside. He folded his hands together on top of the table. They weren't ink-stained, but they were rough. His nails weren't manicured and buffed like those of Monsieur Constantine or any of the young men Gabby had been acquainted with in London. She had a feeling that Nolan Quinn wouldn't be caught dead in a pair of dove-white gloves or holding a silver-topped cane.

"I can't. At least, not entirely. The Alliance might not like you knowing everything there is to know about it. But since you're already involved . . . ," Nolan said, unfolding his hands and holding them up in a gesture of defeat. "What if I told you that the version of heaven and hell you believe in—the version most of the world believes in—is wrong? What if I told you there isn't just one devil to fear in some fiery pit, but limitless demons that find their way to the earth's surface? Wouldn't you want someone to be aware of them? Someone who can fight them?"

The dining room was so quiet and still, it sounded as if it had been plucked from the rest of the rectory and submerged in water. Gabby stared at Nolan, waiting for him to break into one of his maddeningly coy grins. He couldn't possibly be serious.

But Nolan matched her stare, lips taut as a tightrope, waiting for her reaction.

He *was* serious.

"Are you that person?" she finally whispered. "You fight . . . demons?"

Nolan snapped into motion. He snagged a croissant from a tray and stood up. Gabby did as well, her napkin falling to the carpet.

"Where are you going?" she asked, before remembering that Vander had gone to fetch their phaeton.

Nolan came around the table. He bent before Gabby and retrieved her napkin.

"Hôtel Bastian. Follow me with your sister as soon as possible." He handed her the ecru linen. "Allow only Luc to drive you there."

Nolan disappeared into the foyer and out the front door before Gabby could utter another word.

CHAPTER ELEVEN

Gabby closed the book Vander had given Ingrid and rested her palm on the black cloth cover. Ingrid waited as her sister took deep, even breaths. Gabby knew everything now, about the hellhound, the gargoyles, the Underneath. Well, almost everything. Ingrid hadn't been able to tell her sister about the lightning that Luc said she'd conjured. Ingrid still wasn't completely sold that she *had* made lightning. It would explain the heat on her palms, the singed fur on the hound, the ballroom she'd destroyed in London. But she still couldn't accept it. She was too frightened to accept it.

Gabby's patience snapped. "Luc? He's a gargoyle? The very human-looking boy who is currently at the reins and driving us to Hôtel Bastian is secretly a *gargoyle?*"

Ingrid buried her hands deeper in her ermine muff. She understood Gabby's disbelief. If she hadn't witnessed it firsthand, she would have had trouble believing it, too.

"I don't know why he's a gargoyle, but he is. He called himself a Dispossessed."

Gabby slipped the book onto Ingrid's lap. She had been reading it for the last hour while she and Ingrid had waited for their mother to ready herself for a trip to the *poste*. She was finally sending that telegram to their father. Surely he would set out for Paris. Ingrid closed her eyes and fought a surge of nausea. It had taken him years to accede to Mama's plans for a gallery here. What if he decided to end it and sweep them all back to London?

"Was he hideous?" Gabby whispered.

Ingrid leveled a firm stare at Gabby. "He saved my life. Twice." She let out a long breath and softened her tensed shoulders. "It doesn't matter what he looked like."

Oddly, Luc's gargoyle form hadn't been hideous. He'd been a beast, yes, but a majestic, fascinating beast. Ingrid hadn't been able to stop thinking about him. Even more strangely, she longed to see him shift again.

A whistle came from the driver's bench. Ingrid had felt wretched when she'd overheard their butler, Gustav, reporting to their mother that Bertrand was nowhere to be found. Gustav suggested that the old man had taken off in the middle of the night, though for what reasons, no one could guess. The Alliance had even gone so far as to clear Bertrand's belongings out of the carriage house.

"A little advance notice would have been nice," their mother had muttered, her voice carrying from the sitting room to the upstairs hallway where Ingrid and Gabby had been eavesdropping.

The horses came to a shifty stop. The new animals looked remarkably like the slaughtered ones. The Alliance—whoever they were—had to have sizeable resources to have so quickly and quietly covered up the hellhound attack.

"So," Gabby said softly. "Luc has to protect us?"

Ingrid set the book aside, her eyes fastened on the door. "He's bound to anyone living on the abbey grounds."

"Then where was he yesterday when I found Henri's body?"

Ingrid felt horrible about the evening before. Gabby had been trying to tell her about Henri's murder and Ingrid had brushed her off.

"You weren't in any immediate danger, were you?" Ingrid asked.

Gabby's fire went out. "No, I suppose not."

The latch snapped down and the door opened. Luc stood aside, without extending his hand to Ingrid. Perhaps he didn't know to offer it, Ingrid thought, but suspected she was being too generous. Where Bertrand had been polished, like a fine gentleman's shoe, Luc was churlish, like a scuffed, sole-worn brogan.

Ingrid gathered her skirts and navigated her way to the curb. Gabby followed.

"Are you coming with us?" Ingrid asked Luc.

He raised his eyes toward the upper floors of the apartment building. "I don't think so," he replied. "But I won't be far if you need me. I'll know if you do."

"How is that?" Gabby asked.

Luc frowned. "I'll feel it," he answered.

Ingrid hooked her arm through Gabby's. "Let's go, then."

Luc remained by the landau, but Ingrid felt his eyes on her as she and her sister made their way up the freestone steps. Gabby must have noticed as well.

"Is there something going on?" Gabby whispered. She opened the door and dragged Ingrid into an oval-shaped foyer.

Ingrid extracted her arm. "Yes, quite a lot, actually."

Gabby tilted her head. "Sarcasm doesn't suit you, Griddy." She no doubt enjoyed using that nickname. Gabby then clarified, "Between you and the driver. Gargoyle. Whatever he is."

"Of course not!" Ingrid paused. "And his name is Luc."

Spots of crimson erupted on her cheeks, but thankfully, only one was visible. Gabby had helped Ingrid better hide the raw pink scrape behind a veil of well-positioned curls.

"I knew it," Gabby said. "Have you gone completely mad?"

"I'm sure I don't know what you're talking about. Let's just find Mr. Quinn." After turning in a full circle in a failed search for a door, Ingrid fled for the winding iron staircase.

Gabby rushed up the steps behind her.

"I told myself I'd never come back here, not after finding Henri. Keep going," she advised as they reached the second floor. She pulled Ingrid to the next flight of steps.

Ingrid expected an open landing with a handful of doors and another set of stairs—from outside she'd counted five stories—but the marble steps ended directly in front of a door covered by an intimidating grid of iron bars. Where was the access to the next two floors?

Behind the bars there was a panel of wood. The door looked like it had been thieved from the torture dungeon of some ancient castle.

The wood was so dense Ingrid had to pound her fist against it to make any discernible noise. She inched forward, putting herself slightly in front of Gabby. Gabby, in turn, nudged her sister's protective arm back. They were squabbling silently, each one trying to get closer to the door, when the panel of wood behind the iron grid slid aside.

Both girls gasped.

A face scored with puffy pink scars appeared. It belonged to a young man, his slate-blue eyes staring at them from behind a pair of wire-rim glasses. He slammed the wood panel shut. A moment later came the telltale sound of sliding locks and rattling chains, and then the door creaked open.

"The Sisters Waverly, I presume?" The young man swept out his arm, gesturing for them to enter. "Nolan and Vander said you would be coming."

Ingrid composed herself. "Yes, thank you."

She and Gabby stepped into the apartment. Voices drifted from the main rooms, located down a short entrance hall. To her right was a window that overlooked the street. She held back the impulse to go to it and check on Luc.

"I'll take your things," the young man said, the offer gentle and polite.

Ingrid wished she hadn't stared at him like she was a cheap circus-goer. His face and neck were badly scarred, the pink injuries still relatively fresh, but his manners were impeccable as he accepted their velvet capes.

He led them down the hall, which was upholstered in pale-green damask with metallic gray stripes. The cloth worked to muffle the voices inside the apartment, but Ingrid could still make out Nolan's brogue.

Gabby and Ingrid followed the scarred man out of the hall and into an immense room. It looked like a giant factory loft, stretching long and wide, divided only by exposed, floor-to-ceiling wooden beams. The beams created the feeling of rooms without the need for doors or walls.

Vander was in one of these rudimentary rooms. He and Nolan were leaning over a zinc-topped table covered with loose papers. Two girls stood nearby, one of whom Ingrid recognized. It was the girl from the café, the one Henri had been speaking to. She leaned against a whitewashed brick wall, her ankles and arms crossed in a relaxed, boyish fashion.

"They're here," the scarred man announced. Vander looked up from the sprawl of papers and immediately came out from behind the table.

"You're all right?" His long strides took him through a sectioned-out sitting room enclosed by overflowing, waist-high bookshelves. He reached Ingrid within seconds, and to her astonishment, he grasped her shoulders. Vander held her slightly away from him and inspected her cheek.

"I couldn't ask at breakfast with your mother and Constantine listening, but are you hurt? Did the hellhound harm you?"

Ingrid's response lodged in her throat. Her mouth opened wordlessly and she emitted a choking noise. Vander dropped his hands and stepped away.

"I'm sorry, I was just worried," he said.

"No, I'm sorry, I didn't expect—"

"I shouldn't have . . ." Vander garbled the rest of his apology. Ingrid's mortification was complete.

Gabby cleared her throat in a none-too-delicate way and walked around them, toward the rest of the group.

"I'm not hurt," Ingrid said softly as they followed Gabby. The wound on her leg felt too private to admit. Having Luc's eyes and hands on her calf earlier had been awkward enough. She didn't want Vander or Nolan to insist upon a look as well. Besides, the punctures had scabbed already. Luc's blood, as revolting as it sounded, must have sped up the healing.

"Good. I was told that you had, uh"—Vander faltered—"help? Last night?"

He watched Ingrid, as if to measure her reaction.

"Do you mean the gargoyle? Luc?" she asked.

The crowd around the table, including Nolan, fell quiet. Vander took off his glasses and stared at her.

"You know it was Luc?"

"That's impossible." The café girl came forward. "The Dispossessed don't reveal themselves to humans."

"But he did," Ingrid said.

The girl regarded Ingrid closely, her hand resting on the slim hip of her baggy breeches. The boyish trousers didn't fool Ingrid. The girl's nails were perfectly manicured, her white blouse crisp and spotless, and the Zouave jacket was of a tight weave. She cared for her appearance.

Ingrid also noticed a carefully folded scarf of vivid red tied around her waist. The same as Vander's. Looking around, Ingrid saw that they all wore the red scarf in one fashion or another. Around the waist, looped around the neck, or diagonally across the chest, like on the scarred young man. Ingrid realized it must be the mark of the Alliance.

"What are they doing here, anyway?" the girl asked, flicking her hand in the air. She turned to Nolan. "The Alliance is an underground army, not a social club."

"I didn't notice anyone wearing party clothes," Gabby cut in with an equal amount of sass. "The only reason we've come is because Mr."—she caught herself—"*Nolan* said he knows where our brother is. So where is he?"

Ingrid arched a brow. Her sister was a regular little monarch when she wanted to be. Nolan rested his big hand on the girl's shoulder and smiled at Gabby as if he'd had the same thought as Ingrid.

"Chelle, of course, meant to say welcome to Hôtel Bastian, Paris Alliance faction headquarters," he said, his hand dwarfing Chelle's willowy shoulder. He gave it a squeeze. Chelle speared him with her slightly upturned eyes and shrugged out from under his hold. Nolan ignored her. "I know it looks a bit empty at the moment. The place is usually swarming, but a number of us have been called off to Rome for the summit."

Ingrid figured the summit was something important having to do with the Alliance, though she really didn't care. The only thing that interested her was finding Grayson.

"Most of us live here, although there are some, like Vander, who choose to live separately." Nolan cocked a grin and eyed Vander. "When will you leave that crummy flat above your shop?"

"And share all day every day with you?" Vander returned. "I'm afraid I'm not ready for that kind of commitment, dear."

Chelle had rejoined the second young woman beneath a rack suspended from the ceiling. Pans, colanders, and ladles hooked onto it like copper charms. The second girl, with a single long braid thrown over her shoulder, looked only marginally more accepting of Ingrid and Gabby's presence.

"What is it that you do, Mr. Quinn?" Ingrid asked. "Luc mentioned the Alliance last night, so you must know about the gargoyles. And demons. What more is there?"

He kicked out a stool next to a glass-fronted cabinet and

propped a foot on the seat. He leaned forward, his tall black boots in need of a shine. "More than I can explain in one visit. It's a lot to take in, Lady Ingrid. And please, call me Nolan."

He flashed her what he no doubt meant to be a charming smile. She ignored it.

"We're not leaving without answers." Ingrid hated how she always needed to prove to people that she was stronger than she appeared.

Nolan nodded. "Understood. I'll tell you what I can without breaching Alliance law. But I need your word that what we say stays between us. You can't breathe a word to anyone. Not your mother, not your servants. The Alliance is invisible, and it goes to great lengths to remain that way. There are a few apartments on the second floor like Henri's that we can use for entertaining citizens," he said, looking pointedly at Gabby, who steamed red. "But the rest of the building is off-limits. Trust me, if there were any senior Alliance members in the city right now, you wouldn't even be standing here."

They were taking a risk bringing Ingrid and Gabby in on whatever it was they knew about Grayson. The gratitude for it felt hot and full in her chest.

"You have our word," Gabby declared for them both. Nolan nodded.

"What we do is straightforward. We hunt and destroy demons," the girl next to Chelle immediately said. She stepped away from Chelle's side. "They come up through fissures from the Underneath and prey on humans all over the world. Think of the Underneath as a hellish kind of second Earth, with countless portals into our world. We're trained to either destroy them or send them back." She gave a half shrug. "I prefer the first option."

"Most of us were born into the Alliance," Chelle tacked on with unwarranted defensiveness. "We come from generations of members."

Ingrid couldn't tell if she sounded proud or resentful.

"That's all splendid, but what we really care to know is where we can find Grayson," Gabby said.

Nolan lowered his foot from the stool and stood tall. "Your patience is truly virtuous, Gabriella." She scowled at him, but he pretended not to notice. "Yes, we know where your brother is."

There was a catch. Ingrid heard it, like the jeering pluck of a discordant violin in a finely tuned orchestra.

"I should begin with what happened yesterday," Nolan said. "We believe a Dispossessed had a hand in Henri's death."

"But gargoyles protect humans," Ingrid said. That was what Luc had led her to believe, at least.

"The humans they're bound to, yes," Nolan replied. "The Angelic Order rules over the Dispossessed, assigning them to their individual territories. Whatever happens beyond those territories is usually of little interest to them."

"And most of the Dispossessed adhere to a hands-off code when it comes to unguarded humans, or humans who belong to another gargoyle," Vander added. "But not all of them. This building isn't marked with *les grotesques*—we prefer not to tie any gargoyles to us in that way. So any gargoyle who wanted to do Henri harm would have had access to him."

Gabby shouldered her way around Nolan and moved toward the table. "But don't you work with the gargoyles? It would seem you have similar interests," she said as she peered at the papers. She looked at ease, while Ingrid was so tense it felt like a stiff board had been strapped to her back.

"We protect Paris as a whole, and while some gargoyles hunt for the fun of it, most only look after their own human charges," Vander clarified. "Still, we do try to work together. When we can."

The last bit hadn't sounded so convincing.

Ingrid looked at Nolan. "You mentioned an Angelic Order? You mean to say the Dispossessed are like angels?"

Chelle's and Nolan's short, coarse bursts of laughter matched.

"Not at all," Nolan explained. "We don't have contact with the Order—we *are* only human—but from what the gargoyles have imparted, they're little more than slaves to the angels."

God's angels held slaves? It sounded so wrong. So hypocritical.

"Then why do you think a gargoyle killed Henri?" Ingrid asked.

Nolan crossed his arms and cupped both elbows as he looked at Vander. He gestured for the bookseller to explain.

Vander stepped forward and removed his glasses. Without them, his features changed drastically. His jawline strengthened and his lashes became more visible, making his pale, wheat-colored eyes brighter, like sunshine.

"It's not easy to explain," he began. "But seeing how you've already survived a hellhound, know about gargoyles, and apparently also know their shape-shifting nature, I'm guessing you'll be able to handle it."

He gave her a lopsided smile. She saw hope in it and nodded encouragement.

"I have an ability," Vander proceeded. "You saw a demon last night, but you only saw its physical form—its body. When I see a demon, I see something no one else can."

He raised his hands and held them apart, fingers spread, as if he were holding a ball. "Every demon gives off glimmering particles invisible to human eyes. It's a dust, surrounding them like an aura. When they move, they leave these particles behind. It eventually dissipates, but only after time has passed. A few hours, usually."

Ingrid's lips parted, but she had nothing to say. Vander could see demon particles? He had an *ability*? She thought of her hands and what Luc had said she'd done with them. Ingrid clasped her hands before her, her palms damp.

"Vander calls it demon dust," Nolan added.

"And yesterday, after the youngest Waverly finally left Henri's flat," Chelle said, stressing *finally* and targeting Gabby with one of her daggered glares, "Vander came for a look."

"Gargoyles aren't demons, but they are supernatural creatures. They leave behind a sapphire-colored dust," Vander explained. "There were strong traces of it around Henri's flat."

Gabby lightly shifted some papers on the table, no doubt to have a better look at them. Chelle propelled herself from the wall where she'd been leaning and gathered all the papers into a haphazard pile, swiping them away from Gabby's reach.

Vander placed his glasses back on the bridge of his nose and wandered to one of the street-side windows spilling light over the unvarnished floors.

"The Dispossessed leader here in Paris, an old gargoyle named Lennier, knows what's happened. He was supposed to have convened all the Dispossessed this morning." Vander peered down at the curb. "Did Luc say anything?"

Luc had been silent as a clam so far that morning. Ingrid had thought it was because of what had happened the night before. He'd shared something vital with her. He'd brought her out of the dark. Not only that, but he'd also done her a favor. Had he not shown himself to her in the abbey, Ingrid had no doubt she would have driven herself mad wanting to know more about the gargoyle that had rescued her. She might have even started to believe she *had* gone mad.

"He hasn't said anything," she answered. "Could you please just tell us where our brother is?"

Vander left the window and moved toward the low couches and overstuffed chairs in the sitting area.

"Why don't you sit," he said.

No. That wasn't what Ingrid wanted to do at all. People always wanted you to sit when they had bad news to share.

Gabby left the kitchen table and joined Ingrid. They followed

Vander to the couches, where the scarred young man was sitting with an open book in his lap. He'd been so quiet, Ingrid had all but forgotten him. He closed the book and got up, a polite gesture if the girls wished to sit.

They didn't.

Nolan leaned his forearms atop one of the bookshelves and said to Vander, "I'll tell 'em, mate."

"Tell us what?" Gabby asked. Ingrid heard the panic beneath her sister's irritation.

"When your brother went missing from that dinner, Luc went to Lennier, who then came to the Alliance. Lennier asked us to help look for Luc's human. First thing we did was go to the house. It belongs to a viscountess, Lady Ormand," he said.

Ingrid recognized the name. Her mother's childhood friend, Lady Genevieve Ormand, had a house in Paris. Of course. She wouldn't have hesitated to invite Grayson to a dinner.

"We walked around a bit," Nolan went on, his head bowed over his propped arms, his black hair nearly covering his eyes. "Vander saw the dust trail leading out a rear door and into a courtyard. He followed it into the mews running behind the houses and saw where it had mingled with another shade of dust about three houses down."

A demon. Ingrid's fingers went numb. For the first time she felt the cold of the open, drafty apartment. She felt Gabby twining her hand around her elbow.

"We have every reason to believe that your brother was taken to the Underneath," Nolan said.

"No," Ingrid whispered. It was such a common reaction. To deny tragic news, to insist that it wasn't true. But Ingrid met genuine despair and regret as she looked into each of their faces. They were telling the truth.

And Luc had lied.

The night before, inside the abbey, he'd pretended not to know where Grayson was. Yet he *had* known—he must have. He should have told her instead of protecting her from the truth. Ingrid wasn't sure how, but she was certain that that was what Luc had been doing. Protecting her.

"The Underneath?" Gabby's fingers now strangled her arm. "But that's the place where demons live. If our brother is there . . . he's dead?"

He wasn't. Ingrid knew it instinctively. They'd shared a womb. They shared a birthmark. A life. Ingrid would know if he'd died. The same way Luc claimed he'd know if they were in danger. She'd just *feel* it.

Nolan abandoned the bookcase and came toward them. "We can't be sure."

Ingrid, however, was. "He isn't dead. Don't ask me how I know, I just do. So"—she raised her chin—"how do we get him out?"

Her question was met with guarded silence.

"It's not as simple as that," an even voice replied. It belonged to the man who'd opened the door for them. He stepped forward, entering the conversation for the first time. "We don't trespass into the demon realm. It's against Alliance law, and for good reason. We can each take on one or two Underneath creatures at a time, here, in our world. We can only imagine what kind of attack we'd encounter if we stepped inside their world."

"Can't the Angelic Order help?" Ingrid persisted. "If there are angels, shouldn't they want to protect Grayson? Save him? Shouldn't they care?"

She didn't like the second round of silence any more than the first.

"They do care," Nolan answered with perceptible caution, as if the angels might be listening at that very moment. "To a point."

"It sounds strange at first, but angels really aren't all that different from the gargoyles," Vander said with a confidence that Nolan hadn't shown. "They serve God, obey his commands, deliver his messages, and bring judgment, but God ranks the below humans. From what we've learned from the Dispossessed, it's inspired a kind of resentment among the Order. They do what they must for God's precious humans, but they don't go above and beyond."

Ingrid knew a little about the scriptures, and the claims that God favored humans over everything, even his angels. But the idea that it was real—that Luc had contact with *angels*—left her thunderstruck.

"Trespassing into a demon realm, a place that would sap angels of their power, is definitely considered above and beyond," the scarred man said.

Chelle waved a hand impatiently. "What does it matter? It was a hellhound that took him. Vander saw its dust. No one could survive a beast like that."

Vander pinned her with a black stare. "We don't know that for certain."

"Yes, we do. Most hellhound victims end up just like the body the police found on boulevard Saint-Michel this morning: in small pieces."

"Enough, Chelle," Nolan barked.

But Chelle wasn't finished. She shifted her eyes, as hard and dark as basalt, toward Ingrid. "We come across one or two hellhounds every month, sometimes every other month. Yet here we are discussing two attacks in one week, and the intended victims happen to be brother and sister."

Ingrid peeled her eyes from Chelle's and turned to Vander. "And you want to know why."

He stepped forward. "Not just that. We want to help protect you. In case the hellhound comes back."

Ingrid shuddered at the thought of having to see that beast again.

"How many hellhounds are there?" she asked. "You said you saw dust leading away from Lady Ormand's home the night Grayson disappeared, and more dust in the mews. There were two hellhounds, then?"

Could two come for her?

Vander and Nolan exchanged a guarded look.

"No. Every species of demon gives off its own colored dust. The two streams of dust I saw were from different, uh . . . creatures," Vander replied.

"What other creature?" Ingrid asked.

He sighed and took off his glasses. "Your brother."

Two heartbeats, maybe three or four, passed before Ingrid took a breath. Before anyone in the apartment took a breath.

"I don't understand." Ingrid shook her head as if to clear it.

Vander forgot himself and closed the space between them. He took her shoulder with one of his hands, though not with the same intensity as before. "Grayson left a faint amount of dust. I noticed it the first time I met him. It's why I brought him here, to meet Nolan and the Alliance."

Gabby left Ingrid's side and stepped up right beneath Vander's chin. She broke his grip on Ingrid. "You're lying."

. He looked down the fine Roman lines of his nose at her. "I'm not. I know I can't prove anything, but I'm *not* lying."

Ingrid pulled Gabby back with a gentle tug on her wrist. "But you said supernatural beings give off dust, not humans."

Chelle's irascible voice sounded from the open kitchen behind them. "Go on, Vander, just tell her and let us get back to work. It will be sunset in three hours and we haven't decided who takes the Ninth and the First tonight."

"Tell me what?" Ingrid asked, turning back to Vander.

He ran a hand through his hair. "Some humans do have this dust. Not many, but some. We call them Dusters. Your brother was one." He sighed. "And you're another."

All Ingrid saw in the next few seconds was her sister's mouth, wide with shock. Then Gabby laughed.

"Ingrid does not have demon dust!"

Ingrid squeezed her fists tighter. Her palms, no longer damp, felt warm, as if she'd turned them to a glaring July sun. Grayson had demon dust? *She* had demon dust?

Vander was wrong. She couldn't handle it. She couldn't handle it at all.

"I'm sorry, Ingrid," he said, and not even his dropping her title for the first time was able to stir her. "You might not want to believe it right now, but you do have demon dust. You and your brother . . . well, you're not exactly human."

They had all been girls.

And every one of them had arrived screaming.

Grayson tested his footing as the newest girl's screams vibrated against his eardrums. His legs were surprisingly stable as he loped toward the cave opening. He hadn't been beyond the low arched entrance yet. The hooded woman hadn't bound him, but he was a prisoner just the same.

The girl's shrieks should have brought out his chivalrous nature. Hadn't he always held doors for ladies, stood when a woman entered a room, maintained a proper tongue? Grayson should have gone in search of the girl, ready to fight the monster assaulting her. But the monsters . . . there were so many of them here.

Grayson stayed put by the cave entrance, a hand braced against one side of the rough arch. If he stepped out, what manner of monster would he be met with? He'd already seen so many passing by the mouth of his cave. Some walked on two legs, like men, but he could see, in the blue flashes of light, that there was always something wrong with them. One had stood erect, but in place of arms there had been giant pincers, and a smaller set clicked wildly where its mouth should have been. Other creatures scuttled like gargantuan cockroaches, and some slithered with stumpy lizard arms and thick, undulating tails.

The girl's screams reverberated through the tunnel outside Grayson's cave. He leaned his forehead against the packed-dirt wall. He'd lost count of how many girls he'd heard screaming since he'd woken in this cave. Since the fanged man had started punching holes in Grayson's flesh. Whatever the black liquid being injected into his bloodstream was, it was changing him. He should have wanted to help the girls. He should have felt remorse when each girl eventually stopped screaming. But it just wasn't happening. Instead, he found himself smiling. Laughing.

Wanting to make them scream louder.

CHAPTER TWELVE

Monsieur Constantine's chateau was the last place Gabby wanted to be that morning. It was set on the outskirts of the city, near one of the old walls enclosing Paris. It was a place, Luc had so genially told them as they waited in the carriage for their mother, that had once been dangerous. Packs of wild wolves had once stalked the woodlands surrounding Paris; during the winter months, desperate and starving, the wolves would often prey on the livestock belonging to poor farmers who made the border-lands their home.

"Sometimes, if livestock ran thin," Luc had added with a gleam of mischief in those green eyes of his, "the wolves' prey would end up being the farmers themselves."

Gabby was positive she did not like Luc.

He steered the landau through an opening between two stone pillars. They marked the entrance to Constantine's chateau—which was, Gabby noted with relief, nothing like a poor farm plagued by wild wolves. The brick-and-stucco-sided mansion looked like it was at least a century old. The gravel drive leading up to it cut through a pasturelike front lawn, complete with paddocks and grazing horses.

"Monsieur Constantine must be a very successful salesman," Gabby mumbled.

"We don't speak of money, Gabriella," her mother said tightly. But Gabby could plainly see her appraising the grand home and grounds.

Constantine's invitation to his home, Clos du Vie, had arrived at the rectory before dinner the evening before. He had insisted they come for tea. His peaceful chateau, he'd written without an ounce of shame, was a balm to frayed nerves.

Gabby suspected the man was smitten with her mother. Her father hadn't yet sent a reply telegram, but Gabby thought he might want to step to it.

"Perhaps it's just a family home," Ingrid said.

Gabby watched her sister carefully. She hadn't said much since returning from Hôtel Bastian the afternoon before. Gabby supposed being told you were *not exactly human* was plenty cause for a lengthy silence. She still didn't believe what Vander had said, though. How could Ingrid have demon dust? Or Grayson, for that matter? How could they have it when Gabby did not?

Ingrid, looking out the window, furrowed her pale brow. Gabby followed her gaze up to the mansard roof. Adorning the front two corners of the sloping roofline were stone gargoyles. So Constantine had a guardian as well. She wondered if the old man knew, but quickly decided he couldn't. Chelle had told them that the gargoyles hid in plain sight. How many of them were here? Perhaps they were members of the chateau staff.

Gabby felt a leap in her pulse. The thoughts should have made her feel as if she belonged in Bedlam. Instead, they sent out an electrical charge. She wanted to know everything about the Alliance, the Dispossessed, demons, and the Underneath. The idea of it all actually being *real* exhilarated her.

The landau drew to a stop in front of a set of steep gray quartz steps. Gabby was the last to exit, and Luc seemed all too eager to release her gloved hand and turn his attention back to Ingrid. His concentration on her sister's face didn't flag as their mother readjusted her fur wrap and commenced mounting the steps to the front entrance.

"I won't be far," he said to Ingrid, quietly enough so their mother couldn't hear. He'd said the same thing to Ingrid the day before at Hôtel Bastian. Luc might have been bound to protect all of the souls living beneath the rectory roof, but the way his eyes prowled Ingrid's face led Gabby to believe that protecting anyone other than her sister would be a burden to him.

"Girls," their mother called. "Don't dawdle."

They started up the steps but certainly did dawdle. Gabby waited until their mother was well ahead to touch Ingrid's arm lightly. "Do you believe what they say? About the Underneath and Grayson and how no one can reach him there?" she whispered.

Ingrid kept their conversation hushed. "I believe *they* believe Grayson is beyond rescue."

"However?" Gabby prodded.

"However," Ingrid said, linking her arm with her sister's, "he's not their brother, and they can't possibly love him like we do. We can't give up on him, Gabby."

It wouldn't do to start sniffling in the entranceway to Constantine's home, so Gabby battled back the tears stinging her eyes. Her sister hardly ever spoke like this to her—as if they were confidantes. Partners of sorts. Gabby felt her throat thicken with a ridiculous sob. She choked it down.

"We *won't,* Ingrid," she assured her just as their mother widened her eyes at them in another plea to hurry up already. Ingrid's arm slipped from Gabby's, but Gabby still felt the press of it as the maids took their cloaks. They were of one mind then, with one goal: get to Grayson and bring him home.

The butler led them down a few twisting hallways with

shining parquet floors. When at last he led them into a room, a wave of humidity lapped against Gabby's cheeks. They had entered an orangery.

Three surrounding walls of glass and iron had been built at a slant to form a massive greenhouse. Inside was a jungle of potted orange, lime, and lemon trees, glossy eucalyptus, vivid bougainvillea, flowering bamboo, and a number of other shrubberies and flowers Gabby couldn't identify.

"This is marvelous!" her mother cried, her voice echoing off the glass.

Monsieur Constantine stepped out from a path winding through bamboo stalks. His gray hair, beard, and clothing were completely drab compared to the lush colors surrounding him.

"Lady Brickton, mesdemoiselles, *bienvenue*. Welcome," he said, spreading his arms wide. "I am glad you have come, but I must apologize—"

At that moment, two more people emerged from the bamboo. Gabby's eyes immediately rested on the dark-haired one; his locks hung limply in the humidity, his jacquard tie loosened and his coat cast off. A sheen of sweat glistened on his forehead and nose. Any other man would have looked rumpled and pitiful in just a vest and damp shirtsleeves.

Not Nolan Quinn.

If possible, he managed to look even more masculine in the junglelike climate. He met her surprise with a lift of his lips. Her blood purred as it rushed through her ears. Gabby wasn't sure if she was nettled or secretly pleased to see him.

"I've had two unexpected visitors," Constantine continued. Beside Nolan, and looking just as handsome despite his fogged glasses, was Vander. "Though I am afraid they bring no new information regarding your son."

Their mother's petite shoulders drooped. The small fold of loose skin beneath her jaw tightened as she swallowed her disappointment.

"I wish we could bring you better news, but Grayson's trail is completely cold. There isn't a single lead to work from," Nolan said.

It wasn't entirely a lie. Grayson's trail had gone cold because he no longer existed on Earth. But there *were* leads. Nolan and Vander knew exactly where her brother was.

"My lady, mesdemoiselles, come. Sit. Please." Constantine took Gabby's mother by the hand and led her through a natural archway of vines and moss to a garden table and chairs. He called for tea and cakes. Gabby's stomach clenched. She was impatient. Restless. And the humid air was starting to close in on her.

"Monsieur Constantine, do you have outdoor gardens that my sister and I might stroll through? I find I need air."

"Of course," he said, handing Charlotte into a green iron chair. It looked about as comfortable as one of the abbey's wooden pews. "My vineyards are gently sloping. I don't imagine you will tax yourself strolling them. Messieurs, will you accompany the young ladies?"

Gabby stifled a frustrated sigh. She'd wanted a chance to continue the hushed conversation with Ingrid from earlier.

Vander and Nolan both made stiff, proper bows of acquiescence. Gabby took Ingrid's arm and followed the two young Alliance members through the bamboo stalks, toward a glass door. Gabby stepped from the South American jungle into a brisk northern winter. Her body didn't take it lightly.

Gabby let go of Ingrid's arm and tried to warm herself by striding quickly toward the vineyard rows. They began about a full hectare away from the glassed-in orangery, atop a knoll crusted with snow.

No one spoke until they had reached the first row of trellises, the grapevines heavily pruned for the winter. They were so spare and cut back, Gabby could see through one line of trellis to the next and the one after that. As they turned into the first row, her boots squished a few remnants of the summer crop.

Nolan had fallen into step behind her. He emerged in her peripheral vision.

"What are you really doing here?" Gabby asked.

"Constantine believes we're in the middle of an investigation, and I've learned it's best to keep up appearances," he said.

"But you're not really. I mean, you're not investigating anything. You took on the case as a way to get closer to Ingrid. Because Vander says she has that dust," Gabby said, keeping her tone down. A quick look behind them showed Ingrid and Vander conversing a few paces back.

"You make it sound as if I'm doing something malicious, and for my own benefit," he replied, matching her strides. "I apologize if you think accepting the job to investigate your brother's disappearance was underhanded, but I needed a legitimate way to meet you and your sister. You have to admit, the first time we met was rather debauched."

Gabby reached for the folds of her cape and realized she hadn't sent a footman to retrieve it before leaving the orangery. Glancing back, she saw Vander draping Ingrid's shoulders with his shabby tweed coat. Her sister tugged on the floppy lapels to bring it closer around her neck.

"I apologize, but I haven't a coat to warm you," Nolan said, picking up on her thoughts like some sort of magician.

"I haven't a need for one," she replied.

"You're a prickly little juniper, aren't you?"

He sounded amused, just like the time he'd observed she had *a bit of flint* in her. It had almost been a compliment. She ignored him this time, too.

"You say it isn't safe, but if I wanted to go into the Underneath, how would I get there?" Gabby asked.

Nolan smirked. "And delusional as well, I see."

She stopped and set her shoulders in a firm line. "This isn't a joke. Someone has to go after my brother and rescue him, and it's clear your lot hasn't the interest or the backbone. Tell us how to enter the Underneath and my sister and I will do what should have been done days ago."

He propped his hands on his hips and turned his eyes skyward, that infuriatingly mocking grin still on his lips.

"Aye, that's brilliant. I'll just send a girl and her sister into the demon realm because I'm too lily-livered." He dropped his eyes and pierced her with an uncharacteristically harsh gaze. "Grayson is beyond rescue. You don't go into the Underneath unless you're brought there, and when that happens you're as good as dead."

Gabby checked over her shoulder. Ingrid and Vander had stopped walking and were far down the row behind them, deep in conversation.

"You told us he was alive," she challenged. "Were you lying?"

Nolan hesitated, again eyeing the clouds. "First cowardice, now lying. What else do you plan to accuse me of before this lovely stroll concludes? Treason? Murder? Failing to heed fashionable clothing trends?"

Gabby fairly growled with annoyance before making a brisk turn around the bend in the vineyard row. Nolan came up on Gabby's heels.

"Luc has been told—by an angel—that Grayson is alive, and we have no reason to doubt he's telling the truth," he answered.

She kept walking, her boots mashing leftover grapes into the crusted grass. "If he's alive, we'll get to him. Ingrid and I won't stop."

He hooked her elbow and reeled her to a halt. He stood close enough for Gabby to trace the musk of his skin. Vanilla and sandalwood. It did something funny to her knees, and she was glad he held her firmly.

"He's not coming back, Gabriella, and you'd best understand that no Alliance, let alone any privileged young girls, is going to enter the demon world to get to him. I won't allow it."

She tightened her jaw and spoke through clenched teeth. "And *you'd* best understand that I'm not giving up on my brother."

She jerked her elbow free and surged down the vineyard row away from him.

"So you're saying Grayson and I have this demon dust, but Gabby doesn't?" Ingrid asked as she and Vander slowly followed her sister and Nolan. The other pair was marching quickly, already far ahead of Ingrid and Vander, as if the stroll were a military drill.

Vander pulled his arms free of his knee-length coat. "That's right."

"Oh no, please," she said, raising her hand to stop him. "You'll be too cold."

He laughed and continued to shuck his coat, leaving him in only ivory shirtsleeves and a green vest the color of a billiard table's baize. "Don't you know that the male epidermis is a half-centimeter thicker than the female epidermis? I read it somewhere once," he said, holding out his coat. "Honest. It's all in the research."

Ingrid raised a brow, knowing full well he was lying. And something about that warmed her. She stopped to let him drape his coat over her shoulders. It settled with an unexpected weight.

"You're a horrible liar," she said once they'd started walking again.

"But I'm a perfect gentleman," he returned.

Ingrid smiled as she closed the floppy lapels tighter around her neck. Something hard in the coat's lining clinked against her side when she moved.

"There are others, you say, besides Grayson and me?"

Vander crossed his arms to warm his hands as they walked. Ingrid felt guiltily warm.

"Yes, but it's not something I see every day. Still, there are a number of Dusters." He took a sideways glance at her. "Including me."

Ingrid faltered to a stop and gaped at him. "You?"

Vander smirked. "Since I was sixteen. Before that, I couldn't see it around me, or anyone else, for that matter. But now . . ." He held out his arms and rotated them appraisingly. "I have to say, we make a pretty pair. Your pearl dust, my multicolored dust. Close together like this, we look like a rainbow snowstorm."

Ingrid wished she could see the dust the way he did. "But why? I mean, there must be some sort of connection between everyone who has this dust. Something that sets them apart from those who *don't* have it. Is it something we inherit?"

Vander tucked his arms close to his body again, folding them tightly. His muscles strained against the seams of his shirtsleeves. Either his shirt was a size too small or Vander's build was thicker than Ingrid had first realized.

"No, it's not passed from generation to generation, that much I know. Nolan and I have been investigating. We began with me, in fact. We marked down everything, from my sex and coloring and ethnicity to where I live, what languages I speak, where I was born, and so on. So far we've only narrowed it down to two consistent commonalities." Vander glanced at her. "You were born in Paris, weren't you?"

Ingrid stopped walking. "How did you know that?"

Vander's eyes brightened with victory. "Because so far all the Dusters we have dossiers on are under the age of twenty and were born in Paris."

"But I thought you were an American."

Up ahead, Ingrid saw her sister rush into the next vineyard row. She knew her sister's body language. Gabby was angry about something.

"Actually, I was born in Paris," Vander said. "Parisian mother, American father. We moved to the Pennsylvania countryside when I was a baby. I came back a few years ago, thinking to study at the Sorbonne."

"Gabby was born in London, not Paris," Ingrid explained.

"My parents used to keep a home here and my mother wanted to be close to her mother when her time came."

Talk of childbirth with a near stranger—and a boy at that—brought a blush to Ingrid's cheeks. Vander went silent.

"What are you studying at the Sorbonne?" she asked to change the subject.

"They've shut down their theology program, so nothing at the moment. I'm studying on my own for now, maybe applying to a seminary somewhere in the future." Vander cupped his hands and blew into his fists to warm them.

A seminary? Ingrid stared at him in amazement. "You're going to be a *priest?*"

Vander laughed, probably used to that reaction. "A minister, actually. I'm Protestant." He grinned at the utterly rude expression of astonishment her face refused to drop.

"But you have demon dust. Can ministers have demon dust?" she asked, knowing the question was just as rude as her expression.

Vander shrugged. "I don't see why anyone would need to know I have it. It's not as if a lot of people do. The Alliance, and that's it. The Dispossessed know I can see dust, but they don't know I have it myself. I'm probably much safer that way."

But the gargoyles wouldn't mistake Vander for a demon just because of his dust. Would they?

"Let's keep walking," he said, and guided her forward.

He blew into his fists again. Ingrid tried to take off his coat to return it to him, but he laid his arm across her shoulder to stop her. "A half-centimeter thicker, remember?"

He kept his arm draped across her shoulder a beat longer than was proper. Enough to turn Ingrid's stomach into a kaleidoscope of feelings: unease, excitement, guilt. Guilt? She puzzled over that. She wasn't doing anything wrong, even if he did aspire to the clergy.

Still, she edged away from his side. "But I am human. If I weren't, Luc would have known."

"He can only be bound to humans who live within the abbey and rectory, yes. So you are, at least partially, human. Besides, if you weren't, you wouldn't even be able to step on hallowed ground."

It sounded awful. *Partially human.*

Like Luc.

"Do you know Luc at all?" The question gave away her interest in the gargoyle, and she was instantly sorry she'd asked Vander.

"Not very well. From what I've been told, he's just come out of hibernation." When Ingrid suddenly came to a stop, he explained, "Whenever a gargoyle's territory is abandoned for a long-enough period and he isn't needed, he slips into a kind of idle sleep. He turns hard, almost like a stone statue of himself. Luc's just woken from something like thirty years of hibernation."

Ingrid covered her shock by searching through the trellis into the next vineyard row. Luc had been in hibernation long before Ingrid had even been born. He might look like a boy of eighteen or nineteen, but exactly how old was he? How long had he been protecting the inhabitants of the abbey? She wondered if she was different from any of the other humans he'd protected. Probably not. But knowing that Luc was close, knowing that he could sense the things she was feeling and find her at any given moment, gave her the tiniest of thrills. It was more intriguing than anything she'd ever experienced.

"Ingrid," Vander said with a note of caution. "Luc may look like a human, but he isn't one. Not anymore. None of the gargoyles are, and from what I know about them, they aren't admirers of humans. In fact, most of them are bitter and resentful of the humans they're forced to protect."

"Forced?" Ingrid asked distractedly as she saw Gabby rush

past on the opposite side of the trellis. Nolan walked slowly behind her.

"They didn't choose to become Dispossessed. They're turned into gargoyles as punishment for a sin they committed when they were alive. An unforgivable sin."

"What sin?" she asked.

"I'm not sure you really want to know." The melodrama in Vander's tone exasperated her.

"I wouldn't have asked if I didn't," she ground out.

Before Vander could reply, Ingrid saw something dark ripple through the parallel rows of trellis. A shadow, gone before she could focus. But then she smelled it: the stench of rotting meat and soured milk.

"Vander," she whispered. He'd already gone stiff, his arm stretched across her front as if it could shield her.

"Stay behind me," he whispered.

Ingrid took a frantic look through the vineyard trellis, searching for Gabby. Her eyes landed on her sister's periwinkle taffeta skirt, farther down the next row. Nolan had positioned himself in much the same way as Vander, guarding Gabby's front.

The black shadow darted fast behind the square-patterned trellis three rows beyond. The hellhound came into full view as it leaped over a section of trellis, splintering the wooden frame with its whiplike tail.

"Blade!" Nolan shouted, wrapping Gabby close to him and pulling her through a break in the trellis, back into the first row.

Vander ripped his jacket from Ingrid's shoulders. Before she could utter a word, he drew a gleaming silver sword from a sheath sewn into the jacket's lining. That was why it was so heavy! Vander gripped the handle of the arm-length sword and, taking Ingrid's hand, dragged her toward Nolan and Gabby.

The hellhound bounded into the next vineyard row, leaving only one row as a buffer.

"It's daylight!" Vander tossed Nolan the silver sword. "What is it doing out?"

Nolan caught the sword with expert precision and then released Gabby, thrusting her toward Vander and Ingrid.

"I don't know. Take them back to the chateau. Now!"

Gabby screamed as the hellhound pounced down into the neighboring row, less than ten paces from where they stood. Ingrid grasped her sister's arm and stumbled backward.

"No! We can't leave him," Gabby said, trying to wrench her arm free.

Vander herded them back, face taut with focus. "He can take care of himself. And he'll fight better without distractions. Let's go!"

Ingrid had dragged Gabby's resisting feet less than a yard when a pair of black wings swept over them like a low, racing cloud.

The gargoyle smashed into the oncoming hellhound's chest just as the beast cleared the top of the trellis. They thrashed through the woodwork and grapevines as they struck out at each other, talon and claw.

Luc's gargoyle form was even more gruesome in daylight. His obsidian scales were a shade grayer, and instead of appearing smooth and silky like before, the plates were coarse and weathered. As Luc battered the hellhound into the next vineyard row, another dark form wavered in Ingrid's peripheral vision.

Nolan saw it at the same moment and swiveled into a defensive stance, sword extended. A second hellhound was hurtling full bore down their row, all red lantern eyes, froth, and fangs. Nolan advanced to meet it, emitting a war cry that made the hairs on Ingrid's arms prickle stiff. The hound sprang from the ground, its front paws looking as if they were going to soar right over Nolan's head. He sliced at the hound's front legs. The hound growled and spit and lashed out at Nolan with one of its long slanted fangs. Nolan went down, rolling into a trellis post.

The hellhound stopped to lick its wounded front legs but then turned its lantern eyes toward Ingrid, Gabby, and Vander.

"Run," Vander whispered. "As fast as you can."

But Ingrid's feet wouldn't work. The beast was so big, and Vander didn't have a weapon to use against it. Only blessed silver or holy water would work, Luc had said.

"Water!" Ingrid jammed her hand into her skirt pocket. She grasped the small mother-of-pearl perfume bottle and black-netted atomizer that she'd transferred Luc's water to. She shoved the bottle into Vander's hand.

"Use this," she said. He looked blankly at the perfume bottle. "It's holy water!"

Vander had only just grasped the bottle with understanding when another pair of obsidian wings hurtled into the vineyard row and collided with the second hellhound. The impact drove the hellhound into the ground, its back plowing a rut in the grass. Of course! One was Constantine's gargoyle, and the other was Luc. But the two gargoyles were nearly identical, each one dark-winged and dogheaded. Ingrid looked between the two. Which was Luc?

The first gargoyle was still struggling with the other hellhound and seemed to be losing. The hound worked the gargoyle beneath its massive paws and slashed at a wing with one of its slanted bottom fangs. Black liquid spewed from the gargoyle's wing, and its anguished screech rent the air.

"Luc!" Ingrid screamed. A mistake. The hound whipped its lantern eyes toward her.

Without hesitation, Vander tore through the wrecked trellis to distract the demon. At the same moment, Gabby shoved away from Ingrid and started for Nolan's prostrate form.

Ingrid practically ripped the sleeve of Gabby's dress as she flung her sister behind her. "Stay back!"

"But the sword!" Gabby cried. The silver blade gleamed beside the rut the hellhound's back had carved into the grass.

Ingrid released Gabby's sleeve and lunged for the ebony hilt herself—she couldn't let her little sister attempt to fight this beast. Ingrid enclosed the smooth ebony in her fist and lifted the silver blade, surprised by the weight of it. Down their vineyard row, the second hellhound batted the new gargoyle away with a strike to its doggish head. The hellhound reared back and charged toward Ingrid.

She raised the sword with both hands and held it out before her. A sudden current of electricity traveled through her arms, into her hands, and then, as if it had nowhere else to exit, streamed from the silver tip of the sword as a white flare of lightning. The bolt struck the hellhound in the chest just as Ingrid's back hit the ground.

She lifted her head in time to see the beast burst into a cloud of emerald cinders.

CHAPTER THIRTEEN

The landau rocked violently on its springs as Luc wrestled into his trousers. He'd left his clothing on the floor of the carriage the moment Ingrid's panic had surfaced, along with Gabby's. Constantine's stables had been quiet and deserted, a safe place to coalesce. But it had still been daylight. Transforming into gargoyle form while the sun was up wasn't something the Dispossessed liked to do. The demon hounds shouldn't have been out before dark, either.

Luc's body buzzed, an aftereffect of the reverse shift. He laced his boots, his fingers fumbling. He had to get inside Constantine's house. The humans had fled there after the attack, and he had to find Ingrid. First she'd thrown lightning from her hands, and now she'd sent a streak of it from the conduit of a blessed sword. The blast had struck the hellhound with enough force to send it back into the Underneath, and possibly even destroy it. The remaining hellhound had taken off after that, as had

Luc and Gaston, the gargoyle who ruled over the old chateau and vineyards.

Luc barged out of the landau and through the stable doors. His boots crunched over the white and tan rocks of the circular gravel drive, which surrounded a meticulous topiary. He made his way to the side of the chateau and down a set of scuffed steps to a foundation-level door. This was the entrance to the servants' floor, one level up from the basement, root cellar, and furnace and plumbing rooms. Luc knew Clos du Vie well. The old Sorbonne professor he'd guarded had known the previous owners and had visited often. Though none of those visits had ever been quite as eventful as this.

The innards of the chateau were alive and well, filled with steam and clanging pots and purposeful voices. The scullery maids and laundresses eyed Luc as he stormed through the halls, past the long tile-and-copper kitchen and the steamy laundry room with rectangular windows near the ceiling, now open to vent the humidity. They saw Luc's status in the clothes he wore and paid him little attention.

Luc smelled mushrooms and sage from the kitchen, rose soap from the laundry, and the sweat of Constantine's servants. His sensitive nose traced it all, including Ingrid's earth, sweet grass, and that additional, mysterious tang. He closed his eyes and breathed it in deeper. She was in the orangery.

The chiming at the base of Luc's skull came just seconds before he ran headlong into Gaston, who was exiting the single lavatory on the servants' level. Constantine's gargoyle and personal valet was eternally middle-aged, and damned with receding black hair. Like Luc, he was a member of the dog caste. It brought relaxation between them, but not necessarily friendship.

Gaston was favoring his left side, his arm drawn in against his ribs.

"You were injured?" Luc asked.

"A torn wing." Gaston shrugged. "It will heal, but not if I continue having to coalesce. It's quiet here, Luc. Quiet is the way I like it."

It was also the way Luc liked it, though he hadn't been lucky as of late.

Gaston inclined his head. "I saw what your human did with the blessed sword."

Luc had suspected as much. He also suspected Gaston would bring the news back to Lennier. Luc licked his lips and asked, "Might I ask you to forget what you saw?"

"And what about what I heard?" Gaston asked. Luc frowned. "One of your humans called out to me when I was injured. She called me Luc."

Ingrid. She'd mistaken Gaston for Luc. Easy to do, considering their gargoyle forms were nearly identical.

"How does she know what you are?" Gaston asked.

"She can be trusted," Luc said, unwilling to part with anything more than that.

He tried to measure Gaston's reaction, but the gargoyle had never been easy to read. His deadpan expression hardly ever changed. He held Luc's intent stare before finally jerking his head toward the servants' stairwell farther down the corridor. "Take your humans and get them off my territory. The demons targeted them today, and I won't have any of my humans here caught in the crossfire."

Luc raised his hands in surrender. "They'll be gone as soon as I can manage it."

When on another Dispossessed's territory, you did as you were told. Luc understood Gaston's devotion to his humans. He also understood how much Gaston probably despised those feelings, unwanted as they always were.

Luc climbed the steps, which were carpeted to muffle the sounds of servants' hard leather shoes, and emerged into a wide first-floor hallway. The floors were polished so brightly they reflected his image. He looked terrible, his shirt half tucked-in, his hair an unkempt crop of black curls. He'd forgotten his coat in the landau.

His trace on Ingrid led him down the imposing hall, past gilt-framed portraits of dour-looking old men, a display of ancient swords, a few elephant tusks, and a collection of exotic feathered and beaded masks. Luc heard voices ahead and stopped at the entrance to the orangery.

The jungle warmth of the room took his breath away. There were plenty of places to hide in this orangery, and Luc quickly wended his way through the vine-laced trees, dripping moss, spiked shrubbery, and then a thicket of bamboo. Through the pale-green stalks he saw flashes of purple and blue: the bright dresses of the Waverly girls. He also heard the concern in their mother's voice.

"We should call for a physician," the lady said. "What if the wolf was rabid?"

"It showed no symptoms of rabies. I'm not worried about infection," the injured Alliance member, Nolan Quinn, replied. Luc saw him reclining on one of Constantine's garden benches. Nolan resembled his father, someone Luc had known and disliked before his last hibernation.

"But the wound requires stitches," she insisted. "Doesn't it require stitches, Monsieur Constantine?"

Luc edged closer to the open path. He needed to catch Ingrid's attention.

"Sutures might be a wise idea, Monsieur Quinn," the old man said. "This is quite a gash."

"Gabriella, Ingrid, I told you to avert your eyes," their mother scolded. Luc saw them more clearly now. Ingrid and her sister had been pushed back, apparently to keep them from glimpsing Nolan's bared torso. They stood near the bamboo.

Luc cleared his throat lightly. Ingrid and Gabby both turned. As soon as Ingrid's eyes found him, she nudged her sister.

"Monsieur Constantine, might I have directions to your lavatory?" Ingrid asked.

Luc retreated, knowing the bamboo barrier wouldn't shield them well from the others. He waited for Ingrid behind the thick trunk of a tree, the low branches draped with a furry, bright-pink moss. She parted the moss, saw him, and rushed over.

"You're all right," she whispered, and threw her arms around his neck. "I saw the hellhound tear at your wing, or at least I thought it was you, and there was blood—this black, strange blood."

She continued to hold him, her arms tense around his neck and shoulders. He stood stiffly, uncertain what to do. He breathed in, taking in the scent of her hair. Luc let his arms settle around her waist and his hands slid to where a trail of satin buttons skimmed the small of her back.

Ingrid's breathing hitched. Her embrace turned rigid, but she didn't let go of him. "I didn't know if you were the first gargoyle or the second," she said softly, her breath reaching through his shirt to heat his skin.

Luc closed his eyes. The warmth spread through him like fever. His mouth moved against the silk of her forehead. "I was the second."

The touch of his lips brought Ingrid's chin up. Her eyes were fierce with something Luc didn't understand. Confusion? Fear? Luc pressed his palms tighter against the ridge of buttons. He didn't want her to be afraid of him.

He brought Ingrid closer. Close enough to lower his head and brush the tip of his nose across hers. His top lip had barely grazed hers when something fixed and buried deep inside of Luc stonewalled. He jerked his head back as if something sharp and fast had lashed at him.

What was he doing?

Luc released his hold around her slim waist and took a wide, fast step backward. Ingrid stared at him, her lips parted in surprise.

Luc quickly looked around, making sure Gaston hadn't for some reason come up to the orangery. What had he been thinking? He could have been seen. The Dispossessed had their laws, and taking liberties with a human was more than just a shameful breach of honor—it was a punishable offense, for both the gargoyle and the human involved.

Luc took another step away for safe measure. Ingrid tried to regain her composure, her shoulders having lost their usual eloquent posture. She looked disoriented.

"Why did you stop?" she asked.

When had young women become so forward?

A flippant reply made it to the tip of Luc's tongue before he saw something in her face.

He'd hurt her. He'd made her think something was wrong with her, and now she looked so damn vulnerable. He wouldn't lie to her, too.

"I had to," he answered. "Because of what I am. This curse. It isn't allowed."

Ingrid pressed her lips together in thought. She took a timid step toward Luc. "And if you weren't cursed?"

He couldn't help the small laugh that burst out of him. Not cursed? If that were the case, he'd be long dead and buried. And in hell. When Luc thought of that place, he knew enough to be thankful that he hadn't been sent there. But what would it be like to be in his original body permanently, without having to coalesce, without having to protect?

"It isn't an option," Luc finally answered, raising his hand up just enough for Ingrid to understand she shouldn't come any closer. "Do you think I'd be this if I didn't have to be?"

Instead of waiting for her answer, Luc plowed onward. "How did you make lightning come out of the sword?"

It took a moment for Ingrid to grasp the change of subject. "I don't know. It felt like lightning struck it. I didn't mean to do it, I just took up the weapon before Gabby could—you have no idea what it's like to have such an impulsive sister."

The shutters closing off Luc's past rattled. Another unwanted image of Suzette leaked out. "I have more than an idea, actually."

Ingrid frowned. "You have a sister?"

He focused, angry he'd let slip a thought like that. "*Had*. And lightning didn't strike the sword. You made it yourself."

Ingrid shook her head. Her hairpins had come loose in the vineyard attack. Blond loops hung haphazardly around the scrape on her cheekbone.

"I don't know how. Maybe it has something to do with the dust Vander says I have."

Luc turned his ear toward her, hoping she hadn't just said what he thought she had. "Dust?"

Ingrid nodded distractedly, glancing back through the mossy veil as if Vander Burke, the Alliance Seer, would be there. "He calls it demon dust. He says I have some, and that my brother does as well. I don't understand what it means, though."

"Humans can't *have* demon dust," Luc immediately said, voice rising.

All the Dispossessed knew Vander Burke had the uncanny "gift" of seeing the dust demons gave off, and he used it to help hunt them. But he only saw dust around demons. Never humans. At least, that was what he had always told the Dispossessed.

"But Vander said—" She cut herself off, her brow furrowing.

"You shouldn't have told me this." Luc tried to control his building frustration. "First lightning, now dust? This changes everything, Ingrid. It's wrong. *You're* wrong. I don't know what to make of you."

He ignored the quiver of her lips and instead remembered the unidentifiable tang beneath her gorgeous scent. Repulsive yet intoxicating. It had to be the dust.

Luc broke from her injured stare and started through the

moss, heading for the orangery door. "We need to leave the chateau. Constantine's gargoyle wants us gone. Convince your mother that it's time to go."

He didn't stay to hear her reply. He'd been overly harsh with her, but it was for the best. She was already a target for the hellhounds, she made lightning with her hands, and now she had demon dust, the mark of unearthly beings. When it came to the other Dispossessed in Paris, all three strikes were against her. If Luc had been foolish enough to kiss her, that would have been a fourth. He had to protect Ingrid, even if it meant protecting her from his own kind.

CHAPTER FOURTEEN

The single seat in the basket phaeton had Gabby and Ingrid thigh to thigh with the scarred young man they'd met a few days before at Hôtel Bastian. His name, they'd learned that morning when he'd arrived at the rectory, was Tomas. He had bowed to their mother, explaining that he was a friend of Detective Quinn (Gabby had held back a snort at the ridiculous title). He had given their mother a note from Nolan, and it had explained that while he was recovering well from the wolf attack, he felt dreadful about interrupting what was supposed to have been a restorative visit to Clos du Vie. He introduced Tomas via the note and asked if Tomas might be allowed to make up for the lost day by showing the young ladies the sights of Paris.

"Of course, it would be a pleasure if you would join us," Tomas had said, again bowing with flair. Charlotte had taken one look at his little phaeton and declined—a reaction Gabby was sure Tomas had hoped for.

"My apologies for the close quarters," Tomas said from his seat between the sisters.

Gabby was thankful for a little distance from Ingrid. Her sister wasn't telling her much of anything about what had happened the afternoon before in Monsieur Constantine's vineyard. Gabby had asked how lightning had come out of the sword, and Ingrid had shrugged and said she didn't know. Gabby had asked what Luc had wanted to speak to her about in the orangery, and again Ingrid had shrugged and said something vague.

Tomas pulled back on the reins as the horse veered around a bend in the road and drew to a stop just outside Le Livre Rouge. Gabby shivered despite the pelt that he had stretched over their laps.

"Is Nolan really recovering as well as his note claimed?" Gabby asked, picturing again the lengthy tear along his torso, the vivid blood seeping from the wound and spreading through the fibers of his ruined shirt and vest.

The hellhounds had been enormous, just as Ingrid had said. And the gargoyles, though hideous and vicious, had been magnificent, like dark-winged angels sweeping in to the rescue.

"He's better than well," Tomas answered. "Any day Nolan Quinn can show off a new battle wound is a victorious day for him."

As he maneuvered around Ingrid's legs and descended to the curb, Gabby wondered if Nolan would feel the same way should those wounds be as visible as the ones scoring Tomas's face and neck.

"Thank you for driving us, Tomas," Ingrid said as he helped her down.

Gabby took his hand next and let him lead her to the curb. It was difficult to look beyond the jagged pink lines, some of them curving into hooks near his jaw. But when she tried, Gabby saw that Tomas was rather attractive. He was the oldest member of the Alliance she'd met so far, perhaps a few years Nolan's senior.

"They're waiting for you inside Vander's flat. Take the stairs behind the counter," Tomas instructed as he opened the shop door for them. He remained outside, though Gabby wasn't sure whether it was to guard the horse and phaeton or the Alliance members in the bookshop.

Before Ingrid could slip behind the counter and through the door, Gabby snagged her wrist and pulled her to a stop.

"I want answers," she said quietly. "And if you shrug your shoulders at me one more time, I'm going to take them in hand and shake you silly."

Ingrid turned around and faced Gabby. She wore her "I don't have to tell you anything" expression.

"The lightning. What was that?" Gabby asked. She held Ingrid's gaze, giving her the "I'm not backing down, so out with it" expression. It was amazing how much they could say to one another without words.

Ingrid softened her stare. "I don't know how I did it. Honestly, Gabby, I don't. But I've done it before. I—I think a few times." She licked her lips. "At Anna's house. The engagement ball. I think I did more than just knock over a candelabra."

Gabby took her sister's forearms in surprise, completely forgetting that she was angry with her. "The fire? You think you started it with lightning?"

Ingrid nodded. The humiliation and guilt she'd worn like a mourning cloak for weeks after the disaster at Anna's home once again settled in her eyes, her brows pulling together into a pained scowl.

"It must have something to do with the demon dust," Gabby quickly said, wanting to put her sister at ease.

"What happened to Anna—" Ingrid started, eyes tearing.

"Was an accident," Gabby interrupted. "Her injuries have healed and she's getting married, and you have to stop blaming yourself."

The fire wasn't Ingrid's fault. The dust. It had to be the dust. What, exactly, did it do to her? What could it *make* her do? The people whose voices traveled from Vander's upstairs flat seemed like the only ones who might know the answer.

"Come on," Gabby said. She led her sister through the door behind the counter and up the steps set directly to the right.

The stairwell brought them into the back corner of a large room, and there they found Nolan, Vander, Chelle, and the other Alliance girl. Gabby's eyes skipped to Nolan. He sat upright in a four-poster bed, his back against the headboard, his long legs stretched before him.

Chelle was perched on the edge of the mattress, her arm draped around Nolan's broad shoulders, her mouth up against his ear. As she whispered, her lips practically nibbled his earlobe. When Nolan took his turn whispering into Chelle's ear, the southern region of Gabby's stomach felt as if it had caught fire.

"Good. Tomas was successful in sneaking you out of the rectory," Vander said, drawing her gaze. He walked past two open trunks filled with books and came over to greet the sisters.

"What do you need to see us for?" Gabby asked, the ice in her tone spearing Vander. He gave her a wide berth.

"Put simply, we want to know more about what Ingrid did yesterday with my sword." Vander removed his glasses and hooked them on his pinky, propping his hands on his hips. He peered at Ingrid. "You didn't appear overly surprised that one of nature's most powerful elements shot from my blade when you pointed it at that hellhound."

Ingrid moved farther into Vander's flat. It was stuffed with a mishmash of sofas and plush armchairs, a paper- and trinket-strewn rolltop desk, steamy glass terrariums, bookshelf upon bookshelf, and, of course, the bed on which Nolan reclined.

"It's happened before," Ingrid allowed, her hands clasped in front of her, her purse dangling from her lace-trimmed wrist.

Chelle repositioned herself on the mattress edge, bringing her legs, clad once again in breeches, up to her chest. She took her arm from where it had rested along Nolan's shoulders and wrapped it around her knees.

She looked so blazing comfortable there. The fire continued to smolder inside Gabby's stomach.

"She's like Vander, then, with demon dust and a subhuman power," Chelle said.

Gabby leaped to her sister's defense. "*Sub*human? You make it sound as if this dust makes her less human than the rest of us."

With a deliberate coolness, Chelle rose to her feet. "That is because she is; she and Vander both. They have demonic dust and strange powers, and we're trying to find out why."

Gabby wondered about Grayson, if he had a hidden power as well. No one had mentioned it yet.

"And"—Nolan spoke up—"we'd like to explore how Ingrid's ability might be useful to the Alliance."

Gabby tried desperately to keep her mouth shut. She pinned Nolan with a savage glare. *Useful.* As if Ingrid were some sort of shiny object that had caught his attention.

"You want Ingrid to help you fight demons?" she asked.

"Perhaps," Nolan replied. "If she's willing."

All eyes turned toward Ingrid. She stood immobile by Vander's messy desk. "Will it help us get our brother back?"

Gabby felt as if everything inside of her—every organ, every blood vessel—had inflated to the point of bursting. She wanted to be the one to shoot lightning from a sword. Why couldn't she have demon dust, too?

"No, but it will help keep others from losing people they love," Nolan answered. "You and your sister need to understand there is no getting Grayson back from the Underneath."

"I won't accept that," Ingrid said, her face a cold, emotionless mask. This was Ingrid as an iron shield. Immovable and stubborn.

Unfortunately, Gabby had already been down this particular road with Nolan. She ground out her frustration with a quick stroll through Vander's cluttered room, letting Vander and the other Alliance girl talk about ways that, even without Grayson, they could help Ingrid find out more about her "gift." As if having a gift—rather than her brother—were some sort of a consolation prize.

Gabby came to a stop at a second desk, this one a slightly inclined davenport. A folded, unopened newspaper covered the face of the hinged top, and a few drawers along the side of the desk were open and overflowing with more papers and folders. Something silver gleamed from within the recess of one drawer.

Gabby drew closer. It was a blade. Short, about the length of her palm from fingertip to wrist, and tapered to a wicked tip. Behind her, Nolan had come into the conversation, telling Ingrid that she didn't have to fight if she didn't want to. Chelle argued that anyone with a special ability should be required to put it to use. The other girl briefly piped up to say that she agreed with Nolan. Vander asked everyone to calm down.

They were all distracted, and Gabby seized the moment. She gripped the silver blade by its brushed metal handle and slipped it inside her cloak into her skirt pocket. The silver was most likely blessed, and from what she'd learned, it would be effective against a demon. Perhaps she did have some unknown gift buried within. She wasn't sixteen yet, after all, and Ingrid had told her what Vander had said during their walk in the vineyard—about not being able to see dust until after he'd turned sixteen. Gabby's birthday was so close, and those hellhounds so hideous.

She said a silent apology to Vander for stealing the dagger, but considering the disorganized state of his flat, he might never even miss it. Ingrid certainly wouldn't allow her to keep a weapon like this if she knew. Gabby would learn how to use it on her own.

When she finally turned back to the others, Nolan was looking at her. Her chest constricted and she quickly pretended to be interested in the newspaper on the davenport, running her finger beneath the boldly printed headline. Gabby translated the words.

It was about one of the missing young women. She searched the banner for the date, and saw that it was today's paper.

"Maybe it's unwise to be taking anyone out for night training right now, especially a girl," the other Alliance girl said.

"*We* are girls, Marie," Chelle replied. "And we've been out the last few nights patrolling, haven't we? You're worrying over nothing."

Gabby picked up the paper. "Not necessarily. Have you read this?"

The others turned to her, as if they'd forgotten she was among them.

"What about it?" Chelle asked, thoroughly annoyed. Gabby held the paper out, though she knew no one would be able to read the small type from a distance.

"The body they found in pieces on boulevard Saint-Michel two mornings ago—the one you so delicately brought up the other day at Hôtel Bastian? It's been identified as one of the missing girls," Gabby answered.

Vander crossed the small room, his foot knocking aside an empty wire birdcage, and took the paper from her hand. He read the first inch of the printed article quickly.

"And another mutilated body was found in the new Métro construction pit just last night," Vander summarized, his eyebrows vaulting. "A young female. No word yet if she is also one of the missing girls."

Ingrid, her cheeks flushed from so much talk about her training for combat with demons, came to Vander's side. "Was it a hellhound, like Chelle said the other morning?"

"There's no way to know for sure without seeing their dust, but it certainly sounds like it. Hellhounds can be a bit . . . ah, messy at times," Vander answered.

"It couldn't have been hellhounds," Marie said, nervously fiddling with the end of her long braid.

"Why not?" Gabby asked.

"They don't hunt in manic sprees like this," she answered, swishing her braid over her shoulder.

"I beg to differ—Ingrid's been attacked twice in one week," Gabby returned.

Nolan sat forward on the bed. He winced and gripped his side. "Marie's point is valid. Five or six young women have gone missing in the last two weeks, and hellhounds aren't usually sent out on attacks so often."

Chelle went back to Nolan's side, watching him attentively now that he'd shown a sign of pain. Gabby suppressed a groan.

"*Sent out* on an attack?" she asked.

Chelle, however, didn't bother to suppress *her* groan. "Hellhounds are like hunting dogs. They're like the Dispossessed, they don't think or act for themselves, but follow orders from their master. They need to be commanded."

Ingrid faced Chelle with a belligerent glare. "The Dispossessed aren't dogs."

Marie also spoke up. "Hellhounds and gargoyles are not the same and you know it. We work with the Dispossessed every day, Chelle. We should treat them as equals."

Chelle belted out a short laugh. "Don't start up again, Marie. You know you're in the minority. Maybe in Rome you wouldn't be, but the rest of us here are all for the proposed regulations."

"To treat gargoyles as slaves?" Marie said.

Vander held up a hand. "Can we avoid a clash of political opinion right now?"

Chelle and Marie sealed their lips, but each sent the other a small, bashful smile: a peace offering between friends.

Vander rolled up the newspaper. "I've never heard of any demon master ordering so many attacks in so short a time, but the mutilated bodies certainly sound like the work of a hellhound to me. If all the missing girls have actually been taken by hellhounds . . . well, then it's possible we have an infestation."

An infestation of hellhounds. It sounded as ominous as the plague or yellow fever.

"The hellhounds might even be deviating from their masters' commands," Vander continued to muse. "Perhaps they've been drawn to Grayson and Ingrid in particular because of their dust."

And maybe because of Vander's dust, too. He'd been with them in the vineyard, after all. This could make sense—if anything about demon attacks could possibly make sense.

"How do we find out?" Gabby asked.

Vander went to the davenport. Gabby prayed he didn't look at the stack of drawers on the side of the desk and notice the dagger missing.

"A customer came in about an hour ago and mentioned another girl had been reported as missing from her home on la Place de la Concorde just this morning. I think I should go and see if there are any traces of hellhound dust there."

Nolan shifted on the mattress and took something out of his pocket. He threw it to Vander, the lusterless silver object arcing through the air. "Take my badge. See if it can get you inside the home. Why don't you bring Ingrid with you in case a hellhound makes another daylight run," he said, then added, "And give her a blade."

Gabby's pulse fluttered as Vander reached for the davenport. To her relief, he only lifted the inclined top.

Inside the compartment was a long black box fitted with a silver buckle clasp. Vander unlatched the box and opened it. A deep-blue velvet lining held a gleaming assortment of silver blades, daggers, and six-pointed throwing stars, and a pair of swords with two curved prongs bowing out from their handles. Gabby breathed in and stared at the silver weaponry the same way she might the jewelry cases at Harrods. It was beautiful. She wanted to run her fingers over all the polished silver.

"The weapons room at Hôtel Bastian has a better selection,"

Vander said as he lifted another, more impressive dagger from its velvet cushion. He extended the handle toward Ingrid and smirked. "This should be more effective than that little perfume bottle of yours, though."

Ingrid shrank back a step. "But I don't know how to use it."

Vander didn't lower the proffered weapon. "You've managed so far with a sword, haven't you?"

Ingrid spread her gloved fingers across the lace overlay of her blue skirts and shook her head, eyeing the dagger as she would a scorpion. "That was an accident."

Vander took one of Ingrid's hands in his and placed the handle of the dagger in her palm. He closed her fingers around it. "Humor me."

He let go and Ingrid, after a moment, tucked the dagger away.

"We'll have Tomas take us," Vander said as he threw on his coat, the swing of the panels revealing a flash of the silver sword fastened into the lining.

Gabby started forward. There wasn't enough room in the phaeton's basket seat for her as well. "So what am I supposed to do, stay here?"

Cooped up in a shabby flat above a bookstore with Nolan and Chelle nuzzling one another's earlobes?

Ingrid followed Vander to the stairs. "I promise, we won't be long." She pinned her with a knowing look. "*Stay put,* Gabby."

As if she were some troublesome dog taken to wandering off! Gabby turned her back and went to the window to cool down. She watched her sister with an unusual prick of jealousy as she and Vander climbed into the phaeton with Tomas and drove away.

"I'll check in with you after my shift," Chelle said, more gently than usual. A tone reserved just for Nolan, surely.

"I have to go, too. I have to prepare for the party in Montmartre tonight," Marie said.

Gabby heard their boots shuffling around behind her. Sounds

of their departure. They were leaving. Which meant she and Nolan would be stuck in Vander's flat. Alone.

Mother would not approve, and Ingrid would have stayed behind or squeezed Gabby into the phaeton had she known Chelle and Marie were leaving so soon. As their footsteps faded down the stairs and the shop bell jangled, Gabby felt Nolan's eyes boring into the back of her cloak. She stood stiffly at the window. Out on the sidewalk, Chelle and Marie pecked one another on the cheek before walking off in different directions, their strides confident. They weren't worried about being without a chaperone. *They know how to fight.*

"You're angry." Nolan cut through the uncomfortable silence. Gabby kept her nose to the window.

"And you're a master at reading body language," she replied.

His laugh was a deep rumble of thunder. It reminded Gabby of a midsummer rainstorm breaking an unbearably humid London afternoon.

"We have an hour and a quarter together, maybe more," Nolan said, the bed rustling as he shifted his weight. "I know how we can put it to use."

Gabby spun around and pierced him with an icy glare, but then saw his puckish grin.

"You can be my nurse," he finished.

Gabby scowled at him and started to turn back to the window. But the sight of Nolan's fingers undoing the top clasps of his club collar stopped her. He then rucked up the bottom of his shirt, lifted it over his head, and tossed it aside. Nolan sat before Gabby, his chest and arms completely bare—and absolutely marvelous.

"Put your shirt back on!" she shouted, her eyes riveted to the impressive sculpturing of Nolan's stomach and pectoral muscles. Innumerable scars covered his smooth skin. Some of the scars were new and pink, while others were faded white lines.

"On? But then you couldn't help me clean the wound."

Nolan got to his feet, a hand bracing the gauzy bandage wrapped around his torso. Gabby, fresh out of sardonic replies, tried not to stare at the coil and spring of his muscles as he unwrapped the bandage. The gash was more gruesome than she'd imagined. It ran from his ribs to just below his navel. Black floss had been used to stitch up the curving track. It would leave perhaps his worst scar yet.

He ran a tender hand over the seam and peered down at himself. "What do you say, lass? Are Benoit's stitches as ugly as they look from this point of view?"

Well, they certainly weren't handsome.

"Who is Benoit?" she asked. Nolan smirked at the way she had evaded answering.

"Our surgeon. He has a private practice, the kind with no questions and no police." Nolan reached for a black glass bottle on the bedside stand. "And he always has a full stock of mercurite."

He uncorked the bottle and held it out to Gabby.

She went forward and took the bottle, careful not to make contact with his hand. He settled back on the bed and turned onto his right side, leaving the gashed left half of him visible. Nolan raised his arm, the crook of his elbow propped against his forehead. He waited. Gabby stood still, staring at his bared skin.

"I see you're speechless. Is it my cutting physique or the nasty scars? Funny. You don't strike me as the weak-stomach sort." His devilish grin brought her back to her senses.

Gabby sat down on the edge of the bed and splashed the wound with the mercurite. Nolan ground his teeth as the antiseptic, a thick silver liquid, beaded up and rolled smoothly along the curving seam in his skin. His eyelids puckered to slits as the globules slipped between the floss stitches.

"What is mercurite?" she asked, bringing the bottle to the tip of her nose.

Nolan took her wrist and forced it down. "You don't want to breathe it in. It's liquid silver and mercury. The combination purges demon poison once it enters your system. The mercury surrounds and absorbs the poison, and the silver destroys it." He winced. "Of course, the mercury is poisonous, too, but at least it'll kill me at a much slower pace."

"That's barbarous," she said. "Isn't there anything else you can use?"

Nolan shrugged. "If I had a gargoyle protecting me, I could use his blood. It has the same healing properties as mercurite, without the aftereffects—you know, blindness, organ failure, insanity, those petty things. But I don't have a gargoyle, and they're only allowed to heal their humans. I don't need gargoyle blood anyway. Dangerous or not, I'd rather use a human method. Most of the Alliance would."

Gabby set the bottle on the stand. "How much exposure to mercurite can a person endure?"

Nolan lowered his arm, his expression darkening. "It varies. Some can tolerate more than others."

There was a hitch in his voice that told Gabby there was more to that answer. But he wasn't going to tell her what it was.

"And you're proud of all these scars?"

Nolan reached for his shirt. "I wouldn't call it pride, but they're a part of who I am. What I am. What my whole family is, really."

She stood up from the edge of the bed and Nolan followed her, his shirt draped over his forearm.

"You can't ask Ingrid to be a part of this," Gabby said, keeping her eyes level with his, not on his bare skin. "It's too dangerous. And what about Grayson? Did you ask *him* to join you as well? Does his demon dust give him an ability like Ingrid's?"

Nolan threw on his shirt and buttoned it from the single stud at the center of his club collar down. He stared at her, no puckish grin now, just earnest blue eyes and a solemn frown.

"If Grayson had a gift to go along with his dust, we weren't aware of it. You sound jealous, Gabriella. What, would you like an invitation into the Alliance, too? Do you think you're a fighter?"

She liked the way his lips moved when he said her name, but not the way he mocked her.

"Of course not," she answered, hesitating to remind him that she was a lady, and ladies don't fight.

And yet, in the vineyard she had wanted to dive for that sword in the seconds before Ingrid did. She *would have* fought.

He tucked in his shirt and stalked away from the bed.

"Could I?" Gabby hedged. "I mean—could I actually fight with the Alliance?"

Nolan went to the desk, his trousers and shirt wrinkled, his hair mussed. He picked up the newspaper Vander had put aside.

"Absolutely not," he said flatly, eyes scanning the print. "Alliance law says you have to be at least sixteen to train, and I bloody well know you're not there yet."

He slapped the paper down, striking the desktop.

Gabby put her hands to her hips. "I'm barely two weeks from my sixteenth birthday. There aren't any senior Alliance in Paris, you said so yourself—they're all in Rome. You could begin training me now."

If she wanted to fight. Did she? The notion gave her a surprising thrill.

"Why, do you think it will get you closer to being able to enter the Underneath and rescue your brother?" Nolan asked, looking at her from over his shoulder. "It won't. It doesn't matter anyway—you're not joining the Alliance, Gabriella. We're just here to protect you. At least until we determine why these hellhounds are coming after you and your sister, and how to stop them. You'll have Alliance and Dispossessed surrounding you at all times. You'll be safe. You don't need to fight."

But what if I want to? Gabby drew in a stunned breath. Had she really just thought that?

The bell on the door to Vander's shop jangled.

"Patrons," Nolan sighed, and she couldn't help but think he sounded a bit relieved. He started for the stairs. "I'll be back."

He disappeared down the stairwell and Gabby heard him speaking in stilted French to the customers.

She sat on the edge of the bed again and felt the press of Vander's silver blade in her pocket. Did Nolan think her too pampered to fight? Too *privileged,* as he'd accused her the afternoon before? *We're just here to protect you.*

Gabby knew the truth of it. She *was* pampered. She was most definitely privileged. But if there was one thing she was not, it was a damsel in need of rescuing.

Maybe this Alliance idea was something to look into.

CHAPTER FIFTEEN

The interior of Lennier's suite looked as though it had been frozen in time from the days when Hôtel du Maurier had been a luxurious home.

The vines that ran rampant throughout the rest of the mansion had never entered the fourth-story rooms where Lennier resided. Instead of crumbling, water-stained plaster, the walls were smooth and papered in a print of green foliage. There were throw rugs and cushioned Louis XVI chairs, a sofa and console, candles and books, and a tall case clock softly ticking between two intact casement windows.

The chandeliers hanging in the center of the main room and in the two adjoining rooms were polished and fitted with wax candles. The lack of electricity was the only hint that this was not a suite in a posh Paris residence.

That and the enormous albino gargoyle standing before the flickering hearth.

Luc, wearing his human skin, stepped inside and closed the

door behind him. Yann and René were there, along with Marco, all in human form. Marco was lounging in one of the silk Louis XVI chairs by the draped windows. He looked like a bored monarch, Luc thought, with one leg thrown over the curved arm, his opposite knee bouncing impatiently.

"You need a watch, brother," Marco said.

"I was keeping an eye on my charges," Luc replied, not divulging that they had been ferried off to the bookshop where the Alliance Seer lived.

When Ingrid had been walking with Vander Burke in the vineyard, Luc, eavesdropping on her emotions from his place in the stables, had felt an effervescence in her pulse. Again that morning, Luc had felt it bubbling when she entered the bookshop. Something sour and heavy had sunk into Luc's stomach and stayed put.

Ingrid was fond of the Seer.

He took a step farther into Lennier's rooms and saw, with another heavy stone settling in his stomach, that Gaston was also present. So he'd gone to Lennier after all. Luc wasn't surprised. When the summons to the common grounds had arrived that morning, he'd suspected Gaston was behind it. He was only relieved that not all of the Dispossessed in Paris were present this time.

Lennier's white-scaled form shifted slowly back into his stooped human frame. It was like watching candle wax melt. Seeing something hard and resilient turning to a soft, malleable substance. An old man once again, Lennier lifted his black robe from the fluted arm of the sofa and wrapped himself in it.

"It's not often that I'm required to shift." Lennier's husky voice rattled like a reed in the wind. "I like to keep myself primed in the event I'm needed."

He shuffled over to the console table and the hard wooden chair before it. Only after he'd seated himself did he look at Luc and acknowledge him with a short nod.

"Gaston has told us what occurred at Clos du Vie," Lennier said.

Gaston stood straight-backed next to the tall case clock. He looked every bit the servant.

"Hellhounds don't usually emerge during daylight," Yann said. He stood in the opening to the next room, arms crossed over his embroidered velvet waistcoat.

"It was a targeted attack on your humans," René added, from where he leaned against the wall opposite the windows.

"On his *human,*" Marco corrected. He straightened himself in the chair and rose to his feet. "They want the fair-skinned girl. Not the dark-haired one, not the mother, none of the servants. Just her."

Lennier lifted two of his wrinkly fingers, a signal that he was about to speak. "Could it have something to do with her ability to conjure lightning in her hands?"

No mention of the sword? Luc met Gaston's even expression. He'd informed Lennier of the attack, but had he not mentioned the debacle with Vander's blade?

"Perhaps," Luc answered, because Lennier's questions must always be answered.

Marco crossed the room to the hearth, his eyes riveted to Luc's. It wasn't an unfriendly gaze, but a searching one. He knew Luc was holding back information.

"You've fought a lectrux demon before, haven't you, Luc?" Marco asked.

"I have," he answered. Lectrux demons were rare but nasty. They were enormous, multilegged creatures that scuttled around low to the ground like cockroaches. When they leaked up from the Underneath they usually traveled through the city's intricate sewer systems, preying on the vermin found there. Rats, mice, wild dogs, and stray cats. Sometimes vagabonds. The lectrux stunned its prey with an electrical shock before settling in to devour it.

"Don't you think it's curious your girl and a demon from the Underneath share a common power?" Marco concluded.

"It's a coincidence, at best," Luc answered, but the cogs and wheels inside his mind were shifting. Luc hadn't before thought of the similarities between Ingrid's lightning and a lectrux demon's.

Telling them about Ingrid's demon dust now would be a damning mistake. To the Dispossessed, having a demon power and demon dust could equal only one thing: being a demon. Vander was the only one who could see the dust, but a gargoyle's sense of smell was acutely perceptive. Ingrid might not smell anything like a demon, but she did have that mysterious tang Luc had puzzled over. Could it be her dust? He couldn't remember it on Grayson, but he *had* had that bitter scent of green sapling bark. If any other gargoyles—like Marco—got close enough to Ingrid now, would they be able to smell it, too?

"You do know, brother," Marco began as he came away from the hearth, "that if she is anything other than human, you're not bound to protect her."

Then she must be human, Luc thought, because he found himself more determined than ever to keep her safe.

"Marco is right," Lennier said. "The girl is unnatural. She may be your human charge, but if she has the powers of a lectrux—"

"She doesn't," Luc growled.

The room fell quiet and seemed to drop in temperature. Lennier stared at Luc, his nostrils flared. *No one* interrupted Lennier.

"One of your humans has already slipped through your fingers," René said, easing them back into conversation. He smirked. "Would it be so difficult to allow a second one to do the same, especially one who has a demon power? There are any number of hellhounds on a rampage right now, snatching young women left and right. The humans strolling through my park think it's a bloodthirsty murderer, but we know better, don't we?"

Marco's dark eyes flashed. "You need to be relieved of her,

Luc. There is something wrong with your human—if she can even be called that."

The muscles in Luc's shoulders and back tensed, and the ridge of his spine swelled involuntarily.

"You both have it planned out so neatly," Luc said, trying to control the pop and spread of his ribs, the sensation of his femurs aching to lengthen.

As if Luc could step back and allow a hellhound to take Ingrid. As if any gargoyle could stand by and watch his human attacked.

Something dawned on Luc. "Have any of the girls who have disappeared had a Dispossessed to guard them?"

A moment skipped by before Lennier answered, "No gargoyle has lost a human charge lately other than you."

René sighed. "What is your point?"

Luc approached Lennier's desk. "Do you believe it's a coincidence that the hellhounds taking these girls have avoided gargoyle territory?"

"Perhaps they knew which properties to avoid," Gaston said, speaking for the first time. Until then he'd acted like a well-trained servant—silent as a piece of furniture.

Lennier looked from one man to the other. A glimmer of interest lit the tarnished blue of his eyes.

"What does this matter?" Marco cut in. "The hellhounds aren't our concern. Your girl and her demon power are what interest us right now."

Luc pivoted to face him. "She doesn't have a demon power."

At least, he sincerely hoped she didn't.

Marco started toward Luc, a fire lighting his step. Luc went forward to meet him, adhering to instinct rather than good sense. Marco could crush him with one well-aimed blow.

"If she turns out to be anything other than human and you continue to harbor her," Marco began, his good humor having iced over completely, "you will have a problem on your hands."

Problem was putting it mildly. The Dispossessed would treat Ingrid like a demon, and they would tear through Luc to get to her.

"Stay clear of my territory," Luc said, the urge to coalesce tightening his skin, threatening an eruption of scales. "And stay away from Ingrid."

She swept her hand over Grayson's feverish brow. Her touch felt like mist, chilling his skin. The coldness burrowed into his skull. It calmed him as he rested his head in her lap.

Grayson was becoming used to her, the sight of her hooded figure looming in the entrance to the cave no longer something to fear.

"I took a chance on you," she said softly. Her fingertips stroked the space between his eyebrows, which was no longer creased with pain. "I wanted you to be something unrivaled. But I had eyes on you in London. We saw you, Grayson. We saw what you did to that girl."

Grayson's eyes flew open. His body tensed. He didn't want to remember her. He'd worked so hard to forget. To pretend it had all been a nightmare.

"You shared the same thirst as my other beasts, but not their form. How could you lead them, how could you be their superior, if you were trapped—*stunted*—within your human body? You required my help, and my mongrels have been making your blood stronger, giving you the ability to properly quench your thirst. I am sorry that it has hurt," she cooed, her fingers turning in wide figure eights through his short hair.

Quench his thirst. She knew his secret. She knew the ugly truth of why his father had sent him away from London.

His father's panicked bellow throbbed through his memory, along with the muddy stink of the Thames, the bitter taste of blood coating his mouth. *Satan's child! What have you done to this girl?*

"You are almost ready now," the hooded woman whispered. "As am I. My infusions are taking longer than I had hoped. My mongrels can be so careless with their tasks. If they bring back the vessels at all, they are usually half drained of the blood I require." She rubbed the skin behind Grayson's ear with new aggression. "Never mind that. We will both see daylight soon. Have patience."

He would do as she said. Daylight soon. Good. Grayson felt caged and restless. He'd find himself pacing the cave—sometimes on all fours. When he stopped he'd feel the hunger gnawing at him. Or was it thirst, as the hooded woman had called it? He couldn't be certain. He just knew what he wanted. One thing more than any other.

Blood.

CHAPTER SIXTEEN

It turned out the young woman who had most recently gone missing was the privileged daughter of an established Paris family. Ingrid gazed in awe at their palatial town house near the Tuileries and la Place de la Concorde. It was twice as stately as Waverly House and practically glowed with old wealth and status. As she nervously straightened her miniature blue top hat and veil, the front door opened and a bleary-eyed butler looked out at them expectantly. Vander flashed Nolan's silver-plated badge, which he'd pinned to his vest, before letting his coat fall back into place in order to conceal it. Ingrid doubted the badge was authentic, but Vander received little more than a fatigued sigh from the butler.

He played the part of the sober, middle-class investigator well, with his unadorned brown tweed frock coat and well-worn bowler hat. Vander certainly didn't look like the minister he hoped to be one day. *A seminary*. Ingrid couldn't picture him wearing a clerical collar or vestments. He seemed more suited to the role of investigator that he currently impersonated.

The butler and Vander conversed in French, and while Ingrid wasn't really knowledgeable, she thought Vander's French smooth and confident. Perhaps better than Gabby's. The butler eyed Ingrid curiously when Vander gestured to her, no doubt with the planned introduction of her as Vander's secretarial assistant. Standing at his side in her bright-blue silk walking dress and fashionable hat, she didn't look secretarial at all. She didn't feel her usual self, either, though. The silver dagger in her purse was the main reason for that, she suspected.

Whatever Vander said worked, for the butler stood aside and let them enter the home's foyer, resplendent with carved marble columns, rose marble floors, and a trickling fountain set in an alcove. They followed him through an equally impressive hallway.

"He said Madame and Monsieur Brochu left about an hour ago, after the police cleared out," Vander whispered as they hooked a right down another hallway, this one glassed in on the left with a view of the courtyard and gardens.

The butler exited through a pair of glass doors and held them open. Ingrid stepped outside, the snow a lacey pattern over the colorful glaze of an Italian mosaic walkway. It edged a sunken garden, and Ingrid didn't have to walk far before a handful of servants bundled against the cold came into view.

They held buckets of water, steam rising into clouds, and were busy scrubbing the side of the house. Ingrid froze. Their wet sponges and rags were rubbing at dark-red stains splashed upon the pale freestone exterior. Another servant held a shovel and was scooping up a trampled area of pink-tinged snow. He let the colored snow slosh off into a metal bin before straightening and running the back of his sleeve across his damp eyes.

Blood. The servants were cleaning the traces of their mistress's spattered blood.

Ingrid suddenly remembered the article about the pieces of girls that had been found.

The butler said something to Vander, his white-gloved hand gesturing to a trellis that climbed to the second, terraced story of the town house.

"The police think Miss Nicolette descended from her bedroom by way of the trellis," Vander translated. The butler stood aside and allowed them to walk on while he fell behind.

Ingrid's stomach rolled as she watched a footman wring a torrent of deep-red water from his sponge. "She was attacked on the ground."

And there was so much blood. "Have they found her yet?" she whispered, fearing there would once again only be dismembered bits left to identify.

Vander walked along the mosaic path lined with potted holly and evergreen shrubs. "The butler says no."

Ingrid followed. "No girl would have climbed down from her room to meet a stranger. She must have known whoever it was." A chilly wind buffeted her cloak.

"It's here," Vander said, removing his glasses. He squinted against the sparkling reflection of the sun hitting snow crystals. "There's barely a particle left, but the dust is here." He met Ingrid's gaze. "A deep reddish-orange. It was a hellhound."

Ingrid strained to see more than the hard-packed snow glinting like diamond chips. "But that makes even less sense. How could a hellhound tempt a girl out of her home in the middle of the night?"

Ingrid had woken the past two nights to nightmares plagued by images of greasy fur, jaws dripping with saliva, and red illuminated eyes. In her nightmares she was running, her nose filled with a putrid stench, hot breath on her back. It didn't matter that when she climbed into bed at night she let her mind settle on images of Luc, both his human form and his gargoyle one. It didn't matter that she would then turn her thoughts to Vander, his hay-bale eyes, and the fiercely gentle way they held Ingrid captive. She would still wake to the horrific memory of the hellhounds.

"Maybe it is a person committing these crimes after all, but a person with demon dust, like us," Ingrid ventured.

Vander put his glasses back on. "This was a hellhound. They're the only demons who leave dust this color."

Ingrid wrapped herself deeper inside her cloak as Vander, sat-isfied, finally turned to leave. They trailed the butler through the resplendent hallways once again, back into the foyer and through the grand front door, which was then shut and locked with a final *clunk* and a *click*.

Vander started down the steps. Tomas was waiting at the curb with the horse and phaeton, the fringed ivory canopy flut-tering in the cold breaths of wind. Ingrid wasn't ready to leave just yet. She touched Vander's arm, drawing him to a stop. "She's dead, isn't she?"

He frowned but didn't answer. He didn't have to. With a bloodbath like that, Miss Nicolette's fate was obvious.

"If she was taken and . . . and *killed* by a hellhound, and if the other girl mentioned in the paper was torn apart by a hellhound—"

"Don't forget the dismembered body found in the Métro sta-tion last night," Vander put in, though he hadn't needed to. Ingrid couldn't have forgotten about a dismembered body.

"Then does that mean hellhounds have taken and killed all of the girls who've disappeared lately? And why would they take Grayson but not kill him? Because I know he isn't dead. He may be in the Underneath, but he's alive."

Vander stepped back up and came level with Ingrid's eyes. "He was alive last Luc heard from the Order, but Ingrid, that could change at any given moment. Hellhounds aren't the only demons he's facing in the Underneath. You should be prepared."

Ingrid felt confident for the first time all day. She raised her chin. "My brother is still alive."

Vander narrowed his eyes. "How can you be sure?"

The answer to that was more a feeling than anything she could explain with words. How could anyone without a second half understand? Grayson was more than a brother. He was an extension of her.

"I just *know*," she answered. "And I know he's scared."

"If he's in the Underneath he has reason to be," Vander said, offering his elbow for Ingrid to clasp. She looped her arm through and started down the steps. She liked how easy things were with him.

Ingrid let herself lean in closer to him. "I can't leave him there."

Vander sighed. "There's nothing you can do, Ingrid."

She'd promised Gabby that she wouldn't give up. She started to pull her arm free. "I know that I can get through to the Underneath if I have demon poison in my veins."

Vander caught her arm and pinned it against him. "Who told you that?"

The fierce glint in Vander's eyes told her to keep Luc's name to herself.

"It's true, isn't it?" she asked.

"It doesn't matter." His usual composure threatened to fray as he grasped her arm tighter. "Untreated, the demon poison would kill you within an hour or two—that is, if the Underneath demons didn't get to you first. Even the best-trained Alliance fighter wouldn't dare enter the demon realm. Ingrid, no one who's been taken there has ever come back."

She stood her ground. She hadn't looked at Vander so closely before—at the squared-off contours of his chin, the fullness of his lower lip, the straight plane of his nose. Ingrid had known he was handsome when she'd first met him in the bookshop. But this close, this intimately, Vander Burke was more than that. He was striking.

On top of that, he was human. And he wasn't cursed.

Neither of them spoke. The top buttons of Vander's collar were undone in that tousled way he had about him, exposing the velvet cream of his skin. Pure curiosity caused her eyes to drift, and as they did, she saw strawberry marks on his neck. Two ovals. One slightly lower than the other, like inked index and middle fingers pressed upon paper side by side.

Ingrid drew back, stunned. They were identical to the birthmarks she and Grayson shared on their calves.

Without thinking, she lifted her hand and pressed her fingers against the two ovals. Vander stiffened, but didn't pull back.

"It's a birthmark," he explained, his hand coming up to cover hers.

"But"—Ingrid took a breath—"I have the same one. Grayson and I . . . we have it too."

"A birthmark?" Vander asked, his hand still clapped over hers.

"Not just *a* birthmark. *This* birthmark."

Ingrid slipped her hand out from under his, but Vander kept the two ovals covered with his own. He shook his head. "I'm sure that isn't possible."

"But it is," she insisted. Of course, proving it would mean lifting her skirt and baring her leg. "I can't show you, though. It's . . . well, it's somewhere . . . private."

Vander let go of his neck, shock widening his eyes.

"Not *too* private," Ingrid quickly added, realizing there were a number of private places on her body that Vander could be envisioning. "My leg. Calf, actually."

His lips bowed and she saw a new expression behind his smile: mischief. "Another time, then."

She blinked, speechless. He filled the awkward silence. "Maybe the birthmarks have something to do with our dust."

She liked how he spoke of their dust as if it was one and the same. It reminded her that she wasn't entirely alone in this.

He brushed away the wave of hair she'd positioned over the

healing scrape on her cheekbone. "I wish I knew how to bring Grayson back for you."

Ingrid stared breathlessly at him, surprised at how much she wanted Vander to keep his hand exactly where it was. But she knew he shouldn't. They were in plain sight where everyone, including Tomas, could see. Ingrid lowered her chin and stepped out of his hold. The moment she did, the walkway and the wide square beyond came into focus, along with the dark stamp of a figure standing at the gate.

Luc pushed it open and stormed toward them. His eyes dropped to the hand with which Vander had just been touching Ingrid. Vander drew his shoulders up and met Luc head on.

"Luc?" Ingrid's pulse jumped the way it always did when she saw him.

He flicked his surly grimace her way, and she wondered if he could sense her reaction to him. The thought made her cheeks burn, especially after the way he'd treated her in Monsieur Constantine's orangery.

Luc turned to Vander. "Does she really have the dust?"

Vander, ever composed, answered calmly and simply, "Yes."

"Have you told anyone?"

"Other than the Alliance here in Paris? Of course not. I'm not an idiot."

Luc lifted his chin in assessment. "If the Dispossessed knew—"

"I'm well aware of what would happen if the rest of your kind knew, Luc."

Ingrid butted her way into the conversation. "*I'm* not aware."

"I didn't realize the two of you were so close," Vander said, the last word barbed. "Or else I would have advised you not to tell Luc about your dust."

Ingrid remembered the sneer of disgust on Luc's face after she'd told him, the things he'd said. Vander had kept his dust a secret from the gargoyles for a reason, and now she wished she'd done the same.

"Lennier and the others are already questioning how human you are," Luc explained. "If they knew about the dust, they might be convinced you're more demon than human."

"And what would happen if they decided that?" She figured the answer wasn't going to be a good one.

Vander placed a hand on Ingrid's back and shouldered past Luc, bringing her with him as he headed for Tomas's phaeton. "If they come after her, they'll have the whole of the Alliance to deal with."

Luc's caustic laugh followed them. "A half-dozen Alliance against hundreds of gargoyles? You wouldn't know what hit you, Vander Burke."

Ingrid wheeled around. "Stop it—both of you. I think we've agreed that no one is going to say anything about my dust, so quit arguing."

Luc slammed the iron gates shut behind him. He peered over his shoulder at the town house. "What are you doing here?"

Tomas took Ingrid's hand and helped her into the phaeton.

"Another girl was reported missing. This is her home," she answered.

Vander climbed up after Tomas. "You should inform Lennier that hellhounds have been snatching up these girls, not a human. The hounds are probably acting autonomously, mangling the girls here, on Earth's surface, or taking them back into the Underneath. A little of both, perhaps."

"Vander saw the hellhound's dust," Ingrid said. Luc's attention came to rest solely on her.

"Did he?" Luc asked, sarcasm thick. *The same way he saw* your *dust?* she imagined him thinking. Was that why Luc was so riled? Did he see her as more demon than human now? Ingrid straightened against the cushioned back of the bench, unexpectedly hurt by the thought.

"The gargoyles need to be more vigilant of the humans within their territories," Vander said as Tomas took up the reins.

Ingrid met Luc's green stare, and in it she saw a solemn vow. A vow, she suddenly realized, that had been there, in those eyes of his, ever since the first time they'd met hers. Luc's vigilance wasn't optional. It wasn't something Vander needed to remind him of. No gargoyle would ever waver when it came to protecting his humans. And with that, the knowledge of something else came to her almost instantly.

"Wait," Ingrid said, sitting forward. "These girls . . . They didn't have gargoyles."

The corner of Luc's mouth rose with surprised pleasure. He'd wanted her to figure it out.

"What?" Vander asked.

"She's right," Luc said, still staring at Ingrid, his expression impervious. "If they had, their gargoyles would have fought to the death to protect them."

Just as he would for her.

Vander sat forward. "So they knew which homes to avoid."

Tomas lowered the reins. "No. Their masters knew which homes to avoid."

"If they were acting on orders, yes. But what if they were running rampant?" Vander braced an elbow against his thigh and ran a hand through his hair. "Maybe the hellhounds had help."

"Maybe," Luc said, his tone pensive. "Lennier says you think a gargoyle killed your Alliance friend?"

Vander straightened his back. "I don't think—I know. I saw the dust, Luc."

"So if there's a gargoyle out there breaking all sorts of rules, maybe it's also helping the hounds," Luc said

"Can a gargoyle do that? Kill a human and help a demon?" Ingrid asked.

The wind flipped up the collar of Luc's coat, an outdated double-breasted style that looked as though it had been stashed away for thirty years, then shaken out when he'd risen from hibernation.

"It's frowned upon," Luc said. "But it happens."

"Far too often, according to the Euro-Alliance. They're meeting about proposed regulations as we speak. But that's another topic entirely." Vander motioned to Tomas and the reins. "Let's go back to the shop. You need to get Gabby and Ingrid home to the rectory."

Tomas slapped the horse's flanks and they started rolling forward. Ingrid swung around, watching Luc as the phaeton drove away. *I won't be far.* He'd told her that a few times now. She realized then just how much of a comfort those words were.

"Do you really think the gargoyle that killed Henri is helping these hellhounds?" Tomas asked Vander as he steered their horse left, slowing for a nanny guiding a covered pram across the road.

"It's not so far-fetched an idea, especially if the gargoyle was brash enough to defy Lennier's rules in the first place," Vander replied. His fingers tapped the tops of his knees, in either deep thought or deep impatience.

"And you think that all of this is somehow connected to the hellhound that took Grayson Waverly, and the ones that came after Ingrid?" Tomas asked.

"I do," Vander answered. "I don't know how just yet, but I do." He leaned back and turned his head, looking past the rigid plane of Tomas's shoulders to Ingrid.

She didn't understand any of it. Why a gargoyle would help a demon; why a hellhound would take Grayson and kill a handful of young ladies; how she and Gabby figured into everything. She didn't understand, and neither did Vander. And that only made her more afraid.

Vander looked away. "Drive faster, Tomas."

CHAPTER SEVENTEEN

Gabby reached the imposing door on the third floor of Hôtel Bastian and brought down her fist.

She hoped Nolan wasn't home. He'd driven her mad the day before, what with his practically begging Ingrid to join the Alliance and his outright refusal to extend Gabby the same invitation. He might rethink that decision if she could prove her ability to fight. That was the hitch, though. She couldn't fight.

Not yet, at least.

Gabby was about to knock again when she heard voices approaching on the other side of the door. She stepped back as it opened. The female Alliance member, Marie, and a ruggedly handsome man filled the entrance. Marie was smiling up at the stranger. His mouth was drawn into a roguish smirk. Until they both saw Gabby on the landing.

Marie's smile wilted. "Gabriella?"

The man beside her inspected Gabby from head to foot. His brow creased with a look of distaste. Or was it hostility?

"Is Tomas in?" Gabby asked, avoiding the man's eyes.

Marie and the stranger shuffled out onto the landing, allowing Gabby to slide into the apartment.

"In his room," Marie answered, and without another word, she started down the steps.

The man followed her after throwing Gabby another cool look. He was muscular and handsome, and he radiated arrogance. Not a playful and cocky arrogance like Nolan's, but something colder. He hadn't uttered a word, but she knew she didn't like him.

Gabby closed the door and walked the cushioned hallway toward the loftlike room. It was empty. On the opposite end of the long, open apartment, there was a hallway bordered by drapes, all on taut ropes fastened to ceiling hooks. They cordoned off what looked like makeshift rooms. There were still two floors above this one, she remembered, and wondered where the stairs were.

She walked through the sitting room and kitchen, and past a second, larger sitting area on the left. The couches and chairs set inside the inverted alcove looked like they were used more often than the first set of chairs and couches off the entrance hall. A man's shirt had been thrown over the arm of a frayed chair, a pair of high-heeled boots left on the floor. Newspapers littered the seat cushions and tabletop, along with a mirrored compact and a half-drained bottle of brandy.

Gabby stopped to stare at the still life. She was struck by something that should have been obvious before: Alliance members lived here, both male and female. They slept and ate and lounged here, together, as roommates. It was sordid and modern and thoroughly exciting.

And Gabby could picture herself there among them.

One set of faded, red-striped curtains was half parted. A hand shoved the curtain the rest of the way along the rope line.

"Marie, don't forget—" Tomas stopped speaking when he stepped into the hallway and saw Gabby.

"Oh," he said, clearly taken aback at the sight of her. The

pink grooves marking his face and slipping beneath his collar tightened as he craned his neck to peer behind Gabby.

"Marie left," she offered. Gabby kept her questions about the arrogant stranger to herself. She didn't have time to veer off course. Her mother would be gone from the rectory for only another hour or so. "I've come hoping to talk to you."

Tomas's startled expression only deepened. "Have you? Well then. You should come in."

Tomas gestured to the makeshift room, and then disappeared inside. She followed, but hesitated by the open curtain when she saw it wasn't just a room, but a bedroom.

Tomas gave her an encouraging smile. "You don't have to stand in the hallway."

The sleeping cot and mussed pillow said otherwise. "I really should," she answered.

Tomas laughed. When he did, Gabby found it easier to see past his scars, to the handsome face behind.

"As you like," he said, sitting in a wheeled wooden chair in front of a trim writing desk. He stared at her expectantly.

Nerves made her stomach do a jig. What had she been thinking? Tomas was going to laugh at her. Feeling the need to stall, Gabby took a testing step inside. It wasn't far. Just a step. A bare brick wall directly opposite the entrance had an arched window, and each curtained side wall was packed with boxes and crates. In one corner stood a tall filing system.

"What is all this?" Gabby asked, genuinely curious.

Tomas stood up and took a glance around. "It's part of my job for the Alliance. I keep an ongoing registry of the Paris Dispossessed. We like to have a sense of their numbers and locations, when we can."

She went farther inside and turned to the six-drawer-tall filing system, plus numerous stacks of boxes, presumably filled with more files. The sheer number within view gave Gabby an idea of how many gargoyles there actually were. It left her speechless.

But then she felt a hand drop into her skirt pocket, brush against her hip, and retract. Gabby whirled around and saw Tomas holding up the silver blade she'd taken from Vander's desk.

"You really shouldn't steal," Tomas said lightly.

Gabby put her hand against her skirt pocket. "How did you know I had that?"

With one hand behind his back, Tomas flipped the dagger into the air. He caught it with precision. "I saw the weight of it in your skirts."

He'd been inspecting her skirts? Gabby didn't know what to make of that, so she ignored it and got to the point: "I came here because I want you to show me how to hunt demons."

He didn't miss a beat. "Why? So you can enter the Underneath and fight your way to your brother, slaying every demon in your path?"

Gabby sealed her lips, obstinate in the face of opposition. Tomas lowered Vander's blade.

"Ah. That *is* what you want," he said, tapping the blade against his leg. "Fighting skill alone isn't enough. First off, you need demon poison in your veins in order to enter the Underneath. If you are not treated, the poison will kill you."

"Then I'll bring mercurite to treat it."

Tomas's expression remained steady. "No maps of the Underneath have been charted. If the demon realm is even a fraction of the Earth's size, how will you find him?"

Gabby could feel her logic thinning. She didn't want to give up on rescuing Grayson. But what if they were right? What if he was beyond rescue?

Two steps delivered Tomas right in front of Gabby's nose. He held out Vander's blade as if he wanted her to take it back. She did, and slipped it in her pocket again. Tomas was too close, but oddly, she didn't feel uncomfortable. He wasn't a threat.

"You haven't asked me what happened," he said.

Gabby blinked. "What?"

"My face. You haven't asked about the scars."

Their mention brought her eyes to them, but she quickly looked away. "Of course I haven't. It would be unspeakably rude."

Couldn't the two of them just pretend they weren't there at all?

"It was an appendius demon," Tomas said casually. "I crossed paths with it on the Champs de Mars. You should have seen it. The appendii can have any number of arms, and this one had six. They were at least this thick." Tomas held his hands about a foot apart. "And as long as I am, measured head to toe. Each arm was tipped with a horned spike in place of hands. I destroyed it." He ran one of his palms across his jawline. "But not before it did this."

Gabby pursed her lips, imagining Tomas stumbling back to Hôtel Bastian, his skin a bloody, flayed mess.

"Why are you telling me this?"

He focused on her eyes, coming back to the present. "Because if you want to fight demons, you need to know what they can do." Tomas, barely moving a muscle, produced a silver blade in his palm. He'd ejected it from his jacket's sleeve. "And you'll also need to know how to hit them where they are the weakest. The appendius's horns are nearly impenetrable, so it's a waste of time and energy to try and slice them off one by one. Its weak spot is in the center of each arm, where nothing but soft cartilage does what our elbows do."

Tomas caught Gabby's hand in his own and slapped the handle of his blade into her palm. "Pretend you're holding a full-size sword, because you don't want to get any closer to an appendius than you have to."

Tomas then got behind her, keeping hold of her hand and bracing her arm with his own. He wrapped his other arm around her waist, holding her close to him. She took in a short gasp as he raised the blade into an attack position.

"The arms are thick everywhere but at the cartilage joint," he said, his breath tickling the back of her ear. "You have to move fast. A swift, concentrated lunge"—Tomas took her whole body with him as he surged forward—"and a flick of the wrist"—he rotated her wrist, the blade cutting through the air in front of them—"and you'll lop off the dangerous half of the appendius's arm."

Gabby's heart pounded, a grin creeping along her lips. With the way Tomas had moved her body in time with his, she had almost been able to see the blade severing the demon's arm.

Tomas kept his hold, his arm parallel to hers, his body tight against her side. She twisted her head to look at him. He smiled, a mischievous fire flickering behind his wire-rim glasses.

"Do you want to go again?" he asked.

Gabby would have blushed had she not been having so much fun. "Yes."

"No."

The husky voice came from the entrance to the makeshift room. It split Tomas's hold on Gabby as effectively as a blessed blade. Gabby let go of Tomas's weapon and it clattered to the floor.

Nolan stood in the curtained doorway. Gabby hadn't heard his approach. Tomas's voice had been filling her ear.

"What is this?" Nolan demanded. "Tomas?"

Tomas stooped to pick up the dropped blade. "It's nothing. Gabby and I were simply . . . visiting."

"Visiting," Nolan repeated, the muscles along his jaw coiling. "Is that right?"

Gabby stepped around the cot, toward the curtain opening. "I should leave."

Ingrid would have noticed her absence by now, and her mother might even be on her way back to the rectory. Plus, the dark fury in Nolan's stare made her nervous.

He held up his hand to bar her way. "I want to speak to you first." He then looked at Tomas. "Privately."

Gabby stood in silent awe as Tomas cleared his throat, loaded the blade back into his sleeve spring, and edged by Nolan.

"I'll make myself scarce," he said, briefly meeting Gabby's stunned gaze. An apology flashed in his eyes, and then he looked away and headed down the hall of curtained rooms.

"You can't kick him out of his own room!" Gabby cried.

"Considering my family owns this building and allows Tomas to live here, I'm certain I can." Nolan stood aside, holding the curtain for Gabby. "If you'll come with me."

It wasn't a request.

Nolan walked farther along the curtained hallway, all the way to the last cordoned-off room on the left. He reached the split in the curtains and shoved them open before sending Gabby an impatient glare. She pressed her shoulders down and took calm, infuriatingly measured steps toward him. She was going to get an earful, and it wasn't going to be pleasant. But Tomas had taught her something. *Her first lesson.* She'd hold on to the thrill it had given her for as long as she could.

When Gabby at last reached Nolan, his patience shattered. He grabbed her arm and winged her through the curtains. She stumbled to a halt, tripping over the rise of a throw rug.

"How dare you!" Gabby shouted. She immediately turned to leave, but Nolan blocked her.

"What were you and Tomas doing?" All his usual mirth and mischief were gone. He was well and truly angry.

It brought her up short. "Nothing. We were doing nothing." As if she had to explain anything to him. "Nothing that happens to be any of your business."

Nolan stepped closer. "You should be at the rectory. Not here, in Tomas's room. You don't know him."

Gabby retreated, her heels tripping on the rise of the rug again. Nolan's room was a haze around her. She was too angry to see anything clearly.

"You may hold authority over Tomas, but you don't over me."

"This isn't about authority," he said, herding her back farther across the rug as he moved closer. "People have died, Gabby. Do you not remember finding Henri's body?"

The back of Gabby's skirts knocked into something low, a table, perhaps. Something made of glass crashed down and rolled onto the rug.

"What about the hellhounds that came out in the middle of the day, do you remember those?" Nolan battered.

"How could I forget them? Of course I remember! Why are you being such a bully?" Gabby shoved her hands into Nolan's chest and pushed him.

He sucked in a short breath and tucked a hand against his left side. Gabby remembered with a jolt of hot guilt the nasty wound hidden under his shirt and waistcoat.

"Oh!" Gabby slapped a hand over her mouth. "Oh, I'm sorry! I forgot. Oh, I didn't mean it."

She reached for him, hoping she hadn't damaged his stitches. Nolan caught her by the wrist and held her hand at bay. She expected him to throw her arm back and curse her carelessness, but he didn't. His fingers tightened, bonding against the lace cuffs. He bowed his head as he worked to even his breathing.

"Why do you have to be so bloody pigheaded?"

"I am not—"

Nolan tugged Gabby against him and smothered her protest with a kiss. His lips moved tentatively over her mouth, hers stunned and graceless, her hands clenched into fists against his chest.

He was kissing her. *Kissing* her. She had most definitely not seen *that* coming.

Nolan hooked his arm around her waist and brought her closer against him. It felt entirely different from when Tomas had gripped her. Nolan held her as if a riptide were trying to steal her away from him. A low, hungry groan rose up his throat—and

Gabby gave in. Her fingers fanned out across his chest and she returned the kiss, her lips turning soft against his.

It was glorious. *He* was glorious, and Gabby rushed to keep up with all the different sparks lighting her skin where he touched her: on her back, where his hand trailed to the curve of her spine and rounded out to cup her hip. The base of her neck, where his fingertips climbed to the pins holding up her dark hair.

The *zip* of metal sliding along rope pulled her from the warm haze building around them. Nolan's head snapped up.

Chelle stood in the split between the curtains, her eyes glazed with tears. She threw the curtains together and stalked away, her boots pounding the floor as she ran.

Nolan let go of Gabby and backed away, running a hand through his tousled curls. "Oh, hell."

Gabby stared at him dumbly, her lips stinging, her body buzzing.

"Go back to the rectory," Nolan said on his way toward the curtains, still swinging violently from Chelle's thrust. "Just, please, go back and stay there. Stay on hallowed ground."

Gabby had no words; she barely felt a thing at all, numb from the lips down. Nolan was leaving her. He was leaving to chase after Chelle.

Nolan stopped at the curtains, as though he wanted to say something more. But after a moment's pause, he left and ran down the hallway. Away from Gabby—who felt like the biggest fool in all of Paris.

CHAPTER EIGHTEEN

None of the Waverly women wanted to be in this carriage.

And yet, they were all tucked inside the landau, wearing their finest dinner dresses, their toes freezing because *fashionable* slippers could not also be *warm*. None of them spoke, their thoughts spinning off in divergent directions, along with their eyes.

Ingrid stared out the window, watching her sister and mother in her peripheral vision as the dark streets of the Right Bank blurred by. She searched for red sparks down slim alleyways, dark wings spread out like canopies atop buildings. But there was nothing. Everything looked mundane now that she knew to search for something supernatural.

If it were any other dinner, Ingrid would have asked her mother to beg off the invitation she'd accepted before even leaving London. But this dinner was taking place at Lady Geneviève Ormand's home, the very place from which Grayson had been abducted.

Vander and Nolan had already investigated and there was

nothing more to be gained from a visit to the house, but Ingrid still itched to be there. To see what Grayson had seen, to feel what he'd felt inside the home. She hoped just crossing the threshold into Lady Ormand's foyer might let her feel closer to him. She missed him so much. Without him, it felt like a part of her had been detached and set upon a shelf, out of reach.

The news that the countess was returning to Paris to open a new gallery had demanded that her friend, Lady Ormand, host a dinner party in her honor. Lady Ormand had invited scores of Parisian artists, including, rumor had it, Henri de Toulouse-Lautrec, all for their mother to mix and mingle with to talk up the gallery.

Only, the gallery was the furthest thing from any of their minds now.

"Must we stay long?" Gabby asked.

She had been despondent ever since she'd returned to the rectory the morning before. Ingrid hadn't had the heart to be angry with her for leaving hallowed ground, or to badger her with questions. She got the feeling Nolan Quinn had something to do with Gabby's sullen turn but couldn't be sure. Before Grayson had started rebelling, Ingrid had been able to read his emotions with precision. In a way, she'd always felt entitled to know what he was thinking or feeling, and he'd treated her the same way. But it wasn't like that with Gabby.

"I plan to speak at length with Lady Ormand about the night of her last dinner," their mother replied. "I doubt a single officer went to her home to interview her. I'll do so myself tonight."

Ingrid turned from the window. There was hardly any point for Mama to interview her friend, and she didn't wish to stay at this dinner any longer than necessary. "Papa's telegram finally came today, didn't it? Won't he be coming with someone from the London police to do that?"

She'd seen the telegraph messenger leaving the churchyard that afternoon, but her mother had closed herself in her rooms until just before departing for dinner.

"Yes, what did the telegram say?" Gabby asked.

Their mother's cheeks turned a light puce. "I do not wish to discuss his telegram."

Gabby and Ingrid shared a bewildered look.

"Mama, please," Ingrid said.

Charlotte inhaled sharply. "He thinks I'm inflating a problem that doesn't exist. He was adamant that *no* police be involved, especially Scotland Yard. He said to leave things alone."

Surely Mama was exaggerating. Ingrid couldn't believe her father would brush off the disappearance of his only son.

"But . . . you're not going to?" Gabby pressed.

Their mother's anger with her husband cut a path toward Gabby. "Of course I'm not. Your father's instructions were inane. I have no intention of obeying them."

Ingrid couldn't fathom it. Why would Papa treat Grayson's disappearance so lightly? He and Grayson had often been at odds, but Grayson was still his heir.

The landau went through a gated entrance, toward a brilliantly lit three-story home. Lady Ormand's mansion, near la Place des Vosges, spoke clearly of old wealth and good taste. Footmen holding trays of Champagne were stationed along the two flights of steps curving up to a columned loggia.

"Let us be upbeat, girls," their mother said as the carriage came to a stop in the front courtyard.

Luc opened the door. Ingrid took one look at him and wished she could stay in the landau for the next few hours instead.

She hadn't set foot off hallowed ground the day before, but Luc had still watched her closely. Every time Ingrid had passed one of the rectory windows looking out over the churchyard, she had seen him. He'd stood guard all day, either within the door to the carriage house or in the loft, the door rolled open to the biting weather. Countless times Ingrid had considered going to him, but she hadn't been able to fabricate a reason for the visit. He would have seen straight through to the hurt brewing inside her.

She'd wanted him to kiss her in the orangery. Just like she'd wanted Jonathan to love her. But both of them had refused her. Was it as Gabby had said? Was she really an iron shield? Or could there truly be something wrong with her? The humiliation of it burned.

Luc extended his hand to Ingrid, the white driver's gloves a part of his new livery along with a proper coat, waistcoat, and pinstriped trousers. He was meticulous, right down to his polished black brogans. But the servant's attire looked like a costume. It didn't suit him.

Shimmering black scales and a pair of powerful wings did.

Gabby and their mother primped and rearranged their skirts and wide-brimmed hats while Ingrid hung back beside the carriage door. They didn't notice when Luc stepped up behind her and whispered, "There's a gargoyle here."

Ingrid started to turn toward him, but he stayed her with a hand to her elbow. In the shadows of the lamps and Japanese-style lanterns brightening the courtyard, no one would have seen his touch.

"Who?" she whispered, lips barely moving.

Electric light shone through the windows of Lady Ormand's home with an abrasive glare. It glinted off the string of carriages around the center fountain and a quartet of dinner guests taking the curved stairs to the right, a heavy gloss of Macassar oil in the men's hair and impressive baubles dripping from the ladies' earlobes. The doors to the home swung open for the guests, and Ingrid could imagine the anxiety her brother must have felt. He would never have admitted to it, but he would've been nervous attending a dinner here alone. She could nearly feel the traces of his discomfort, left behind like demon dust.

"I don't know," Luc whispered as Ingrid's mother and Gabby exchanged pleasantries with the couple stepping from the carriage directly behind theirs. "The home isn't marked, so he's not a guardian. He's inside. A guest, maybe. I can feel him."

Her heart staggered a beat. Could it be the rogue gargoyle? Luc must have felt her fear. He slipped his hand from her elbow to her wrist, then wound his fingers through hers. To conceal the breach of propriety, he brought Ingrid's arm behind her back.

"I'll get to you if you need me," he whispered, the press of his fingers a tangible version of his pledge. She wished neither of them was wearing gloves. The feel of his skin against hers shouldn't have been the foremost desire in her mind, but it was. Luc sapped her of all reason, it seemed. And his touch made it difficult to breathe.

"I know you will," she said.

Her mother and sister started to bow out of their conversation with the other dinner guests.

"Stay indoors," he said. Luc dropped Ingrid's hand a split second before her mother's eyes landed on her.

"It's only for a few hours, Ingrid. You must try to be social, at the least," her mother said.

The air chilled her back now that Luc's body no longer warmed it. But he would get to her. She trusted his promise. She trusted *him*.

As she followed her mother and sister to the front door, the strings of her small purse cut into her wrist. It was heavier than usual. The perfume bottle wouldn't seem too out of place within a lady's bag. The short silver dagger was another story entirely.

Ingrid kept a hand on her dangling purse as the butler and maids greeted them and checked their cloaks, then gestured toward the twisting set of marble stairs that led into a spectacular ballroom.

At the entrance, though, Ingrid came to a tripping halt. Guests swarmed the room, glittering with rubies and sapphires and diamonds, wrapped in taffetas, silks, and chiffons. Conversation rose into the air and droned alongside the strains of a violin-and-cello duo playing somewhere behind the crowd.

"Ingrid?" Gabby touched her arm. "What is it?"

Ingrid's mouth went dry. She hadn't been inside a ballroom since the fiasco at Anna Bettinger's home. She remembered the flames eating the drapes, branching out to the walls, the cream molding turning black, the potted shrubbery catching fire, people screaming, careening toward the exits.

Luc would be feeling the rush of her blood, the drumming of her pulse; he might think she was in trouble. Ingrid shook off the irrational fear and forced herself to step inside the ballroom.

"I'm fine," she said. Her mother and sister appraised her. Then, apparently satisfied, they faced the crowd.

The high polish of the parquet floor reflected clouds of brightly colored skirts, hips draped with ruffles, heavily boned bodices sewn with pearls, hems trimmed with gold braid. Men wore white gloves and black tailcoats, and young ladies flapped feather and lace fans coyly in front of their décolletages.

"There she is," their mother said, her chin high as she peered across the room. Ingrid followed her gaze to a tall woman in a dress with capped and puffed sleeves. Lady Ormand was easy to spot, with a bright-blue peacock plume spearing her bun and flapping above the horizon of heads.

"Come, girls," their mother instructed. "I'll introduce you."

She took off through the crowd, expecting the girls to follow. Ingrid started to, until Gabby yanked her to a halt.

"Look, over to the right. By the potted palms."

Ingrid did, but saw only a group of guests being served by a waitress. "What about them?"

Gabby pulled on her arm again. "The waitress, Griddy. *Look* at her."

Ingrid pursed her lips, about to tell Gabby once again to drop the nickname. But then the waitress turned her round tray of fluted Champagne glasses toward them. The glasses trembled and sloshed the moment she laid eyes on the Waverly sisters.

Ingrid almost didn't recognize her, what with the white-aproned uniform and long black skirt instead of a red scarf looped around her neck.

"Marie," Ingrid said. "What is she doing here?"

"Serving Champagne, obviously," Gabby answered. "Or maybe the Alliance is here, watching us? I mean, this is the place Grayson went missing from. Perhaps they have an eye on it. On us."

The shock registering on Marie's face said otherwise. She dodged to the right, behind another circle of guests.

"I'm going to speak to her." Gabby squeezed Ingrid's arm before letting go.

"But mother wants to introduce us." Ingrid tried to snag her sister gracefully, but Gabby slipped away like a curl of butter.

"I'll be just a few moments," she called back, then disappeared behind a large woman wearing a pillowy dress of pale violet. The woman's girth, accentuated by far too many bows and ribbons, sealed off Gabby's escape route.

Muttering an oath, Ingrid searched for her mother. She spotted a flash of her viridian dress across a dance floor. But just then a waltz struck up and couples slid into Ingrid's path. Wheeling skirts soon twirled Ingrid's mother from view.

"You look lost."

Ingrid startled at the smooth, unfamiliar voice. A man stood at her side, clad in a pristine black dinner jacket and an embroidered scarlet vest. His dark complexion spoke of Italian pedigree, his tall, robust frame of athletic ability. His eyes were a shade similar to the amber liquid he swirled in his glass tumbler. His gaze slowly swept over Ingrid's face.

"Excuse me?" she asked.

He took a sip of his drink, then said, "You're searching for someone."

There was something mesmerizing about his voice. It was confident and easy and purposeful. He also seemed aware of the effect it had on her, and he cut a wolfish smile.

"I'm not," she lied. Nothing would sound more juvenile than admitting she was looking for her mother.

"Good," he said, setting his drink on the tray of a passing waiter. "Then perhaps you would permit a dance?"

He presented his hand. Ingrid stared at his scarlet gloves, and then met his warm amber eyes. "You know I cannot. We haven't been properly introduced."

Actually, Ingrid realized, she hadn't been introduced to anyone. She had no dance card tied around her wrist or tucked inside her handbag as she would have had in London, no chaperone to oversee whom she danced with and whom she avoided. Besides, this was a *waltz*. Young ladies couldn't go off waltzing with just any random man.

"The element of mystery is one I thoroughly prefer," he said. In a brazen move, he took Ingrid's hand and led her to the dance floor.

"But it isn't—"

"Done. I know. The rules ought to be changed. It is a modern world, after all. The dawn of a new century."

He said the last bit with mock excitement, as if he couldn't care in the least about the approach of the twentieth century.

The waltzing couples took notice as he and Ingrid joined in late. He held her right hand extended, his left palm flat against her shoulder blade. Her left hand rested on the solid muscle of his shoulder and, true to an intimate waltz, he pulled the length of her right side tight against him, from thigh to breast. *If Mama were to see* . . . Ingrid scanned the crowd as they twirled counterclockwise.

"That was far too easy," he said, urging Ingrid's right foot back and to the right.

She moved mechanically, her waltz graceless. "What was?"

He kept the proper, stiff hold of his chin, but peered down at her. "Getting my hands on you."

Ingrid immediately locked her legs. She tried to pull away, but his fingers tightened around her hand. His sly grin vanished, his left arm now an unyielding hook around her shoulders and ribs.

"Now, now, calm yourself, Lady Ingrid. You're not in any danger." He smiled and nodded to a passing couple. "We can't have Luc storming the ballroom in his scales, can we? Take a deep breath and know that I mean you no harm."

"How—?" Ingrid answered her question before she'd even finished forming it. *This* was the gargoyle Luc had felt.

"How do I know you're aware of his nature?" he finished for her. "It was only a matter of time, considering you'd decided to take up with the Alliance. But Constantine's gargoyle told me how you gave yourself away, shouting Luc's name in the vineyard when the gargoyle was in fact Constantine's own—a Dispossessed called Gaston."

Of course. She'd thought the injured gargoyle had been Luc. She hadn't realized that the gargoyle had heard her shouting Luc's name.

"Why should I trust that you mean me no harm?" Ingrid asked, trying to calm the mad rhythm of her heart. She didn't want Luc to sense anything. Of course, it was probably too late for that.

The man swung her counterclockwise, his dance steps liquid and graceful while hers were distracted and bumbling.

"I should take that back. I *am* murdering your toes at the moment." He peered down at her feet. "Do us both a favor and climb onto mine. No one will see."

"I will not. I'm most certain everyone would see."

The man sighed and simply lifted her from the dance floor and set her back down so that she balanced on the tops of his shoes.

"There. Much better. Now I can honestly say I won't harm you."

He twirled them among the other dancers, Ingrid's skirt swirling and fluttering, keeping rhythm with her stomach and heart.

"Who are you?" she demanded.

"My name is Marco," he answered, the proper waltz affording him a sly glance down at her. "I'm one of Luc's friends."

Luc didn't seem the sort to collect friends, especially not a man like this. "You're lying."

Marco laughed, drawing the attention of a passing couple. "Very good, Lady Ingrid, indeed I am. Luc doesn't like me. He doesn't trust me. So I knew that if I was to find out how you create electricity at your fingertips, I would need to ask you myself." He paused. "That was my asking you, by the way. You may answer at any time."

He glided them through the perfectly timed dancers. From the mezzanine, they all must have appeared like cogs and wheels rotating, spinning, and gliding in sync. Ingrid's legs moved with his, and she felt like a little girl standing on the tips of her father's shoes as he led her in a silly dance.

"And what if I don't answer?" she asked, knowing she couldn't mention the demon dust, or that she suspected the lightning she'd made was connected to it. "What if I have no idea how I can do it or why?"

Marco's amber eyes clouded. "You know something, Lady Ingrid. I've existed long enough to know what lies look like upon a human's face."

She hoped he hadn't learned to read minds, too.

Ingrid deflected Marco's question. "How long have you existed?"

Marco answered swiftly. "I lived twenty-seven years as a human, and so far four hundred and fifty-three as a Dispossessed." He pressed her side closer against him, the rock of his muscles intimidating. "Long enough to learn how to properly infiltrate a party. It's also long enough to know when someone is stalling."

"I have nothing to tell you. I can't explain it."

If Marco was the rogue gargoyle, he might try to lead Ingrid out of Lady Ormand's home, the same way Grayson had been led out. Ingrid glanced at the people lining the dance floor. Did Marco want Gabby as well? The weight of her small purse did little to calm her. Blessed water and silver daggers wouldn't protect her from a gargoyle.

Marco loosened his grip and allowed Ingrid a few inches of space between them. "Did you know, Lady Ingrid, that there is an Underneath demon that has your particular ability?" he asked casually. "It's called a lectrux demon. It hunts using lightning to stun its prey, and then it eats its catch whole and living."

Ingrid recoiled. Marco readjusted his grip and brought her back against his chest. A demon had her ability. And Ingrid had demon dust. *Was* she a demon of some sort? But how could that even be possible? Her parents were human, her sister free of dust. What had made Ingrid this way?

Marco tilted his head toward her neck, and Ingrid heard him breathe in. "You're human," he murmured. "But a human's scent is only supposed to give us information—what you're feeling, where you are. Yours does something more." Marco twirled them off the dance floor and ground their feet to a halt. He breathed in Ingrid's scent again. "It makes me *feel* . . . adoration . . . aversion. Such conflict."

Ingrid stepped off the tops of his shoes, away from the hungry shine of his eyes. A prickle of heat flared up at the center of each palm. *Not now,* she hissed to herself. Marco released her. "Luc's fascination with you is a dangerous one."

"He isn't fascinated with me," she whispered.

That seemed to amuse Marco. He inspected her closely again. "I think I will take you to Lennier. He might know what to make of you."

"I'm staying here." *Stay inside,* Luc had said. She couldn't be led out like Grayson had been. Like the other girls. Marco was certainly handsome and charming enough to have enticed impressionable girls to climb out of their bedroom windows in the middle of the night.

Ingrid's fingers tingled and then throbbed. Her shoulders itched. Heat swarmed to the tips of her fingers, pushing and buzzing, and the more she worried about how to stop it, the less control she seemed to have. It was going to happen again. Here, in another ballroom. What if she hurt someone, as she had the last time? What if this time, instead of Anna, it was Gabby or Mama?

Marco cocked his head and released her as if he too could feel the bubbling of her blood. The tips of her fingers felt like they were splitting open, and in one hot burst, all the energy swelling within her drained. Thin branches of electricity attacked the lightbulbs in the ballroom's chandelier. They forked off to the bulbs in the sconces on the walls, up through the mezzanine. The room fell into blackness and a collective scream rose up, along with the fizz and spit of the dozens of blown bulbs.

Marco seized Ingrid's arm. "Thank you very much, Lady Ingrid."

In the pandemonium, no one noticed him as he tore through the crowd. They didn't see Ingrid struggling in his grasp or hear her cries for him to release her. Marco reached a pair of balcony doors and threw them open, heaving her out into the brisk night air.

"It doesn't matter where you bring me, I'm not telling you anything!" she screamed. Her voice reverberated off the two wings bracketing the home's back courtyard.

Marco wrapped his arms around Ingrid and forced her up into the crook of his arms. "You'll find I can be very persuasive."

With that, Marco placed his foot atop the balcony railing and with an inhumanly powerful thrust, launched himself into the air. It felt like they were falling for ages, instead of dropping just one story. Marco landed with the poise and stealth of a feline. He sank into a crouch, his arms and chest cushioning Ingrid against the impact.

"I wondered how far I'd get," Marco muttered.

With an ungracious toss, he rolled Ingrid out of his arms. She crashed to the ground and cowered, waiting to hear the wet growls of a hellhound, to smell its rot. How easily he'd taken her. It was pathetic, really.

But the only thing Ingrid heard was the crunch of boots crossing the crust of snow. Ingrid raised her head and saw Luc coming toward her, his eyes pinned on Marco. He moved with predatory focus—and he was already starting to undress.

Gabby saw the offshoots of lightning a millisecond before the bulbs in the chandelier exploded, followed by the pops of shattering wall sconces. Screams erupted in the ballroom as sudden darkness blinded the guests. She pulled herself out of the clutches of the horrid dance partner she'd been landed with.

"Lady Gabriella?" the young man called. Gabby sidestepped and ducked away from the sound of his voice.

Earlier, she hadn't gotten farther than the edge of the dance floor before she'd lost sight of Marie entirely. And then her mother, along with Lady Ormand and Pierre, the viscountess's third son, had found her. As soon as the two mothers had stuck them together on the dance floor, Gabby had spied Marie darting within the crowd, toward a swinging door. The kitchens.

Gabby headed for them now, her muddled path lit only by the oil lamps and candles the servants were hastily lighting to ease the chaos. Her toes had been trod upon and her arms and ribs elbowed by the time she made it to the doors. She barged through, and met with a full kitchen already lit by candles and gaslights. The electricity must not be wired throughout the whole house, Gabby reasoned, and set about looking for Marie.

She spotted her near a copper counter lined with fizzing Champagne flutes and hors d'oeuvres. Marie was just picking up a drink tray when she saw Gabby.

"What are you doing back here?" Marie barreled toward the swinging doors. "You can't be in the kitchens."

Gabby followed her back into the frenzied crowd in the ballroom. There were more lights now, though smoke and the acrid odor of burnt wires filled the air.

"Why are you serving drinks?" Gabby asked.

Marie scowled at her. "Because I'm not to the manor born, *my lady*. I have a living to make."

Gabby didn't have a ready response. She had expected something much more clandestine. Something having to do with the Alliance.

"Oh. I'm sorry. I thought—"

"Marie?" Both Gabby and Marie turned to greet Lady Ormand. Gabby's mother was at their hostess's side.

"Oh, gracious, Gabriella, Pierre was quite upset he'd misplaced you," her mother said. Gabby repressed a groan. "Have you found your sister yet?"

"Marie, please tell the kitchens we'll be cutting dancing short and will be taking dinner immediately," Lady Ormand instructed.

Marie curtsied. "Of course, my lady." She shuttled back through the swinging doors.

"I really must find my butler. This is dreadful, Charlotte. I don't know what could have happened. The wiring was installed just last year."

Gabby searched the calming crowd for Ingrid. She had an idea of what might have happened but couldn't find Ingrid in order to ask. Gabby followed her mother and Lady Ormand as they wove their way toward the ballroom's main doors.

"My lady, was that waitress a member of your staff?" she asked, eliciting a suspicious glance from her mother.

"She isn't," Lady Ormand answered. "Though I have thought about having my housekeeper extend an offer. She's a fine waitress, one of the best employed by the catering service I use for my dinners. I'll have my housekeeper send yours the contact for them, Charlotte."

Gabby's mind worked backward at a furious pace. "Did she work at the dinner party from which my brother disappeared?"

Her mother and Lady Ormand stopped to peer at her.

"Yes, she did. Why?" Lady Ormand asked.

Her mother squared her shoulders. "What is this about, Gabriella?"

But Gabby didn't quite know herself. Marie had been at the dinner Grayson had disappeared from, but hadn't Nolan said that some gargoyle had been the one to approach the Alliance and inform them? Why hadn't Marie done so?

"I just thought that perhaps she saw something irregular," Gabby fibbed, and shrugged lightly.

The two women continued toward the exit, promptly dismissing Gabby's speculation. Why hadn't Nolan mentioned that Marie had been there? Did he even know? She thought she might be overreacting, but something felt wrong. Like she had discovered a secret, one that Marie had kept from everyone.

CHAPTER NINETEEN

"**I** should have known it would be you," Luc growled.

He peeled off his livery jacket and flung it to the ground. He saw Ingrid wobble to her feet, disoriented from the leap Marco had taken from the balcony. Luc's shoulders and collarbones began to quiver and shift. In a matter of seconds his muscles had bunched and bulked, the black wool vest and white-collar shirt stretching with the growth.

"Keep your skin on, brother," Marco said lazily. He held up his hands in surrender. "None of us mean the girl any harm. We just want Lennier to meet her."

Luc saw them now. René and Yann. Of course Marco's little pets would be with him. Yann moved up on Ingrid's left, and René took a position in front of a darkened set of doors that led inside the home.

"She's not going anywhere," Luc said, a deadly sort of calm settling over him. His shift had paused for the moment, but it was unsteady. Like an ocean wave rolling toward shore, building and growing until it was a thin blade, inevitably going to crash down.

Ingrid's breath clouded the air as she stumbled toward Luc. The fingertips of her white opera gloves were singed black, the fabric destroyed, so that her pale-pink nails poked through. Yann stepped across her path, keeping her from the safety of Luc's side. Ingrid shied to the left, toward the house, but René blocked her way. She was cold, her heartbeat wild. Luc felt the thrash of it inside his chest, an echo beating out of rhythm with his own heart.

"You can come with us, brother," Marco went on. "She'll be under your protection the whole time. Of course, if Lennier determines she has demon blood in her . . ."

Marco didn't finish the threat, but Luc's ribs cracked and pushed apart anyway. He was going to coalesce. He was going to attack Marco—and then Marco, Yann, and René were going to tear Luc to shreds.

But just then Ingrid did something unexpected. She pitched herself toward Marco, her cheeks like tightly folded red carnations. "I am *not* a demon. You said so yourself. I'm human. And the only place I'm going is back inside!"

She pivoted on the heel of one ridiculous little slipper and charged René at the bottom-level doors. Massive when in true form and beefy when in his human skin, René grabbed Ingrid's wrist with one firm hand.

"Let *go*!" Ingrid shouted, following the command with a shriek of pain.

Luc sprinted toward her, mashing his fists into Yann's barrel chest when the chimera tried to intervene. The hold on Luc's shift broke. His spine ridged and his facial bones spread.

"René!" Marco's surly warning came as blue sparks of electricity crackled at the tips of Ingrid's singed gloves.

Luc jammed his heels into the snow as she clawed at René's hand. Forks of electricity traveled from her fingertips, climbing in sparking vines up his arm. A spasm rocked René's body. His mouth, opened to emit a rippling scream, lit in bursts of white and blue, illuminating the bones of his jaw and teeth. The force of the current launched René backward. He landed hard on his side atop a stone vase. It slivered into blocks, creating a landslide of stone and soil.

Luc made a dash for Ingrid at the same moment Yann did. Ingrid saw Yann approaching and held out her hands.

"Stop!" she screamed.

Both Yann and Luc slammed to a halt, as instantly as if a glass wall had been thrown in front of them. An oppressive weight landed hard on Luc's back and shoulders and pressed him low to the ground in a bow. *Irindi.* The angel must have arrived in the courtyard. Yann kneeled beside Luc, panting.

"What's happening?" Yann asked.

Irindi's blinding luminosity hadn't come. The courtyard was dark, cold, and silent, except for René's miserable groaning.

"Stay away from me," Ingrid said, her voice quavering as she shivered.

Luc tried to look toward her, but an invisible hand pushed against his temple, driving his head into a deeper bow. He didn't understand. This was what happened when one of the Angelic Order descended upon the Dispossessed. And yet, they were alone in the courtyard. Alone, except for Ingrid. A girl with demon dust. A girl with lightning for fingers.

The grinding weight on Luc's shoulders and back lifted, and he staggered to his feet. Yann shot up as well, and a look behind them showed Marco rising to his full height once again. René still lay prostrate on the ground, but he was at least conscious.

Ingrid, however, was gone. The doors René had been blocking were now ajar. Luc stared at them, picturing Ingrid as she darted inside while all of them had been bowing in unwilling reverence.

Marco crossed into Luc's field of vision on his way to René.

He met Luc's bewildered expression, his glossed hair falling into slick waves around his eyes.

"Tell me she is human now, brother."

"It is time."

Grayson lifted his head, his back hunched against the wall of the cave. The hooded woman stood in the entrance. He could feel her excitement. Grayson sniffed the air. No. He could *smell* her excitement. The scent landed on the back of his tongue like the fizz of a sugar cube dropped in hot coffee.

"Your blood is stronger now, Grayson Waverly, and I cannot wait any longer," she said. "This will be your test. I hope you do not fail it."

Grayson clambered to his feet, but it felt awkward standing on only two. His hands and head felt too far away from the floor. Something wet dripped down the side of his chin. With a graceless brush of his hand, he swiped it away. Saliva.

"I'm hungry," Grayson said, his voice so near a growl that he didn't recognize it.

"I know, my darling," she preened. She lifted Grayson's arm and led him toward the mouth of the cave. "There is one more girl I need. I must have her and no other, but my pets have failed to bring her to me."

A girl. His mouth filled with another spate of salivation.

"She is protected, but you are different. You will be able to get to her. She will trust you . . . like a brother."

For the first time, Grayson stepped outside his cave. The tunnel was long, with rounded walls and ceilings. It was a giant tube of flickering blue and black light. Unlike before, the flickering now soothed his eyes. It pulsed with all the calming familiarity of a mother's heartbeat.

"Do not harm her. Do not let one drop of her blood escape her veins. I require it."

The thought of blood made his throat hot with thirst. What was wrong with him?

"Bring her back unharmed, and I will reward you. You can satisfy your hunger," she said. Everything inside of him, from his throat to his groin, clenched and twisted. "Bring her back," she continued, "and you can become everything you were always meant to be."

CHAPTER TWENTY

Ingrid passed the foot of her bed on her way to the window. She reached the curtains, glanced into the darkness, and then turned back into the circuit she'd been pacing for the last hour or more, ever since arriving home from Lady Ormand's dinner party. It had been an awful evening, and not only because of what had happened in the courtyard with Luc and Marco and whoever those other two brutes had been. They were gargoyles, that much she knew.

The rest of the party had been excruciatingly dull. The electrical current had filled her with pain to the point of overflowing in the courtyard. She hadn't been able to keep it inside. The need to release it, get it out, had been so strong. Much stronger than any of the other times it had happened. And she'd almost killed the man who had grabbed her. Or perhaps she *had* killed him. She'd run inside before she could find out.

Ingrid wrapped her arms tighter around her corseted waist. Cherie had come to undress her, but Ingrid had sent her away.

She didn't want to go to bed. What she wanted was to gather the courage to sneak out to the carriage house and see Luc. He'd been running toward her when she'd blocked the other gargoyle's hand and sent the current of electricity streaming through him. He'd smelled, she remembered, like burning hair and singed flesh—something Ingrid had hoped she'd never have to smell again.

After she'd electrocuted that other man, Luc hadn't even been able to look at her. Repulsing a hellhound was one thing, but attacking another person was . . . *monstrous*. She felt like a monster. The blackened tips of her opera gloves, which she'd ripped off and shoved into her bag before rejoining the dinner party, were proof of it.

Ingrid stopped at the foot of her bed and sat down, burying her face in her hands. They felt normal now. Soft. Slightly cold. Nothing extraordinary.

A scrape outside her window brought her head up. Ingrid twisted around, wondering if perhaps someone—Luc?—had thrown a handful of pebbles against her window.

She slowly made her way toward it, debating whether she'd be able to go downstairs and let Luc in through the front door or the side kitchen door should it be him. As soon as she pulled back the curtain, though, she knew neither door would suit.

Luc clung to the stone ledge surrounding her window in full gargoyle form. His feet dug into the wooden beam lining the exterior sill while his razor-tipped fingers helped brace his weight on the ledge. His unfurled wings rippled obsidian in the low light of Ingrid's oil lamp, his eyes glimmering jade.

Ingrid's fingers shook as she unlatched the casement window and swung each panel wide. Luc's breath clouded the air. His scaled body was so fascinating that, until then, it had stolen her attention away from his face. Now, eye to eye with him, Ingrid could inspect his gargoyle face closely.

It wasn't much like the ones carved on the abbey's gargoyles. Luc's ears were pointed at the tips like a dog's, but his snout didn't protrude like the noses on the foxhounds her father kept for hunts. The shape of it was still very much human. Luc's eyes were the same, too, though without his normal thick black eyebrows. The scales covering his face and stretching over his head were smaller than on the rest of his body, and tightly knit. He wasn't hideous. Not when she looked at him bit by bit.

Ingrid stepped away from the open window. She didn't need to say anything to invite him in. She was certain he could feel the thrill of his presence throbbing through her veins. She tried to steady her breathing as his wings folded in behind him. Once inside, Luc had to hunch over so the top of his head wouldn't crash into the plaster ceiling.

"What—what are you doing here?" she whispered. Of course he couldn't answer. Not in gargoyle form, at least.

With that very thought, Luc's scales started to dissolve. His wings sank down behind his back as the transformation began, and just like in the abbey, she was mesmerized by how rapidly he changed—and then startled when she realized that he was also nude.

Ingrid turned her back to give him privacy, but her heart sputtered. Luc hadn't been carrying any clothing in his arms.

"You can turn around," he said, his voice low enough that it wouldn't penetrate the old walls and alert her sister or mother.

She quickly crossed to the door and threw the lock in case Cherie decided to return for another try at undressing Ingrid. Slowly, she turned back toward the window. Luc had taken the liberty of shutting and latching it. He'd also taken the liberty of wrapping the thin wool blanket usually spread over the bottom of Ingrid's bed around his waist. She'd been right—he hadn't brought his clothes.

The red and tan plaid of the blanket made it look like Luc was wearing a long Scottish kilt. Ingrid shouldn't have been ogling him, but her eyes were rebellious. His chest was completely bare and right in front of her. How could she not look at it?

"I was in a rush," he apologized. "I didn't think to bring anything."

She tried to say it was all right, but it came out sounding like a drunken slur. The corner of Luc's mouth kicked up in a grin.

"Why were you in a rush?" Ingrid said, recovering, though not nearly fast enough.

He crossed his arms as if to ward off the winter air that had entered her bedroom while the window had been open. "The Alliance is meeting inside the abbey vestry. There aren't any windows in there, so as long as everyone is quiet your mother and the servants won't be the wiser." Luc lowered his eyes and cocked his head, as if listening to something she couldn't hear. "Your butler and lady's maids are still awake. I'll fly you over."

Ingrid wasn't sure she wanted to fly with Luc again. The first time had been terrifying enough.

"I could walk," she said.

"And you could be caught leaving," he quickly retorted. He was right. She'd let Luc fly her over. It was practically just a hop anyway.

"The meeting," Ingrid began, averting her eyes from the smooth skin of his chest and arms. "Is it about what happened tonight? With Marco?"

Luc gripped the folded edge of the blanket and took a step toward her. "I don't think so. Your sister called for the meeting."

Gabby? She hadn't said anything about a meeting before they'd gone to their own rooms for the evening. Then again, Ingrid hadn't told her anything about what had occurred in the courtyard, either.

"Was he going to hurt me? Marco, I mean," Ingrid asked. "He promised he meant me no harm. But what would he have done if this Lennier person determined I had demon blood in me?"

Ingrid hadn't looked up. Her eyes had been drifting over the folds in the blanket Luc wore. His knuckles tightened and turned white where he held the blanket at his hip.

"Gargoyles take pleasure in destroying demons," Luc replied, his voice gravelly. "And like I said before, there are some who take pleasure in harming humans. Marco doesn't have a history of it, but if Lennier had given his permission . . ."

Ingrid closed her eyes. "He might have killed me."

Luc closed another inch between them. "Marco knew he wasn't going to make it past that woman's courtyard with you."

Trusting the hold of the tucked-in blanket, he caught one of Ingrid's hands in his. He held it up between them and laced his fingers through hers. His palm was hot. The warmth kindling low in her stomach had nothing to do with her odd gift.

"Besides," Luc went on, his thumb brushing the tips of her fingers. "I don't think he could have harmed you—and not just because I would have first ripped out his throat."

Tapping every last ounce of her willpower, Ingrid pulled her hand away, untangling his fingers. He was her protector, with possibly more right to this property than anyone else, but he was still in her room at an indecent hour—and even more indecently dressed.

Not that she would dare complain. He might go away if she did.

"Did I kill him?" she asked, her throat dry. "The other man?"

Luc frowned. "René? No. You just stunned him."

Like the lectrux demon Marco had told her about.

"It's not only that, Ingrid," Luc said. "I think, earlier, when you held out your hand to Yann and ordered him to stop . . . I think you controlled him. I think you controlled all of us."

She stepped back. It was difficult to concentrate when she could smell the musk of his skin. It had a heady bite, like Spanish cedar.

"I don't understand," she said.

Luc had cowered in the courtyard. He'd turned away as if the sight of her was sickening. She had mostly been watching him, but she supposed if she remembered correctly, the other two had also dropped into low, cowering crouches. Still, it had been Luc's shunning her that had hurt.

"I think you have power over the Dispossessed. I felt it tonight," Luc said.

He walked to her mirrored vanity and examined the things she'd left out. He ran his fingers over the teeth of one of her carved ivory hair combs. He picked up the silver-framed photograph of Grayson and stared at it a long moment.

"There's something special about you," Luc said. "I didn't feel it with Grayson. I don't feel it with Gabby or your mother, or anyone else."

"Not special," she said, taking the photograph out of Luc's hand. She set it back on the vanity table with unintentional force. "Whatever it is, it's dangerous. Demonic. Not *special*. I have demon dust and demon powers—Marco told me about the lectrux."

He held a finger to his lips to hush her. She checked her voice. "I can do the same thing as a lectrux demon, and I know you've been keeping that from me. You've had more than enough reason to side with Marco and the rest of the Dispossessed, not to mention every opportunity to end me, just like they want. Why haven't you?"

Luc stared at her, his expression unreadable. He lifted his hand and pulled out the ivory comb that secured her hair. The twisted coils came tumbling down, the remaining small pins not enough to hold the weight of her thick tresses.

Luc carefully laid the ivory comb next to its match on the table. She was ready to repeat her question when his hand unexpectedly came back up. Ingrid froze as he grazed his fingers through her hair, scattering a few pins to the floor. Then he gripped the back of her head, his tangled fingers tugging at her hair, and Ingrid thought she could finally read something in the way he looked at her: a longing so tangible that it made her ache.

"I haven't ended you because you're my human."

And then Luc did what he hadn't done in the orangery. His lips found hers. It was a light sweep of a kiss, and Ingrid, who'd quit breathing, feared he was going to stop again. The idea of it knifed through her and her hands itched to reach up, latch on to him, and refuse the retreat.

It didn't come to that.

Luc sank deeper into the kiss. He pressed his lips against hers so powerfully that her mouth could do nothing else but open to him. He tasted her, his tongue a warm spice that reminded her of the jungle inside Monsieur Constantine's orangery. Ingrid felt the heat of the orangery as well. It climbed from her softening legs, turning into a pool of liquid sunshine low in her stomach. She curled her hands around the nape of Luc's neck and clung to him, thinking her knees might very well give out beneath her.

Luc circled her waist with his arm and hitched her tighter against him. The unnatural hardness of his chest was the only thing that reminded her of his other shape. His other life. The rest of him, his mouth, his hands, the satin of the black curls between her fingers, were completely human.

Ingrid slipped her hands back to his chest and felt the skin she'd imagined touching earlier that evening outside Lady Ormand's home, when Luc had held her wrist discreetly behind her back. She'd been aware of him then, her body humming at his touch. But *this* . . . his starving hold on her, the sublime crush of their bodies . . . this was leagues better than she had thought possible.

Ingrid didn't want him to stop.

So, of course, he did.

Luc ripped himself away and Ingrid lost her balance, jarring against the vanity table and knocking over a box of powder. The cover slid off and rose-scented dust clouded the air. He quickly turned away from her, but what was happening to him was unmistakable. Ingrid stared at the planes of his back in horror.

"I knew I couldn't. Ingrid, it's impossible—" His voice cracked into a hawklike shriek.

His spine knuckled and stretched. The velvety skin Ingrid had just been caressing trembled. Across Luc's back, rows of glittering black plates appeared, flipping up in patch after patch, replacing his pale white human skin. She watched until the plates streamed down to the small of his back. Luc loosened the plaid woolen blanket that had covered him.

Ingrid averted her eyes and rushed to the window to throw the panels open. The talons of a gargoyle wouldn't be able to undo the tiny metal latch. By the time she turned back to him, Luc was gone. A creature she could never kiss—couldn't even think about touching in that way—stood before her.

Luc hadn't been able to stop his transformation. *I knew I couldn't.* He couldn't kiss her. Just like he'd claimed in the orangery. And yet he had. A little bit, at least.

Was that all it could ever be? A little bit?

Ingrid moved out of the way as his scaled, muscled legs brought him to the window. He had one foot out on the ledge when his arm hooked around her waist. It wasn't the passionate hold he'd had on her just moments before, but it was earnest. Protective.

Ingrid tucked herself into a ball and clung to him, her knees wedged into her stomach, as he ducked back out of the window and caught the wind with a snap of his unfurling wings. She clung to him, the leathery texture of his scales rough against her cheek as he bounded over the churchyard toward the abbey spires.

This was Luc. This version of him was the dominant one. And he had been right.

It was impossible.

CHAPTER TWENTY-ONE

The vestry felt more like the cold abbey's crypts than a place once used for storing records and holding meetings. Gabby walked the perimeter of the windowless room, running a finger along the glass doors of the floor-to-ceiling cabinets. They were on each wall, crammed with dusty old papers and rolled ledgers, cobwebbed scrolls and molding vestments that hadn't been worn in at least a century. Her finger left a clear trail in the grime.

She hadn't wanted a meeting like this. What she had wanted was to be taken to Hôtel Bastian after her mother had safely retired to her room. But when she'd asked Luc to drive her there he'd been adamant: No one was leaving hallowed ground a second time that evening. They had been lucky not to meet any hellhounds on the drive back to the rectory. He wouldn't push his luck, and instead had offered to bring Nolan to her.

"Stay in the vestry," he'd added. "If you hear someone beckoning you out, don't follow. They're delusion demons. They lure you by using the voice of someone you trust. You'll be off hallowed ground in the blink of an eye."

Gabby had promised to stay put, but the privacy of the vestry bothered her. As she waited alone in the center room in the abbey, lit with only a few prayer candles and an oil lamp, she thought of her last memory of Nolan: him running out of his curtained makeshift room in order to chase after Chelle.

Gabby roughly smudged away the grime her fingertip had picked up from the glass. She mustn't think about it. He'd been improper and presumptuous and she'd been a dolt. She should have stomped on his foot or slapped his cheek.

But then she wouldn't have experienced the most wonderful kiss imaginable. Her only kiss. Gabby had been driving herself mad with worry that she hadn't been able to hold up her end of the kiss. Had she been horrible at it?

Gabby kept pacing the vestry room. She had to quit being such a ninny. She hadn't had Luc fetch Nolan so she could bring up the kiss. There was something more important to discuss: Marie.

She didn't hear the approaching footsteps until they were just outside the thick wooden vestry door. It was flung open on its rusting hinges and Nolan rushed inside.

"Gabby," he said breathlessly, as if he'd jogged all the way from rue de Sèvres to the abbey. "What is it? Are you all right? Luc said it was an emergency."

Vander entered on Nolan's heels, his brown eyes dark with concern. He searched the room. "Where is your sister?"

Before Gabby could answer either of their questions, Chelle walked in, followed by Marie and Tomas. What were they all doing here?

Chelle glared at Gabby, her petite shoulders pushed back and her ungloved hands clutched into fists. She looked like a soldier. "Why have you called for an emergency meeting? You're not Alliance. You don't have the right."

"Gabby didn't call you all here. I did," Nolan said, which brought out specks of color on Chelle's cheeks.

"So you've brought us all here, pulling us off patrol in the middle of the night, because you think whatever she has to say is *that* important?"

Gabby waved her hand through the air. "Stop it! I didn't intend for everyone to come, Nolan."

She glanced toward Marie, who looked as pale as a sheet of Gabby's bleached stationery.

Chelle snorted. "I bet you were hoping to be alone with him."

Tomas stepped between them. "Can we get to it, then?"

But they were delayed once more as her sister arrived. Ingrid's attention went at once to Vander.

"What's going on?" she asked, her lips much redder than usual. They were bright as cherries.

"Where is Luc?" Gabby asked her, nervous with all eyes being on her. "I didn't tell him it was an emergency."

"He's, ah, getting dressed," Ingrid answered, her cheeks turning just as red as her lips.

"Gabby?" Nolan prodded.

She supposed there was nothing to do but come out with it. "I simply wanted to know why no one mentioned Marie had been working at the dinner Grayson disappeared from."

Marie's eyes fluttered shut. Chelle's fierce glare shifted paths and struck Marie.

"You were there?" Chelle asked.

So they hadn't known. Good—Gabby hadn't wasted anyone's time after all.

"I—I—" Marie stuttered.

"You should have told us," Chelle said.

"I know, but I—"

"Are you hiding something?"

"Please, I can't—"

Chelle cut her off. "Can't what?"

Tomas stepped in front of Chelle. "She can't tell us anything if you won't allow her to speak."

He turned his stony expression to Marie. "Take a moment to consider your answer, Marie. But know that we do require one."

He was nearly as commanding as Nolan.

Marie nodded, blinking rapidly. Her chin quivered as she looked imploringly at Tomas, as if pleading with him to help her. He didn't budge.

"It wasn't my idea," Marie finally said, her voice a trembling squeak. "But I didn't have a choice."

Her tears spilled over. She covered her face with her palms. From behind them, she continued, "I love him. I didn't have a choice."

Ingrid and Gabby matched sharp gasps.

"You *love* him?" Gabby repeated, slack-jawed. "Grayson?"

Marie raised her face from her hands with a start. "Grayson? No, of course not. I only promised him a kiss. I had to. It was the only way I could get him to leave the others at Lady Ormand's dinner."

The gasp was collective this time. It echoed around the vestry as Luc entered, fully dressed. His eyes immediately found Marie. He'd heard her confession.

Ingrid lifted her skirt and charged forward, elbowing her way around Tomas.

"*You* led him out of the dinner?"

"Good God," Vander murmured as he took off his glasses. "Marie, you didn't."

Gabby couldn't put a stopper in the fury building inside of her.

"I told him to slip away and meet me in the courtyard before the seating started," Marie said, falling into one of the old chairs around a pitted table.

"But why?" Chelle asked, her anger replaced by incredulity.

"She made a pact with a demon," Nolan answered for her. He curled his lip. "Didn't you?"

Marie was quick to deny it. "Not a demon, no. Not exactly."

"Then please, explain yourself," Tomas said, again as chivalrous as he was firm.

Vander, Gabby noticed, had crossed the vestry room to stand at Ingrid's side. Had Luc's eyes been knives, they would have carved Vander open as he rested a gallant hand on Ingrid's shoulder.

"I never had any contact with the demon," Marie asserted. But then her lip wavered. "René did."

Luc tore his focus from Vander's hand. "René?"

"Who is that?" Gabby asked.

Tomas groaned. "A gargoyle."

Chelle rattled off a string of curse words in her native French. Gabby understood them, but at least Ingrid's ears were spared.

"I'm not surprised a Dispossessed would sink to collaborate with a demon, but how could you help him, Marie?" Chelle grabbed her by the arm. "Why would you betray the Alliance like that?"

Gabby tried to catch up. "So this René is the rogue gargoyle? He led the hellhound to Lady Ormand's home, and Marie led Grayson out into the courtyard?"

"René asked me to help him," Marie said, rubbing away the tears that had streaked down her face. "Grayson wouldn't have gone outside to meet with René, and Luc would have felt his uncertainty anyway. I was supposed to lead him far enough away that Luc wouldn't scent the hellhound. The whole deal was hinged on delivering Grayson to the Underneath."

"What deal, Marie?" Chelle shouted.

She jumped and screeched, "The one René made with the demon master! I don't know anything about the demon, just that it promised to free him from the Dispossessed as soon as something called the Harvest happened."

Luc let out a mocking jeer. "René's a fool. No demon can free a gargoyle from servitude."

Marie's sobs hardened over. She looked daggers at Luc, the same way she had at Chelle the time her friend had likened gargoyles to dogs. "He isn't a fool."

Of course Marie would defend him. Of course she would have helped him. She loved René. She loved a gargoyle.

"He said he'd do whatever it took," Marie went on, playing with the frills of lace around her collar. "For us to be together." She turned to look at Luc. "You know that it's not possible for a gargoyle and a human to . . . well, you know."

If she'd wanted warmth and understanding from Luc, she didn't receive it. Instead, she got thinly veiled contempt. "You think he loves you."

"He does love me," Marie insisted.

"Then you're an even bigger fool than René was for trusting the word of a demon," Luc replied.

He stepped around Ingrid and jerked the vestry door open. He hesitated before turning to Vander. "See that the Waverly sisters stay on hallowed ground. I'm going to find René."

He slammed the door behind him.

"We should alert Lennier," Nolan said to Vander. "Tomas, can you take Chelle and Marie safely back to Hôtel Bastian?"

Tomas bowed like a gentleman, his answer in the short, perfunctory dip.

Nolan stopped next to Marie's chair, her shoulders limp and shaking. "We'll decide what to do about the things you've told us tomorrow. You should be prepared, though—I'll have to contact my father in Rome. It's possible he'll send for you."

Marie gasped and started to cry even harder. The reaction made Gabby wonder about the senior Quinn. He had to be a powerful member of the Alliance, and she wondered what he was like—most likely as arrogant and chafing as his son. But judging by Marie's reaction, perhaps he was someone to fear as well.

Ingrid took Gabby's arm and together they led Vander and Nolan out of the vestry, through the abbey, and to the western transept doors, located on the far side of the abbey. The hedges lining that boundary of the church were unkempt and close to the stone exterior. They caught in Gabby's hair, their thorns snagging and making small tears in her skirts that might be difficult to explain to Nora come morning. She'd worry about it then.

"I'm sorry about how Chelle treated you." Nolan's voice was a loud crack against the still night. "She's been on edge ever since Henri was killed."

"Do you think it was René who did it?" Gabby asked.

"If Henri discovered their secret, yes," Vander said.

And Marie could have led René to Henri's room. Because she loved him. The excuse made Gabby feel ill. That wasn't love. It was wretched and misguided, and Henri and her brother had suffered because of it.

"Do you have a way into the rectory?" Nolan asked.

"I left the kitchen door unlocked," Gabby answered.

"Good," Vander cut in. "Luc wants you to stay on hallowed ground, and for once I don't think he's being irrational or overprotective."

They parted with Ingrid and Gabby at the brick and gravel drive, and the girls hurried toward the kitchen doors. The windows were dark, lit only by the warm orange glow of a low fire in the grate. They made it in without being heard and crept through the house to the front sitting room. Gabby sat heavily on a sofa cushion as Ingrid closed the blue drapes.

"Can you believe it? Marie had an affair with a *gargoyle*," Gabby breathed, suddenly exhausted. "Since when did we take up residence in a horror novel?"

Ingrid swung around from the drapes. "What do you mean by that?"

Gabby flinched at the sharpness of her voice. She was still trying to gather a response when a heavy fist came down on the front door of the rectory. Ingrid and Gabby both leaped.

"What on earth—?" Ingrid said as the next knocks rattled the door on its hinges. The sisters stole a quick look at one another and then raced into the foyer. The incessant barrage was so loud it slammed through Gabby's head and chest, and was most certainly shaking every living soul at the rectory from their beds.

Gabby unlocked the door and started to open it just as Ingrid shouted for her to stop and ask who it was. Too late. The person on the other side pushed against the door and forced his way into the foyer. Gabby and Ingrid scurried backward as a man in tattered and soiled clothing stumbled across the Persian rug. He was barefoot, his hair lank with grime, his hands black as a chimney sweep's.

And yet Ingrid rushed to the man's side.

"Griddy, stay back!" Gabby cried, but Ingrid clutched at the stranger, falling with him as he collapsed. His sheet of greasy hair was swept aside, and only then did Gabby see him, too.

"Oh, Grayson!" Ingrid sobbed, brushing her hand across her twin's forehead and then bringing his head into her lap.

Gabby stared in horror at their brother, immobile on the floor. Grayson had come home. He'd escaped the Underneath.

CHAPTER TWENTY-TWO

The ice floes on the Seine looked like cracked white sheets as Luc flew overhead. They floated slowly downriver, carving the banks of the Ile de la Cité and the connected Ile de Saint-Louis. The Dispossessed charged with protecting the grand Notre Dame Cathedral, a mix of castes and personalities, were all close by. Luc felt their presence as he swooped over the cathedral spire, the verdigris copper statues of the twelve apostles set in tiered steps at the spire's base. A black shadow curled around one statue, giving the apostle a pair of wings.

Luc flew on. René's park was at the tip of the island, a small grassy space that, unlike Notre Dame, with its scores of famous stone gargoyles, had but one gargoyle marking. Most humans who came to the park for the weekend markets probably never noticed it, submerged as it was at the base of a fountain. The stone mouth of a wolfish gargoyle drew in the fountain water at the bottom of the pool, piped it to the top of the fountain, and then jetted it out again.

René was the only Dispossessed assigned to the park, but as Luc touched down next to the fountain, he was certain René wasn't alone. Marco and Yann were probably with him, just as they had been earlier in the evening. It was safest to assume they, too, had struck bargains with the demon master the Alliance girl had spoken of.

"I'm not here to discuss Ingrid Waverly," Luc announced as soon as his reverse shift was complete. Marco emerged alone from a copse of thickly set trees. The bare limbs let through twinkling lights from homes across the river.

"That's a pity. I find I quite enjoy thinking about her," Marco replied as Luc buttoned his trousers. "You should be more careful with your arrivals. We're in a public space, and the humans don't take very kindly to indecent exposure."

Luc searched for René and Yann as he tugged on his shirt. He found them reclining on a park bench.

Marco stepped closer, though neither of them had difficulty seeing in the dark. Their eyes were as keen as a feline's. "If you're not here to talk about your human, what is it that you want?"

Luc turned to the park bench, walking around Marco. "I want to ask René the name of the demon master he's working for."

Yann hurtled to his feet. René didn't so much as twitch.

"Be careful, Luc," Yann said. "Accusing one of your own of something like that can be dangerous."

"I'm only in danger if you and Marco have also made bargains with this demon," Luc replied. "Have you?"

Marco growled and winged Luc aside with a blow to the shoulder. He sneered at him. "Don't insult me again."

Centuries had taught Luc that anger was the only emotion Marco consistently failed to mask. Accusing him of dealing with a demon had swung Marco's body into a rigid half shift. His facial bones had sharpened, his shoulders and hands jointed and lengthened. He'd just proven himself innocent.

"Yann?" Luc asked, ignoring Marco.

Yann's intense stare could have burned someone alive. There wasn't a trace of guilt behind it. "Where did you come up with such a story?"

Good. So it was just René, then.

"I didn't come up with it," Luc answered. "An Alliance girl named Marie did."

René finally reacted, even if just by lowering the ankle he'd had crossed over his knee.

"Is Marie the short and pretty Alliance girl?" Marco asked.

Luc thought to test René's limits. "No. She's the tall and ugly one."

René began to leap from the bench. He caught himself, but not before Marco and Yann had seen him.

"Quite a reaction for a human who isn't strolling through your park," Marco said, and shifted his aggressive stance toward René.

Now was the moment to strike. But just as Luc opened his mouth to speak, Ingrid's scent surfaced, quickly followed by Gabby's, and he faltered, overwhelmed by the sudden onslaught of emotions his humans were experiencing. Happiness. Confusion. He held his muscles tight, prepared for the urge to coalesce. But he didn't need to. They weren't in any danger, though something *was* happening at the rectory. Luc would find out what it was later.

He focused again on René. "Marie told the Alliance everything. How the two of you have become involved. How you accepted the offer of a demon so you would no longer have to be a Dispossessed," Luc said, watching as René fell back, looking like a stray cat trapped in a corner by advancing dogs. "All so you could be with her."

"You've taken a human?" Yann asked, revulsion coating his tone.

"It's a lie," René tried. "I don't have anything to do with the human girl."

"And the demon?" Marco asked, closing in on René's left while Yann approached his right side. "Is that a lie as well?"

René bobbed his head from Marco to Yann. "Of course it's a lie. You would believe this Dog over me? The only one infatuated with a human girl is Luc."

Luc kept his lips sealed. *Infatuation* wasn't the right word for what he felt for Ingrid, though what René said stung. If Marco or Yann knew Luc had kissed Ingrid a mere hour before, in her bedroom . . . if they knew that Luc had longed for more than just a kiss, they would turn on him the same way they were turning on René.

"Then you won't mind if we pay this Marie girl a visit," Marco said, his dark intent palpable. "She really ought to be silenced if all she's going to do is spout off lies about you. Don't you think so, René?"

René floundered. And then caved. Fast. "Leave Marie out of it," he said. "I'll tell you what you want to know."

Yann and Marco shrank away from René as if he had started giving off a foul odor.

"You fool," Marco seethed. "I hope she was worth your destruction."

It was the price René would have to pay.

"It's not just about her!" René cried, eyes wild with anger and fear. "It's what I was promised in return."

"From the demon master?" Luc asked.

"What demon master?" Marco demanded.

René backed up, looking as if he wanted to flee. Yann slammed into his side, throwing René against the fountain rim. The stone cracked.

"Answer the question," Yann ordered.

René cowered, something Luc hadn't thought the Wolf capable of.

"Her name is Axia," he quickly divulged. "Fallen from the Angelic Order nearly two decades ago. She was stripped of her wings and glow, and imprisoned in the Underneath, though I don't know why. I don't care, either. All I know is that she hasn't

243

been able to go to Earth's surface like other demons. But now she's found a way to escape the Underneath, to lead an army of her own making against the humans and the Order."

"What does that have to do with you?" Yann asked.

"She needs a specific kind of blood," he answered. "Female. Untainted and newly matured."

Exactly the sort of blood all the missing girls would have had, Luc thought to himself. No street whores or girls from the slums, whose health and blood might have been less than ideal.

"And what were you going to receive in return for your betrayal?" Marco asked.

René let out a raw, humorless laugh. "It wasn't going to just benefit me, *brother*. I was doing it for all of us. For all the Dispossessed. She promised us freedom from the Angelic Order, from the humans we're slaves to. She promised us life as eternal humans, more powerful than any angel of the Order."

René slowly stood up from where he'd been crouching against the cracked fountain wall.

"So you led Axia's hellhounds to the kind of girls she required," Marco surmised. "And made sure they didn't live in protected homes."

René gave a careless shrug. "Can you honestly say you wouldn't have done the same?"

Marco's clothing strained against his ridging spine, his bulking muscle. Luc felt the same urge to shift and rip into René. But he still had another question.

"Why Grayson, then? If Axia required only female blood, why lead a hellhound to him as well?"

The Notre Dame's south tower bell sent the first of twelve gongs through the night, marking the new day.

"I don't know. It was something about his blood being different. Like his sister's." René changed course, taking direct aim at Luc. "Can you, of all gargoyles, blame me for accepting Axia's offer? Don't you want to be human again? If you weren't cursed, you could be with your human girl. Don't tell me you haven't wished for it."

A slow burning ignited in Luc's stomach and spread outward as the memory of Ingrid in his arms, her lips against his, his fingers buried deep in her hair, came unbidden. Even when Luc had been human he hadn't kissed a girl that passionately. And he hadn't thought it possible as a gargoyle. But the pain of the shift it triggered had surprised him. It had been unexpected. Close to excruciating, almost as if he were an infant gargoyle again, a time when each shift had felt like bones breaking and resetting, his muscles twisting and stretching beyond their capability.

Had the painful shift been worth it? Yes. Had he wanted to keep kissing Ingrid? Hell, yes. But unlike René, Luc would never be able to lead innocent humans to slaughter in order to get what he wanted. Maybe other gargoyles wouldn't have cared, but Luc did. He was different from the rest of them, though he wasn't sure when he'd started realizing it.

"Involvement with a human is forbidden," Luc said in order to deflect René's question.

"As are dealings with Underneath demons," Marco added. "We have our own laws and you've made a mockery out of them. You think we're cursed? You're blind. We are blessed. We are necessary. That necessity gives us power."

"But not enough power to cross into the Underneath," Yann said thoughtfully. "How did you accomplish it? The fallen angel couldn't come to Earth's surface and you couldn't go into the Underneath. So how did you communicate?"

Again, René acted as if he was bored with all the questioning. He rolled his massive shoulders. "A messenger. Axia has a human messenger who can come and go from the Underneath."

He sounded exasperated, as if the others were failing to grasp the intelligence behind accepting Axia's offer.

"I'm finished listening," Marco announced. He began to remove his shirt. Yann followed suit, kicking off his shoes. René backed away, knowing that the moment they shifted, they would attack.

"What human?" Luc demanded as René's clothing tore at the seams. He wasn't even bothering to undress.

"*René!* What human?" he repeated as René staggered backward, away from Marco's and Yann's calm disrobing.

"Alliance," René answered as his face began to shift. His voice would go next.

"Which one? Marie?" Luc asked before he remembered that Marie had seemed to know agonizingly little about the demon master.

René's gargoyle form shredded the human clothing and he immediately spiraled into the air. Less than a second later, Yann and Marco followed, leaving Luc behind in the park.

Alliance.

Luc tore himself out of his clothing and triggered the shift, surfacing Ingrid's scent in a heartbeat. He was streaking over Notre Dame and the icy Seine when his trace on her cleared. She was at the abbey still, but there was something wrong. Her scent was different. He inhaled the familiar tilled soil and sweet grass, but with it came the green flesh of a sapling pine. Crushed tea leaves. And suddenly Luc understood the giddy flood of emotion Ingrid and Gabby had experienced minutes before.

It was Grayson.

His scent blended with Ingrid's now, as if the two distinct scents were actually one. *Because they're twins,* Luc quickly reasoned. For the first time in weeks Luc knew exactly where Grayson was: out of the Underneath, and at the rectory with his sister.

Lady Charlotte Brickton screamed the second she entered the front sitting room. Had Gabby not been there to prop her up, she would have fainted dead away.

"My son!" she cried, prying herself from Gabby's hold. "What has happened to him?"

She pitched forward to where Grayson lay on the sofa, his head in Ingrid's lap.

"Nora! Send Luc for the doctor," Charlotte instructed as Gabby's lady's maid, in her dressing gown and frilled cap, came into the sitting room. She squealed when she saw Grayson, all filth and grit, and then rushed out of the room again.

Gabby ducked into the foyer after her. "Nora," she whispered. "I don't believe Luc is in the carriage house. Wake Gustav and send him on the errand instead."

Nora, though frowning, nodded and left. Gabby went back into the sitting room and found her mother kneeling on the floor in front of Grayson. Her hand made a trembling stroke across his forehead.

"He hasn't said anything," Ingrid explained.

Grayson rolled his head from side to side, his eyes opening to slits. "Ingrid?"

Gabby stood back, not wanting to crowd him. How had he done it? How had he escaped the Underneath?

"My darling, what happened to you?" their mother asked, her hands making an inspective run over his limbs. Other than the filth he wore like a second skin, he seemed in one piece.

"Taken," he answered, his voice scratchy. "Held prisoner."

"Gabby." Ingrid looked up at her. "Some water."

She crossed to the sideboard, to the decanters of water, soda water, and liquor. She splashed some water in a glass and rushed it over. Grayson bucked his head, refusing the drink when their mother put the glass to his lips.

"Escaped," he croaked. "Won't go back."

His eyes had fluttered shut again. Their mother got to her feet and returned the glass to Gabby.

"He needs to be cleaned. Where is Madam Bertot? How has she slept through this? And where is my maid?" She went to the bellpull, a tapestry ribbon near the fireplace, and tugged twice. Gabby had no doubt their cook was already up and heating water in the kitchen.

"Mama, it's the middle of the night," Gabby said. "They were sleeping. Give them a moment."

"I can't abide waiting," she said. "Stay with your brother. I'll be back."

And with that, their mother rushed out of the sitting room.

"She's impossible," Gabby said.

"She's worried," Ingrid corrected. "And so am I. Look at him, Gabby."

She did. Their brother appeared to be in the throes of a fever. Sweat rolled in thin streaks through the grime on his face.

"How did he get out?" Gabby whispered. Ingrid ran her hand through Grayson's matted hair, pushing it farther back from his forehead.

Grayson's eyes opened wide, startling Gabby and Ingrid to full attention.

"Ingrid," he said, chest heaving as he looked straight up into his sister's eyes. "You have to leave. Leave Paris. Now."

He tried to sit up, but fell back. Ingrid pressed his shoulders down to hold him tighter in her lap.

"Leave Paris? Why? Grayson, what's happening?"

"No. No, don't leave," Grayson murmured. "You can come with me instead. Yes, you have to come with me."

Ingrid pressed her palm against his forehead, checking for fever. "He's not making any sense."

"Grayson, what happened to you?" Gabby asked. "We know you were taken by a hellhound."

Grayson craned his neck, rolling his head from side to side as wretched mewling came from his throat. "The teeth. His teeth," he moaned. "He's a monster. I don't . . . I don't want to."

Ingrid sent Gabby a killing glare. "Leave him be. He's delirious. He can explain later."

Gabby swallowed her protest. Of course Ingrid was right. He was delirious. Exhausted. By the looks of him, escaping the Underneath had nearly destroyed him. But Gabby still couldn't shake the feeling that something wasn't quite right. It was like a phantom finger, poking her in the back every time she looked at Grayson. As if she should see something that was plain as the nose on her face.

What an obscene sister she was. To be questioning her brother's homecoming when she should be overjoyed by it. To see him lying in delirium and wonder if she should be afraid.

"Ingrid," Grayson said, clear for the moment. "I need to talk to you." He searched the sitting room until he found Gabby. "Alone."

The wound took a moment to sting. He didn't want her there. He wanted Ingrid and only Ingrid, because they were closer. Because they were essentially the same person through and through. And Gabby was the outsider. Just as she'd always been.

Ingrid parted her lips, seeing the hurt Grayson had inflicted. "Grayson—"

"No," Gabby interrupted. "It's all right. I'll go. I'll . . . wait for the doctor."

"Gabby!" Ingrid fixed her with one of her iron shield stares. "Remember, stay on hallowed ground."

Gabby fluttered her lashes. She couldn't leave the sitting room fast enough. And to think, Gabby steamed as she threw on her cloak, that she'd been willing to enter the Underneath, to lead a rescue mission. She felt like a fool as she stormed out the front door and down the walk into the churchyard. A blithering idiot. Grayson hadn't needed her help and he hadn't wanted it, either.

"Lady Gabriella?" Nora came around the corner of the rectory. One hand clutched the shawl at her neck, and the other a hurricane lamp.

"Has Gustav left?" Gabby asked, still moving toward the

hedgerow. She'd rather wait in the cold than be inside, banished from the sitting room.

"He rode out quick. Didn't even saddle the mare," Nora replied, falling into step with Gabby.

"Good. And my mother, is she harassing Madam Bertot?"

Nora smiled. "Her ladyship is quite distressed."

A tactful evasion, Gabby thought, and continued walking. "He looks awful," she said.

Nora held the lantern out farther to light their way. The clouds were thick, the moon shrouded. "The doctor will set him to rights, my lady."

Gabby didn't make a reply. If her brother had indeed been in the Underneath, no doctor would be able to treat the wounds from what happened to him there.

Nora started to walk through the break in the hedgerow, out onto the curb. Gabby saw her maid's slippers leave hallowed ground and roughly took her elbow. Nora tensed.

"My lady?"

Gabby drew her back behind the hedgerow. "It's improper to stand on the street side this time of night."

The excuse sounded a little more rational than the one regarding hallowed ground and protection from demons. Nora went back to Gabby's side with a quizzical expression.

"Yes, my lady."

They waited in silence, the intersection of rue Dante and rue Lagrange devoid of any traffic, foot or wheeled. Gabby itched to know how Grayson was explaining his departure from the Underneath. Marie had said a demon master had wanted him. How could Grayson have escaped a powerful demon in a condition as pathetic as the one he'd arrived in? Unless he hadn't escaped. Unless he'd been set free.

The clatter of wagon wheels sounded from down rue Dante. The driver of the carriage was going fast.

"Thank the stars," Nora said. "The doctor is already here!"

But Gustav had left barely five minutes prior.

"Wait a moment," Gabby said as the carriage wheels thundered closer.

Nora strained for a view past the hedgerow limbs. "There he is." She waved her hand to flag him down.

"Are you sure it's the physician?" Gabby asked, hesitating at the mouth of the drive.

"Over here!" Nora called, still waving.

She stepped through the hedgerow and onto the sidewalk.

"Nora, wait!"

But her maid was already at the curbside, hailing the basket phaeton barreling toward them.

A gust of hot, putrid wind whirled past the break in the hedgerow, so close to Gabby's nose that she gagged on the foul odor of wet, rotten fur. Nora's scream rent the air as a hellhound crunched her around the waist and swiped her up like a bone.

"Nora!" Gabby screamed as the hurricane lamp crashed on the curb. "Nora, no!"

The hellhound bounded into the street, directly into the path of the approaching phaeton. The driver swerved, but not before the hound had taken another arcing leap to the median at the intersecting rues, Nora looking boneless in its jaws. She emitted another piteous scream.

"Nora!" Gabby cried again. Forgetting the line between hallowed ground and open territory, she started to run after her. Vander's blessed blade was still in her pocket. She might be able to catch up with the hellhound. Save Nora.

The phaeton whipped to a stop in front of Gabby before she could even step off the curb in pursuit.

"Gabby, stop!"

It wasn't the doctor. Tomas leaned across the bench seat, the lights from the rectory barely bright enough to show his scarred face.

"But Nora!"

He'd seen her maid attacked; he was Alliance. For heaven's sake, he could help!

"It's too late," he said. "We could never catch up to a hellhound on the run. Go—back up. Onto hallowed ground."

He directed his horse and phaeton forward, herding Gabby back through the hedgerow opening. She stumbled over the roughly laid stones, her hand still wrapped around the dagger in her pocket.

"But Nora—" she said again.

Tomas cut her off. "There's a demon inside the rectory, Gabby." She stared at him, agape. "What?"

"Marie broke down and told me everything when we reached Hôtel Bastian. I couldn't afford the time to go to Nolan and tell him—I had to come straight here."

Every window in the rectory was lit up, throwing halos of light upon the snowy churchyard.

"Marie told you *what* exactly? That's impossible. No demon can cross onto hallowed ground," Gabby said, already moving up the drive toward the front doors.

Tomas steered his horse and phaeton in front of her. The wheels tore ruts in the lawn as he jerked his mare to a halt.

"This demon can. It's Grayson."

The phantom finger that had been prodding her since her brother's arrival suddenly went still. "What? How did you even know he was here?" she asked.

"I told you. Marie explained it. She said it was happening tonight, that this was the night Grayson was returning—but *not* as a human."

She backed up a step. "That's insane."

"Is it? Have you noticed he's not quite himself?"

His delirium and filth; his sudden release from the Underneath. It hadn't made sense before. But what kind of demon could walk on hallowed ground?

Tomas extended his hand to her. "Get in. I have to take you back to Hôtel Bastian."

Gabby ignored his hand and tried to go around the horse. "But my mother and Ingrid are in there with him!"

"Luc is already on his way," Tomas said with urgency. It stripped him of his usual gentlemanly manners. "He's connected to your emotions, Gabby, and to Ingrid's and those of everyone else inside the rectory. He's already felt everything going on here. He'll arrive in full gargoyle form at any moment. Please. I can't let you go back inside."

"Then I'll stay out here and wait for Luc," Gabby said, her heart thrashing in her chest. She couldn't just leave.

Tomas maneuvered his phaeton so that the steps up to the bench seat were right before her. "All right, I'll take you to Saint-Julien-le-Pauvre, just down the block here. It's hallowed ground and you won't be far from your family. Please, Gabby." He extended his hand once again. "Nolan would put me to the guillotine should anything happen to you."

Gabby looked away from the rectory windows and met Tomas's purposeful stare. He was only trying to help. But Grayson, a demon? Marie had to be wrong. Perhaps she'd lied to get Tomas, one of her guards, to leave. Could Marie have then overpowered Chelle?

"Fine. But I want to come back as soon as Luc arrives. I have to tell them about Nora." Good Lord, how would she explain about Nora?

Gabby took his hand and he pulled her up into the basket seat beside him. Tomas slapped the reins and the phaeton curled back onto the drive, through the hedgerow, and onto rue Dante. But instead of taking an immediate right to go around the block toward Saint-Julien, Tomas continued to go straight.

"Where are you going?" she asked, turning to look behind them.

Tomas slapped the reins to urge the horse onward. The winter wind bit at her scalp like a comb carved of ice.

"They're laying pavement at that end of the street," he answered, eyes firmly on the road ahead.

Gabby tried to recall seeing any workers laying pavement on rue Galande earlier that day.

"I don't think they are," she said.

Tomas hesitated. She watched his profile, lit every few seconds by the glow cast by streetlamps. His Adam's apple bobbed as he swallowed.

He's nervous, Gabby realized.

"It will only take an extra minute," he replied.

Gabby felt the lie rather than heard it. Tomas wasn't being truthful. She suddenly knew that she should never have left the rectory.

She should never have gotten into the carriage with Tomas.

Luc flew closer to the rooftops than he usually liked. The clouds over Paris were filled with snow and ice, and they'd left a frozen glaze on his wings. Beneath the clouds he'd been able to shake off the crust and fly faster.

He had but one block to go before he reached the abbey. He was glad he'd left the Ile de la Cité when he had. As he'd crossed over to the Left Bank, the cloying combination of two of his humans' scents hammered into him—Gabby's hibiscus and water lily along with the tart green apple scent of Gabby's lady's maid, Nora.

He automatically traced them to the rectory, on hallowed ground. They were both terrified of something. Luc tasted the cold metal of their fear in the back of his throat. The odd thing was, he'd felt no fear from Ingrid when he'd called up her scent. Instead, all he felt from her was a mix of concern and joy. No doubt in reaction to her twin's return. Luc wanted to see Grayson rather than just scent him. He was at the rectory, that much he knew. But how had he escaped the Underneath?

Another blast of hibiscus and water lily surfaced in Luc's senses with the power of a speeding locomotive. Nora's green apple promptly evaporated. Luc's trajectory slowed. He tried to call up the lady's maid's essence, but came up vacant once again. Just as he had with Grayson when he'd disappeared. And then again, with Bertrand. Something had happened to Nora.

He tucked his wings back to gain speed and then, moments later, the trace on Gabby shifted. She was no longer at the rectory. She was moving . . . Luc concentrated, and his sixth sense found her. She was on a street off of rue Dante. And she was afraid. Deathly afraid.

Damn.

He conjured Ingrid's scent once more, but she didn't need him. Her sister did. A sister so much like his own. He'd been too late to save Suzette. He'd avenged her, and it had cost him his soul. But he had still been too late.

He'd do anything and everything he could to spare Ingrid that kind of pain.

Luc hooked his right wing and swung around, following Gabby's trail.

CHAPTER TWENTY-THREE

"**T**ake me back."

Gabby waited for Tomas to respond, but he only directed the phaeton deeper into the labyrinth of streets. Shoddy buildings leaned every which way, their roofs steeply pitched. Alleys were gated off, and curtains were drawn against the night. "Tomas? Did you hear me? I want you to take me back to the rectory."

He stared straight ahead, tensing so the reins were close to his chest. "I'm afraid I can't do that."

The carriage rattled her to the bone as it bounded over the street. Gabby's teeth began to chatter.

"You're not taking me to Saint-Julien, are you?"

Tomas's grim expression stayed fixed. He didn't answer as he steered the phaeton to the left, onto a road that held a row of storefronts on one side and on the other, a giant construction pit. A tower crane loomed over the crater that had been dug out of the ground, heaps of soil, rock, and rubble rimming it.

"Where are you bringing me, then?"

She used the next lurch of the carriage wheels to cover the motion of her hand as she slipped it into her skirt pocket. She grasped the handle of the blessed dagger. Gabby didn't know how to use it, her only lesson having been instruction on how to de-limb appendius demons. And her teacher had just abducted her.

"You shouldn't be alone with him. You don't know him." Gabby had thought Nolan was overreacting, but maybe he hadn't been confident he could trust Tomas.

Tomas drove along the road, the ledge of the crater close enough for Gabby to spy a slope of gravel and rock inside.

"Tomas! If you don't answer me, I'll—" She bit off her threat.

Tomas laughed. "What, Gabby? What exactly will you do?"

He truly belonged on the stage. What an actor he'd make! He'd played her for such a fool.

He was still smirking when Gabby yanked the dagger from her skirt pocket, leaned over, and sank the blade deep into his thigh. She felt the tip of the blade pierce tendon and strike bone. Tomas screamed in agony and let go of the reins to deliver a back-hand slap across Gabby's cheek.

The force of the strike propelled her against the winged wicker side of the phaeton. The carriage lurched violently as the horse, spooked and confused, ran off the road and started for the rim of the crater. Tomas flailed for the reins he'd dropped, but it was too late. The phaeton's slim wooden wheels bucked over a mound of gravel and landed hard on the downward slope into the crater, tipping dangerously to the side. Gabby screamed as the impact sent her flying.

A brief moment of weightlessness in the air ended with a jarring crunch. She skidded over the rock rubble, the air pummeled from her lungs, and ground to a stop on her back. She lay still for a moment, uncertain that she was even able to move. From a distance came the distressed snuffles and whinnies of the horse. And a human moan.

Gabby slowly tested each limb. Other than sore ribs and a

burning scrape along her elbow, she seemed to have fared well. Crashing the phaeton had definitely not been her intent. But at least she'd done *something*.

She heard another moan and, searching the construction site, spied the overturned phaeton. The horse was still hitched to it, though the reins were a tangled mess. The wheels spun, the tasseled white umbrella snapped off and crushed like a moth's wings beneath the phaeton.

"Tomas?" Gabby called, fearful he'd lunge from behind one of the scores of steel beams crisscrossing the base of the crater, or from the pyramid of loose brick near what looked like an entrance to a cave.

"Here."

She barely heard the groan coming from the overturned phaeton. Gabby started across the uneven ground, imagining him crouched behind it, waiting to spring out at her.

But he wasn't.

Tomas lay flat on his back, on the dirt and rubble. The rim of the hard wicker seat had landed on his legs and now pinned them to the ground. He tried to sit up and belted out a short wail of pain. The entire weight of the phaeton pressed on his kneecaps.

"Help," he pleaded, his arms stretched toward his knees, fingers reaching. "Help push it off."

Even if she had had enough muscle to lift the phaeton—which she doubted—Tomas would be in no shape to come after her. She was certain both of his legs had been broken. But right then helping to free him was Gabby's only leverage.

"I will—after you tell me where you were taking me and why."

Before Tomas could respond, a piercing shriek came from the sky and a gargoyle landed on the steel chassis. The back draft of air from its wings knocked Gabby to the ground. The whole phaeton shook and creaked, rocking from side to side. Tomas screamed, his cry echoing like the report of a gun. The gargoyle's black wings spread over the length of the chassis like a pooling ink stain.

"Stop!" Tomas wailed. "Get off!"

Gabby pressed her palms into the sharp rubble and stood up, staring in wonder at the gargoyle.

"Luc?" she whispered.

The gargoyle lifted its eyes to hers. Pale jade cut through the night and she knew it was him. She wasn't Ingrid, and yet he'd come for her.

"Please, make him stop," Tomas begged her.

Luc didn't budge.

"Not until you explain where you were taking me," Gabby said.

A guttural sound ripped from the back of Tomas's throat. She shuddered just imagining the pain. Luc's gargoyle form had to have added at least another twenty stone to the weight of the carriage. Tomas breathed heavily, his scarred face pinched so severely it looked like a dried currant.

"Here, for Christ's sake, I was taking you here!" he growled, clutching at his legs. "I didn't want to hurt anyone! Not you, not Henri. It wasn't what I wanted, I swear to you."

Gabby listed to the side. "You killed Henri?"

Luc gave the chassis an intentional rocking. Tomas whimpered.

"No, I didn't kill him. I didn't." He heaved for air. "René was stronger. Henri wasn't his human; he wasn't anyone's human. René could do it without the angels caring, without any other gargoyle caring."

"But why? What did he do to deserve it?" Gabby asked.

"He found out." Agony corded the muscles along Tomas's neck. "The battle with the appendius demon. The one that scarred me. Do you remember how I told you I destroyed it?"

Gabby did. She also remembered the way she'd allowed

Tomas to guide her hand, the way he'd whispered instructions in her ear. She was so angry at being led like a little, eager lamb that she wanted to pound on the phaeton herself.

"I lied," he said. "I didn't destroy it. I lost the battle and it took me . . . it took me to the Underneath."

She walked closer to the wheels and gripped one of the smooth, lacquered spokes, ending its slow rotation. "And you escaped?" she asked, thinking of all the times Nolan and Vander, and even Tomas, had treated the Underneath as a vast, mysterious, and deadly realm. "But how?"

"I struck a bargain with a woman there. No, not a woman," Tomas corrected himself. "An angel. A fallen angel, named Axia. She said if I helped her, she'd command one of her hellhounds to take me back to the surface of the Earth. She'd let me go fast, before the demon poison in my veins spread and no amount of mercurite could save me."

"What did she want help with?" Gabby asked.

Tomas swallowed hard. "Finding pure-blooded girls. Leading her hounds to them. She wanted them for something—something having to do with transfusing her own blood, to make herself more human, able to walk the earth. If I refused Axia's offer, I'd be left to the mercy of the appendius that bested me." Tomas rolled his head to the side so he could gaze up at Gabby. "I didn't have a choice."

Gabby hardened. "Of course you did."

He flashed his teeth in a sneer. "You wouldn't be so brave if you were faced with that slow, agonizing death. The appendius would have skinned me alive. It would have devoured me piece by piece, taking time to digest between meals. No, I didn't have a choice."

A death like that *would* have been impossible to brave. Gabby didn't even want to imagine the pain. The suffering. But a task like the one the fallen angel had given Tomas would have been a slow death as well.

"You made a bargain with a demon, just like René," Gabby said.

Tomas closed his eyes. His glasses had been lost in the tumble down the crater slope.

"No. I accepted Axia's offer, and then René accepted mine after I discovered he and Marie's . . . *affaire.*" He screwed up his face at another lashing of pain. "I saw the opportunity for what it was."

Gabby understood. "You had René lure the girls to the hounds so you wouldn't have to."

He pursed his lips in accord.

"Axia didn't really promise him release from the Dispossessed, did she? You lied to convince him to help you."

Tomas looked at her, lips thin and nostrils flaring. "It didn't take much to sway him. René was desperate. He wanted freedom like no gargoyle I've ever met. I did what I had to. Look at me, Gabby. Do you really think any decent girl would have left her comfortable home late at night to meet someone like me?"

I would have, Gabby thought. After she'd seen past the scars. Before she'd been exposed to his cold, cowardly soul.

"And Axia. She wanted me as well? Is that why you brought me here?" Gabby asked.

The cave, dug out of one side of the crater, had definition now that her eyes had adjusted to the dimness. It was a perfectly arched entrance, neatly bricked around the rim—similar to the underground railway entrances in London. It would explain the steel rails and beams and the mounds of crushed ballast. They were building a new Métro stop here.

"Axia doesn't want you," Tomas answered, his teeth grinding in agony. "Grayson does. The new Grayson, anyway."

Gabby looked up at Luc, who was crouched on the carriage, as still as a stone statue. Thick black plates covered him from head to foot. His talons clung to the chassis as he leaned forward, wringing out another tormented scream.

She turned back to Tomas. "But you were lying to me about Grayson being a demon."

Tomas's cry wound down into little yelps. "I wasn't lying," he wheezed. "Axia is testing him. You're part of his test. You're his reward."

Gabby backed away from the phaeton's wheel. The sound of that last word—*reward*—crawled down her spine and made her shiver.

"What does that even mean?" she whispered.

Darting motion filled her peripheral vision. Gabby twisted around, searching the slope of the crater until she saw two black shapes at the rim, their eyes red as coals.

Gabby reached into her skirt pocket for the blessed blade, but her fingers fumbled around a vacant space.

"The knife!" she cried. It wasn't still impaling Tomas's thigh. It could have been anywhere between the road and the phaeton.

With a battle shriek, Luc launched himself from the chassis. The hellhounds streaked down the rim of the crater, straight toward them. Luc could only fight one of the beasts at a time. The other would be left to Gabby.

And her hands were empty.

CHAPTER TWENTY-FOUR

"**H**asn't the doctor arrived yet?" Ingrid's mother asked as she blew into the sitting room like a tempest wind.

Ingrid still sat on the sofa cradling Grayson's feverish head. His sweat had soaked the pink-orchid silk of her dress straight through to her petticoats, leaving streaks of dirt on her lap.

"Not yet," Ingrid answered. The clock said they had only been waiting for ten minutes.

Their mother came over and peered down at Grayson. She stroked the same soothing path across his forehead and into his hairline that Ingrid's hand had been taking.

Something wasn't right. Not just his fever and ragged appearance, but the expressions playing out on the surface of his face. As Ingrid had watched him sleep, his features had rippled with changing emotions—from fright to sadness to lascivious humor. And Ingrid could feel none of it. No echoes of anxiety, no prickling tears, no urge to smile or laugh as she normally would have when her twin was feeling these things. It was as if the invisible nerve connection, or whatever it was that had always linked them together, had been severed.

"He's sleeping," Ingrid whispered.

He'd closed his eyes just after Gabby had fled from the sitting room, whatever he'd needed to say to Ingrid forgotten. She'd felt his rhythmic breathing soon after. He'd cried out a few times as he'd slipped into unconsciousness, his screams loud enough to wake the dead in the abbey's cemetery plot. Ingrid had thought she'd heard echoes of his screams, but her ears had been ringing and her nerves jumping. She'd expected Gabby to come rushing back in after that, but she hadn't. Grayson had injured her with his dismissal.

Grayson and Gabby had never been close, but this was the first time he'd been truly cutting. It was his delirium. His fever. Ingrid was sure of it.

Lady Charlotte Brickton's hand made another pass over his forehead. Grayson's eyes opened. He slapped his mother's gentle fingers aside. She croaked and staggered backward.

"Ingrid? Ingrid?" Grayson cried, blindly looking about as if he couldn't see her face right above his.

"I'm right here." She tried to restrain his flailing arms. "Right here. You're safe now, Grayson. You're home."

Their mother recovered and went to the sideboard, returning with the glass of water Gabby had set aside earlier. She held it to Grayson's mouth and water streamed past his lips. He gagged and choked, turning his head to the side to spit it out. He snatched the glass from their mother's hand and with a growl hurled it overhead. She screamed as the glass narrowly missed a window and shattered against the wall.

"Water? *Water?*" he bellowed, surging up from Ingrid's lap. He propped his hands on the edge of the sofa cushion and leered toward their mother. He arched his back and rolled his shoulders the same way a frightened, hissing cat would have.

Their mother's parted lips trembled as she backed away, eyes glistening. One of her hands caught up the lace around her dressing gown's collar, the other covering her cheek as though Grayson had slapped her.

"You're raving, my darling. You should drink something," she said, her normally commanding voice feeble.

"I don't want water," Grayson growled, his teeth bared.

Ingrid touched his sleeve timidly. "Then tea, perhaps? Mama is right, you need to—"

"No!" he barked.

Their mother jumped and kept backing toward the drapes. "I'm going to fetch my laudanum," she said to Ingrid. "Keep him calm."

She scurried through the drapes, no doubt planning on taking a teaspoon of the tincture herself. A dose of it would make Grayson relax, if anything could. Ingrid might even need a sip.

He collapsed against the back of the sofa in a slovenly kind of slouch. It was a posture Lord Fairfax, future Earl of Brickton, would never have allowed himself before. He ran a hand over his face.

"Grayson, you should lie down," Ingrid said. Her brother was so out of sorts. The way he'd barked and lunged at their mother had frightened her.

"Ingrid, come with me," he said.

She leaned across the cushion toward him, as far as her stays allowed. "Go with you where?"

"You're in danger," he mumbled, his eyes closing once again. The fever gripped him. What was keeping the doctor? And Gabby—Ingrid glanced toward the drapes. Was she still waiting outside?

"I know I'm in danger," Ingrid said, setting a timorous hand on Grayson's shoulder. "But we're safe here. It's hallowed ground. No demon can touch us."

He laughed. It was short and caustic.

"That's just the thing." He rested his head on the back of the sofa, looking as though he might doze off again. "This demon *can* touch you on hallowed ground, because a part of it is human. Isn't that something? Isn't that remarkable?"

He rolled his head, repeating *remarkable* over and over. He had to be imagining things. If she could clear her head, then maybe she would be able to sense what was going on inside of him. She supposed it was similar to the way Luc sensed her. Had he picked up on Grayson's presence yet? He would have been checking in on her, Ingrid was certain of it. Knowing he could, no matter where he was in Paris, set her mind somewhat at ease. It gave her the sense that she was never truly alone.

"I don't know what kind of demon you mean, but, Grayson—" She stopped. Arguing with him while he was in this condition was pointless.

"Come with me," Grayson repeated. He cracked his eyes open to slits and found her. "Please, Ingrid."

She rubbed his arm, her palm slicking down a layer of dirt on his sleeve. "Of course I will."

Grayson lifted his head. His eyes came fully open. It was the answer he'd wanted, and now that he had it, it seemed to revive him. He caught Ingrid's wrist, plucking it off his sleeve. "Then we must go. Now. Before Mother returns."

With surprising agility and speed, he leaped from the couch, hauling Ingrid with him.

"No, Grayson! Mama's been worried to death about you. We can't just leave."

He kept pulling her toward the foyer. Ingrid dug in her heels, though the rug beneath her slipped along the wooden floor.

"Stop! We can't go anywhere, not right now. You need to—"

Grayson crooked his head and snarled at her. Ingrid shut her mouth and stared at his teeth. The top and bottom canines had grown longer. Sharper. The whites of his eyes were a new, fleshy red, the veins webbed and bloodshot. Ingrid yanked her arm back, but Grayson didn't let go. His hand was a shackle around her wrist, and when she looked at it, she saw more than just dirt and grime. Patches of greasy, yellowish fur fleeced his skin. His nails had pushed up from his cuticles into sharply filed tips. When she met her brother's snarl once again, what he'd said came back to her. She understood it now: *This demon* can *touch you on hallowed ground.*

Ingrid bit back a scream as more patches of fur hatched upon Grayson's cheeks and chin, as cartilage stacked up on his nose until it jutted out into a wrinkled muzzle and his brow became a shelf of thick fur over his bloodshot eyes. Ingrid wrenched back her arm, twisting it until her skin burned.

"What's happening to you?" she asked, praying their mother didn't walk in with the laudanum right then.

Grayson's now black, leathery lips moved, but instead of words, his throat emitted a vicious wet growl. He sounded like a dog. *Like a hellhound.*

His nails bit into Ingrid's flesh with finality and he continued to haul her toward the foyer. She had to stop him. Her blade and perfume bottle of blessed water were still in her handbag in the foyer. Ingrid let up on her resistance and he jerked her through the drapes. She spied her beaded reticule lying on the elliptical table beneath the mirror. It was too far from the front door. She wasn't going to be able to get to it.

The drapes to the dining room flashed open and Maureen, her mother's lady's maid, stepped into the foyer with a tea service. The instant she saw Grayson's mutated face she let out a bloodcurdling scream and launched the tea service at him. His reflexes kicked in and he released Ingrid's arm to intercept the flying silver tray.

Ingrid dove toward her reticule and snapped open the clasp. Her hand landed on the netted atomizer just as Grayson pinched his claws around her other wrist, puncturing her skin. As Grayson whipped Ingrid back toward him she lifted the bottle and crushed the atomizer in her palm. A wide, misting spray blasted into Grayson's face. He recoiled, and for a terrifying moment, Ingrid feared the water was harmless. But then thin tendrils of steam snaked up from the patches of pale yellow and white fur. His skin began to sizzle and pop, and a high, keening wail replaced his husky growling. He let her go so he could cower and clutch his face.

Ingrid wasted no time. She ran outside and started across the lawn of the churchyard. She had to get to Gabby. Had to warn her. But if hallowed ground no longer promised safety, where else could they go? She looked to the night sky as she stumbled over the crust of snow, hoping to see Luc and the grotesque sight of his wings, his changed body. But there were just stars and clouds and a thin sliver of moon.

"Ingrid?"

She looked down in time to avoid a collision with a birdbath. Two figures were coming through the break in the hedgerow. Vander and Nolan broke into a sprint but almost immediately slid to a halt. Their stare traveled past Ingrid to the front door, where Grayson had appeared.

Or at least, *she* knew it was Grayson. He had to have been unrecognizable to Vander and Nolan, who tore back the flaps of their overcoats and extracted their blessed silver. Nolan carved at the air as he raised his sword into a defensive position. Instead of the sword he'd been carrying in the vineyard, Vander wielded a crossbow.

"No!" Ingrid lifted the bottom of her dress and ran in front of the crossbow. "Don't hurt him!"

Vander grabbed her arm and whirled her behind him. He kept his weapon aimed at the half-formed hellhound on the rectory doorstep.

"How did it get on hallowed ground?" Vander asked. Ingrid came forward, again positioning herself in front of the crossbow.

"Ingrid! Stay back!" Vander shouted.

"But it's Grayson!"

Vander nearly dropped his weapon. Nolan, however, kept his sword steady.

"That's impossible," Vander said.

Grayson had almost completely mutated. The yellow-white fur had come in fully on his head and face; his shoulders had broadened, stretching the seams of his shirt until long rips had partially separated the sleeves. His teeth had become miniature versions of a hellhound's slanted fangs.

The blessed water hadn't injured him permanently, only held him off for a few moments. Grayson came off the front steps of the rectory and fell forward onto his hands. He mimicked the stance of a dog.

Or perhaps he wasn't mimicking at all.

"What in God's name happened to him?" Vander whispered.

His arms had lengthened until his cuffs were just above his elbows. With arms and legs roughly the same length, Grayson's spine was a level plane instead of inclined. He looked like a territorial animal as he prowled restlessly at the front door, back and forth, back and forth. He looked so . . . so *wrong* using his hands like front paws, his arms like forelimbs.

"He's a hellhound," Nolan said without a trace of astonishment.

"He can't be," Ingrid whimpered.

"You're right," Vander said, his voice amplified by frustration and disbelief. "He's on hallowed ground and he hasn't burst into flames yet."

"But blessed water hurt him," Ingrid said. She then thought of something else: "Where is Gabby?"

Nolan's poise faltered as his trained gaze left Grayson's indecisive pacing. "She's not inside?"

Ingrid looked to the hedgerow. Had she gone back in through the kitchens? Her stomach kinked into a knot of worry, made tighter by a scream that issued from the rectory door. By the time Ingrid had turned around, her mother was already halfway to the foyer floor in a dead faint, the bottle of laudanum still clutched in her hand.

Nolan looked to the sky. "Gargoyles," he said just seconds before two winged creatures touched down on the snowy lawn in front of them.

Ingrid's heart took a dive. Neither of them was Luc. But she did recognize the cinnamon-colored scales on one. That gargoyle had landed right in front of her during the first hellhound attack. The other was a strange breed, with the body of a lion and the head of an eagle. Its wings were feathered instead of scaled. Ingrid remembered seeing something like it in Vander's book.

The strange gargoyle whipped its lion's tail as it advanced on Grayson. Her brother had arched his back, hackles raised along the furry bulk at the nape of his neck.

"Stop!" Ingrid moved forward over the snow. "Leave him alone! He's human!"

The cinnamon gargoyle curved at the waist and lifted its thin, membranous wings to look back at her. Its brilliant amber eyes roved over her with what felt like slow, burning insolence. Ingrid stepped back. Those eyes were alarmingly familiar.

"Grayson's not human, Ingrid. Not anymore," Nolan said.

She rounded on him. "Of course he is! He's my brother. I don't care if he's been turned into some sort of half demon—he's still Grayson and I'm not going to let anyone hurt him!"

That was when she felt the first spark. It fired from her shoulder. Then a second, matching spark from her other shoulder. They rained down through her arms, past the bends of her elbows, feeling like shooting stars trapped within her skin.

And it hurt. Bloody *hell* did it hurt.

The lion-tailed gargoyle struck first, using its tapered beak to rip into her brother's arm. His sleeve, hanging by threads to begin with, tore off, exposing an arm fully enveloped in fur, now streaked with vibrant blood. The cinnamon gargoyle hung back as the lion-tailed one dove toward Grayson again. Her brother lunged off the ground and made a panicked lash with his clawed hand. The gargoyle knocked him to the blood-speckled snow with a single sweep of its forelimbs.

"No!" Ingrid screamed again.

The two gargoyles continued to circle Grayson. He was half their size, nowhere near that of a normal hellhound. Whatever Grayson was, he was no threat to them. But Luc and Vander had already made it perfectly clear that to the Dispossessed, a demon was a demon, and demons needed to be destroyed.

Ingrid pushed on Vander's arm until he lowered the crossbow. "They're going to kill him. Do something. Stop them!"

He knitted his brows, not needing to tell her that he could do no such thing. Coming between a gargoyle and a demon would likely lead to a quick death. Ingrid didn't want Vander to risk himself.

She ground her teeth as more sparks of pain rocketed down her arms, toward her hands. One spark set off another, then four more, then a dozen. They continued to ignite, growing by exponential numbers, until the searing fire of a live electrical charge filled her. Ingrid knew that when it finally exploded from her fingertips, the lightning was going to be more powerful than ever. She didn't need Vander or Nolan to stop the two gargoyles—*she could do it herself.* She wasn't going to lose her brother a second time.

But the brilliant threads of lightning refused to branch from her fingers. As the cinnamon gargoyle shredded Grayson's shirt and chest with its talons, an odd sensation seized Ingrid. She felt like she was growing taller and wider, inflating like a hot-air balloon. Bursts of electricity detonated in her muscles and veins, making her feel swollen and scorching hot. She stopped breathing as her feet rose off the ground.

And then a shock wave of ice chased out the blistering heat.

Ingrid arched her spine as the hot torture of the last minute ended. Blessed, immeasurable release. She'd never felt such overwhelming mercy.

Ingrid opened her eyes to a blinding white glare. She squinted against the light that had suddenly made the churchyard look like a radiant night carnival. There was silence. Complete silence, and when Ingrid's vision finally adjusted to the glaring light, she saw that everything had stilled.

Her brother was in a guarded stance on all fours. His ears, mutated into wolfish tips, had flattened. Both the cinnamon and feathered gargoyles had dropped to the snow, their wing tips just as low to the ground as their heads. They'd abandoned their attack on Grayson to sink into reverent bows aimed in her direction. What were they doing?

Ingrid turned to find Vander and Nolan bathed in the pearlescent light, but they had backed away from her. Neither of them bowed, yet they were staring at her with expressions of wonder.

"What is it?" Ingrid asked, but her voice was different. It was deep and shuddering—and not her own. She whipped up a hand to cover her mouth, and the glaring white light blinded her again. She tried to shield her eyes, and that was when she saw that it would be impossible to escape the light. Because it was coming from her.

Incandescent beams streamed from her fingertips as if she were Prometheus giving mortals the fire he'd stolen from Zeus. But the light wasn't just coming from her hands. It shone from every part of her, every pore, every strand of hair. Her sleeves glowed; her bodice and skirt illuminated her surroundings like a seaside beacon. Shafts of light flowed out from beneath her dinner gown, casting a wide halo over the ground.

Ingrid couldn't breathe; the mercy she'd felt just moments before now shriveled into a state of panic. The gargoyles bowed to her the same way Luc and Marco and the other Dispossessed had submitted to her in Lady Ormand's courtyard.

Marco. The cinnamon gargoyle's amber eyes, its insolent stare—they had belonged to Marco. His gargoyle form wouldn't look up. Perhaps he couldn't look up. Luc had said she'd held some sort of control over them. But before, she hadn't glowed as brightly; now, she was like a hot filament within an incandescent lightbulb.

Grayson crawled toward the side of the rectory, his body smeared with blood. The gargoyles tensed their wings as if they sensed their enemy's retreat. But they remained doubled over, a position that Ingrid felt—no, *knew*—she controlled. The gargoyles, and only the gargoyles, it seemed, were bending to her will. But how was she doing this? Her light began to ebb as she saw Grayson bound into the darkness between the rectory and the carriage house, toward the cemetery plot and, farther back, the grounds of Saint-Julien-le-Pauvre. *He's gotten away.*

Ingrid felt the ground rush at her. She hit it like a sack of flour, the numbness of her body giving over to a dull, exhausted ache. Her power over the gargoyles shattered. They erupted from the ground, soaring into the air over Ingrid, Vander, and Nolan. The wings on the cinnamon gargoyle folded in and Marco fell toward the ground, shifting from gargoyle to man before he landed, and before Ingrid could wobble to her feet.

"What are you?" Marco stormed toward her, his bared body thankfully draped in midnight. The sudden loss of radiant light had ruined her vision.

Vander came to Ingrid's side. "Stay away from her."

Marco regarded Vander as he would a narrowly avoided pile of manure. "Don't get courageous with me, Seer." He redirected his amber eyes, as luminous as Luc's green ones, at her. "I want to know what you are."

Ingrid wanted to know the same thing. She tried to say as much, but the muscles along her jaw were too slack, too tired, to cooperate.

"We don't have time for this," Vander said, obviously not at all threatened by Marco. "Ingrid, I'm taking a horse from your stables and following Grayson's dust trail while it's still fresh."

Ingrid forced a measure of strength back into her posture. "I'm coming with you."

Vander didn't object. The safety of hallowed ground had been put to the test and had received a failing mark.

"And Gabby?" Nolan asked, his sword still drawn. "Where is she?"

Ingrid searched the entrance to the rectory, hoping to see her sister inside, fanning their unconscious mother's face. But it was just Cherie, Maureen, and Madam Bertot at her side. Maureen held one of her mistress's limp hands, and Cherie and the cook were watching the display on the front lawn with glazed expressions of shock.

"She was waiting for the doctor outside," Ingrid answered, her chest beginning to feel too small. "I told her to stay on hallowed ground. I *told* her."

Vander turned to Nolan and in a low voice said, "The shattered lamp we saw on the curb."

The tip of Nolan's sword sliced into the ground as he let it fall. "The hellhound dust."

The words landed in Ingrid's gut with the force of a fist. "No." Oh, God no. *No, no, no.* Not Gabby.

Marco snorted. "Where is your dear Luc now, Lady Ingrid?"

Nolan lifted his coat panel and sheathed his sword. "He's gone after Gabby."

Yes. Ingrid's pulse rebounded. She struggled for breath. Yes, of course! Luc had gone after her. That was why he hadn't shown up at the rectory. He was busy protecting Gabby. Busy saving her. He had to be. Ingrid couldn't accept anything else.

Nolan took two quick strides and stood before Marco. "Are you able to help us locate Luc?"

Ingrid's eyes had adjusted a little and she saw more of Marco than the dark outline of his unclothed figure. His chest and arms were heavy with muscle, his toned abdomen narrowing in toward the waist. Ingrid's eyes bounced up to his face, where she saw the white of his teeth as he smiled.

"If a hellhound got her on the curb, you're wasting your time. Luc was wasting *his*. She's already dead."

"Don't say that!" Ingrid wanted to shove him for emphasis, but kept her hands to herself.

"She's dead," he repeated, then spread his arms wide in revelation. "Apparently, your commands are only mandatory when you glow."

Marco closed in on her, completely unbothered by the fact that he wasn't wearing a stitch of clothing. He didn't say anything, just cocked his head and inspected her face. He was too close. Too intense. She felt his heat radiating off her own skin and she leaped back a step.

"Lennier would want you to help us," Vander said, inserting himself between Marco and Ingrid.

Marco's bare feet crunched on the snow as he backed up a pace, coolly regarding Vander once again. "Do not speak as if you know what Lennier would want," he sneered. "You will follow the half-breed's dust and Yann and I will search for Luc." Marco took a bow as if he'd just granted their wish. He brought his eyes up to meet Ingrid's. She was adjusting to the darkness and was beginning to see more swaths of his skin. And yet, she couldn't look away from him. "You cannot protect your brother forever, Lady Ingrid."

Vander ignored him and urged Ingrid toward the stables with a nod of his head. Nolan quickly overtook them as they made their way across the churchyard. Ingrid turned back toward the rectory's front door to tell the lady's maids and Madam Bertot to take care of her mother until the doctor arrived, but the cook had keeled over as well, leaving Cherie and Maureen to stare agog as Marco transformed back into a gargoyle. He and the feathered gargoyle ascended into the air and out of view.

CHAPTER TWENTY-FIVE

Grayson reached the construction site, the place the hooded one had instructed him to bring the girl.

He didn't have her.

He'd failed.

All he'd had to do was bring the girl there and pierce her skin—just one small bite was all it was supposed to have taken. One bite and they both would have been able to return to his master. And then, finally, Grayson would have been rewarded.

He wanted his reward. He craved it.

But he wasn't going to get it now. The grounds around the abbey had rejected him the second he'd set foot on them. Scorching heat had washed over his soles as he'd walked up to the rectory and pounded on the front door. The pain had sealed itself inside his skin and quickly climbed through him, clinging like thorns of fire. Burning even beneath his eyes.

And he'd remembered her. He'd known the girl and he hadn't

wanted to hurt her. But even more so, he hadn't wanted to disappoint his mistress. He'd tried to take her. He'd tried and failed.

How would she punish him?

A whine slipped from Grayson's throat and his frantic eyes skittered over the crater in the ground. He felt better here. The sacred fire had left him. He walked the way he yearned to walk, on all limbs instead of only two. Below him, two of his mistress's pets were closing in on another one of the gargoyles. There was an overturned carriage, a man on the ground, and next to him, a girl.

Grayson sniffed at the air and caught her scent. Saliva pooled inside his mouth. He was thirsty. So thirsty.

And he wanted his reward.

The phaeton landed on its wheels with a squealing crash. Luc had launched himself into the air to meet the hellhounds, rolling the carriage upright and freeing Tomas's pinned legs. Tomas lifted himself onto one elbow and followed Gabby's terrified gaze toward the crater's rocky slope, where the hellhounds were scrabbling down toward them. The beasts moved with the same sort of predatory stealth Gabby had once seen in the tigers at the London Zoo. Slow and purposeful. Deadly.

The horse hitched to the phaeton bucked and whinnied, then bolted in the opposite direction, up the slope to escape the crater.

Gabby felt Tomas grab at her hand. "Take it," he said as the cold handle of a silver blade pressed into her palm. Not the one she'd taken from Vander, but Tomas's own weapon. The one he'd taught her with in his room at Hôtel Bastian.

"What are you—"

"I can't move, Gabby. Defend yourself. Strike for the vitals—the heart, the throat, the brain."

Gabby stared at the blade, panic swelling. It was short, barely the length of her forearm. It was too small, too inadequate. How could she battle a demon with this? "I can't!" she cried.

Luc collided with one of the hounds, ripping into it with his talons. Their growls and shrieks drowned out Tomas's insistence that she *must*.

Gabby tightened her grip on the handle. *She must.* She'd die if she didn't at least try.

She turned to face the second hellhound. It was huge and black, its nose and jaws matted with saliva—and it was in midleap, coming through the air at her. Gabby did the first thing instinct ordered. She dove forward as the hound was coming back toward the ground. She slid along the gravel, straight under the beast's trajectory. Clasping the hilt with both hands, she rolled onto her back and held the blade high. The silver melted through the beast's rib cage as though she had sliced churned cream instead of flesh.

A gush of something gluey spilled from the hound's injured sternum. It was warm, vibrant green, and the moment it splashed Gabby's feet and skirt hem it started to bubble and fizz. The hound landed, listing to the side, green sparks showering from the wound. With a vengeful snarl, the hound made another advance.

Something vital, Tomas had said. But with a blade this size, there was no chance she could reach a vital organ unless she risked getting close. It didn't matter. She'd be close enough in a few seconds. The hellhound was coming for her.

She softened her locked knees and bent into a defensive crouch. The demon circled her, and Gabby rotated to match its path. Its red eyes burned brighter, hotter, and she knew it was registering something that surprised it: *The human is going to fight.*

The hound dropped into a crouch as well, its long tail, matted with fur, lashing eagerly. It circled, certainly not expecting her to make the first move. And so she knew exactly what she had to do.

Gabby ran toward it. The hound flinched in surprise before lunging. Again, Gabby dropped and rolled to the side as the hound's front paw came swiping through the air toward her head.

She kept her eyes rooted to that paw, and she thrust out her blade toward it. The silver ate through the hound's flesh and cartilage, cutting the appendage clean off.

The hound stumbled and roared, shambling to the side as it tried to regain its balance. And then a gust of air swept over Gabby's head. A pair of black wings dropped like a curtain in front of her, blocking her from the hound. Luc slammed into the maimed demon. He curled his taloned hands and feet around the beast's top and bottom fangs and ripped them out.

They continued to battle as Gabby searched the crater. Tomas was dragging himself across the rubble, his legs limp and twisted behind him.

A flash of movement on the brick arch above the tunnel entrance stole her attention. The electric streetlamps lining the boulevard outlined the figure of an animal. It supported itself on all fours and was covered with a patchy layer of pale fur. Too large to be a dog, and yet too small to be a hellhound, the creature paced along the top of the bricks lining the tunnel's entrance. Its front and hind legs moved awkwardly, as if it had just learned to walk. And then Gabby noticed the clothing. The animal wore trousers and a torn and bloodied shirt.

As if the thing were actually a human.

Luc continued to beat back the defanged hellhound while Gabby stared in awe at the strange new creature. The clothing looked familiar, even at this distance. Its long tongue had been lolling out over a pair of jutting bottom fangs, but the moment it fixed Gabby in its sights, it reeled its tongue back in. The animal's pointed ears swiveled forward. And then, like gas jets in a theater, the creature's eyes flared with light.

They burned blood-red.

Green bark and tea leaves cut through the potent odor of rotted flesh and fur, distracting Luc just long enough to allow the hellhound to catch his thigh. The demon's claws raked trenches through Luc's thick scales before he could parry the attack. He spiraled into the air, leg aflame. It was the second time within the last few minutes of battle that a scent had distracted him long enough to get him injured. Ingrid had rushed up into his senses, her fear overpowering. Luc couldn't have left Gabby to face these hounds alone. He'd stayed with her, keeping Ingrid's scent with him, letting it tear into his chest as keenly as a hellhound's claw, as he'd been dragged back into the fight. Right now it was Grayson's scent turning his head.

Luc located him quickly, but it took another few seconds to understand what he was looking at. Ingrid's brother was atop the entrance of the new Métro tunnel, but he was no longer in human form. His skin was a patchy coat of fur, he stood on all fours, and the boy had fangs—the fangs of a hellhound.

Grayson's eyes flared red and he took a flying leap off the peak of the bricked tunnel. He lost his balance as he landed, but recovered fast. Grayson had a focus, Luc realized, and he moved like white smoke across the flat crater floor toward it: Gabby.

Luc flew toward them, but his injured leg burdened his flight. Grayson slammed into his sister, whose attempt to defend herself with the blessed blade had been too slow and unskilled. Equally unskilled, Grayson failed to close his teeth around Gabby's neck the moment he'd leaped on her, and it lost him the prize. Luc barreled into Grayson's back, pried him off with an easy pull, and hurled him into a mound of ballast.

He wasn't a hellhound. He didn't reek of one, and he was nowhere near the size of one. But his fangs were angled just the same, his eyes two round burning coals. And like a hellhound, Grayson vaulted up at Luc in a frenzied rage. He was clumsy, though. An uncoordinated swat of his clawed hand opened Grayson up for a rocking blow to his sternum. Luc took it, tamping him back down into the ballast.

Gabby screamed. *The other hellhound.*

Luc pivoted in the air in time to see the three-pawed hound twist its head and clamp its jaws around Gabby's middle. Luc had already ripped out its fangs, so the beast wasn't able to impale her and inject its poison.

That was Gabby's only godsend.

Even with one front paw missing, the hound galloped toward the dark tunnel entrance. Luc propelled himself after the hound, but something hooked the bridge of his left wing. It reeled Luc backward, spinning him out of the hellhound's path and sending him to the ground. Grayson's bestial form clambered atop Luc and he swung his head like a scythe, attempting to rake one of his fangs through the plates protecting Luc's chest. He was a pest, a Lilliputian hellhound. Luc hurled him off, but the hellhound carrying Gabby had already disappeared into the mouth of the tunnel.

Just then, Ingrid's scent spiked through him yet again. She was here.

CHAPTER TWENTY-SIX

Ingrid couldn't see the whorls of her brother's demon dust as she and Vander careened on horseback through the winding Saint-Germain streets. She didn't have to see it to know that Vander could. She could feel his sight in the corded muscles along his ribs and stomach, where she clung to him for dear life. He didn't slow as they approached a fork in the boulevard. He veered right, Nolan's horse loudly bringing up the rear.

They hadn't had time for saddles, so they rode bareback. Ingrid's legs straddled the horse's back in a thrillingly unladylike way, its short, bristly coat warm from exertion. Her blood had never pumped so hard or hot. She'd never felt so pressed for time. They had to find Grayson, had to help him. Had to stop him from hurting someone else. And Gabby. Tears pricked the backs of her eyes. She wanted to dig her heels into the horse's ribs and make the animal go as fast as Luc could fly.

Her worry for her sister, coupled with Vander's near-breakneck speed, made Ingrid's head spin, her stomach churn.

She closed her eyes and buried her face in Vander's back. Feeling her, his hand shot back and gripped her knee. The intimate touch chased the nausea away better than anything else could have.

Their horse turned onto a boulevard that curved around a huge crater dug out of the ground. The boulevard circled it, without a partition to stop so much as a pram from rolling over the edge and down the slope.

A scream sheared through the blare of the horses' hooves hammering the pavement.

Gabby.

Nolan overtook them, hurtling over the rim of the crater and disappearing from view. Vander pulled the reins, leaning back into Ingrid, until they came to a skidding halt at the rim. The crater was lit by the streetlamps well enough for them to see what was happening below.

Grayson was there, still transformed, and he'd hooked his claws into the fringe of a gargoyle's wing. Ingrid didn't need to be closer to see the gargoyle's jade eyes. She already knew his shape, the swarthy shade of his scales. They'd found her brother *and* Luc. But not Gabby.

"Stay up here," Vander ordered, and held out a hand to help her dismount.

"Not a chance," she said, her arms latching tighter around his torso.

"You're impossible, you know," Vander said, and urged the horse forward. Ingrid held on to him as they lurched over the rim and down the slope.

Below, Nolan gave Luc and Grayson's scuffling forms wide berth as he bent over Tomas, who was crawling across the ground. Luc plucked Grayson off his hulking chest and flicked him away as easily as he would a flea. Grayson landed in a pitiful heap. He looked rabid with his spotty patches of fur, frothing mouth, and now two glowing red eyes. He snarled as he lay stunned on the rocky ground.

Nolan dismounted and unsheathed his sword.

"Where is she?" he shouted to Luc, who purposefully glanced toward a yawning black tunnel entrance.

"The Métro," Vander translated. "With a hellhound. The dust leads in."

Ingrid swung her leg over the horse's haunches and vaulted to the ground. She started for the black cave. Her legs were sore from the thrashing ride, but she didn't care. If Gabby had been taken into the tunnel, she would follow. Ingrid hadn't believed she could fight a demon before, but now, she almost looked forward to it. She'd do whatever it took.

"Ingrid!" Vander shouted at the same moment she noticed a white blur coming up on her right. *Grayson.*

A black mantle of wings closed like a husk around her. Luc's chest slugged into her back, buffeting the air from her lungs. His leaden arms folded her against him and they pitched forward, Ingrid's feet sweeping off the ground. She heard a catlike yowl as they pushed against gravity, rising higher above the crater. Pain lanced through Ingrid's shoulder—a phantom pain. A sensation she'd felt so many times that she instantly knew what it meant: the connection with her brother had come back.

Ingrid thrashed. "Stop! Put me down, Grayson's been hurt!"

Luc's wings beat the air, suspending them. Locked in his powerhouse of a grip, Ingrid could see her brother on the ground with a silver dart in his shoulder, his legs and feet digging into the dirt as he writhed in agony. Tomas lay a little farther away, his legs in a wretched state. Nolan disappeared into the mouth of the Métro tunnel, and Vander fitted another blessed silver dart into his crossbow. He'd shot Grayson.

"Vander, no!" Ingrid screamed.

He looked up, the streetlight reflecting off his glasses. His mouth was a severe slash across his face, his lips taut. He kept his weapon aimed, even as Grayson's fur began to slough off in brittle yellow clumps. His fangs withdrew into his gums, and when he opened his eyes, the red coals were gone. His blue eyes were back, fierce with torment.

"Luc, please, put me down. Look at him!" Ingrid begged, the rise and plunge of Luc's wings and body calling up the nausea she'd felt earlier.

Another grating scream resounded from the tunnel. It shuddered through Ingrid, and she felt Luc's muscles tense, too. His instinct was calling him toward Gabby. She needed him.

"Go! You have to go after her, Luc."

He held steady in the air. The coiling of his muscles and the shivering of his scales were physical proof that he was fighting the urge to go after Gabby.

"Luc," Ingrid whispered. "Think of your own sister. You said you had one. I know it was long ago, but *please*. What would you do if it were her?"

An aggravated breath gusted from his snout and he finally descended. Ingrid stumbled as he set her on the ground, and she fell at her brother's side. She pushed her loose hair behind her ear, reminding her of earlier, when Luc had taken out her comb. When he'd kissed her. She looked up at Luc, who hesitated one more second before rising into the air and swooping into the tunnel.

She bent over her brother. "Grayson?" He was human again, the torn clothing and loose mounds of fur on the ground the only remnants of what he'd just been.

He grated his teeth—small, white teeth, not fangs. "What's happening, Ingrid?"

Vander stepped up behind Grayson's head, his crossbow still in hand. "I had to tag him."

She couldn't look at him. He'd done what he had to do, but she was still furious. "You could have killed him!"

"I aimed for the shoulder," Vander replied. "Trust me, if I'd wanted to kill him, he'd be dead." Ingrid had no doubt Vander's aim was that skilled, but she hated seeing her brother in pain. She'd hated seeing him as a demon, too.

"What's happening to him?" she asked, her hand fluttering indecisively around the silver dart sunk into the round bulge of his shoulder. She remembered the light that had streamed from her every pore, beams white as the driven snow. She remembered her power over Marco and the other gargoyle. "What's happening to me?"

Vander stood still and quiet. He let the tip of his crossbow lower toward the ground. He knew more about this hidden world of angels and demons and gargoyles than she did. If he couldn't answer her question, there wasn't a soul who could.

"It hurts," Grayson moaned. Sweat and dirt had darkened his fair hair to a dusty brown and matted it against his forehead. He looked worse than he had when he'd first arrived at the rectory. Twice as feverish, twice as filthy.

Her shaking hands grasped the cold, carved fletching at the end of the dart, and with a wince, pulled it free.

"Ingrid—wait!" Vander's voice registered beneath the wet slurp of the dart being exhumed.

But by then, Ingrid's mistake was clear. In less time than it took for her to drop the silver dart, Grayson's skin had checkered over with fur. His eyes steamed red, and wicked fangs erupted from his gums. He jackknifed up, Ingrid's arm fastened in the crook of his elbow. Her brother's fangs popped through silk and flesh and sank into her muscle. She screamed as heat torched her arm.

And then they were up, Grayson steamrolling forward as he threw Ingrid over his shoulder. She craned her head, saw Vander raise the crossbow, heard his frantic command for Grayson to stop. But then she was falling backward, her arms flailing overhead as Grayson dove forward. Ingrid expected her back to slam against the ground, but instead, she kept going. She kept falling, down, down, through what looked like a hole built of black ribbons of smoke. The sky, the construction site, even Vander's hoarse cries whirled away behind the ribbons.

The heat fired up her arm and boiled through her veins. It reached her face and colored everything she saw red.

The hellhound plunged through the black tunnel, tossing Gabby from side to side as it ran. It held her in its jaws, but the deadly fangs had been torn out. Thank God. Its remaining teeth cut through her dress and pierced her skin with every heaving stride. She could only imagine what damage those fangs would have done.

She was on her back, the hound's hot, wet tongue beneath her. Its jagged molars pinned her at the ribs and pelvis. Gabby tried to hold on to the crushing muzzle but it was slimed with spit and mucus, and she refused to release her grip on the blessed dagger. She hadn't dropped it when the beast had snapped her up like a doll and she wouldn't drop it now.

The demon kept at it, curving through the tunnel as if it knew where it was going. Gabby screamed as the hound's jaws tensed, its molars digging in until she felt the sickening crack of one rib, then another. Tears stung her eyes. She teetered on the verge of panic, but then slowly, slowly, came back to her senses.

Panic would get her nowhere.

She'd already taken one of the beast's paws—each ungainly, lurching step was a testament to the lost appendage. Gabby wasn't going to get any closer to the beast than she was at that moment, but it had her in such an awkward position. She couldn't twist to stab at its throat, and its heart was far out of reach. She wouldn't have been able to see what she was doing anyway. The only brightness in the tunnel came from the hound's crazed red eyes. They flickered like hearth coals, and Gabby wondered if they actually were lit by fire.

Her palm, clammy and cold, tightened around the handle of the knife. It wouldn't be a killing blow, but Gabby would take anything. At least she knew the beasts weren't immune to pain.

She brought her arm up, angled the knife, and sank the blade to the hilt in one of the red globes.

The hellhound's jowls sprang open and the beast roared in anguish. Its remaining front paw plowed into the tunnel floor, bringing it to a halt. Momentum propelled Gabby out of the hound's mouth. She landed hard against an unforgiving surface but launched herself to her feet. She scoured her hands along the rough tunnel wall, following it blindly. The hound's remaining eye flashed into view and out again as it whipped its head around, trying to dislodge the knife she hadn't been able to hold on to. The blessed silver had to hurt; green sparks were spitting out of the wound.

The green flares lit a flickering path, glinting off the steel rails laid into the ground. The rails would lead her out, but first she had to slink past the flailing hellhound. It crashed and thumped against the tunnel walls, growling as its single front paw swiped clumsily for the blade. Ignoring the tight pain in her ribs, Gabby made it past the writhing demon and picked up her pace. She combed one hand through the rock and dirt of the tunnel wall and held the other out before her. Away from the hound's hot, rancid breath, the air was cool and damp.

"Gabby!" A muffled voice echoed through the tunnel.

She slowed. The voice had drifted from behind her, back in the direction of the struggling hellhound. Dread filled her, her lungs heavy as lead. That voice. *Nolan?*

"Lass, where are you?" the voice bounced off the tunnel walls and vibrated against her eardrums.

It *was* Nolan, and if he kept on, he'd cross paths with the hellhound. Gabby started back the way she'd come, but stopped. How had Nolan gotten ahead of them? He hadn't even been at the construction crater to begin with. She slid her heel back. She recalled Luc's warning in the vestry: *"They lure you by using the voice of someone you trust."*

Could that be what this was? A delusion demon? She was

wasting precious time vacillating. No. She was being tricked. It couldn't be Nolan. Gabby stumbled back into motion, her fingertips barely brushing the walls as she ran, lungs wheezing and thirsting for air. She didn't have time for caution. She had to get to the mouth of the tunnel. She had to—

A blow to her back sent her tumbling forward. The heels of her palms plowed the loose ballast, her elbows and knees scraping through the sharp rubble. Her shoulder connected with a steel rail set in the tunnel floor.

The hellhound panted overhead. Its breath reached down like a licking tongue. Each torrid gust fanned her hair and scorched her skin. Gabby rolled onto her back, a deep ache blossoming in her shoulder. The demon's remaining eye blazed through the darkness. It was no longer a round, angry red globe, but the narrow shape of a sickle.

Agony exploded across Gabby's face as the hound's claw raked her flesh. Her head hit the steel edge of the railroad tie and she lay stunned in a motionless heap. She couldn't breathe. Couldn't move. Pain—blunt, undiluted pain—drilled into her, flooded her, until her lungs finally kicked to life. She sucked in air, and though she didn't think it possible, the pain got worse.

Hot, sticky liquid ran down her face—blood. *Her blood.* She gagged as it streamed through her lips and into her mouth, the hound's foul breath chasing up her nostrils. The demon leered over her, making gurgling sounds that sounded like rumbles of laughter.

Gabby moaned, afraid to reach up and cup her face. To feel what the beast had done to her. It hurt. God in heaven, it hurt. Gabby cried out, unleashing the sob that was lodged in her chest.

"Gabby!"

The hellhound's growling clamped off. It stayed silent as another shout for Gabby rang through the tunnel.

Nolan. The *real* Nolan?

Gabby felt footsteps reverberating through the steel railroad beam, the cadence pounding along the base of her skull. It wasn't a delusion demon this time.

"Nolan." Her voice came out a whimper. Blood dripped down her throat, and her hacking cough bounced off the tunnel walls.

She forced her eyes open, and with hazy, uneven vision, saw the beast's eye straining through the dark. It wasn't looking at her.

Down the track, the approaching footsteps skated to a stop on the gravel.

"She got you, did she? Good girl," Nolan said to the beast, his fury a living, breathing thing. It was an animal all its own. "Now come try your best with me."

Gabby imagined what Nolan must look like. His silver sword poised, his ferocious eyes narrowed, taut muscles pulsing along his jaw.

The hellhound's paws scrabbled over the tunnel floor and it heaved itself toward Nolan's voice. Sounds, amplified in the darkness, were all Gabby had to piece together what was happening. A grunt of force from Nolan's throat, the cool chime of air rushing over a silver blade, a short, panicked choking sound from the beast, and then the scattering of gravel as the demon's massive form buckled and fell. An explosion of green sparks lit the tunnel before fizzling back to blackness.

It had happened so fast. The hellhound's rotting stench was gone on Gabby's next labored breath. Her cracked ribs ached, but they were stubbed toes compared to the agony along her face.

"Gabby?" Nolan called, the fear that she might not answer shading his voice.

She gathered as much strength as she could and tried to speak. Instead, she choked on more blood. Nolan followed the sounds, crawling on hands and knees the last few yards until his hands swept over her battered body.

"Oh, Gabby," Nolan murmured. "You're alive, lass. Thank God you're alive." He gathered her into his arms. They were so warm that gooseflesh flashed over her skin. She started to shiver.

"My face," Gabby moaned, the hot, coppery taste of blood coating her tongue. "It tore my cheek."

Nolan lifted them both from the tunnel floor. "You'll be all right, lass. I've got you now." He clutched her tight against his heaving chest and carried her through the tunnel, the wracking shivering she felt setting in more violently.

"Did it bite you?"

She tried to shake her head, but pain drilled through her and she stopped. "Just claws," she answered.

Before he could say anything, a grating shriek echoed through the tunnel and then the whisper of wings met them.

"She's been injured," Nolan said. After a few seconds' pause Gabby heard Luc's footfalls at Nolan's side. He'd shifted to his human form.

"Bitten?"

"No. She doesn't need your blood," Nolan said, not bothering to mask his disdain for the healing practice. "What happened? Why were she and Tomas even here?"

Luc snorted. "The Alliance seems to be having a little trouble with loyalty lately. You'll have to ask your record keeper why he brought Gabby here against—"

The rest of his sentence dropped to silence.

"What is it? Luc?" Nolan asked. He didn't receive a reply.

Gabby wanted to know what was happening, but Nolan's every step ricocheted through her head. She grated her teeth against the pain.

"We're out, Gabby," he whispered to her a few moments later. "I'm taking you to the hosp— Luc!"

Gabby cracked her eyes open and saw the gray night, the yellow-tinged fog circling the construction crater, Tomas still on the cold ground, legs useless behind him—and Luc holding Vander by the collar.

"*Where is she?*" Luc demanded, his fists curled in Vander's coat. Gabby saw Luc's bare arms and shoulders and knew to look no farther south.

"It was Grayson," Vander answered, his voice raised to meet Luc's challenge head on. "She pulled out the dart before I could stop her, and he shifted. He bit her."

Grayson? Shifted? Gabby turned her face away from Nolan's chest, his heart thrumming against her ear. She'd missed something. Something big.

"You let him bite her?" Luc growled.

Vander wrested his collar free from Luc's grip. "I didn't *let* him bite her. He moved too fast."

"Where is she, Vander?" Nolan asked, his chest rumbling against Gabby's ear.

"He—he took her through a fissure." Vander's voice cracked with despair.

Nolan's arms loosened slightly. "No."

Gabby wanted to ask what a fissure was. Where it led. How Grayson and Ingrid had come to be at the crater when they'd last been inside the rectory. But she couldn't stop shivering. Her head tipped toward Nolan's chest and her whole body felt like it was falling over the precipice of a cliff. Her ears rang with the high, shrill wind of a flute. From beneath it came Luc's scathing voice. "He's taken Ingrid to the Underneath."

Gabby left the edge of the cliff and went tumbling in the abyss. The whine of a flute drowned out Luc's voice. Maybe he hadn't said that part about the Underneath. Maybe that had been the first part of a nightmare. But as Gabby lost consciousness, she was clear enough to know she wasn't *entering* a nightmare.

She was leaving one.

CHAPTER TWENTY-SEVEN

Ingrid landed hard on the ground and everything went still. The jarring rise and plunge of her body, slung over Grayson's shoulder, had lasted ages, it seemed. The black ribbons of smoke had given way to flickering, iridescent blue and Ingrid had needed to close her eyes to block the stuttering bright lights.

He bit me.

Ingrid stirred on a hard-packed surface, her head throbbing, her arm burning.

Grayson bit me.

"I hoped you would not fail."

A woman's voice jerked Ingrid out of her stupor. She pushed herself up onto her elbows. Through the pulsing blue-black light, she saw a dark-cloaked figure. The woman's face, deep within the cloak's hood, couldn't be seen.

Her brother lay shivering at the woman's heels, his body curled into a fetal position. All traces of fur and fangs were gone.

He looked like her twin again. His skin glistened with sweat, his teeth chattered.

"What have you done to me?" he whimpered, his face contorted into a mask of devastation. "What have I done?"

Ingrid got her hands beneath herself and tried to push herself up. Her head spun, the pulsating light throwing her off balance. She crashed back to her elbows.

"There, there, my pet," the hooded woman soothed, crouching and scratching behind Grayson's ear. Ingrid watched her from the corner of her eye. "You have not done her any true harm. Her blood will destroy the poison you injected, just as your blood did when you first came to me. I am proud of you, Grayson Waverly. You have brought me my freedom."

Ingrid cringed at seeing Grayson lean into the woman's touch. At the blissful release of tension along his brow.

"Why did you bite me?" Ingrid asked, her throat raw and parched. The air was dry and hot. "Where are we?"

Grayson shot back from the hooded woman's touch and pressed himself against an earthen wall. Ingrid looked around and saw the ceilings were low and rough, the floor and walls all hewn from rock and dirt. Her brother huddled in the corner, rocking back and forth with his hands cradling his temples.

"Don't harm her," Grayson pleaded. "Not like you did the other girls."

The woman's laughter vibrated in Ingrid's eardrums. "Harm her? I would sooner slay all of my hounds than harm this precious girl."

The hooded woman seemed to glide when she moved toward Ingrid. Her robes, brushing along the floor, covered every inch of her. Ingrid would have wondered if a body filled the robes at all if she hadn't been able to see the barest of contours beneath.

"Rest easy, my pet. I no longer require my hounds to fetch me vessels of pure blood. The transfusions have made me just as human as this place made me demon so long ago."

Ingrid tried to sit up again, tried to follow what her brother and the woman were saying. *Not woman,* Ingrid thought. *Demon.* She was a demon. Her hounds had brought her pure-blooded girls and she had what? *Consumed* the blood? It had made her *human*? How was that possible?

Ingrid caught Grayson's crazed eyes from across the room. She could feel his fear. Her stomach cinched tight with it. The connection she'd thought broken had been bridged again. She wanted to crawl over and huddle beside him, but the hooded woman stood in Ingrid's path.

"You have turned out remarkably well, Grayson Waverly. You are nearly ready to lead the rest of my hounds, and I am nearly ready for the Harvest to begin," she said. Ingrid remembered Marie mentioning something similar. "Challenging the Angelic Order is no small task. I will need my blood to be strong. Stronger than that of any of the Order."

The hooded woman lowered herself to a crouch in front of Ingrid. The black void filling the hood was unnerving. It made Ingrid imagine her hand reaching in, deeper and deeper, yet feeling nothing—nothing at all.

"Do you not wish to know what I require from you, my precious girl?" the demon woman asked in a voice so saccharine it made Ingrid shiver. She didn't wait for Ingrid's reply. "My blood."

Ingrid curled her fingers into the dirt floor and prayed to wake up. This was a nightmare; it had to be. The kind you know you're in, but can't figure out a way to escape from. She couldn't be here, with this demon woman, with Grayson. Alone. *Without Luc.*

"You see, Ingrid Waverly, you have kept my blood safe for nearly eighteen years. And now"—the demon woman slid forward until she was inches away from Ingrid's face—"I want it back."

*　　*　　*

There were Dispossessed watching. Luc could feel their presence, even though the construction site was, for the most part, deserted.

The urge to pummel Vander Burke's face was almost impossible to repress. Grayson had bit Ingrid. Had escaped with her into the Underneath, and that worthless human Seer had stood by and watched it happen. If only Luc hadn't gone into the tunnel after Gabby. If only Luc had been able to decide what he'd wanted to do. He would have stayed with Ingrid. He would have blocked out Ingrid's pleas to go after her sister, her words persuading him to remember Suzette, and he would have held her aloft in the sky. He would have kept her safe.

Instead, she was gone. Gone to where Luc couldn't reach her. Couldn't feel her. He immediately tried to surface her scent. It wouldn't come. Her sweet grass and tilled earth, and the mysterious tang that had always driven into him like a punch in the gut. But now, nothing.

He wanted to hurt the Seer. He wanted to feel the satisfying crack of his knuckles against Vander's chin. Luc wanted to feel something other than the strange, draining sensation that he didn't understand.

But the eyes of Paris were watching. To show anger over a lost human, to lash out at an Alliance member, would only lead to rumors. By now, word was spreading fast about René's dalliance with a human. Luc had to handle his reaction carefully unless he wanted rumors about himself added to the fire.

"There's nothing we can do," Nolan said, the open gash along Gabby's cheek tucked against his chest. "I have to get Gabby to the hospital. Benoit's." He enlisted Vander's help to corral the horse.

"We can't just leave her in the Underneath," Luc said, though he knew the protest was absurd. Nolan spared him a sorry look as he mounted the horse and then accepted Gabby from Vander's waiting arms.

"We don't have a choice, Luc." Nolan took up the reins and eased the horse forward. He looked at Tomas, ashen-faced on the gravel. No longer trying to crawl away.

"Vander, take Tomas to Benoit's as well. Don't let him out of your sight. I have questions for him."

Nolan guided his horse up the slope of the crater and departed. Luc and Vander stood in silence, the space between them simmering with hostile energy.

Vander pulled open his jacket and hitched his crossbow into the leather straps tailored to hold it. He looked at Luc, then at the sky. "Put your scales back on."

Modesty. Such a human flaw. Luc followed Vander as he started toward Tomas's limp form. "There has to be a way."

Vander combed his fingers through his hair and spun around. "Do you think I want to leave her there? Do you really think that if there was anything I could do—" He bit off the rest of his sentence, taking a second to calm his fury. "There are too many unknowns. How would I find her? We know nothing of the terrain, the opposition. The only thing we do know is that we need demon poison in our veins and that once it enters our systems the clock starts ticking down. I'd be dead before I even started looking."

He continued toward Tomas, who lay watching them with glassy eyes.

"Demon poison wouldn't kill me," Luc said. It wasn't roses, but it wasn't deadly. Not to a Dispossessed.

Vander huffed a frustrated laugh. "Oh, so you're going to waltz into the Underneath, are you? You wouldn't get both wings through a fissure before a plague of demons turned you inside out." He kneeled beside Tomas, picked up his wrist, and measured his pulse. Vander twisted to look up at Luc, an accusation in his eyes. "And what about Grayson? He's your human, too. He's in the Underneath—*again*. What? No rescue mission for him?"

Luc kept his jaw tight. He hadn't considered Grayson. And earlier, when Grayson had been taken by a hellhound, Luc had simply accepted the loss of his human. He'd accepted the ridicule and waited for his punishment.

But this time, it was different. This time, it was Ingrid.

He felt it again. The draining sensation, like something important had started to pour out of him and he was unable to stem the flow. He was powerless against it.

What was he supposed to do, return to the rectory without Ingrid? Resume his post while she remained trapped in the Underneath, held captive by Axia for whatever reason the fallen angel had wanted her and Grayson to begin with? Luc wasn't bound to her. Not anymore. His responsibility to Ingrid had ceased the second she'd crossed into the Underneath. Any other gargoyle would have let it rest. And maybe, if she were any other human, Luc would have gladly done just that. But he couldn't. With *this* human, he refused.

"If it's demon poison you want, I can help," Tomas said. His voice wasn't more than a wheeze.

"How?" Vander asked.

"You didn't hear his confession earlier," Luc said, not feeling a shred of pity for the record keeper over his crushed legs. "René and Marie aren't our only traitors."

Vander dropped Tomas's wrist. "You—?"

Tomas's gnarled face twisted with even more pain as he raised himself to his elbows. "I'll answer to the Alliance soon enough. But the longer you take to go after Ingrid, the worse chance you'll have at finding her alive." Tomas fumbled for a pocket sewn into his coat's brocade lining. He brought out a small vial. "Take some of the poison. All you have to do is ingest it. Your bloodstream will pick it up fast."

Vander glared at him. "You've done this?"

"I have," Tomas answered with a note of shame.

"But how? No Alliance member has ever gone into the Underneath and come back."

Tomas rolled the small vial between his fingers, focusing on that instead of Vander's face. "Well, now you know of one, don't you? I've taken the poison, just a dash. Enough to cross over, inform Axia of my progress, and then cross back. Finding Ingrid isn't impossible, Vander. The Underneath is nothing like the Alliance has always feared."

Vander eyed the small vial in Tomas's hand with new interest. "How much mercurite did you take after?"

He was going to do it, Luc realized. Vander was going to take the poison and rescue Ingrid. And if Luc was smart, he'd let him.

But Ingrid was *his* human.

Tomas hesitated while lowering himself back to the ground. He let out a sigh. "No mercurite. René cured me."

Vander recoiled from Tomas. "You accepted the blood of a gargoyle?"

"You think that is the worst of my crimes?" Tomas said, laughing grimly.

Luc saw his opening and moved forward to snatch the vial. Vander rounded on him. "Demon poison is forbidden to both of us, Luc. You could be cast out of the Dispossessed for taking it."

Luc felt the other Dispossessed watching him from the roof peaks and chimney stacks along the boulevard. Knew they were curling forward on their talons with anticipation. He uncorked the vial. "And why should that bother you, Seer?"

"The worst that can happen to me is removal from the Alliance," he explained. "It's a sight better than an eternity in hell."

Luc laughed. "Your concern is touching. Be careful—they might remove you from the Alliance just for showing it."

He tipped back the vial, and with one mere sip, fingers of fire began clawing their way down his throat. He swallowed them, nails and all, preferring this kind of pain to the kind losing Ingrid had brought him.

Luc corked the vial and held it out to Vander. "Join me if you want, Seer, but don't count on my blood to cure you once we're in."

Vander stared at the vial, his jaw working side to side as he calculated the risk. Without mercurite, without a gargoyle's blood, he'd be finished. Luc had the best chance of rescuing Ingrid, and Vander knew it. He didn't reach for the poison. Luc tossed it to the ground, beside Tomas.

"Now what?" Luc asked.

"There are fissures everywhere," Tomas replied, his voice weak. "This one is closest to Axia's hive."

Immediately, Luc saw a shivering black pool near the Métro tunnel. It churned with a milky purple current, its surface popping every few seconds with blue showers of static electricity.

"What do you mean by *hive*?" Vander asked, but Luc couldn't wait for Tomas to explain what only he knew of the Underneath. Luc felt a new chiming at the base of his skull, heard approaching shrieks. He had company.

Luc shifted, flipping into his obsidian scales, feeling the drag and slide of muscle and bone. His wings erupted from the slits in his back and unfurled into great black sails. He pushed off from the ground and flew forward, toward the roiling fissure. Without a moment's hesitation, he arched his back and dove through to the Underneath.

CHAPTER TWENTY-EIGHT

I ngrid staggered away from the hooded woman.

"You're mad. I don't have your blood," she said. Her heel hit a rise in the dirt floor and she crashed onto her rump.

Grayson had curled into himself. Her eyes pleaded with him to do something—anything. But he made no move to help her. He did nothing but cower. Whatever the hooded monster had done to Grayson, it had broken him.

Of course he couldn't help her. Ingrid had to help *him*.

"Oh, but you do have it," the woman said. "As did your brother when he first arrived in my hive. I have already reclaimed my blood from his veins, and now I will have yours. I gave it to you and your brother the very day you were born, Ingrid Waverly. I gave the both of you two gifts that day."

Ingrid searched the cavernous room for some sort of exit. The doorway was the only way in or out.

"Gifts?" she repeated, her heart plummeting, panic brewing. "What gifts? Who are you?"

The demon master rose to her feet. "My name is Axia. I was an angel once. A guardian angel. Yours, in fact."

Her robes flowed as she turned to walk a circle around the cavern.

"It is not uncommon for guardians to occasionally give a gift to those they guide into the human realm," Axia said. "Beauty. Melody. Patience. Whatever gift suits the guardian's mood, really. I, however, was much more artful when it came to my gifts, and unlike the other guardians, I was not above collaborating with Underneath demons. They had so much to offer an angel like me.

"For your brother, I brought the blood of a hellhound. For you, the blood of a lectrux. A small slice here . . ." Axia lifted one drooping sleeve and gestured toward Ingrid, and two pricks of pain blossomed on Ingrid's calf. The searing sensation had the shape of her birthmarks. ". . . and a few drops of demon blood to mix with your own. It could not have hurt so very much—you both slept through my ministrations. It was a precious alchemy, my little seedling. The blood prospered over the next sixteen or seventeen years, maturing with you, until finally, it reached its fullest potency."

Sixteen or seventeen years. Vander had been sixteen when he'd started seeing Dust. Ingrid had been seventeen when she'd accidentally set fire to Anna's home. What about Grayson? She clapped a hand over the two burning strawberry ovals on her calf. Grayson mewled in the corner, his dirt-rimmed fingernails digging into his own calf. What had he done?

"You and your brother, and all of my little seedlings, have borne the marks of your demon gifts ever since," Axia said. So they had demon dust because of their gifts, because of Axia. Ingrid and Grayson and Vander and all the other Dusters—an *angel* had done this to them.

"We didn't want these gifts," Ingrid said. How many other Dusters were out there, discovering that they could do extraordinary things? How many babies had Axia gifted?

"No one wants a gift they do not know how to use," Axia replied. "But you will. Soon."

"Why, though?" Ingrid pressed. "Why give us these gifts? You have your beasts, your hellhounds and demons. What do you want with us?"

Axia's robes danced in a breeze Ingrid couldn't feel. The cavern was roasting and dry, her skin thirsty for moisture.

"The creatures here can help me only so much," she answered with a flourish of her sleeve. "They are nothing exceptional. They exist to satisfy their base, primal hungers. They cannot even stay on Earth's surface for any length of time before they must come crawling back to their hives to regenerate. I will require more intelligence, more flexibility in my warriors when I make my stand against the Angelic Order."

Axia's revelation dropped like a stone in water.

"All because they cast you into the Underneath?" Ingrid asked.

Axia laughed. "Of course not. I wanted to be banished. How else was I to set my plans in motion? I was never suited to the Order. They infuriated me, the way they misdirected their power. They could have reigned over the human realm unchallenged. Unchecked. Instead, they treated humans with kid gloves, bowing down to them, coddling them, in the name of their all-powerful God. But do you think they showed such reserve within the Order itself? No, they unleashed their power within their own ranks, with the archangels treating lower angels the way they should have been treating humans."

Her bitterness said it all.

"Lower angels like you," Ingrid hedged.

Axia's swirling robes fell slack. "Even I had enough power to bend humans to my will. Do you have any idea what it is like to possess such supremacy and be forbidden to wield it? To watch the humans destroy a world that was once an Eden?"

If Ingrid recalled her Bible lessons correctly, Axia was speaking of that trifling thing called *free will*. She swallowed back the sarcastic remark, noting the violent undulation of Axia's robes. Ingrid couldn't see the fallen angel's face, but her expressions, her emotions, seemed to play out in the threads of her cloak.

"Why should such powerful beings bow to humans? Humans are lesser than the lowest class of angels. Lower than the Dispossessed. Humans should be serving *us*."

Ingrid couldn't stay silent. "But you're not an angel anymore."

Axia pivoted and streaked to Ingrid's side. "Stripping me of my glow and my wings was merely a symbolic disgrace. An angel's power dwells in her blood. In the Underneath it would have grown toxic, slowly withering away." She lifted her arm, and again Ingrid's birthmark burned. "I needed to safeguard my blood before the Order discovered how I had gifted my infants and cast me out. So along with your demon blood, I added my own blood to the alchemy. You and your brother have kept my bloodline safely hidden. It grew stronger and thrived, saturating your blood until I could finally retrieve it."

Ingrid scrunched herself backward. Her shoulders hit the cavern wall. She had angel blood running through her veins? Mixing with lectrux blood and the human blood she was born with? *"A precious alchemy,"* Axia had called it. And with it came the ability to form electricity in the palms of her hands, to glow, and to force gargoyles to their knees.

"Who else did you give your blood to?" Ingrid asked, thinking again of Vander, of all the other Dusters he had seen.

"None but you and your brother. I knew you would both be safe. Tell me—have either of you ever taken ill? Have your wounds always healed quickly?"

Ingrid caught her breath.

"Even demon poison will not kill you when left untreated, like it would others."

Axia's sleeve drifted forward. The place where her hand should have been was a gaping black hole. The border of the sleeve brushed along Ingrid's cheek in a caress and a damp chill quenched her skin's thirst.

"What am I?" Ingrid whispered.

"You are everything I am going to be: an alloy of power. This place has made me a demon, the vessels of untainted blood have made me human, and after I reclaim my blood from your veins, I will again be an angel."

"The Harvest," Ingrid murmured. *My little seedling,* Axia had called her. "You're going to use the babies you gifted. But for what?"

The cool mist of Axia's touch fell away. "Do not trouble yourself with my plans, Ingrid Waverly. At the moment, I require only one thing from you."

Ingrid set her jaw. Axia wanted her blood. Blood the fallen angel had just described as containing a triumvirate of power. Perhaps Axia hadn't imagined that Ingrid would catch on. Perhaps she'd believed Ingrid would be like Grayson, trembling in fear.

"I'm not going to give you anything," Ingrid ground out.

The frenzied strobe of the blue and black lights flecked Axia's robes. "Do not test me. I have already reclaimed my blood from your brother and I am not without my old strength."

But Ingrid was stronger. She could feel her superiority in her veins. It was the same weighty sensation she'd felt in the churchyard when the gargoyles had been attacking her brother. Crackles of static electricity traveled the lengths of her arms. The pain the lightning had induced earlier was there again, but Ingrid didn't mind it as much. With the pain came added power, and at the moment, Ingrid would use whatever she could harness.

"I thought you might prove difficult at first," Axia said, her buttery voice hardening.

Ingrid expected Axia to lunge at her. Instead, her robes shuddered. A writhing, pale white mass slithered from the billowing hem. It was a serpent, its body as thick as a gargoyle's scaled thigh. Ingrid stared as the serpent skated out from Axia's robes and coiled before her into rounded stacks. The serpent's eyes glowed like a pair of pearl marquise beads. It flattened its neck into a curved hood and brandished a pair of wicked fangs.

A windfall of electricity stung the tips of Ingrid's fingers just as the serpent jabbed its head forward. Ingrid threw up her hands to block the oncoming fangs and seized the serpent's hood, as wide and regal as a pharaoh's headdress. A floor-shaking quake of lightning streamed from her fingertips, and the force of it sent the serpent into a backward spiral. Its stacked coils unraveled wildly as a chain of blue electric pulses flickered through the albino scales.

The serpent thudded to the dirt floor, twitching. Axia's creaseless robes hovered behind it.

"You surprise me, Ingrid Waverly," she said, her voice tight and vicious. Axia surged forward, her robes swelling out as menacingly as the serpent's hood. But Ingrid's hands were numb and powerless. She had spent every last prickle of electricity on repulsing the pale serpent.

Axia came to a halt just inches from Ingrid. Her robes seemed to suck her backward, a weight pulling them tightly against her surprisingly thin form. Axia and her robes crashed to the floor, tangling into the limp coils of the demon serpent. Grayson kneeled behind them, clutching two fistfuls of Axia's robes.

"Ingrid, run! Go!" He yanked on the fabric balled in his fists. Axia's hood fell back.

The fallen angel screeched as her head, as bald and translucent as the serpent's scales, was revealed. Her hideous face—if it could even be deemed a face—was nothing more than a canvas of corpse-white skin, stretched tight and thin over jagged bones. Her eyes were a bottomless black, abnormally wide and round, and unblinking. She didn't have eyelids or eyebrows, or any hair at all. Her saucer eyes completely dwarfed her nub of a nose and the black gash that served as her mouth.

"*Go,* Ingrid!" Grayson screamed again. Ingrid's muscles jumped, itching to follow his command. But she couldn't.

"I'm not leaving you!" she shouted back.

Axia shrugged off the shock and with a flick of her robed sleeve sent Grayson hurtling through the air. He hit the cavern wall and slumped into a heap.

The angel turned her gruesome face toward Ingrid, who was still sapped from defeating the serpent. Ingrid had thought she had more power. She'd thought . . .

Axia laughed then, a high, thin whistle of air. It tunneled through Ingrid's head, burrowing deep into her skull. So deep she feared she'd never escape the sound of it, in this life or the next.

Axia's mouth stretched wider and blacker. It was all Ingrid could see as the fallen angel came for her.

Ingrid's scent slammed into Luc the second he shot out the narrow end of the churning whirlpool. He'd entered the fissure nose first, wings pleated to build speed. Once through, he shook out his wings and dug his heels through the air. Luc flooded his senses with Ingrid's scent while taking in his first glimpse of the Underneath.

He felt like an idiot.

For as long as Luc had known there was an Underneath, he'd imagined it as an expanse of land cratered with bubbling pools of magma the color of iron held over a smithy's flame. He'd imagined geysers of steam and fire, islands of barren rock crammed with writhing demons of every shape and size. Like a fool, he'd pictured a human's version of hell—and he'd been utterly wrong. There was no brimstone or hellfire. No streams of molten rock or trolling demons.

The reality of the Underneath was that it was a vast city of hives. They were enormous, some the size of the abbey, long and tapered like a caterpillar's cocoon. Others were wide and globular like a beehive, the size of the Panthéon. They looked as if they hung suspended from a darkened ceiling, but the spaces between, below, and above the hives were inky black and impossible for even Luc's eyes to cut through. The only reason Luc could see the hives at all was because the walls of the nests flickered with volleys of blue and white light that pulsed through each one as silently as a spate of heat lightning.

The city of hives, eerily quiet, stretched on and on. Luc spun midair and saw more hives clustered behind him. His senses, raised to a new level of awareness, traced no approaching demon. No sign of life outside the nests at all. Everything seemed to exist inside the hives. Axia's hive, the record keeper had said, would be the one closest to where the fissure had emptied.

He surfaced Ingrid's scent again and landed a trace. A wide hive, roughly twice the size of the abbey, called to him. She was in there. And she was terrified. Oddly, the spike of her pulse, the blood humming through her veins, thrilled him. At least she's alive.

He flew toward the hive. The thin, flickering walls appeared devoid of any openings. Luc wagered the entrance lay at the tapered bottom.

Hesitation meant death.

He spiraled toward the tip, saw the black abyss leading in, and hooked into an upward draft. He entered a tunnel, the pulsing lights brighter and sharper than they'd been outside the hive walls. Luc kept his speed up as he traveled through the wormlike hole, his wings tucked close to keep them from scraping on the rounded walls. He couldn't risk injury, not now. The tunnel branched off here and there, leading either down more wormholes or into vast chambers. And while the hive had been still when he'd first entered, he now felt rumbles of life. Awareness of his presence sprang up in the wake of Luc's wings.

He kept his hold on Ingrid's scent. He let it reel him in, let it choose which tunnels he veered into. His focus was unshakable, until a chiming at the base of his skull threatened to sever it.

He wasn't the only gargoyle in Axia's hive.

In the warren behind him, Luc heard a roar of building chaos. But he was too close to Ingrid to stop and backtrack. He glided through a curve in the tunnel and immediately stretched out his wings.

She was pressed against the wall of a cavern, cowering before a pale, bald creature in thick robes. The thing was crawling toward Ingrid on its hands and knees, over the rubbery coils of an immobile crypsis serpent. Grayson's bloody form lay crumpled in the corner.

Ingrid saw Luc a split second before the bald creature's enormous black eyes found him. Luc's chest rumbled. His throat filled with a floor-trembling shriek; a call to battle for the demon, whatever it was. He thought he'd seen every Underneath demon, but this one was new. Yet despite its hairless head, ugly as a newly hatched eagle's, and the coarse, bloodless skin stretched tight over it, the creature was strangely familiar.

Luc pushed off his heels and prepared to ram it. The demon threw out its robed arm and Luc slammed into an invisible wall. Then the wall crumbled onto him. He crashed to the floor of the cavern, the unmistakable weight of an angel's power sealing him to the dirt.

"Luc!" Ingrid screamed.

This creature wasn't a demon. It was an angel. It had to be Axia, the one René had spoken of.

Luc struggled against the oppressive weight, craning his neck to see what he'd never seen before. An angel without her glow, without her blinding white light and dimly fogged contours. And to his astonishment, he *could* see her. She wasn't strong enough to keep his head bowed in submission, or his eyes diverted from her repulsive face. She had to have angel blood in her veins—if she didn't, she would never have been able to force him into submission. But she was nowhere near as potent as Irindi. Even Ingrid had been better able to subdue him.

"Leave him alone!" Ingrid screamed, and then heaved herself toward the robed figure.

Luc shouted for her to stop, but the command gargled through his vocal cords and came out an abrasive growl. A ghostly white hand jutted from the end of Axia's sleeve and raked the column of Ingrid's throat. Ingrid clamped a hand over her neck, blood beading through the spaces between her fingers.

Luc rounded his spine and shoved against the weight bearing down on his wings. He tried again, this time attempting to crawl forward instead of pushing up. The weight gave a little. Luc edged closer, watching as Axia brought her spiked fingertips, stained with Ingrid's blood, to the shapeless gash above her chin. A long black tongue slithered out and took a tentative lick. Then, as Luc watched, the black flesh of her tongue cleaved in half, each half thinning out to sharpened points. The forked tongue looked serpentine as it flicked over the blood-covered barbs of her fingertips.

What kind of angel drank blood? Luc trudged forward, the weight of the boulder on his back shrinking with his every breath. With a ravenous snarl Axia leaped forward, and her hold on Luc instantly severed.

Her reptile tongue lashed toward Ingrid's neck, but Ingrid was fast. She caught the angel's crescent-shaped temples with her hands and pinned the creature a hairsbreadth from her bleeding neck. Ingrid screamed as sudden jets of blue lightning forked through the angel's translucent skin, creating what looked like a tangled pattern of ice-encrusted briars. The gaping black holes that served as Axia's eyes exploded in a fountain of blue fireworks. Her howl and Ingrid's screams matched, vibrating through the cavern, shaking the floor, the walls, even Luc's vision.

Axia toppled backward and landed on the thick coils of the

crypsis. Her robed body lay motionless. Threads of gray smoke spiraled into the air.

"Luc." Ingrid rolled her head toward him, her arms falling limp at her sides. He closed the space between them and scooped her up. She couldn't even raise her arms to grasp him.

"Grayson," she said, her face buried in the ridged plates of his chest.

Ingrid's brother was barely stirring in the corner. Luc folded his wings and circled the forms on the cavern floor in order to get to him—he was his human, after all. But with Ingrid and Grayson side by side, both of their sagging bodies clasped under his wings, Luc felt something he'd never felt for one of his humans before. The feather weighting his right arm, the blond tresses swaying loosely, the scent of a soft, springtime dawn—he'd come into the Underneath for *this*. For her. He wasn't supposed to favor one human over another.

But he did.

He favored Ingrid. He *wanted* Ingrid.

A shriek snapped Luc back to clarity. He was suddenly aware of the chaos rocking the rest of the hive, the slow stirring of the crypsis serpent's coils, and the jerky twitching of Axia's robes. Ingrid had only stunned the serpent and the fallen angel. The two would be rising soon. Luc had to leave. Now.

He tucked his humans tighter under his arms and flew from the cavern. Without a scent this time to lead him through the tunnels, Luc relied on the shrieks of the gargoyles whose presence he'd felt earlier.

He made his way down through the hive, toward the exit and the sounds of his brethren. Down a curved tube and around a hairpin hook to the left, Luc practically threaded wings with Yann. The chimera veered out of Luc's path before Luc could catch his wing on any of Yann's feathers, the edge of each colorful plume trimmed with fine-toothed razors. Yann brought his wing down as soon as Luc passed, and sheared through the torso of a demon. The creature's halves slid apart and shattered into a cloud of shimmering dust.

Luc saw Marco's sunset-red wings ahead, his talons shredding the arms off an appendius. His long, powerful tail whipped away three black-winged corvites before their hooked bills could nip his scales and flood him with their poison.

Luc didn't know why or how Marco and Yann had risked coming into the Underneath. He didn't have time to care. He shot past Marco, aiming for a black hole at the end of the tunnel.

As he closed in on the exit, a figure swerved out of a chamber and into his trajectory. It was a man—or at least, it had the carriage of one until it came at Luc, morphing its shape in one instantaneous motion. One second, it was a man; the next, a hellhound.

His arms full, Luc extended one leg, intending to take the beast down with a crude slash of his talons. The hellhound bounded over Luc's head instead, and he felt the beast's slanted fangs rip through the cartilage of his wing. The strength went out of it and he swung sharply to the left.

He heard the squelched whine of the hellhound moments before Marco's wings overtook him, tufts of hellhound fur and blood sticking to his talons. Without asking, Marco took Grayson's unconscious form from Luc's flagging side and plunged through the hive's exit. Luc, still clinging to Ingrid, beat after them, with Yann bringing up the rear.

The spooling fissure churned with misty ribbons of gray, black, and deep purple. Luc followed Marco's tail toward the siphon's tip, but his lame wing slowed him. Yann swooped past Luc, and as he did, his shaggy lion paws clipped Luc's injured wing. Pain seared through it, but Yann hauled Luc into the whirlpool and kept his claws fastened on him as they fought against the current, toward the surface of the fissure.

They broke through, and with the pressure of the downward

spiral gone, all three Dispossessed rocketed into the sky, streaked blue with the coming dawn.

Luc heard the clanging of bells, the blare of whistles. He scanned the crater, but the Seer and lamed record keeper were gone. Yann loosed his claws from Luc's wing, his charity spent. Luc drooped to the side, but one wing was enough. Speed didn't matter anymore, just obscurity. He flapped the single wing and pushed higher into the sky, following Marco, still clutching Grayson's limp form, above the chimney stacks and zinc roofs. He cradled Ingrid against him, felt the echo of her heartbeat inside his chest, and cut a path toward the rectory.

CHAPTER TWENTY-NINE

Gabby played with the lace fringe at her wrist and stared at the sitting-room wall. Earlier, she had been seated near the window overlooking the churchyard, but the glass had reflected her face.

She hadn't been able to stand it.

She'd moved to the settee shoved into the corner of the sitting room where she hoped she might not be seen if anyone parted the peacock-blue drapes and looked in.

She wanted to be alone. Completely and utterly alone. Forever.

The steel grommets slid along the drapery rod, signaling an end to Gabby's dream. Ingrid spotted her instantly.

"You aren't invisible over there, you know," she said.

Gabby pulled on the lace at her wrist and felt it rip. She sighed and let go, tucking her knees closer to her chest. "Leave me be."

The newly formed scabs beneath the linen dressing killed—positively murdered—whenever she moved her jaw. The three deeply carved tracks ran parallel from her eyebrow to the corner of her mouth.

"We've kept everyone away for days, Gabby," Ingrid said gently as she crossed the sitting room to the velvet settee. The past three days had been awful. The dark smudges of exhaustion beneath Ingrid's eyes attested to that.

Nora's body—at least, parts of her body—had been discovered on a quay along the Seine. The police had come to the rectory, as had a flock of reporters, but Ingrid had kept them at bay, and Grayson and Gabby hidden in their rooms. Before that, at Benoit's, Nolan had known the police wouldn't be contacted. He'd known no questions would be asked.

Nolan. Gabby's throat cinched tight. Her cracked ribs, bound tightly beneath her dress, ached.

"I'm hideous," Gabby whispered. There. That was the truth of it. The hellhound's claws had mangled her face. She wanted to take the wool throw spread over her feet and cover her head with it.

"You're alive," Ingrid countered. And Nora wasn't.

No. Gabby wasn't dead, and she wasn't so idiotic to wish that she were, either. But she'd lost her face. Her beauty. She knew she shouldn't be so vain—the thought left a sour taste in the back of her throat—but she couldn't help it.

Gabby never would have admitted it before, maybe because she hadn't thought it mattered, but she'd used her appearance for everything. She'd charmed people with her smile and with the dark, mischievous glittering of her eyes. Her skin had been naturally sun kissed and smooth. She'd *liked* her looks. She'd had no idea how much of her confidence had been linked to them. Until now.

"How is Grayson?" Gabby asked, wanting to take her thoughts in a different direction.

"Better," Ingrid answered. "Much better, actually. He hasn't shifted form for nearly a full day now."

Gabby had been confined to her bed until that morning, so she hadn't seen Grayson yet. He'd been shifting erratically, from hellhound to human, since coming out from the Underneath. Gabby had heard his roars, his yelping cries, and was certain anyone passing by the abbey and rectory had decided Mama was in fact opening a torture chamber rather than an art gallery.

"And Mama?" Gabby asked. The relief Ingrid had showed over Grayson's progress floundered.

Ingrid let out a long breath, absently touching the linen bandage wound around her neck. Axia's fingers had left deep scratches, but they were nothing like Gabby's gouges.

"She's still pretending what we told the police and the reporters is true."

Nolan and Vander had helped fabricate the story. Gabby had been with Nora when a crazed man had attacked—the one who must have abducted and killed those other girls, they suggested. He'd used a three-pronged weapon to slash Gabby's face before making off with Nora. And when the police inquired about Grayson's return, Charlotte had said her son hadn't been missing after all; he'd come back to the rectory after a week of debauchery, just as the French police had suggested he might.

Purposely looking the fool would normally have been impossible for Gabby's mother, but she'd been too disturbed by everything she'd seen to object: gargoyles in the churchyard, her son as a furry beast, her beautiful daughter's marred face. She'd played the role of scattered, anxious mother to perfection.

"What now?" Gabby asked. The question wasn't just with regard to her face.

Ingrid straightened her back and took a breath. "We'll wait for Grayson to get better, and for your wounds to heal. Papa will be here in a few days. I suspect we'll have to lobby on Mama's behalf to keep on with the gallery. She'll want a way to distract herself."

Gabby wished for some of her sister's confidence.

"She can't run away from the truth forever," Gabby muttered, instantly knowing her sister was going to chuck the statement right back at her. Gabby was running, too. Hiding behind the closed door of the rectory. Behind her bandages.

But Ingrid stayed quiet, only reaching across the settee to cover Gabby's hand with her own.

"I haven't said it yet, but I don't know what I would have done if that hellhound had . . . if it had—" Ingrid swallowed the rest of her sentence and squeezed Gabby's hand.

"You can thank Luc. If he hadn't ripped out its fangs, you'd be mourning more than my beauty."

Ingrid huffed a laugh. It hurt too much for Gabby to smile, but she watched her sister closely. Gabby had noticed the lilting smile on her sister's face at any mention of Luc. And there it was, lingering on her lips again.

"Ingrid," Gabby said, pushing herself up a little taller. Her sister looked up, the smile having vanished.

"What is it?"

Luc is a gargoyle, Gabby wanted to blurt. He wasn't even human. He wore his old human form, and yes, it was an attractive one—but that was what he'd looked like when he'd been *alive*. If Gabby had it all straight in her mind, Luc's human form wasn't the one Ingrid was drawn to. It was the black-winged, black-scaled beast he became.

"What is it, Gabby?" Ingrid asked again, one pale brow pressed down with worry.

"It's just . . ." Gabby hesitated. The bell on the front door cranked out its grating alert, interrupting her.

"It's nothing," Gabby finished as she heard their butler, Gustav, walk through the foyer.

"Are you certain?" Ingrid asked. "Because you can tell me anything. You know that, right?"

Gabby nodded, feeling silly. This was Ingrid, after all. The most practical, most sensible person Gabby knew.

The peacock drapes parted and Gustav's rotund frame filled the doorway.

"Lady Gabriella, you have a visitor. Monsieur Quinn."

Gabby heard a cough and a voice murmuring in the foyer. Gustav cocked his head back to listen, and then faced forward once more with an afflicted look.

"*Mes excuses—Detective* Quinn."

Gabby rolled her eyes. She could just picture the smug expression on Nolan's face. She didn't want to see him. She wasn't ready to feel his gaze upon her as he remembered how she used to look.

Ingrid gave Gabby's hand another soft squeeze and rose from the settee.

Gabby had known she wouldn't be able to hide from him forever. If not for Nolan, she would have died. She would thank him and then let him be on his way.

"Thank you, Gustav," Gabby said. The butler raised his eyebrows in surprise and then slid aside to admit the visitor.

She turned her face away as Nolan stepped into the sitting room.

"Lady Ingrid," he said as she passed him on her way to the foyer.

The drapes closed and Ingrid's and Gustav's footsteps faded. Nolan stood still. Gabby kept her face turned away, and the silence grew.

Gabby licked her lips. "You're not a detective."

"Not officially. You'd be surprised how many people don't bother to check into that," he replied. He crossed the room, the floor creaking under his weight.

"Monsieur Constantine, for example," Gabby said. "And my mother. You swindled them both."

"To swindle, one must accept monetary reward. I'm afraid I'm just as poor as I was at the beginning of all this."

The thought of life before *all this* made Gabby ache with longing. But she couldn't go back. Couldn't regain what she'd lost.

"I'd hoped you'd let me in this time," Nolan said, his voice soft and serious.

He'd tried to visit at least twice a day since the night at the Métro construction pit.

She felt him come up beside the settee. Even with her face turned toward the pink velvet cushion, she knew what expression he wore. His eyes, fathomless pools of blue, would be fixed on her, the muscles along his strong jaw tensed, and his chin lifted slightly, as if he could urge her to look at him without commanding it.

"I'm leaving for Rome tomorrow."

Gabby turned her head halfway before she remembered he'd be able to see her bandages. It was so far from anything she had imagined he might say.

"Rome? Why?"

He lowered himself onto the edge of the settee. Unable to look him in the eye, Gabby stared at the way his knees pulled at his fawn-colored trousers.

"There's going to be an inquiry about everything that's happened here. The Directorate needs to know about Axia." He paused before adding, "And about your sister and Grayson."

About their special blood and unnatural abilities. Ingrid had told Gabby and everyone else how Axia had gifted a number of infants with the blood of different demons, allowing it to mature as they aged, and how that blood lent them the traits of whatever demon Axia had chosen for them. Now, those infants were the Dusters Vander had seen, including Vander himself. But Ingrid and Grayson were different from the rest. In addition to their demon gifts, they had harbored angel blood all their lives. Axia's blood. The fallen angel had reclaimed Grayson's portion but had apparently failed to retrieve Ingrid's. The Alliance leaders would surely need to know.

"And I need to escort Tomas and Marie to their trials," Nolan said after a moment of silence.

Gabby remembered Tomas as she'd last seen him: dragging himself along the ground at the Métro construction crater. She also imagined the torturous death he'd faced before, in the Underneath. To be stripped of his skin and devoured alive . . . Who wouldn't have begged for mercy? She couldn't condone what he'd done, but she felt sorry for him anyway.

"What will happen to them?" she asked.

Nolan unclasped his hands and formed them into fists. "The Directorate has a strict policy when it comes to treason. They don't forgive it. Ever. There's a reformatory in Rome. I'm sure Tomas and Marie will find themselves living there for a long time."

Gabby let out a relieved breath. She'd been hoping their punishment would be more humane than the one the Dispossessed had leveled against René. Ingrid had told her that a few other gargoyles had destroyed him. Apparently, gargoyles weren't immortal. They didn't hold with treason, either.

"Gabby." Nolan sighed her name. "Why won't you look at me, lass?"

She closed her eyes against the vulnerability he'd allowed himself to show.

He pitched his voice even lower. "Is it about what happened between us?"

No. She didn't want to think about that kiss. About him running after Chelle. Not now.

"Nolan—"

"I shouldn't have left you standing there like that. Lord knows I shouldn't have, but I wasn't thinking straight. I've hurt Chelle enough as it is. I made the mistake a while ago of thinking our friendship could be something more."

"Stop, I don't—"

Nolan cut her protest off. "I ended things fast. It wasn't working, at least not for me. But Chelle didn't see it the same way."

The thorns that had started twisting against Gabby's heart loosened.

"I hurt her. I hurt you. And I'm sorry for it. For all of it." He didn't touch her but stretched his hand over the velvet cushion until it was parallel with her hips. "Can't we start over? Go back to bickering instead of this . . . this bloody silence?"

"I don't want you to look at me, Nolan," she admitted, her humiliation stripped bare. She'd always been honest with him before. She wouldn't change that now.

"Why?" He sounded truly puzzled, and Gabby felt the urge to kick him in the shin.

"Isn't it obvious?"

He cupped her chin and tried to lift it up. She jerked out of his grasp. Both hands came at her then, his palms hot on her cheeks. He held the bandaged side of her face as he might an injured dove.

"Do you have any idea what went through my mind when I realized a hellhound had snapped you up and taken you into that tunnel?" He spoke with ferocity. Gabby stopped squirming. "I thought you were dead. I thought I was too late, too human and inadequate, and that I'd find pieces of you scattered about. If I'd found you like that, if I'd lost you . . . it would have undone me, Gabriella Waverly."

Slowly, Gabby lifted her eyes to look at him. He was so close to her, the tip of his nose nearly touching hers. His savage expression startled her.

"So if you're under the impression that when I look at you, all I'm bound to see is a set of scars, you're a bloody fool."

Gabby parted her lips. "Don't call me a fool."

"Don't hide from me again," he said, just as serious as before.

She nodded, and he let his hands slide gently from her face. He sat back, holding her gaze as if it were a test. He raised an eyebrow.

"I'll be away for your birthday."

Gabby straightened her shoulders and slid her feet to the floor. "My birthday?"

"You said it was coming up, right?" Nolan asked.

She'd mentioned it only once. And he'd actually remembered.

Nolan stood and went to the sideboard, where there was a black rectangular box, long and flat with a silver clasp. He took it and returned to her, getting down to one knee. If not for the size of the box, Gabby would have been having heart palpitations thinking he was about to propose marriage.

With notable reverence, Nolan slid the box onto Gabby's lap and undid the latch for her. His hands retreated and he stayed still, kneeling before her, waiting. When she didn't move, he huffed a laugh.

"If you don't want your gift . . ." He made as if to take the box from her lap. Gabby slapped his hands and clutched the box to her. He bit back a pleased grin.

She opened the lid and took a sharp breath. Nestled on a bed of burgundy velvet was a silver sword the length of her arm. The blade was so polished that her bandaged face winked back up at her. Gabby ran her fingers lightly across the silver filigree cross guard and down the grip of inlaid mother-of-pearl. The pommel, a hollowed sphere of silver scrollwork, was magnificent— a crowning extravagance on an already stunning sword.

"Nolan," she whispered, lifting the air-light sword with the same reverence he'd shown in presenting the box.

"I had it blessed this morning," he said, still on one knee. "I was wrong about you, Gabby. You have more than just flint in you. You've got the fire." He shifted himself onto the settee. His leg pressed against hers. "If you think you'd like to train—"

"I do." Her heart swelled. The rush made her feel dizzy after so many melancholy days.

"When I return from Rome, then," Nolan said with a crooked smile. He lifted his hand to her bandaged cheek again. His thumb swept in a gentle arc. "You'll be sixteen, so it won't be entirely inappropriate."

He stilled his thumb, a meaningful glint in his eyes. Gabby knew he wasn't speaking of just demon hunting.

He angled his head and pressed his lips to her forehead, just above her brows. His mouth traveled lower, caressing her so gently his kisses landed like goose down. Nolan's lips carefully traced the bandage covering the plowed lines that would permanently mar her skin. Lines he claimed not to care about. Gabby hoped he meant it. She wouldn't always have this bandage to hide behind.

Nolan's lips came off the linen and hovered over her mouth now, his eyes seeking hers. He was waiting for her to accept him. Waiting for her to trust him. It was Gabby's move.

She wrapped a hand around the dark curls at the nape of his neck and pulled his lips to hers.

Grayson was still asleep, and Ingrid was worried. He'd had few moments of consciousness since Luc and Marco had delivered them to the rectory. Mama had been sitting with Grayson the morning after their return when he'd rippled in and out of a shift. Thankfully, Luc had been standing watch in the hallway and had heard her mother's screams.

Of all wretched things, they'd had to chain Grayson's ankles and wrists to the bedposts. Then Luc had needed to chain the bedposts to the wall. Her brother was out of Axia's hive, but he was still a prisoner to that demon world. For days he'd shifted erratically, muscles bulking and fur sprouting one moment, gone the next, his teeth rising and sinking until his gums bled. He was in agony. And Ingrid could feel it all. When Grayson moaned in pain, the tight, prickling awareness bunched up Ingrid's own muscles along her shoulders and neck. It made her feel ill. Even in her room, down the corridor, she knew when his body was suffering a shift.

She didn't mind. She'd rather feel his every ache than nothing at all.

Ingrid sat in Grayson's room, her legs curled beneath her in a chair, and stared at the peaceful expression on his face. His brows, constantly knitted in pain over the last few days, were now flat and smooth. His lips were loose and full instead of thin and pale. Finally, he was starting to look like her brother again.

Ingrid hugged her knees to her chest and watched him breathe. Grayson was clean, his hair blond instead of dirt-brown. Mama had scrubbed his nails, shooing Maureen away when the maid had tried to take over. And thanks to Luc, the bites that had scored his body were healing with unnatural speed.

Vander and Nolan agreed that the bite marks matched those of a hellhound. It had been injecting him with poison, perhaps. The violent shifts his body had been through, Vander theorized, were likely symptoms of Grayson's body becoming used to going without the poison. But Grayson couldn't heal entirely on his own. Without angel blood in his veins, he'd been left vulnerable, and he'd needed Luc's help.

Ingrid had insisted on staying in the room when Luc slit his forearm and captured his blood in a glass vial. Once Luc had rubbed the blood into Grayson's wounds, they had immediately started to close and scab.

She hadn't seen Luc since. He was keeping watch, though. Somehow, she felt his eyes on her even when he wasn't in sight. But he hadn't come to her room or perched on the window ledge in full scales, like before. He hadn't come to her at all.

A knock landed on the door. Ingrid hoped it wasn't Gabby retreating like a scared animal from her visit with Nolan. The boy was mad about her, and Ingrid was quite certain the feeling was mutual.

"Come in," she called, and the door creaked open.

It was Vander.

Ingrid sprang from her seat, feeling as if she should give him a report of some kind. "It's been nearly twenty-four hours now. I think it might be over."

Vander should have taken a room at the rectory, for all the time he'd been spending at Grayson's side. He'd started reading to Grayson's unconscious form, claiming that wherever her brother's mind was, his ears could still hear everything around him. Mostly, Vander read passages from the Bible and from his theology texts. A few times Ingrid had stood outside the door listening. Vander's voice soothed, like cool water coursing over sunbaked river stones. Ingrid had closed her eyes and let his voice run over her, too. She didn't know if he'd make a grand orator like some ministers she'd heard, but he'd make a kind one. One she'd want to listen to, no matter what he preached.

Behind his spectacles, Vander's eyes roved over Grayson's frame.

"His dust is almost back to its normal rose color, instead of that vibrant green when he was . . . different," he said. Ingrid swayed with relief. But Vander didn't look very happy or hopeful.

"What's wrong?" she asked.

Vander turned to face her. "I'm sorry. I'm just trying to understand everything about Axia and this Harvest of hers. What it all means. Why she gave us demon gifts. How the Alliance needs to prepare."

When Ingrid had told them all the truth about her blood—how it contained the trinity alloy Axia had spoken of—they'd listened in rapt silence before barraging her with questions. The problem was, Ingrid didn't have answers to most of them. She knew a few things—that the angel blood kept her unusually healthy and strong, that the demon blood gave her lightning—but not what Axia planned to do to undermine the Angelic Order.

"She's already taken back her blood from Grayson," Ingrid said, touching the bandage wrapped around her neck. "She said she only gave it to us, but what if she was lying? What if she gave her blood to other infants as well and is able to gain more strength by reclaiming it from them?"

Vander came to Ingrid's side and stood with her at the foot of Grayson's bed.

"Right now, I only care to make sure she doesn't get her hands on you again. The rest of it, we'll figure out in time." His fingers brushed her wrist, bringing out a flare of heat there. "When did you last eat? Or sleep?"

Ingrid searched her memory but couldn't recall when she'd last taken more than tea and toast. And she'd avoided sleep altogether, fearful of nightmares about Axia and her pale serpent.

Vander tugged on her wrist. "He's safe, Ingrid. Come."

He led her out into the corridor, clicking the door shut behind them. It was quiet, the only noise the constant tick of the tall case clock set at the top of the stairs. Ingrid crossed her arms and leaned against the cracked, plaster wall.

"I couldn't kill her," she said. "Axia, I mean. I was fighting for my life, for Grayson's and Luc's, and yet I couldn't kill her. I know you want me to join the Alliance and use this ability of mine, but I don't think I can kill anyone, or anything."

And she felt guilty about it, too. Vander, Nolan, and the rest of the Alliance were always ready to face a demon threat. It was what they lived for. She'd witnessed their agility and strength and fearlessness. Their purpose. Her own sister had even started to show an interest in becoming one of them. But Ingrid didn't feel that same drive. She didn't wish to hide from the dangers she now knew existed; she just didn't like the violence involved in confronting them. She wondered if Grayson would want to fight once he came around. Or maybe he'd given back Vander's ancient book because he hadn't been able to cope with the reality of it all.

"No one is asking you to kill anything. This life isn't for everyone."

Vander covered her hands with his. An unexpected current of electricity sparked through her veins.

"But I'm still a part of it. This whole household is a part of it. My mother. The servants. They don't know Luc is a gargoyle, but they've seen gargoyles. They know they exist."

"And they understand the importance of secrecy. Nolan and I took care of explaining everything to them." Vander drew her closer, the stinging in her arms slowly fading. "You're a part of this world now, and I'm not sorry for it. Mostly because it's *my* world, and I want you in it, Ingrid."

Even if he hadn't said the words, she would have known how he felt. She had known, she supposed, ever since that day at Hôtel Bastian when he'd taken her by the shoulders and inspected her scraped cheek, worry planted deep in his eyes. He wanted her in his world. And she definitely wanted him in hers.

Vander leaned forward and pressed his lips against her forehead. Ingrid closed her eyes and drank in the feeling of his mouth on her skin. He was such a study in contrasts: An aspiring clergyman who knew how to wield a sword. An impoverished shop owner who carried himself like one of England's finest landed gentry. There was so much more to Vander Burke than met the eye. Gabby's first impression of him—that he was a dreadful bore—couldn't have been further from the truth.

Ingrid wanted him to hold her, to keep his nose buried in her hair, his lips pressed against her forehead. But the thought of tilting up her face and allowing him to kiss her properly landed like a stone in her stomach. Because what she wanted, what she truly craved, was a kiss from Luc.

Ingrid pulled back. "I want to be a part of your world, too, Vander, I do. But I . . . I just don't know as what." She forced her eyes up to meet his. He didn't look crushed, but his eyes held a hint of injury. It pricked at her. "Not yet," she added.

Vander shifted his jaw to the side in contemplation. He didn't let go of her, but kept her arms crossed over her chest, her hands trapped beneath his.

"I see the way he watches you," Vander said softly. Ingrid's heart sputtered. He meant Luc. Who else watched her?

"He has to," she answered. "I'm a human on his territory; he doesn't have a choice."

Vander cocked his mouth into a half grin and let go of her. "Trust me, Ingrid, I know all about the Dispossessed. I know their rules and duties, what they're forced to do versus what they want to do." Ingrid stepped back at the fire igniting behind Vander's glasses. "Luc didn't *have* to take demon poison and fly after you into the Underneath. The moment you crossed over you were no longer his human charge. He was no longer required to do anything for you. Any other gargoyle would have sat back and waited for his punishment, gladly suffering an angel's burn just to be rid of his human charge. But not Luc. He went after you anyway, he and those other two Dispossessed. They all went after you of their own free will."

Ingrid flinched as Vander slapped his hat back on. He breathed in deeply, as if to extinguish his fire.

"I know gargoyles," he said, much calmer than before. Much more like the Vander she was used to. "I know you can't trust them, not completely."

"But they saved my life. *Luc* saved my life. You said so yourself: he didn't have to do it—he chose to."

Vander brooded over this for less than a second. "And don't think the rest of the Dispossessed in Paris won't be questioning why."

She hadn't considered that by saving her life Luc, Marco, and the other gargoyle, Yann, might have been putting themselves up for judgment. Maybe that was the real reason Luc had been keeping his distance.

"They might look like humans half the time, but they aren't. They have their own ways. Relationships with humans aren't tolerated," Vander said. Averting his eyes, he added, "Besides, they aren't . . . well, they aren't physically possible. At least, not in the intimate sense."

Her cheeks turned scarlet. "Vander!"

Heat stung his cheeks next. "I thought you should know in case Luc tries—"

"I already know, thank you." At Vander's stiff glare, Ingrid stumbled to add, "Marie made it very clear."

He went still and flexed his fists. He didn't look entirely convinced, but he let it go and turned toward the top of the steps.

"I'll come back tonight to check on Grayson. If that's all right. I mean, if you don't mind my coming."

This wasn't what Ingrid wanted. This awkwardness. Him thinking she didn't want him there. Of course she wanted him to come back. She didn't know what she'd do without him. She rushed forward and threaded her fingers through his. Ingrid clutched his hand, holding it low between them, knowing the gesture was wildly improper. But she didn't care. The thought of Vander leaving angry with her—or worse, hurt by something she'd said or done—made her feel hollow.

Vander tensed in surprise, but only for a moment. He raised her hand and, with his pale caramel eyes locked on hers, brushed a kiss over the ridge of her knuckles. Her breath hitched and she relaxed her grip. He pulled away, tipped the brim of his bowler, and turned to leave. Vander didn't have to say anything. Ingrid knew he'd be back.

CHAPTER THIRTY

Luc was in the stables, running a brush along the muscled haunch of one of the Waverlys' horses, when Irindi's light slammed into him. The brush clattered to the cobbled stone floor and his knees followed, the angel's presence bending him into the obligatory bow. The horse whinnied and bolted to the far end of the stables, but the animal couldn't escape Irindi's glow. It saturated every corner, every board, every mound of hay.

Luc had wondered how long he'd have to wait for Irindi. Now that she was here, he knew that the difference between her strength and Axia's was immeasurable. With most of her angel blood running through Ingrid's veins, Axia had been too weak to even hold a gargoyle in submission, let alone challenge an archangel like Irindi. Of course, that only meant that Axia would be coming for Ingrid again.

"It has been decided," Irindi began, her monotone voice thrashing the trees outside with a sudden wintry gale. "Your human charges outweigh your capabilities."

Luc's heart seized. He surfaced Ingrid and let the rhythmic beat of her heart fill his chest. Irindi should take him from the abbey. He needed to go. He knew he did. Ingrid wasn't just a human charge. She wasn't even completely human. She was more. To Luc, she was so much more. And that made her dangerous.

"You will soon be joined by another Dispossessed. The two of you shall better serve the humans residing upon this territory."

Luc flinched under the weight of Irindi's glow. He hadn't truly wanted to be separated from Ingrid, but another gargoyle? Here? Sharing his territory, his humans? He'd rather have an angel's burn than that.

"Who?" Luc dared to ask.

Irindi surprised him with an answer. "It is undecided." Her hollowed-out voice ebbed before she spoke again. "The Order wants to know why you consumed the poison of a demon and entered the Underneath. It is a sin to defile your body so and enter a place of desecration."

Luc had known the Order wouldn't overlook it. He'd already appeared before Lennier, along with Marco and Yann. They had taken the last drops of poison in the record keeper's glass vial and then followed Luc through the fissure to the Underneath. Without them, Luc, Ingrid, and Grayson wouldn't have made it out. His injured wing was sore, the gash still healing. Luc could only hope he wouldn't be called upon to coalesce in the next few days.

Marco had claimed that an urge to provide brotherly protection had driven him and Yann into the fissure after Luc, but Luc knew Marco well enough to know he'd had another reason. He wanted to know what it was. Lennier, always erring on the side of peace with the Alliance, had praised the three of them rather than punish them. Luc didn't expect the same lenience from the Order.

There was nothing to do but tell the truth.

"I went to retrieve my human charge." He was fast to catch his blunder. "My human charges."

Irindi's glow pulsed. "It was not a required action."

Her voice was as cold and unfeeling as her words.

"I went of my own free will," Luc replied, daring her to challenge him. He wouldn't apologize for going after Ingrid. For the first time in his life—his very long life—Luc hadn't been willing to let one of his humans go.

The weight pressing Luc's shoulders into a penitent bow lightened a degree.

"You have an affinity for the child christened Ingrid Charlemagne Waverly."

Affinity was a chaste way to describe what he felt for Ingrid, but then again, this *was* an angel.

Luc knew the rules of the Dispossessed when it came to affinities for humans, but not the rules of the Order. He didn't know if they would punish him for caring for Ingrid. The truth of it was glaring. He'd gone into a place of desecration to save the life of a human when he hadn't been required to do so. And he'd kissed that human. He wanted her for his own. Surely the Order, as all-seeing as they were, was aware of that.

"Affinities are rare among the Dispossessed, and they are not sanctioned. They court complications, Luc Rousseau, and that is especially true with this particular human."

She knew about Ingrid's blood, then. She'd probably known all along. Luc wondered what Irindi and the rest of the Order thought of a human with both angelic and demonic powers—if they thought or cared at all.

Irindi stayed quiet, and the gale of wind outside softened to a zephyr. She'd strung Luc on tenterhooks. He prepared himself for the angel's burn, for the slow, scorching fire to carve a path through the flesh between his shoulders.

"The valor you displayed in the realm of desecration is recognized by the Order. Your failure to properly protect the children christened Gabriella Honora Waverly and Nora Margaret Rossdale will go unpunished this once. However, take care that you do not favor one human over your others. I will not forgive it in the future. The Dispossessed will not, either."

Luc bowed deeper to Irindi, even though she'd lessened the weight on his shoulders. There he'd gone again, thinking only of Ingrid and forgetting entirely to fear an angel's burn as recompense for Gabby's mangled face and the death of her lady's maid.

Valor. He'd displayed *valor* when he'd rescued Ingrid and Grayson. It was the closest Luc had come to receiving praise from Irindi in all his gargoyle years.

Fancy that.

The incandescent glow vanished and Luc raised his head. He grabbed the horse brush on his way up, but the animal shied, refusing to come back over to Luc. He gave up and threw the brush on a shelf.

He'd displayed valor, but it hadn't been enough. Another gargoyle was still due to join him at the abbey, and when he arrived, it wouldn't just be Luc's every action and indiscretion under observation. The new gargoyle would be able to sense Ingrid just as keenly as Luc did now. A low rumble rolled through his chest like thunder. He didn't like the idea of anyone sharing his connection to her. He could have passed off the possessive notion as a gargoyle trait, if he had felt the same way about any of the other humans living at the rectory. Of course, he didn't.

This thing with Ingrid had to stop. Now. Before it either drove him mad or got him slaughtered, like René. He'd done wrong by her. He'd been selfish when he'd kissed her, teasing her with the hope that maybe this curse of his wouldn't matter after all. He'd kissed her just to know what she tasted like. He'd touched her just to know how she felt against his human skin instead of his reptilian scales. But he'd had no right to lead her to believe there could be more.

What did Ingrid see in him, anyway? His true form was revolting, and she had to know by now *why* he was a gargoyle. He'd killed that priest, the one who'd hurt Suzette, over three hundred years ago, but the length of time between then and now didn't matter. The crime had attached itself to Luc. He'd shoulder it forever.

Ingrid deserved better than selfish kisses and an empty, hopeless future. Even if the Dispossessed allowed it, she deserved to be more than Luc's human obsession. He would end it, cut himself off from her. He could better protect her then. That was all Luc was. It was all he could ever be. Her watchman. Her guardian.

Her gargoyle.

Luc was avoiding her. Ingrid decided to wait until after dinner to do something about it. Once Gabby and their mother had gone upstairs to sit with Grayson and spoon-feed him some of Madame Bertot's poultry consommé, she wrapped herself in her cloak and slipped out of the rectory.

The churchyard was still and cold, the air stiff enough to fracture. Her heels crunched along the brick and gravel drive as she made her way toward the carriage house. The arched windows gleamed with a changing orange light. Ingrid had planned what to say, and she repeated it to herself once again. She would thank Luc for saving her life. For saving Grayson's life. She would inquire whether he had been punished for entering the Underneath. And then she would leave.

Or stay.

It depended on how Luc reacted to her being there. Ingrid hoped he wanted her to stay. She missed him.

Ingrid pushed open the carriage house door and crept inside. The fire in the stove glowed and crackled, throwing off enough heat to warm Ingrid's legs as she climbed the bare-board steps to the loft. Beams, darkened and chinked with age, supported rafters strung with a network of ropes and pulleys long out of use.

Pigeons cooed within the shadows of the domed roof, and the hayloft door had been rolled open.

Luc sat on the edge of a bed in the center of the loft. His feet were on the floor, his elbows propped on his knees. He kept his back to her.

"You snuck out."

Ingrid took a step into the loft. "I haven't even left the property."

Luc stood without looking at her and sauntered toward the loft door, away from the bed. It was just a burlap-covered pallet thrown over a canvas cot frame. The only other piece of furniture was a weathered humpbacked sea chest. The place wasn't just spartan. It was empty. This was how Luc lived. *Empty*. It made her chest ache for him.

"It would be easier for me if only one of you left hallowed ground at a time," he said. Ingrid heard the shade of annoyance in his voice.

So he had been punished after all. What had Vander called it?

"An angel's burn," she answered herself aloud. Luc turned his head, showing his profile. "What is an angel's burn?"

He returned to staring out the loft door. "It's how Irindi punishes us if we fail our human charges. It leaves a brand on a gargoyle's scales so that every other Dispossessed knows of your failure."

A mark of shame, Ingrid thought. She tried to remember whether Luc's scales had a brand anywhere, but he had always been moving so fast. She looked at his wings first, along with his legs and arms and chest. And those deadly talons.

"Were you punished for Gabby's injury and for Nora? Or for saving me from the Underneath?" she asked, realizing he could have suffered humiliation and pain all because of them. Because of her.

He leaned against the ribbed tin door, rolling it farther on its wheels, and gazed at the smoky night sky. "No. Apparently, I was quite heroic."

Ingrid exhaled in relief and lifted her lips in a shy grin. "I could have told you that."

The compliment failed to turn Luc around. He was avoiding her eyes now, too.

"It was nothing. I didn't have a choice."

That wasn't true and Ingrid knew it.

"But you did. Vander explained the rules to me. You didn't have to take that demon poison. I wasn't even your human any longer."

Luc released a contemptuous chuckle. "Vander isn't a gargoyle." He twisted around and finally leveled his bright-green stare on Ingrid. "He doesn't know anything about me."

The winter air coming through the loft door consumed the heat from the stove. Ingrid crossed her arms under her cloak. Luc's stare was cold, too, but it held something. A trace of uncertainty. Maybe disappointment. Did he not want to be their gargoyle any longer? Ingrid had to admit, it wasn't an easy post. He'd woken up from a decades-long hibernation to a veritable disaster zone.

Could he leave? Could he ask to be reassigned?

The thought of it sent a firestorm of electric prickles through her arms. Her emotions were at fault. With any intense feeling she had now, it was as though her arms had been plugged into live wires at the shoulders. She flexed her fingers to work out the prickling.

She couldn't imagine another gargoyle at the abbey. It had taken her long enough to get accustomed to the idea of having Luc in tune with her, ready to shift forms and protect her. Now she was more than just used to it. She liked it, and she wished she could have the same connection with him. Knowing he was there, on the other end of her senses, made her feel safe.

Luc turned back to his sky gazing.

"How old are you?" she asked. She should have known sticking to her planned topics of conversation would be impossible.

He came away from the loft door and faced her with a slanted grin.

"You snuck out of the rectory to ask me how old I am?"

She raised her chin. "No. I snuck out of the rectory because you've been avoiding me."

So much for being furtive.

Luc smoothed out his grin. "I've been this way for three hundred twenty-seven years. If you count the seventeen years I lived as a human, I'm three hundred forty-four." He propped up one of his thick eyebrows. "In June." He paused. "Why do you ask?"

She averted her eyes and ran her fingertips over the humped lid of his sea chest. "I was curious whether in all your years you'd ever seen another gargoyle ripped apart as René was."

Ingrid took a timid glance up. Luc had turned even more somber, if that was possible. He slowly nodded. "It's happened."

"Because they fell in love with humans?"

She knew the question was transparent but refused to feel embarrassment for it. He'd kissed her. He knew her feelings—he'd *felt* them.

Luc shouldered past her and headed for the steps. "I thought Vander explained the rules. No gargoyle can love a human."

She spun after him. "René loved Marie."

"René *used* Marie," Luc countered. "Gargoyles can't love. The ability dies with their human soul."

He kept on descending the steps. Ingrid rushed to follow.

"You're lying," she said. The accusation echoed through the carriage house. It wrenched Luc to an abrupt halt. He gripped the banister and turned around, jade eyes gone dusky. He looked livid.

"You—" she started, suddenly uncertain. He pinned her with the old look of loathing from the first few times they'd met. "You kissed me."

He took the few steps separating them, his feet landing hard on each board. He ran his broad hand over the banister, knuckles white, and stopped on the step just below, his face level with hers. Inches away. She felt his breath on her lips and remembered the wild way he'd tasted. Like the jungle inside Monsieur Constantine's orangery.

"If anyone discovers I kissed you, what happened to René will happen to me. How am I supposed to keep you safe if I've been torn limb from limb and cast into the Seine? And you don't even want to know what they'd do to you, Ingrid."

She felt sick. One kiss? One kiss was all it would take for Luc to be sentenced to death? "I—I didn't know."

"You're just a human. You're not supposed to know." He didn't blink. He only stared at her with those eyes of his, sharp as diamonds, and just as cold and hard.

"I'm not going to kiss you again. And unless it's to protect you, I'm not going to touch you, either," he said, his voice dead and detached. He started back down the steps. "Go away, Ingrid. Go back to the rectory. I have to prepare for a new roommate. Another Dispossessed. It seems you're too much for one gargoyle to handle."

He reached the floor but paused there, his back to her. He hung on to the curved lip of the banister for a moment, his hand pale against the dark walnut. He stood long enough for Ingrid to think that he might turn around. That he might say something and give her a shred of hope, as impossible and hazardous as it would be. She would take it, too. Instead, he stung her once again.

"Gargoyles don't love, but that doesn't mean they don't lust. That's all it was, Ingrid, and that's all it would ever be. So make it easier for yourself and leave me alone."

Luc let go of the banister and disappeared into the recesses of the carriage house. Ingrid swayed in place, as if he'd had her coiled in rope and just spun her free.

She tried to remember if he'd ever said anything else, made any mention at all about caring for her. But she couldn't come up with anything other than what he'd told her in her room: *You're my human*. That was all she was, then. She'd been a fool, just like she'd been a fool back in London, convincing herself that Jonathan was falling in love with her.

Ingrid stumbled down the stairs and out of the carriage house, slamming the door behind her. A shiver of static forked from her shoulders and popped at the tips of her fingers. She didn't flex her hands or shake her arms to erase the sensation this time. She wanted to let it out. She was suddenly ravenous to send lightning streaking from her fingertips. She didn't care what she aimed for: the crab apples to her left, the angelic statuary to the right. If Luc stepped into her path, she'd gladly fling her lightning at him. She just wanted it gone, so long as it took every last sickening feeling of idiocy with it. She had let herself believe. And she had let herself be crushed.

Ingrid didn't feel the stiff cold now. She burned hot with pent-up electricity. She barely heard the rattle of wheels and tack as a carriage pulled through the break in the hedgerow. It was Monsieur Constantine's brougham. Their estate agent's driver slowed as he steered alongside Ingrid, and then came to a complete stop. She waited for the footman to jump down and open the door. Constantine's domed gray felt hat appeared, followed by his walking cane and the rest of his gray-suited figure.

He tipped his hat to her and smiled. "Good evening, Lady Ingrid."

Ingrid's mother had sent a note to Constantine, telling him of Grayson's return. He must have come to check in on them.

She managed a feeble smile. "And to you, monsieur. Mama is inside tending to my brother."

Ingrid started walking, expecting Constantine to fall in step with her.

"Thank you, Lady Ingrid, but I have come to speak to you."

Ingrid's heels dug into the gravel as she turned back to him. His gray mustache twitched as he grinned.

"And I see I've arrived at a most auspicious time. You're practically sparking at the fingertips, mademoiselle."

Ingrid instantly curled her hands into tight fists. "How could you possibly . . ." She caught herself. Constantine wasn't part of the Alliance. He was just a . . . a *human*.

He belted out a laugh, short and crisp. "I know a great deal more about demon gifts than any member of the Alliance, I assure you. Yours is most exceptional."

Constantine took a step forward and Ingrid scuttled backward. He held up his hands, gloved as well as any upper-crust gentleman's would be.

"I meant no deception, mademoiselle. I went to great lengths to find a protected home for you and your family. I knew I couldn't find a safer spot than sacred ground guarded by the Dispossessed."

Ingrid stared at him, speechless. He'd chosen the abbey on purpose? And he'd led them to Luc.

"Please, I simply wanted to observe you and your brother," he said. "And, if I can be honest, earn your trust."

"I don't know you well enough," she replied. And how exactly did *he* know about *them*?

"Being conservative is a wise choice," he replied, unruffled. "As will be learning how to live with your gifts. Aren't you at all curious how to do so? How to control them? I must say, at the moment you look ready to take down a hellhound with one zap." He flicked his fingers out in front of him for emphasis.

Ingrid gaped at him, the sensation of a thousand needles pricking her skin from the inside fading fast. Who was this man? He knew things. Quickly, Ingrid suspected he knew much more than she did.

"Can I get rid of it?" she asked breathlessly.

He clasped his hands behind his frock coat. "I'm afraid it doesn't work that way. At least, it hasn't for the others like you. Those marked with demon gifts of their own."

Ingrid wouldn't have gone so far as to say she trusted Monsieur Constantine, but he'd at least drawn her curiosity. He'd also gone to lengths to choose a safe place for her family to live. Why would he have found them a protected dwelling if he wished to harm her?

"All right," Ingrid said, raising her chin. "Then I want to know how it does work."

He took a deep breath and nodded once, clearly pleased. "I shall gladly teach you. Now, perhaps we should go indoors." He took a tentative glance toward the carriage house. "My gargoyle, Gaston, tells me that your gargoyle's protective nature is one to be reckoned with."

So he knew about Luc, too. She turned her back on the carriage house and accepted Constantine's proffered arm.

"Don't let him trouble you," she said as they started for the front door.

Ingrid certainly wasn't going to trouble herself with him any longer. Vander had been right. She couldn't trust a gargoyle, not completely. Maybe she couldn't trust the strange Monsieur Constantine, either, but it wasn't the same—she wouldn't be trusting him with her heart.

If he could teach her about her gift, show her how to use it, then she wouldn't have to rely so much on the Dispossessed. She could protect Gabby and Grayson and Mama from whatever creatures the Underneath belched up. Ingrid would need to know how to protect herself, too, because Axia wasn't gone. She'd be coming back for her blood. And the next time they met, Ingrid would be ready.

ACKNOWLEDGMENTS

My first bit of thanks has to go to my agent, Ted Malawer. When I first told Ted about my idea for this book it sounded embarrassingly vague (*"It's about real, living gargoyles . . . in Paris . . . in the 1890s. And they, like, protect humans. Or something."*). But being the spectacular agent that he is, Ted embraced the vague (*"You had me at 'gargoyles' and 'Paris.'"*). Thank you, Ted, for guiding me through this project from start to finish, and for sticking with me through the good, the bad, and the exceptionally awesome.

Next, a huge thank-you to Krista Marino, Beverly Horowitz, and everyone at Random House who has shown *The Beautiful and the Cursed* some serious love and affection. I've wanted the chance to work with Krista and Delacorte Press for many years, so I feel honored to have had this experience.

Thank you in spades to my mother-in-law, Charley, and my sister, Lisa, for taking care of my youngest daughter (aka the Attachment) on a regular basis so I could have some quality time with my laptop—writing a hundred thousand words in three months required a lot of it!

To my critique partners, Maurissa Guibord and Dawn Metcalf, thank you for your insight, wisdom, and general glee regarding this project. It reminded me just how lucky I am to have you in my corner.

To Megan LaCroix and Cindy Thomas, thank you for caring enough to email me every now and again to make sure I'm still breathing.

To Camille Bocquillon, a Facebook friend who was generous enough to help me translate English passages and words into fabulous French, *merci beaucoup!*

To my parents, Mike and Nancy Robie, thank you for encouraging me to follow my dreams. As we always say, "Never give up. Never surrender." And no, Dad, there are no dwarves in this one either. . . .

And of course, to Chad, Alexandra, Joslin, and Willa. Sometimes I sit back and marvel at how blessed I am to have the four of you in my life. You each give me so much love and joy. Thank you.

The saga continues
in
The Lovely and the Lost
Spring 2014

About the Author

Page Morgan has been fascinated with *les grotesques* ever since she came across a black-and-white photograph of a Notre Dame gargoyle keeping watch over the city of Paris. Her subsequent research fed her imagination, and she was inspired to piece together her own mythology for these remarkably complex stone figures. Page lives in New Hampshire with her husband and their three children.